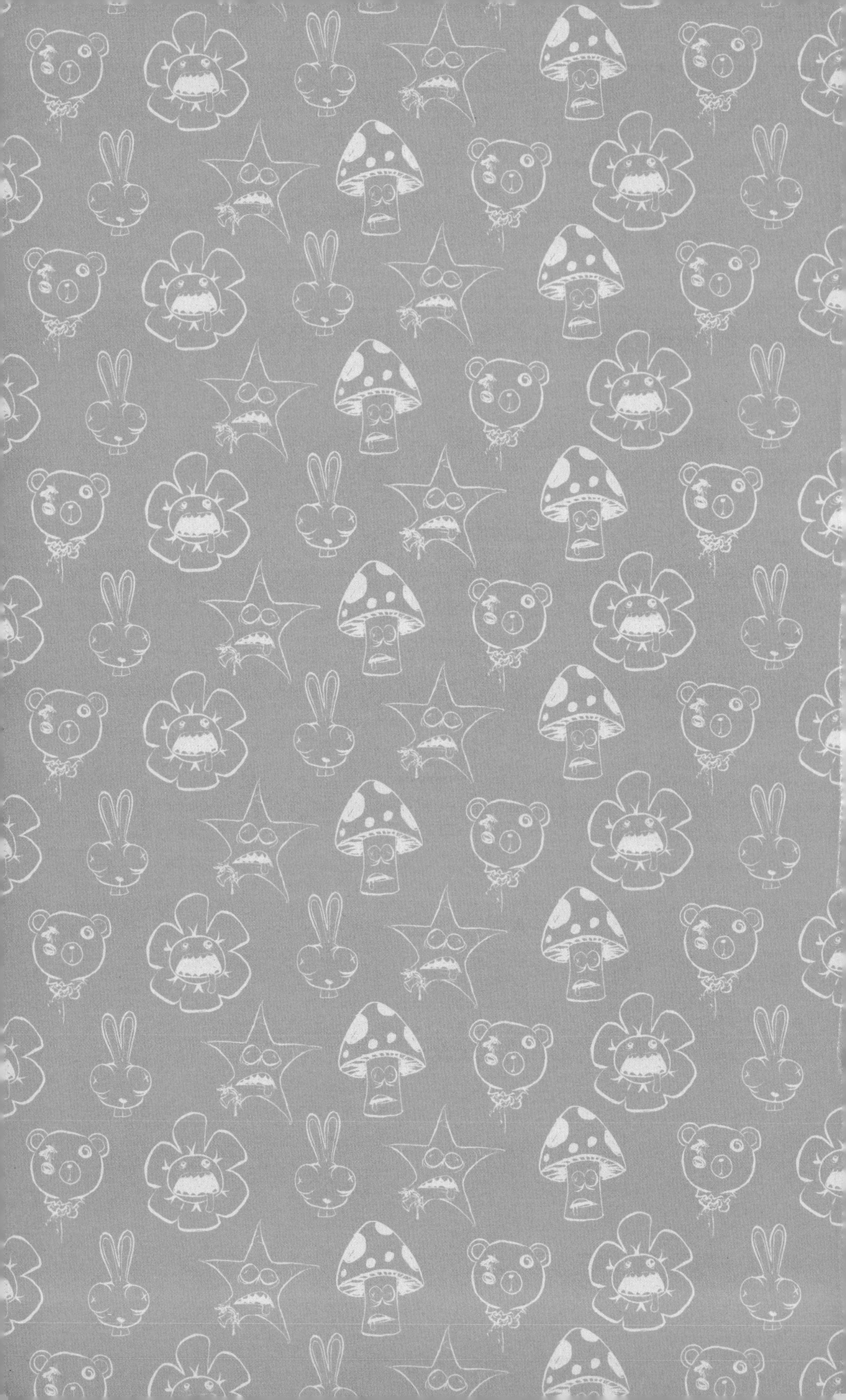

"Oh my! She killed my husband! Did you see that? She killed him so fluffing hard! I wonder if she'll autograph him!"

- Filthy, recently
widowed peasant

Written and Drawn by
SKOTTIE YOUNG

Additional Art in Chapter Eight by
JEFFREY "CHAMBA" CRUZ

Coloring by
JEAN-FRANCOIS BEAULIEU

Lettering & Design by
NATE PIEKOS
OF BLAMBOT®

Logo Design by
RIAN HUGHES

Image Comics, Inc.
Robert Kirkman – Chief Operating Officer
Erik Larsen – Chief Financial Officer
Todd McFarlane – President
Marc Silvestri – Chief Executive Officer
Jim Valentino – Vice-President
Eric Stephenson – Publisher
Corey Murphy – Director of Sales
Jeff Boison – Director of Publishing Planning
   & Book Trade Sales
Jeremy Sullivan – Director of Digital Sales
Kat Salazar – Director of PR & Marketing
Branwyn Bigglestone – Controller
Drew Gill – Art Director
Jonathan Chan – Production Manager

imagecomics.com
Meredith Wallace – Print Manager
Briah Skelly – Publicist
Sasha Head – Sales & Marketing Production
   Designer
Randy Okamura – Digital Production Designer
David Brothers – Branding Manager
Olivia Ngai – Content Manager
Addison Duke – Production Artist
Vincent Kukua – Production Artist
Tricia Ramos – Production Artist
Jeff Stang – Direct Market Sales Representative
Emilio Bautista – Digital Sales Associate
Leanna Caunter – Accounting Assistant
Chloe Ramos-Peterson – Library Market
                    Sales Representative

Standard Cover, ISBN: 978-1-63215-887-1
Big Bang Comics / Forbidden Planet Variant Cover, ISBN: 978-1-5343-0162-7
Newbury Comics Variant Cover, ISBN: 978-1-5343-0163-4

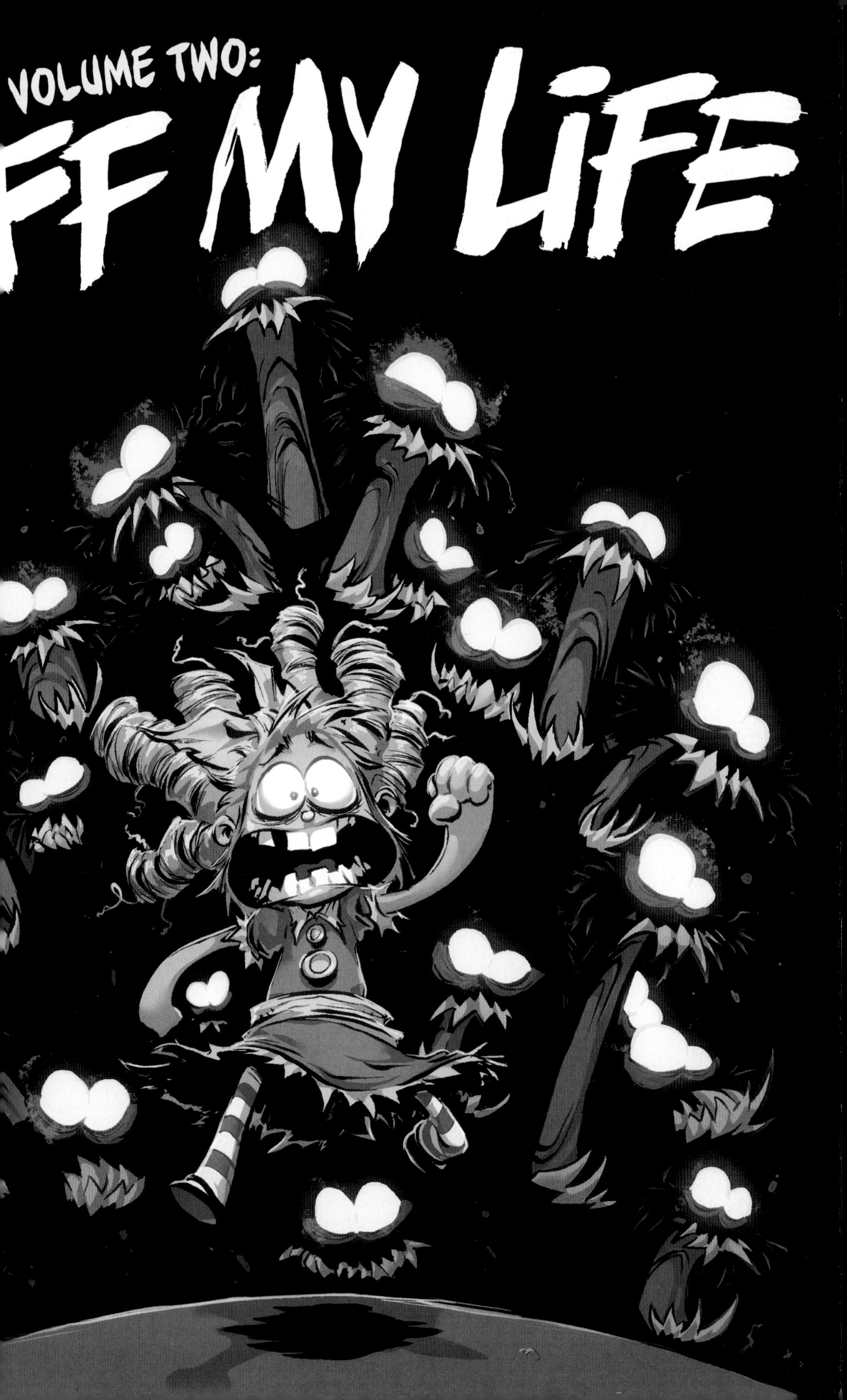
VOLUME TWO:
FF MY LIFE

SIX

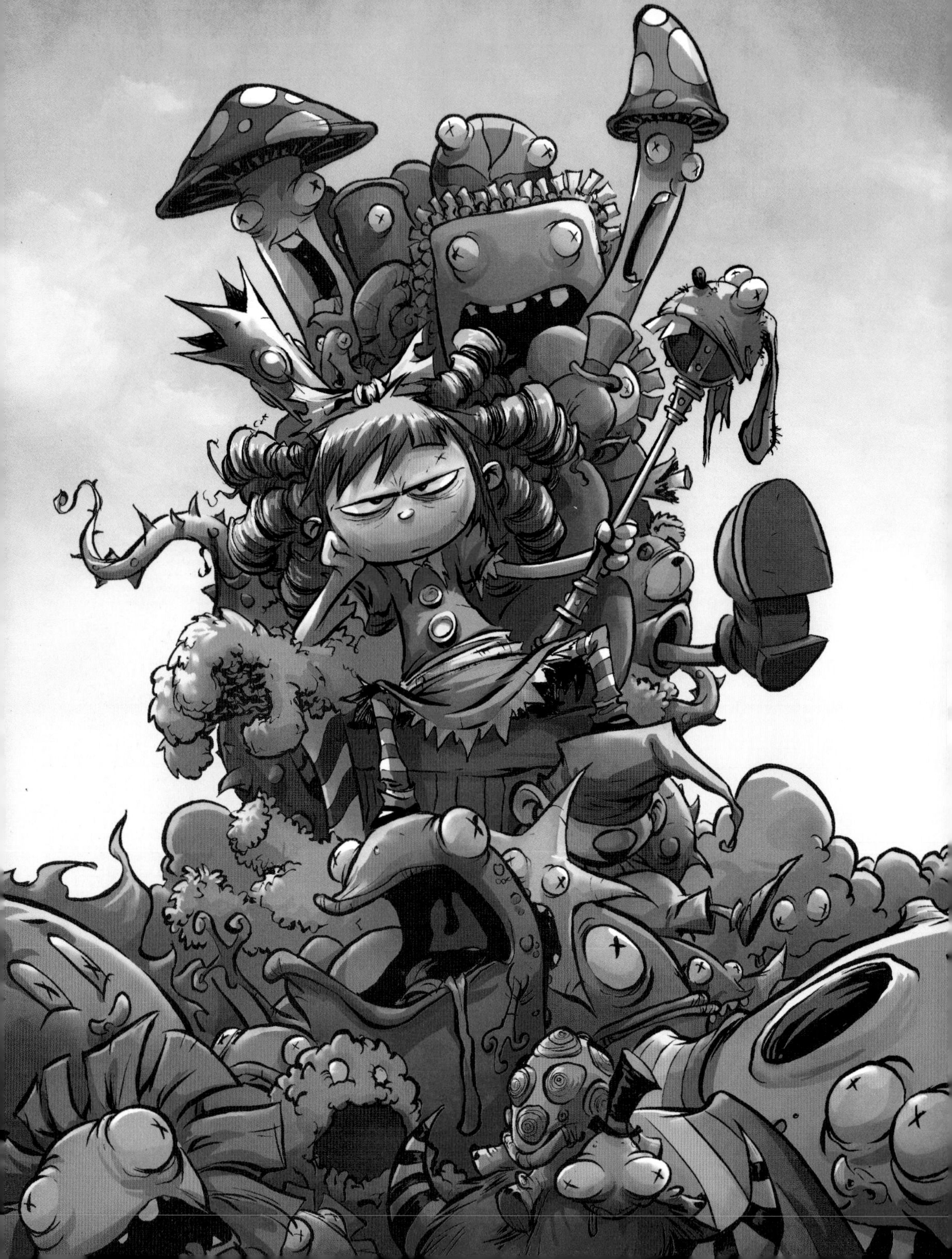

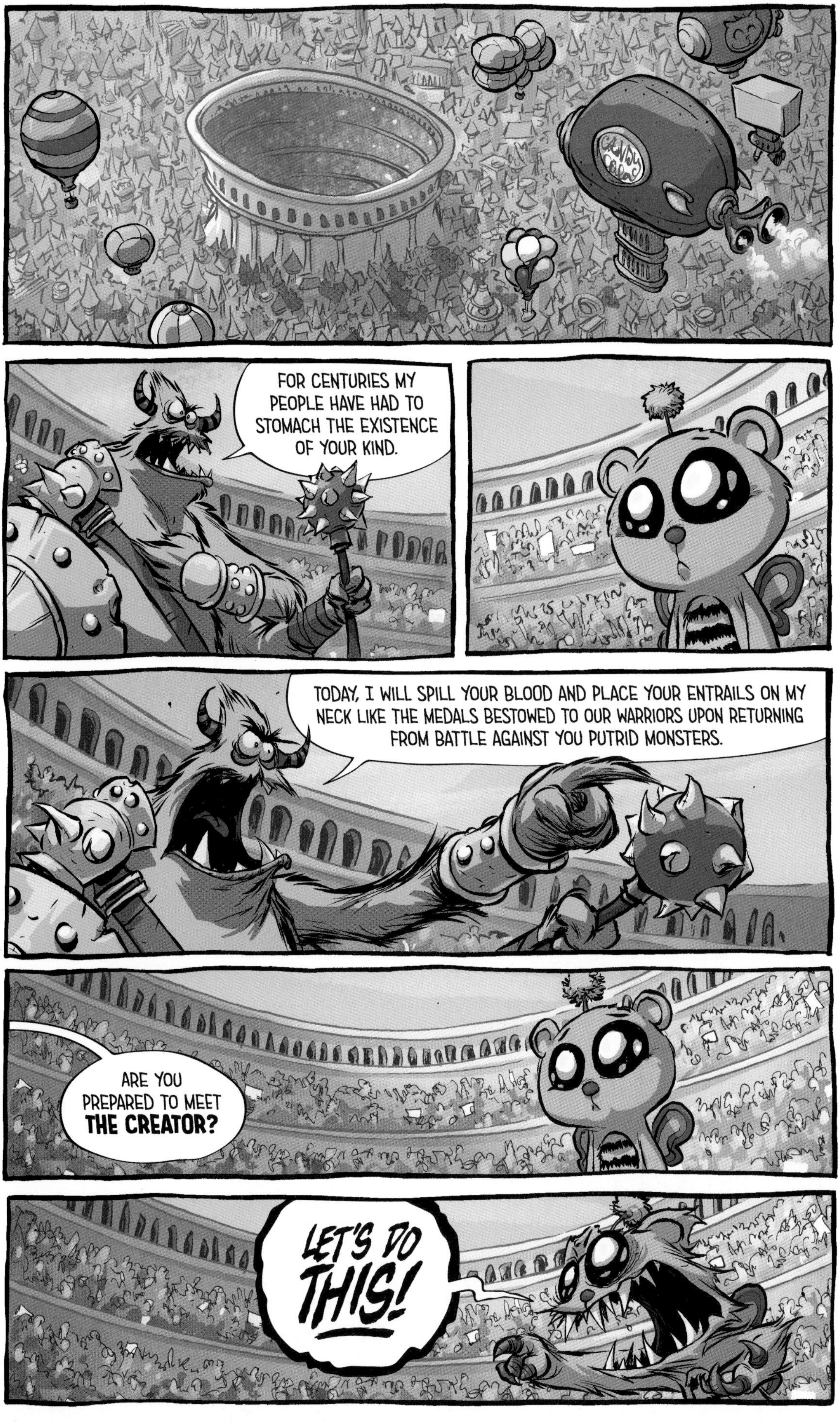

FOR CENTURIES MY PEOPLE HAVE HAD TO STOMACH THE EXISTENCE OF YOUR KIND.
TODAY, I WILL SPILL YOUR BLOOD AND PLACE YOUR ENTRAILS ON MY NECK LIKE THE MEDALS BESTOWED TO OUR WARRIORS UPON RETURNING FROM BATTLE AGAINST YOU PUTRID MONSTERS.
ARE YOU PREPARED TO MEET **THE CREATOR?**
LET'S DO THIS!

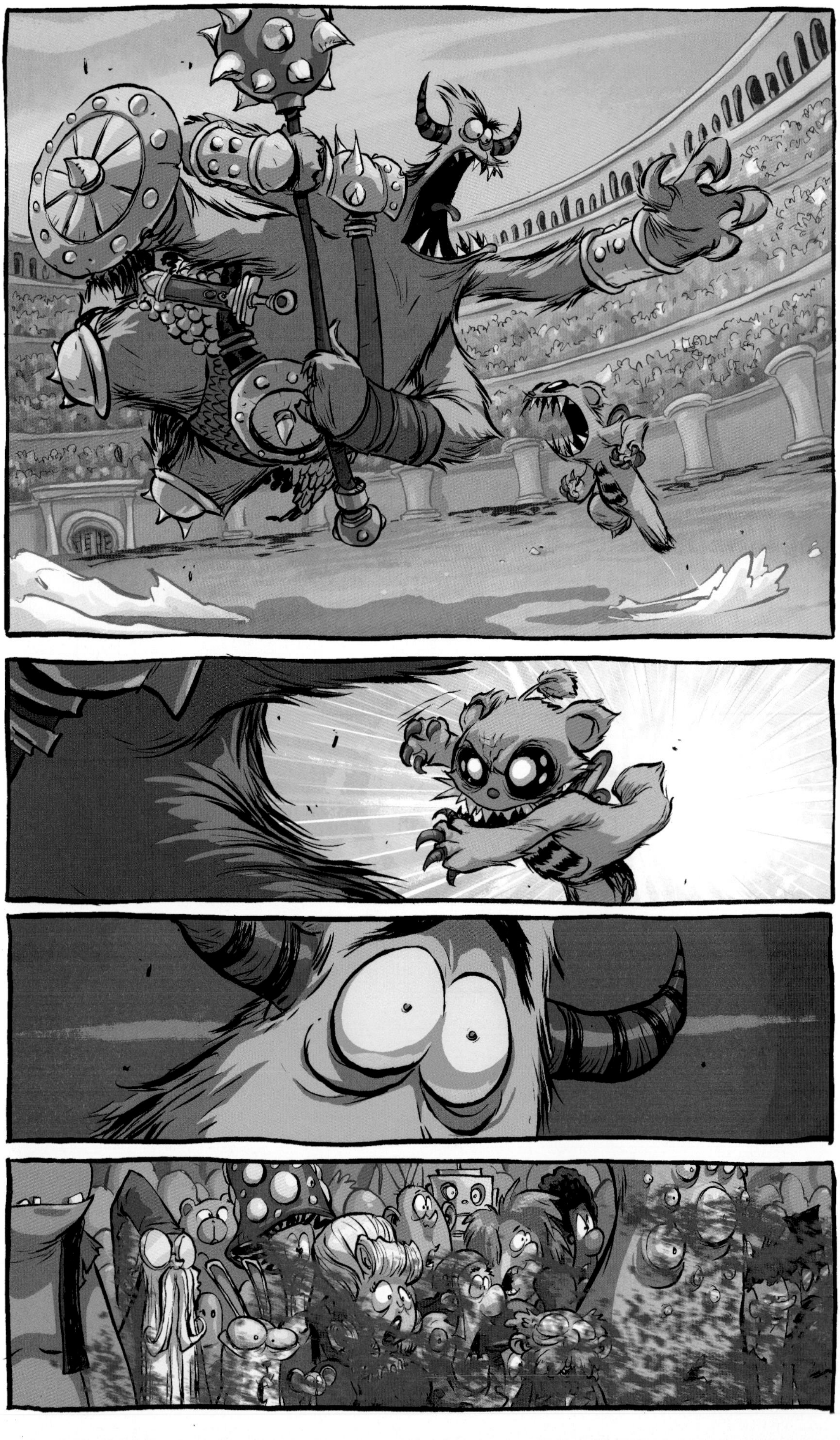

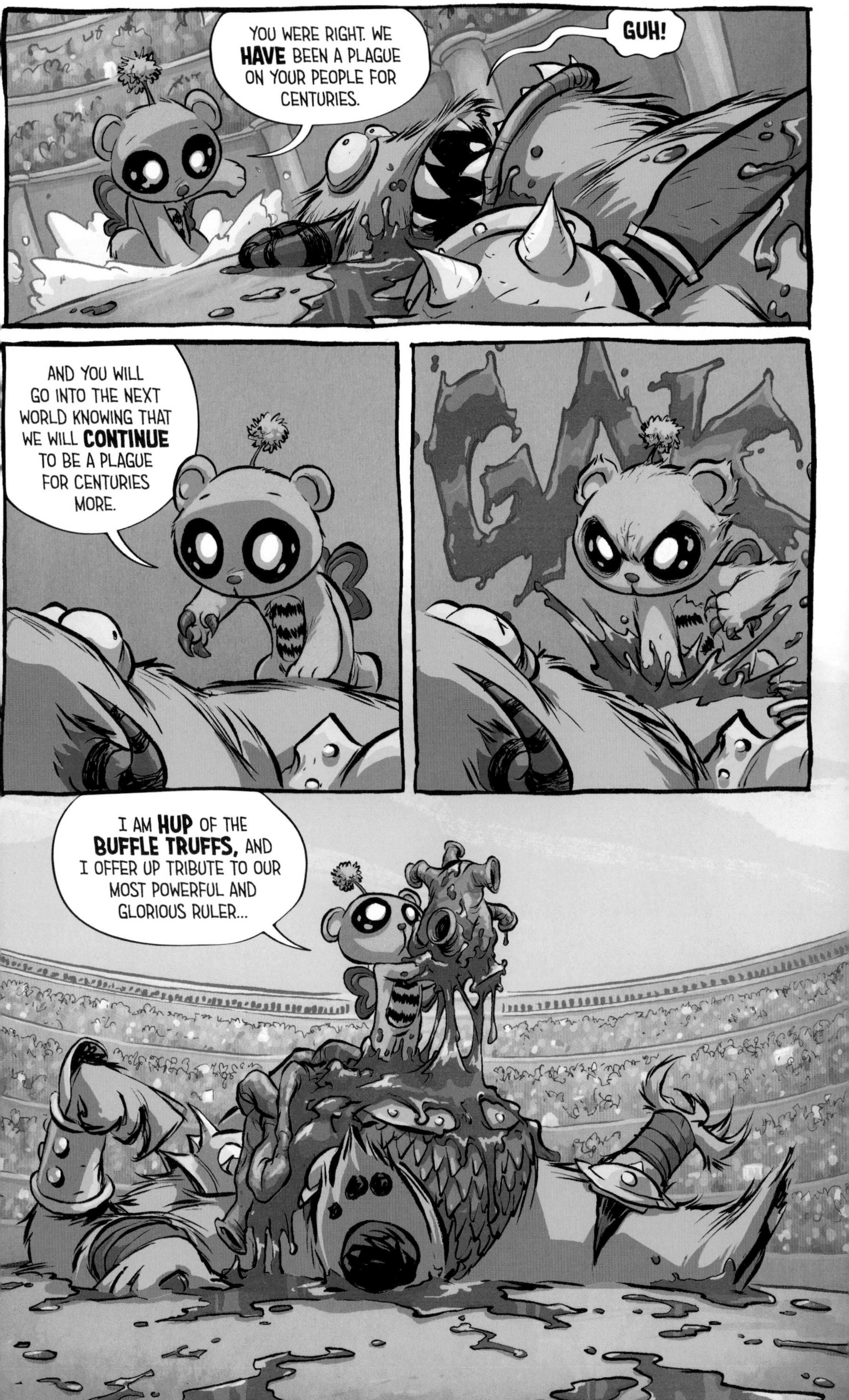

YOU WERE RIGHT. WE **HAVE** BEEN A PLAGUE ON YOUR PEOPLE FOR CENTURIES.
GUH!
AND YOU WILL GO INTO THE NEXT WORLD KNOWING THAT WE WILL **CONTINUE** TO BE A PLAGUE FOR CENTURIES MORE.
GAK
I AM **HUP** OF THE **BUFFLE TRUFFS,** AND I OFFER UP TRIBUTE TO OUR MOST POWERFUL AND GLORIOUS RULER...

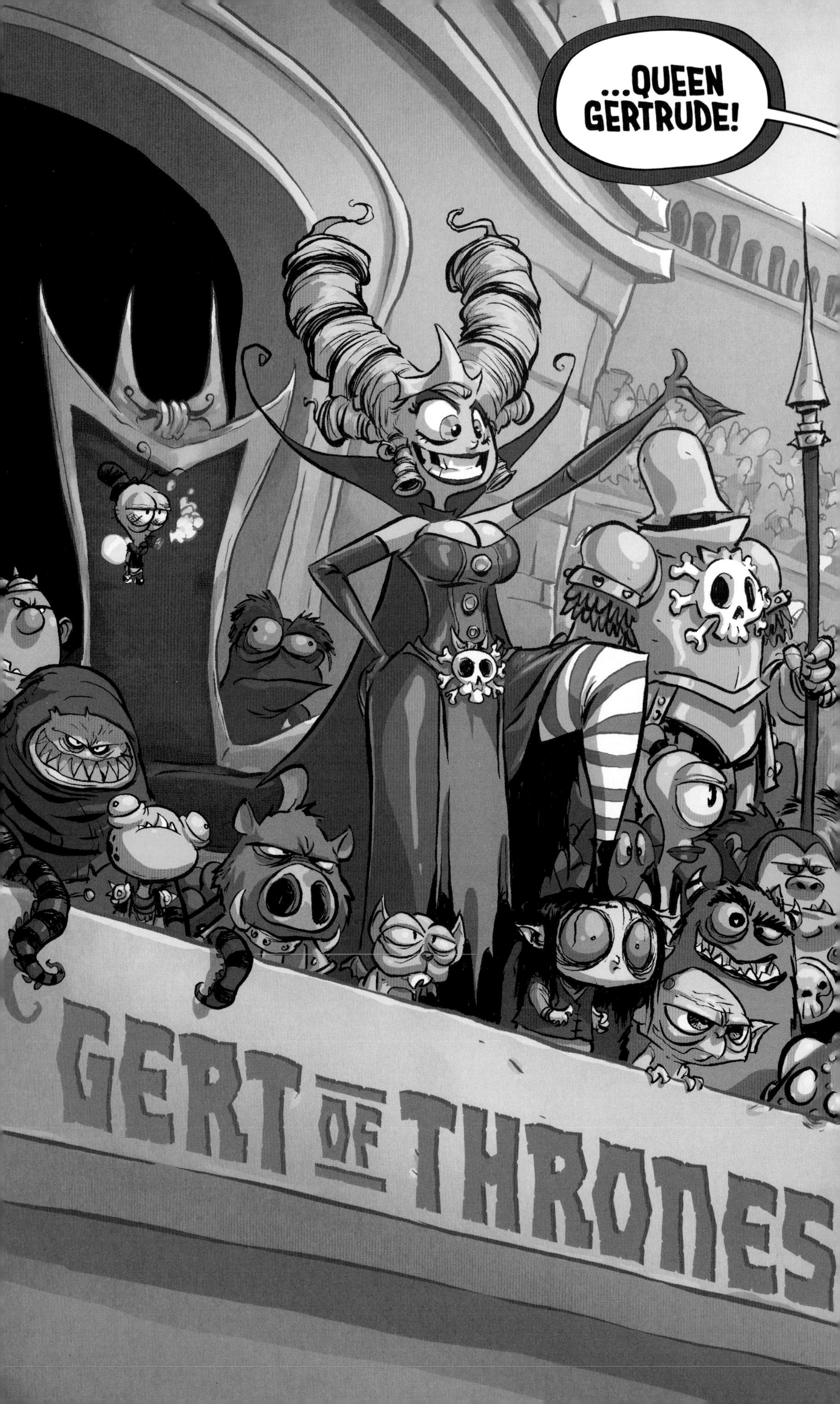
...QUEEN GERTRUDE!
GERT OF THRONES

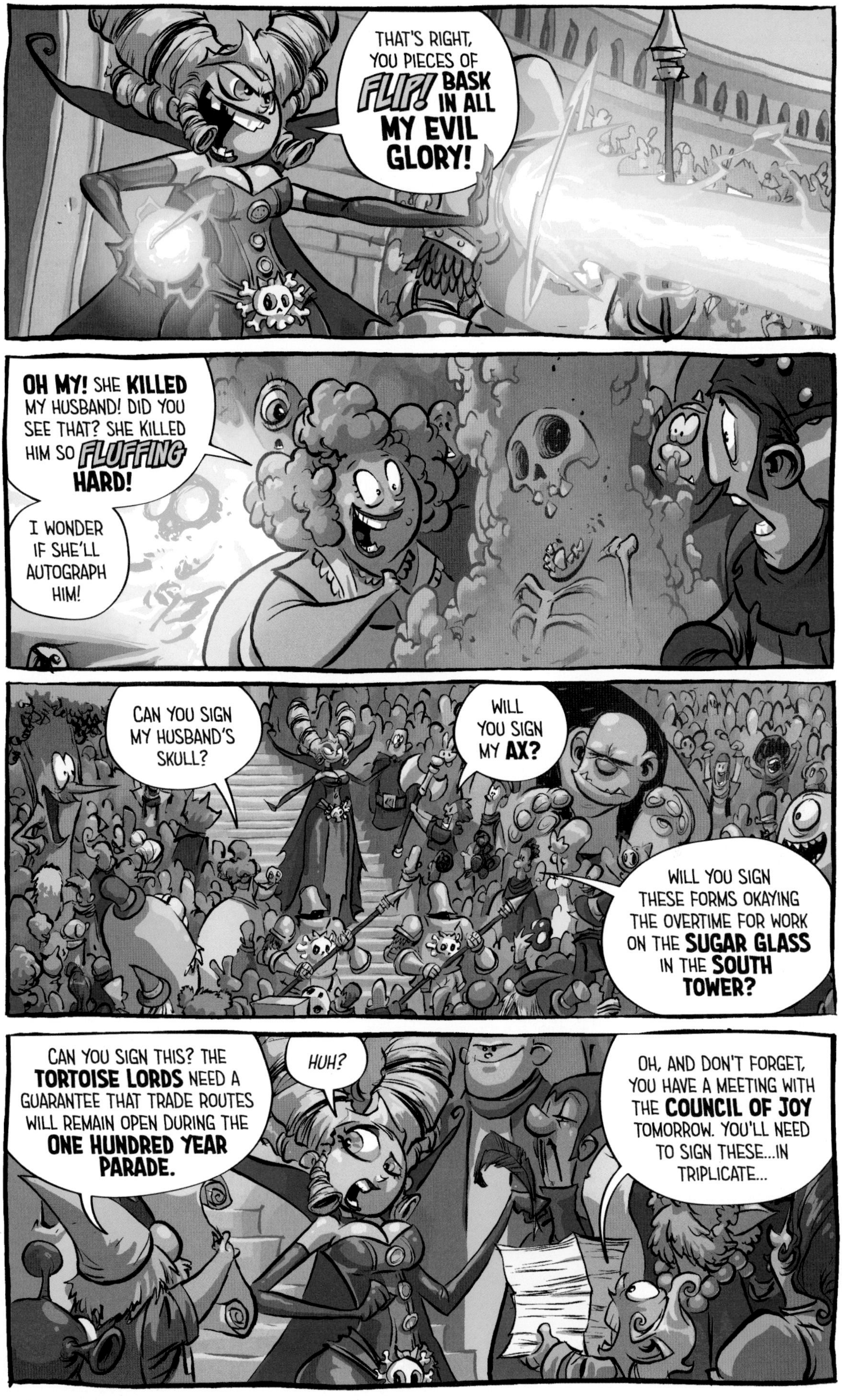
THAT'S RIGHT, YOU PIECES OF FLIP! BASK IN ALL MY EVIL GLORY!
OH MY! SHE KILLED MY HUSBAND! DID YOU SEE THAT? SHE KILLED HIM SO FLUFFING HARD!
I WONDER IF SHE'LL AUTOGRAPH HIM!
CAN YOU SIGN MY HUSBAND'S SKULL?
WILL YOU SIGN MY AX?
WILL YOU SIGN THESE FORMS OKAYING THE OVERTIME FOR WORK ON THE SUGAR GLASS IN THE SOUTH TOWER?
CAN YOU SIGN THIS? THE TORTOISE LORDS NEED A GUARANTEE THAT TRADE ROUTES WILL REMAIN OPEN DURING THE ONE HUNDRED YEAR PARADE.
HUH?
OH, AND DON'T FORGET, YOU HAVE A MEETING WITH THE COUNCIL OF JOY TOMORROW. YOU'LL NEED TO SIGN THESE...IN TRIPLICATE...

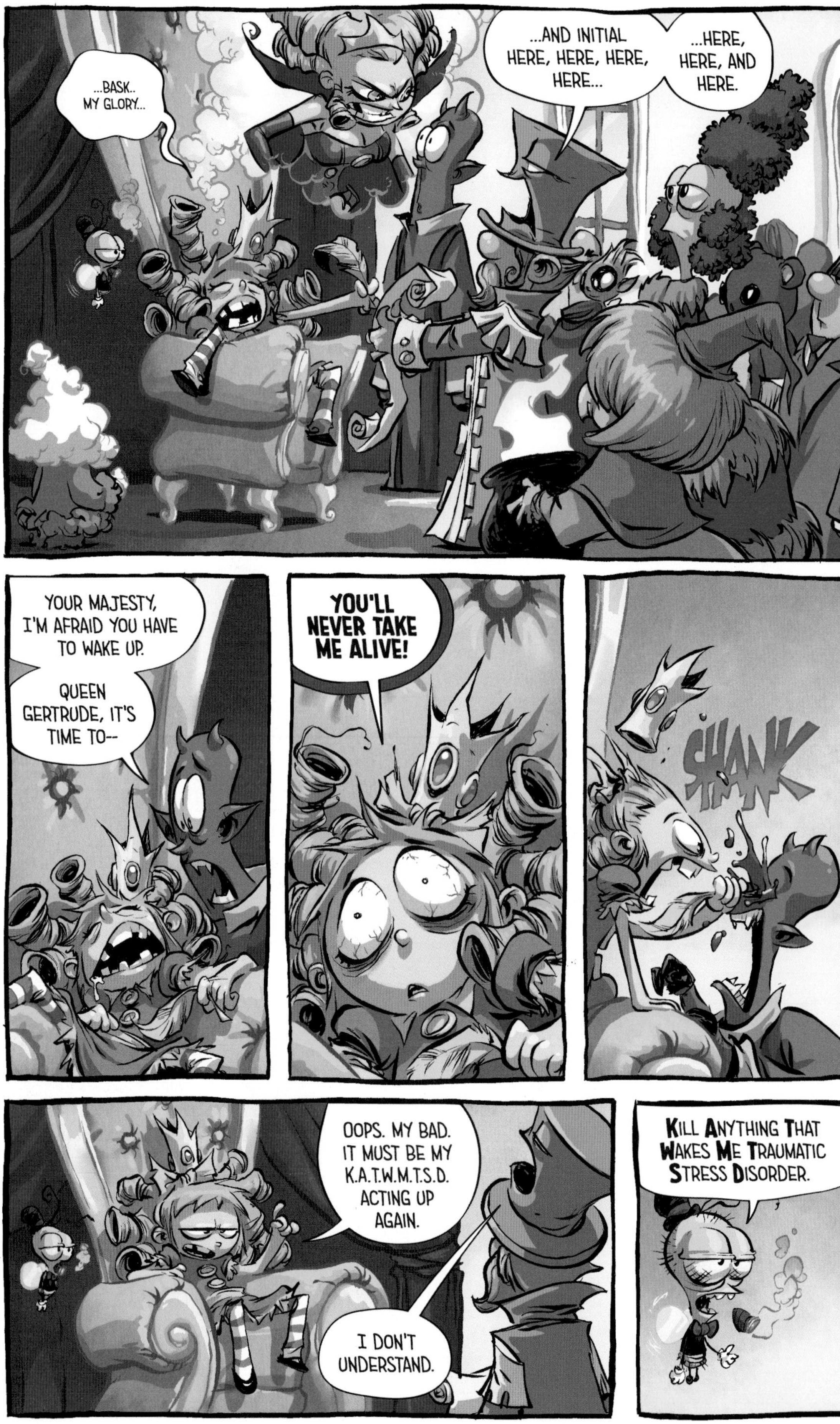
...BASK.. MY GLORY...
...AND INITIAL HERE, HERE, HERE, HERE...
...HERE, HERE, AND HERE.
YOUR MAJESTY, I'M AFRAID YOU HAVE TO WAKE UP.
QUEEN GERTRUDE, IT'S TIME TO--
YOU'LL NEVER TAKE ME ALIVE!
SHANK
OOPS. MY BAD. IT MUST BE MY K.A.T.W.M.T.S.D. ACTING UP AGAIN.
I DON'T UNDERSTAND.
KILL ANYTHING THAT WAKES ME TRAUMATIC STRESS DISORDER.

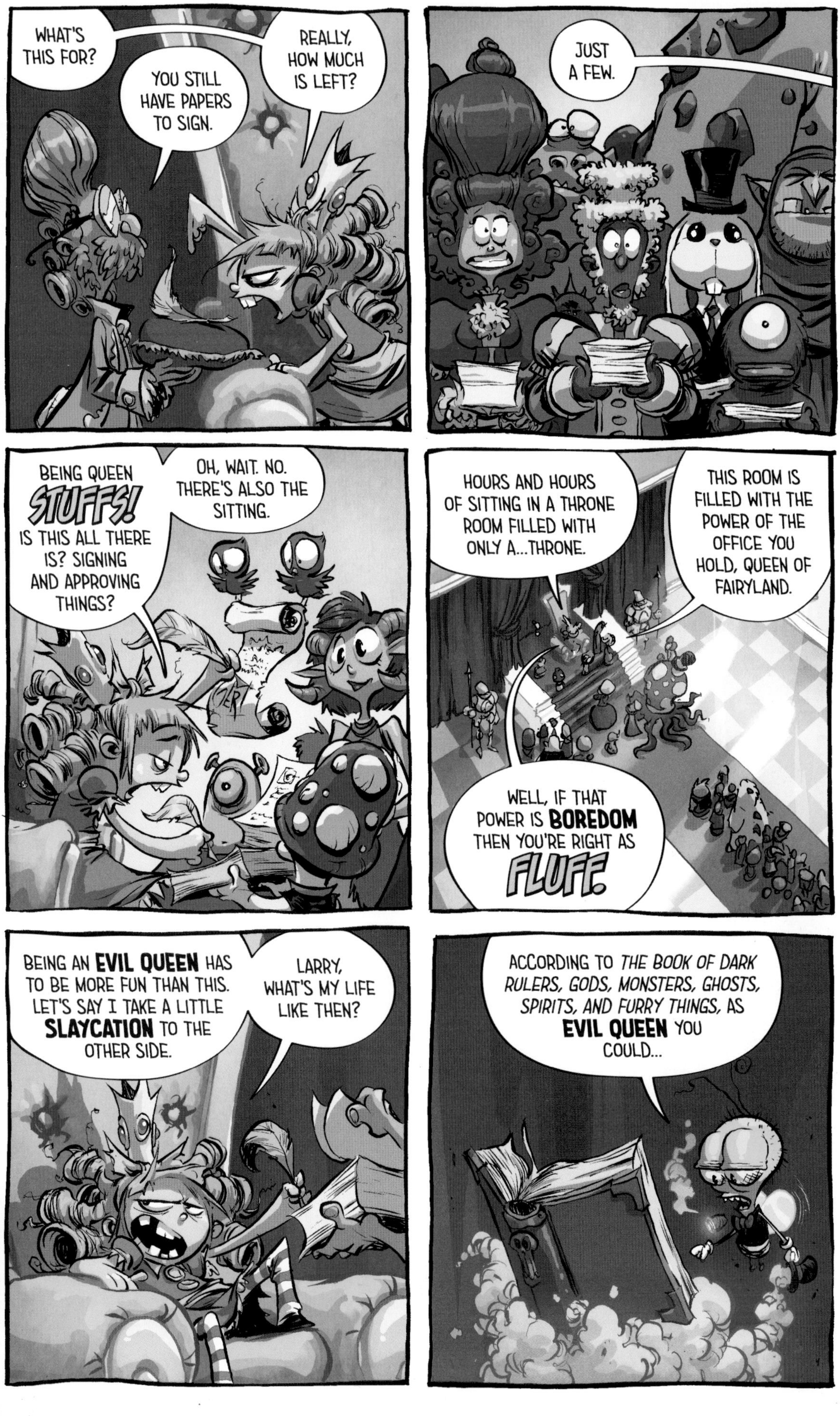
WHAT'S THIS FOR?
YOU STILL HAVE PAPERS TO SIGN.
REALLY, HOW MUCH IS LEFT?
JUST A FEW.
BEING QUEEN STUFFS! IS THIS ALL THERE IS? SIGNING AND APPROVING THINGS?
OH, WAIT. NO. THERE'S ALSO THE SITTING.
HOURS AND HOURS OF SITTING IN A THRONE ROOM FILLED WITH ONLY A...THRONE.
THIS ROOM IS FILLED WITH THE POWER OF THE OFFICE YOU HOLD, QUEEN OF FAIRYLAND.
WELL, IF THAT POWER IS BOREDOM THEN YOU'RE RIGHT AS FLUFF.
BEING AN EVIL QUEEN HAS TO BE MORE FUN THAN THIS. LET'S SAY I TAKE A LITTLE SLAYCATION TO THE OTHER SIDE.
LARRY, WHAT'S MY LIFE LIKE THEN?
ACCORDING TO THE BOOK OF DARK RULERS, GODS, MONSTERS, GHOSTS, SPIRITS, AND FURRY THINGS, AS EVIL QUEEN YOU COULD...

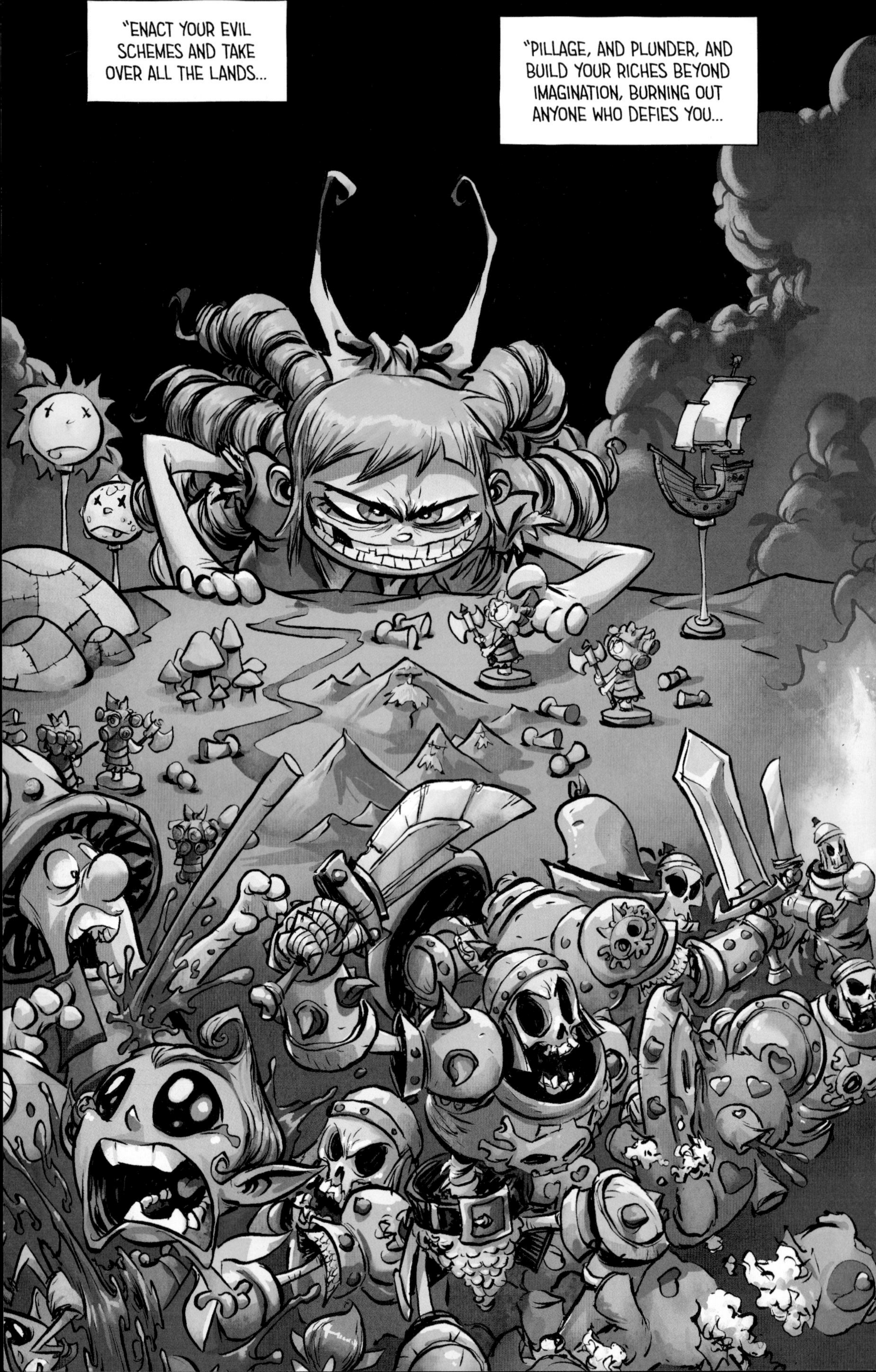
"ENACT YOUR EVIL SCHEMES AND TAKE OVER ALL THE LANDS...
"PILLAGE, AND PLUNDER, AND BUILD YOUR RICHES BEYOND IMAGINATION, BURNING OUT ANYONE WHO DEFIES YOU...

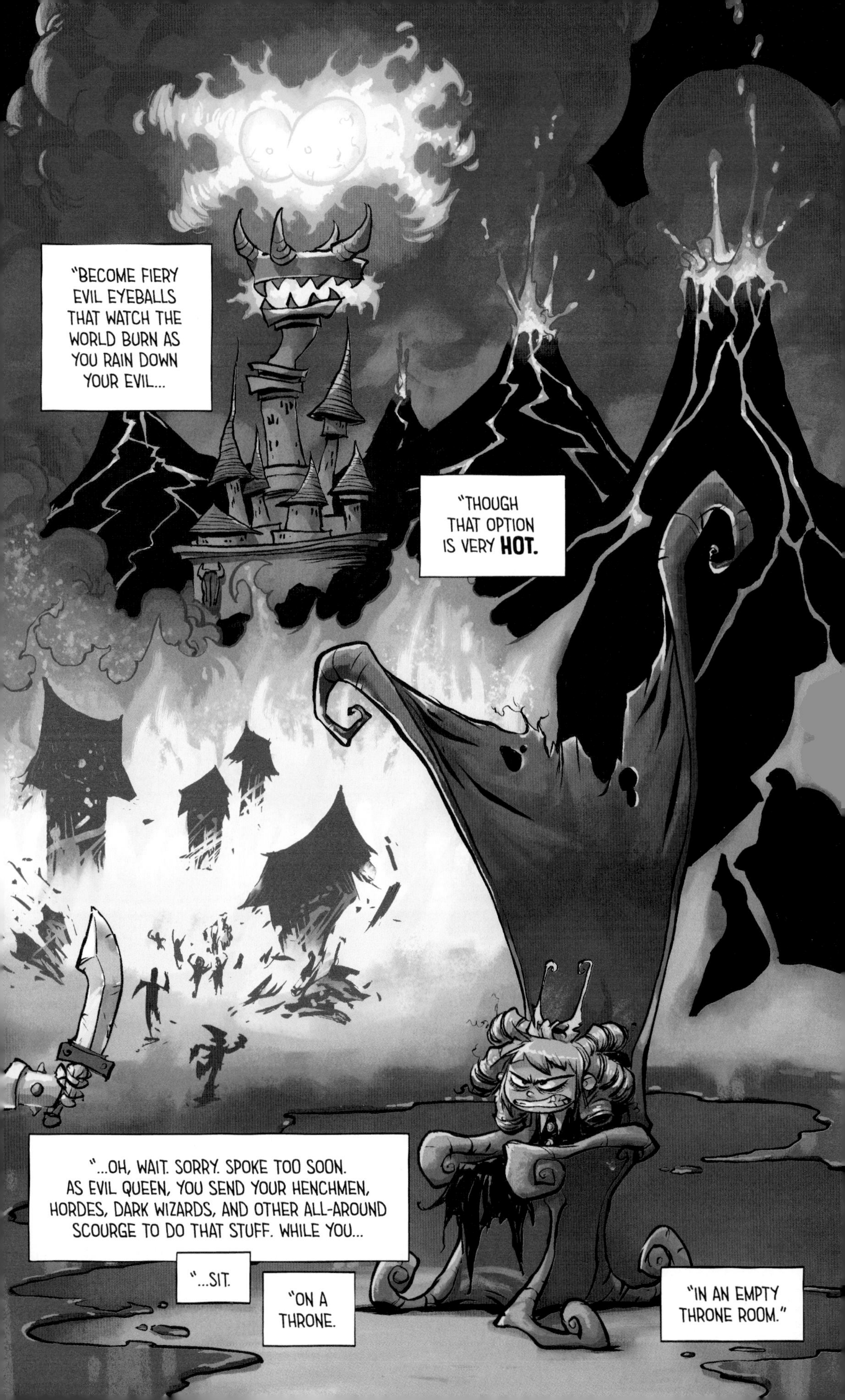
"BECOME FIERY EVIL EYEBALLS THAT WATCH THE WORLD BURN AS YOU RAIN DOWN YOUR EVIL...
"THOUGH THAT OPTION IS VERY **HOT.**
"...OH, WAIT. SORRY. SPOKE TOO SOON. AS EVIL QUEEN, YOU SEND YOUR HENCHMEN, HORDES, DARK WIZARDS, AND OTHER ALL-AROUND SCOURGE TO DO THAT STUFF. WHILE YOU...
"...SIT.
"ON A THRONE.
"IN AN EMPTY THRONE ROOM."

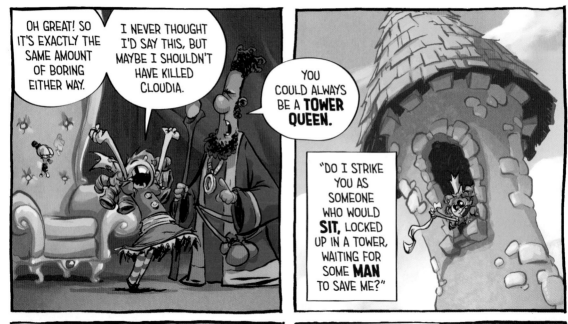

OH GREAT! SO IT'S EXACTLY THE SAME AMOUNT OF BORING EITHER WAY.

I NEVER THOUGHT I'D SAY THIS, BUT MAYBE I SHOULDN'T HAVE KILLED CLOUDIA.

YOU COULD ALWAYS BE A **TOWER QUEEN.**

"DO I STRIKE YOU AS SOMEONE WHO WOULD **SIT,** LOCKED UP IN A TOWER, WAITING FOR SOME **MAN** TO SAVE ME?"

OR DO YOU THINK I WOULD BREAK MYSELF OUT, FIND THE ONE RESPONSIBLE FOR PUTTING ME THERE, AND DO THINGS TO THEIR INSIDES THAT WOULD MAKE **DARKETH DEADEATH** PUKE HIS SOULLESS GUTS OUT?

UH...THE SECOND ONE?

CORRECT.

LARRY, WHAT'S ON THE AGENDA TODAY? I'M IN THE MOOD TO **QUEEN THE FLUFF** OUT OF SOMETHING.

YOU'RE CLEANING THAT UP YOURSELF.

"WE HAVE THE **LILY'S LUNCH** NOW...

"...THEN WE HAVE A COMMENCEMENT SPEECH TO GIVE AT **HARBINGERS SCHOOL OF WITCHES AND WARLOCKS.**"

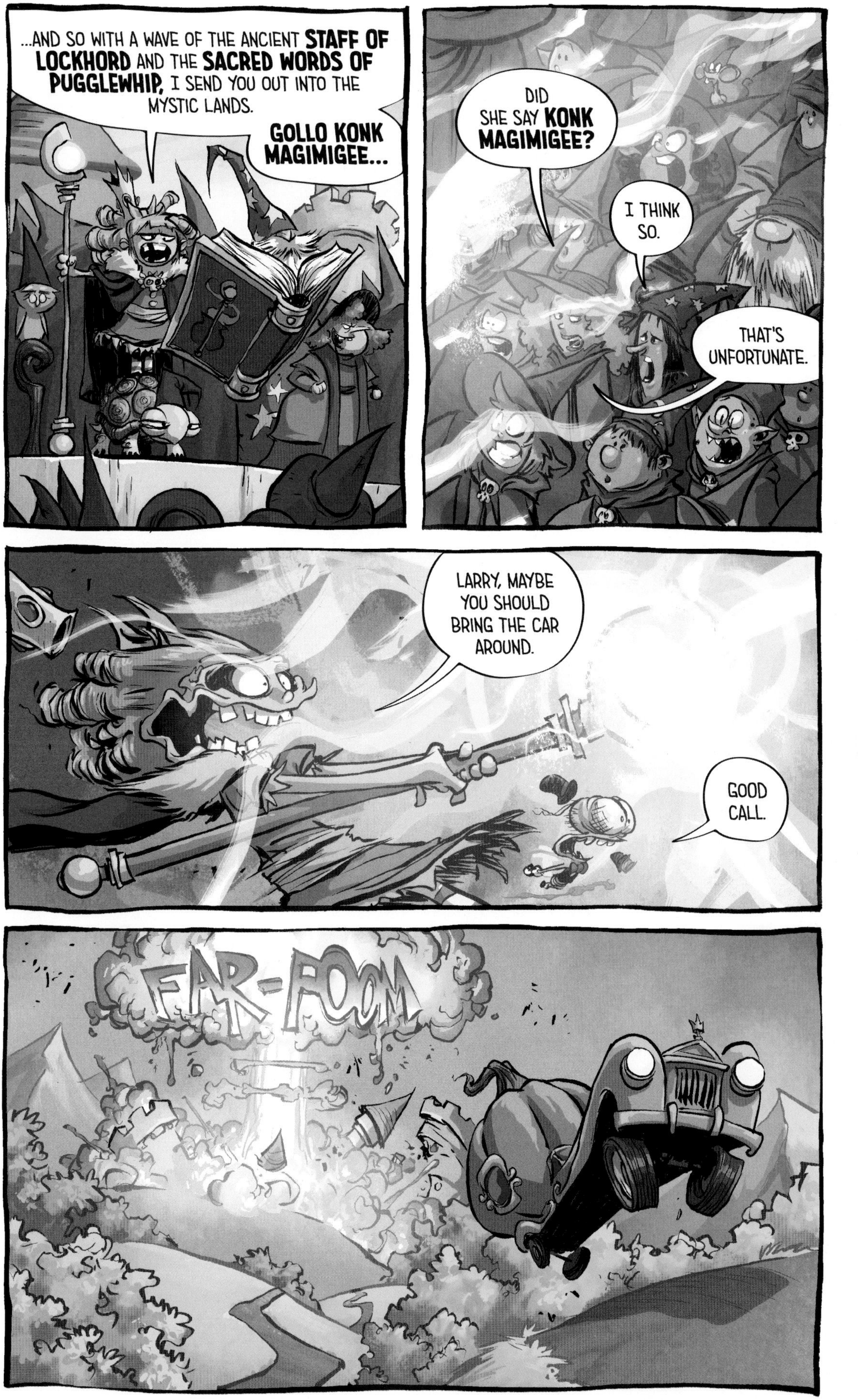
...AND SO WITH A WAVE OF THE ANCIENT **STAFF OF LOCKHORD** AND THE **SACRED WORDS OF PUGGLEWHIP,** I SEND YOU OUT INTO THE MYSTIC LANDS.
GOLLO KONK MAGIMIGEE...
DID SHE SAY **KONK MAGIMIGEE?**
I THINK SO.
THAT'S UNFORTUNATE.
LARRY, MAYBE YOU SHOULD BRING THE CAR AROUND.
GOOD CALL.
FAR-FOOM

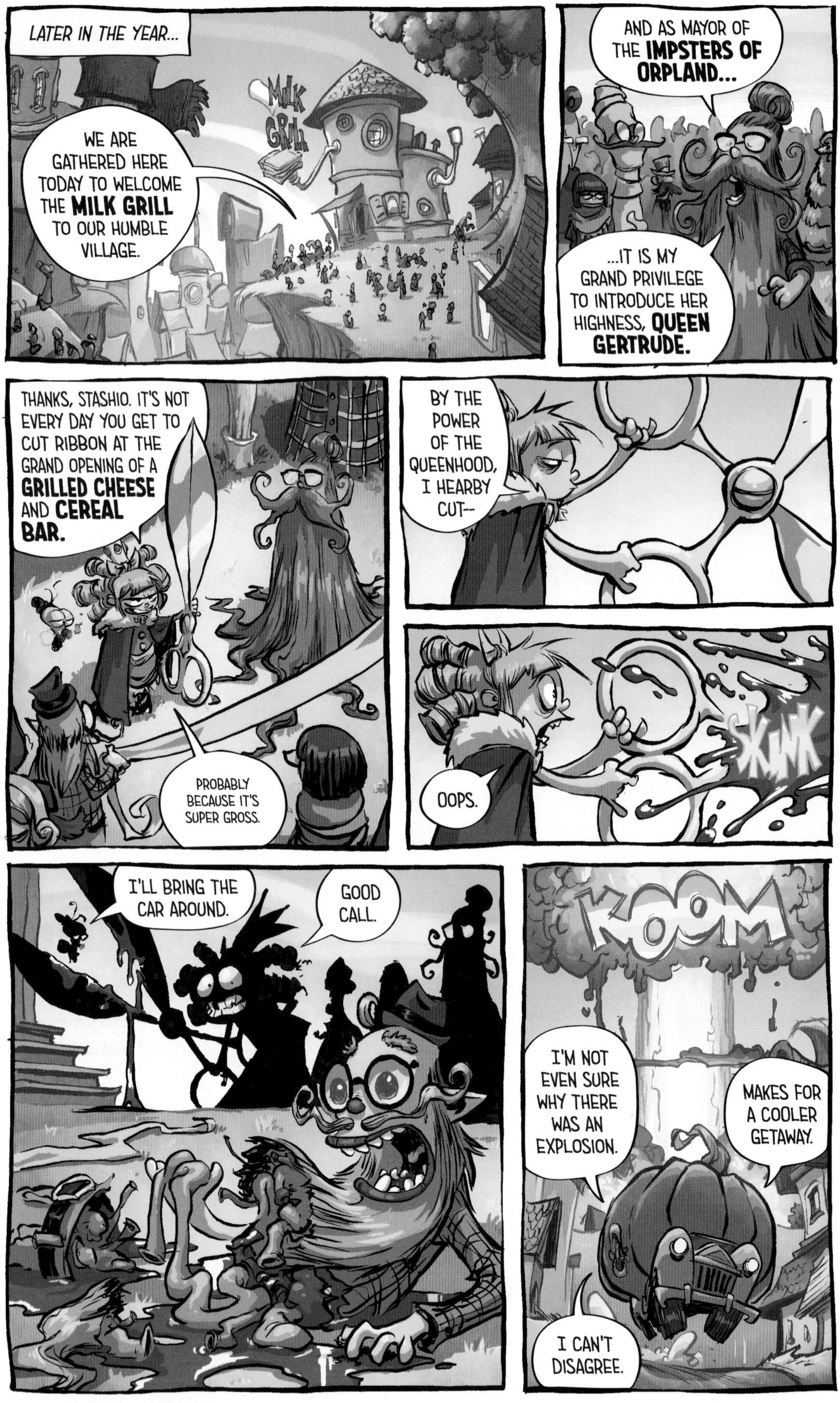

LATER IN THE YEAR...
MILK GRILL
WE ARE GATHERED HERE TODAY TO WELCOME THE MILK GRILL TO OUR HUMBLE VILLAGE.
AND AS MAYOR OF THE IMPSTERS OF ORPLAND...
...IT IS MY GRAND PRIVILEGE TO INTRODUCE HER HIGHNESS, QUEEN GERTRUDE.
THANKS, STASHIO. IT'S NOT EVERY DAY YOU GET TO CUT RIBBON AT THE GRAND OPENING OF A GRILLED CHEESE AND CEREAL BAR.
PROBABLY BECAUSE IT'S SUPER GROSS.
BY THE POWER OF THE QUEENHOOD, I HEARBY CUT--
SKLINK
OOPS.
I'LL BRING THE CAR AROUND.
GOOD CALL.
KOOM
I'M NOT EVEN SURE WHY THERE WAS AN EXPLOSION.
MAKES FOR A COOLER GETAWAY.
I CAN'T DISAGREE.

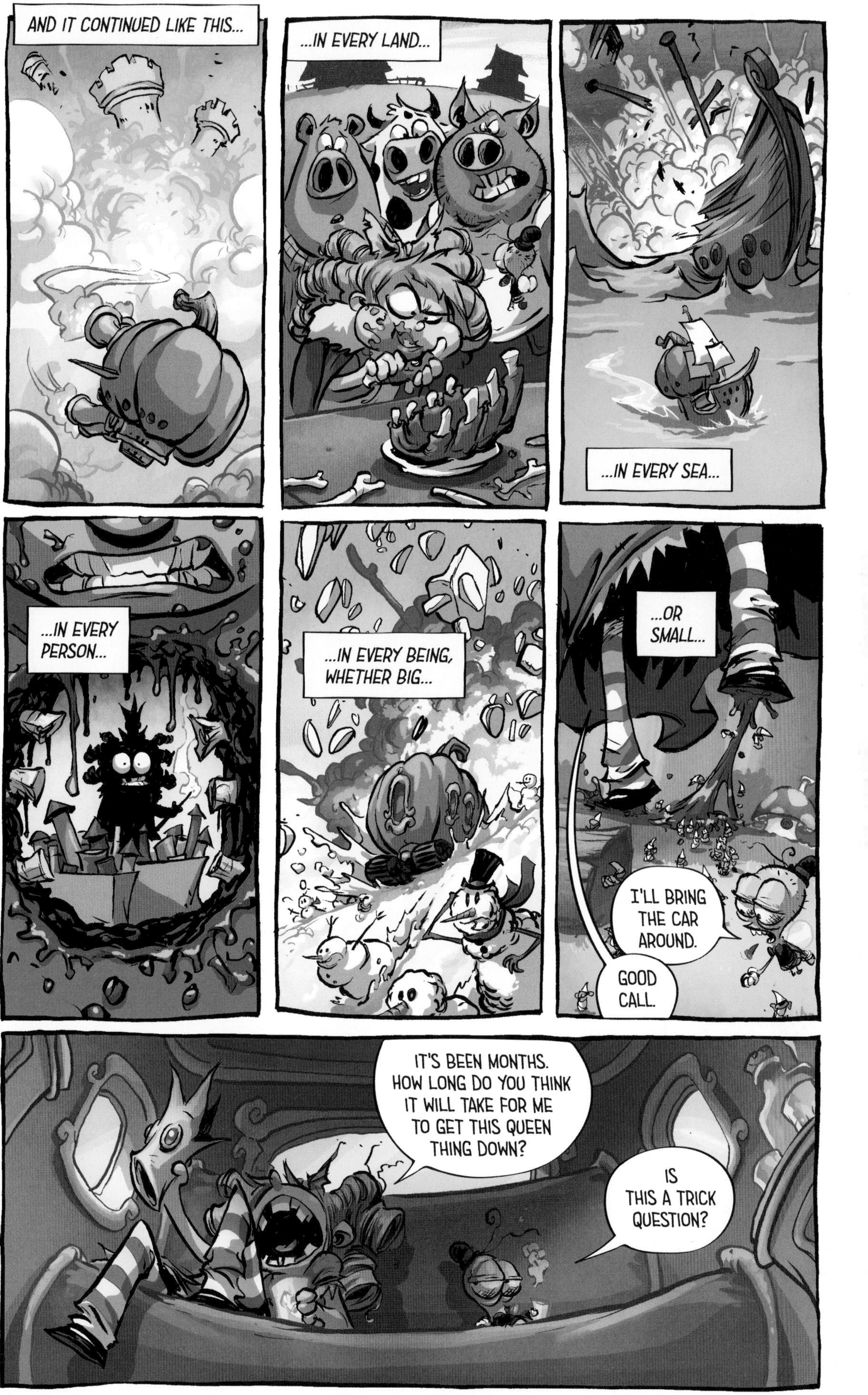
AND IT CONTINUED LIKE THIS...
...IN EVERY LAND...
...IN EVERY SEA...
...IN EVERY PERSON...
...IN EVERY BEING, WHETHER BIG...
...OR SMALL...
I'LL BRING THE CAR AROUND.
GOOD CALL.
IT'S BEEN MONTHS. HOW LONG DO YOU THINK IT WILL TAKE FOR ME TO GET THIS QUEEN THING DOWN?
IS THIS A TRICK QUESTION?

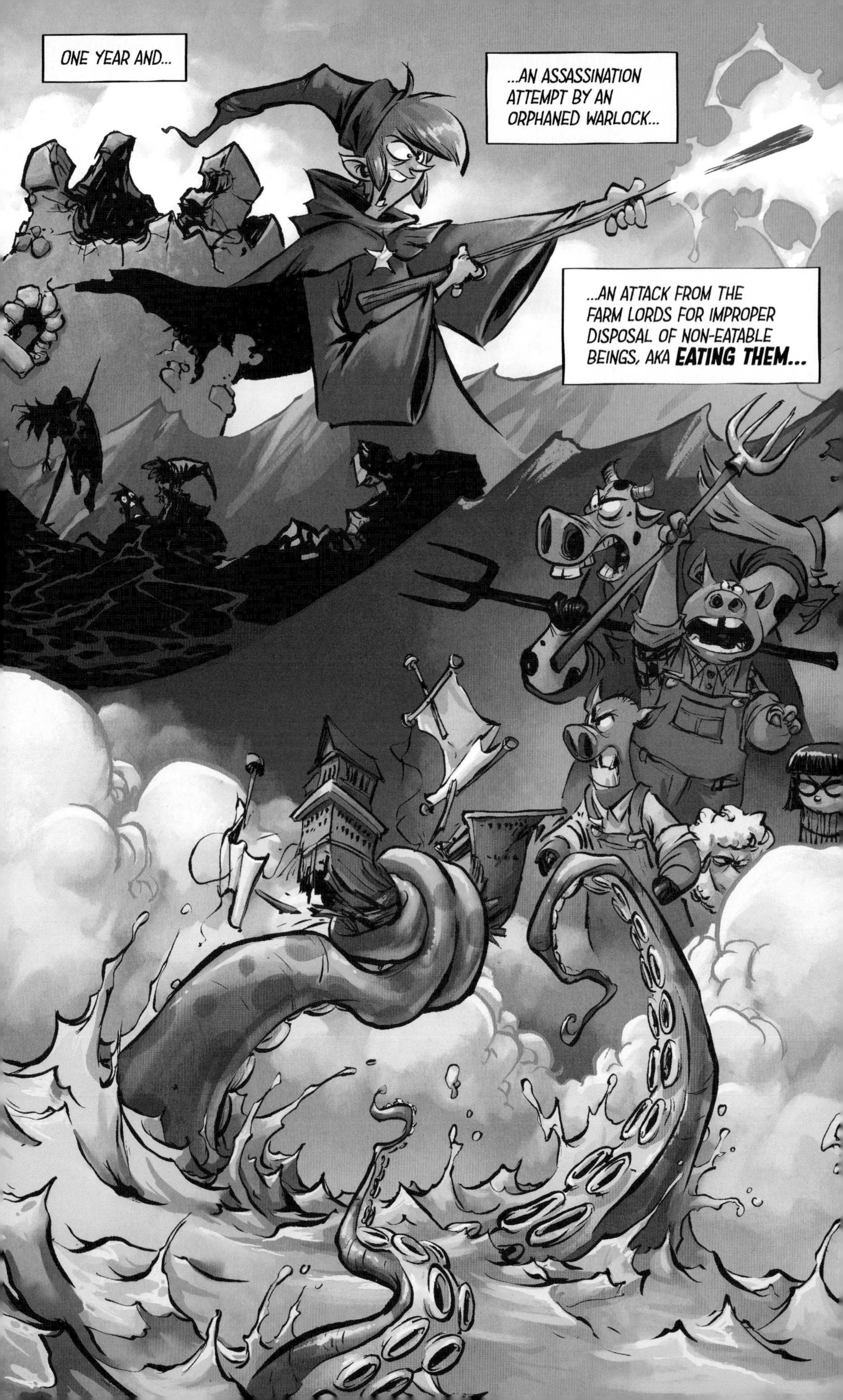
ONE YEAR AND...
...AN ASSASSINATION ATTEMPT BY AN ORPHANED WARLOCK...
...AN ATTACK FROM THE FARM LORDS FOR IMPROPER DISPOSAL OF NON-EATABLE BEINGS, AKA **EATING THEM...**

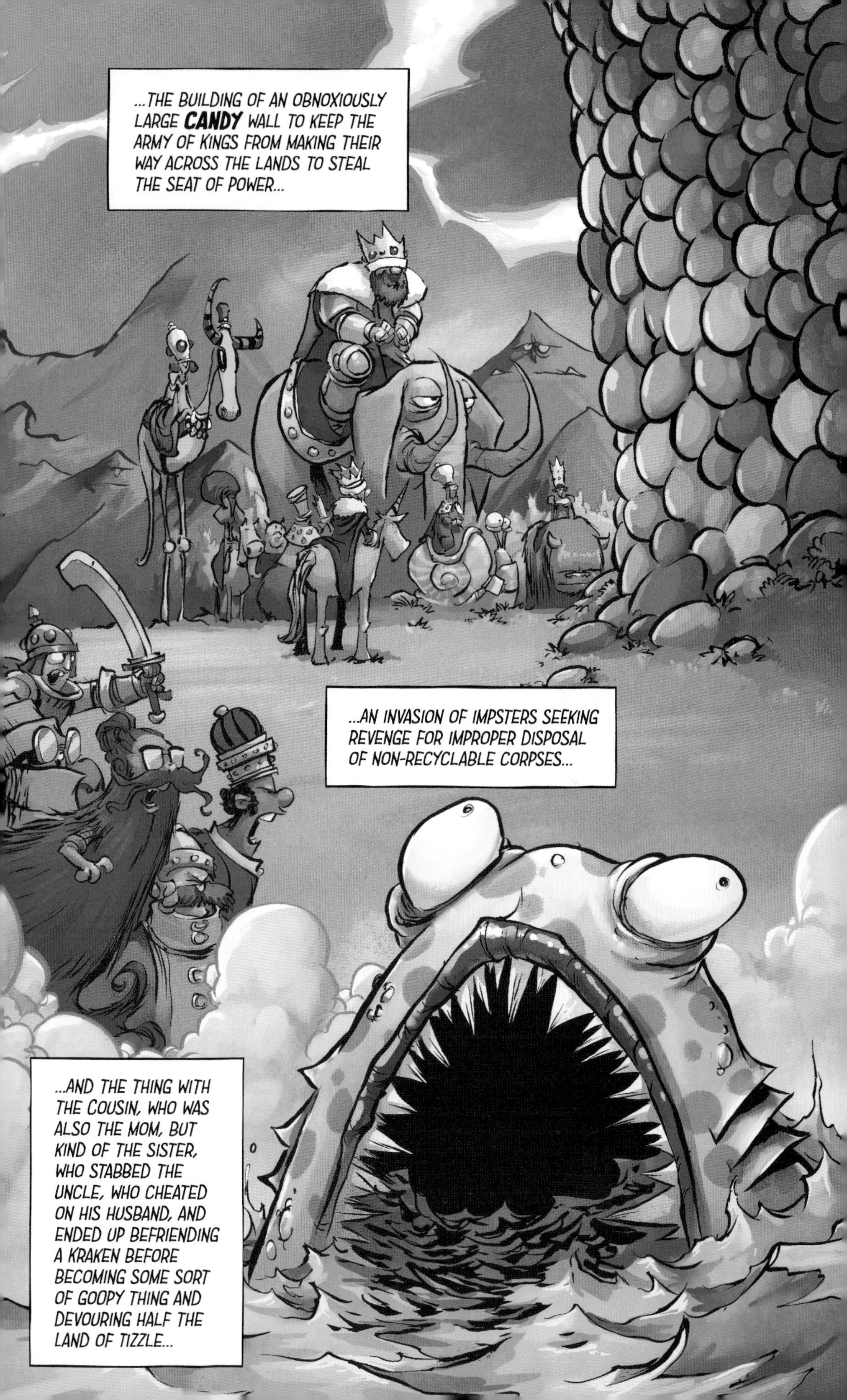
...THE BUILDING OF AN OBNOXIOUSLY LARGE **CANDY** WALL TO KEEP THE ARMY OF KINGS FROM MAKING THEIR WAY ACROSS THE LANDS TO STEAL THE SEAT OF POWER...
...AN INVASION OF IMPSTERS SEEKING REVENGE FOR IMPROPER DISPOSAL OF NON-RECYCLABLE CORPSES...
...AND THE THING WITH THE COUSIN, WHO WAS ALSO THE MOM, BUT KIND OF THE SISTER, WHO STABBED THE UNCLE, WHO CHEATED ON HIS HUSBAND, AND ENDED UP BEFRIENDING A KRAKEN BEFORE BECOMING SOME SORT OF GOOPY THING AND DEVOURING HALF THE LAND OF TIZZLE...

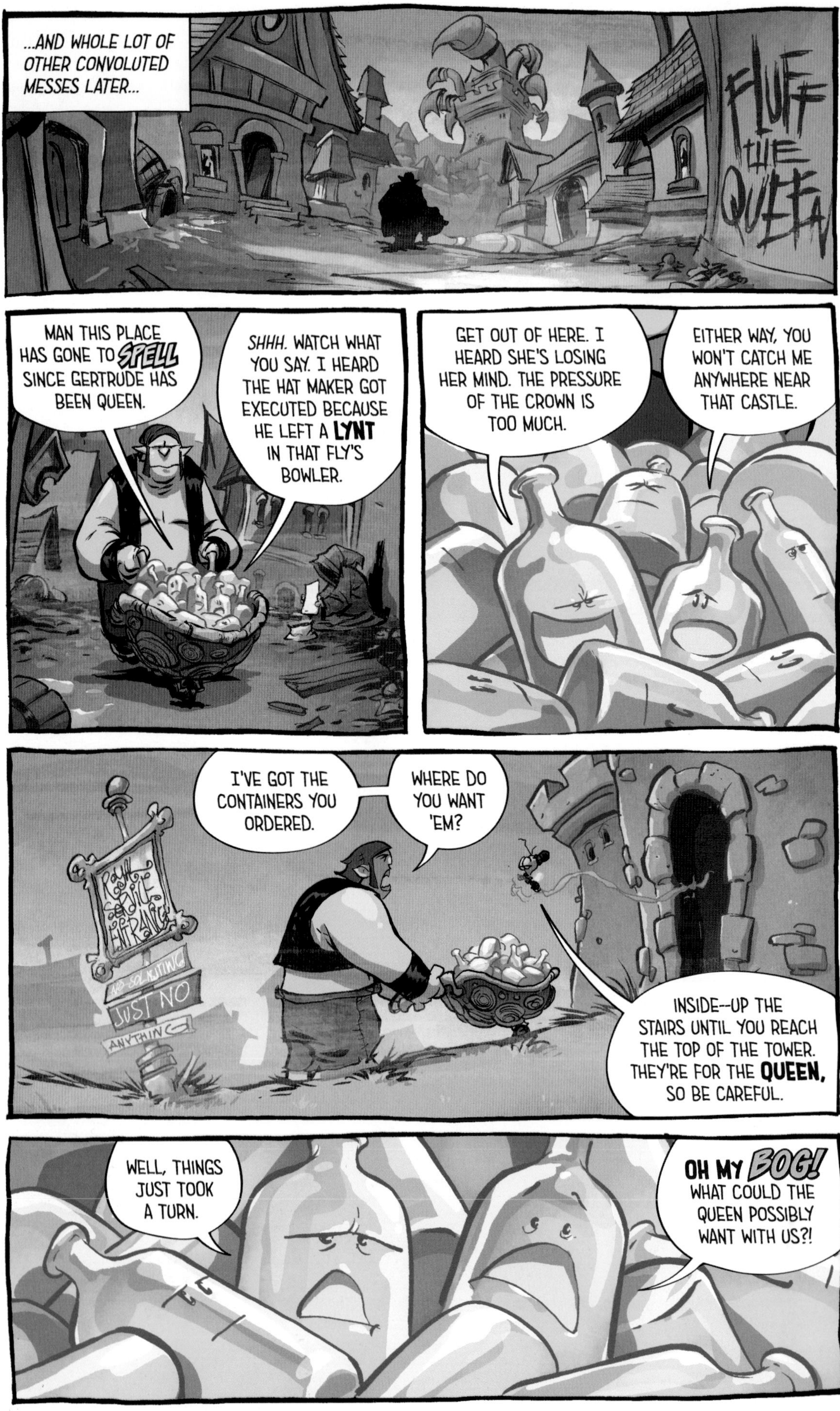

...AND WHOLE LOT OF OTHER CONVOLUTED MESSES LATER...
FLUFF THE QUEEN
MAN THIS PLACE HAS GONE TO SPELL SINCE GERTRUDE HAS BEEN QUEEN.
SHHH. WATCH WHAT YOU SAY. I HEARD THE HAT MAKER GOT EXECUTED BECAUSE HE LEFT A LYNT IN THAT FLY'S BOWLER.
GET OUT OF HERE. I HEARD SHE'S LOSING HER MIND. THE PRESSURE OF THE CROWN IS TOO MUCH.
EITHER WAY, YOU WON'T CATCH ME ANYWHERE NEAR THAT CASTLE.
I'VE GOT THE CONTAINERS YOU ORDERED.
WHERE DO YOU WANT 'EM?
JUST NO
ANYTHING
INSIDE--UP THE STAIRS UNTIL YOU REACH THE TOP OF THE TOWER. THEY'RE FOR THE QUEEN, SO BE CAREFUL.
WELL, THINGS JUST TOOK A TURN.
OH MY BOG! WHAT COULD THE QUEEN POSSIBLY WANT WITH US?!

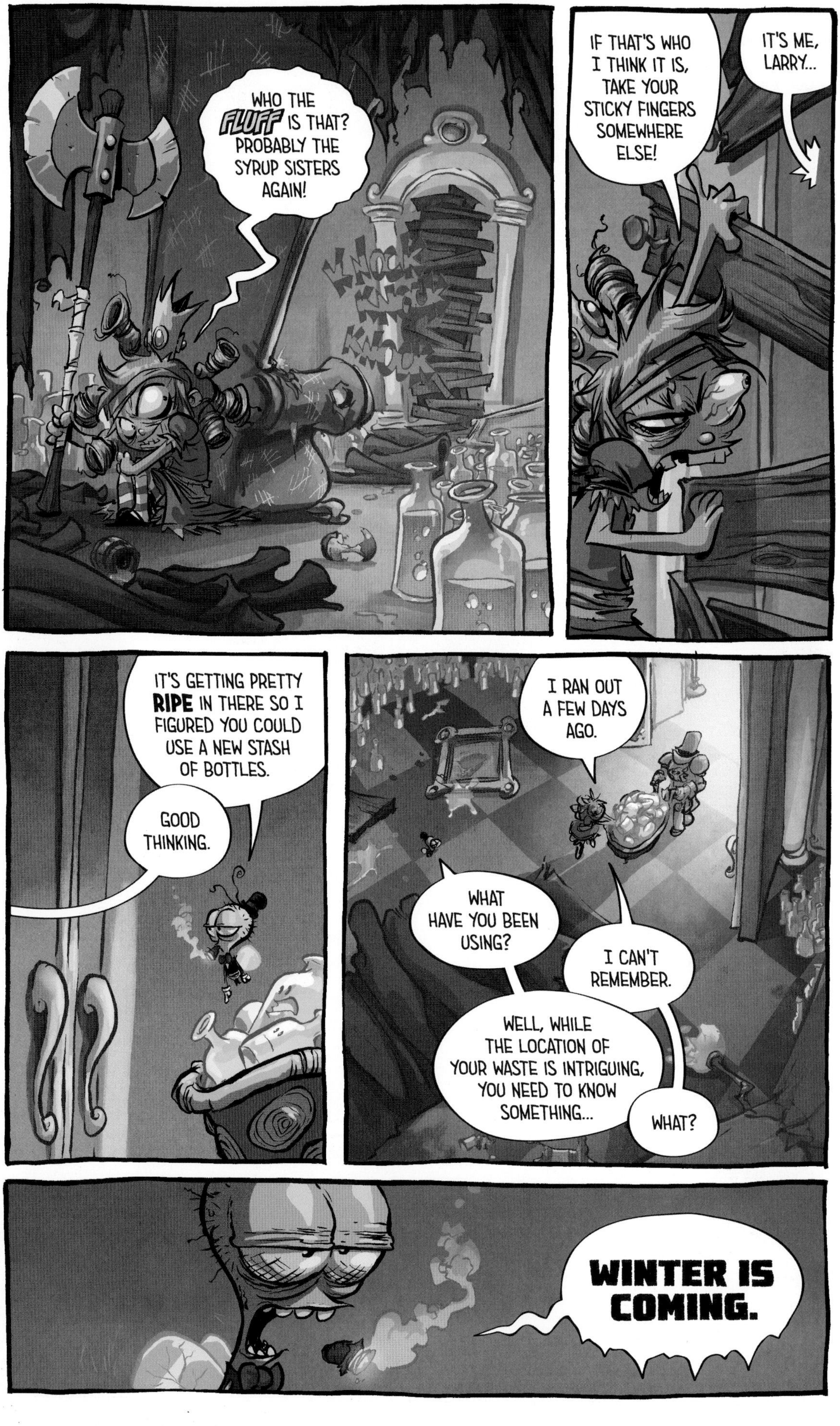
WHO THE FLUFF IS THAT? PROBABLY THE SYRUP SISTERS AGAIN!
KNOCK KNOCK KNOCK KNOCK
IF THAT'S WHO I THINK IT IS, TAKE YOUR STICKY FINGERS SOMEWHERE ELSE!
IT'S ME, LARRY...
IT'S GETTING PRETTY RIPE IN THERE SO I FIGURED YOU COULD USE A NEW STASH OF BOTTLES.
GOOD THINKING.
I RAN OUT A FEW DAYS AGO.
WHAT HAVE YOU BEEN USING?
I CAN'T REMEMBER.
WELL, WHILE THE LOCATION OF YOUR WASTE IS INTRIGUING, YOU NEED TO KNOW SOMETHING...
WHAT?
WINTER IS COMING.

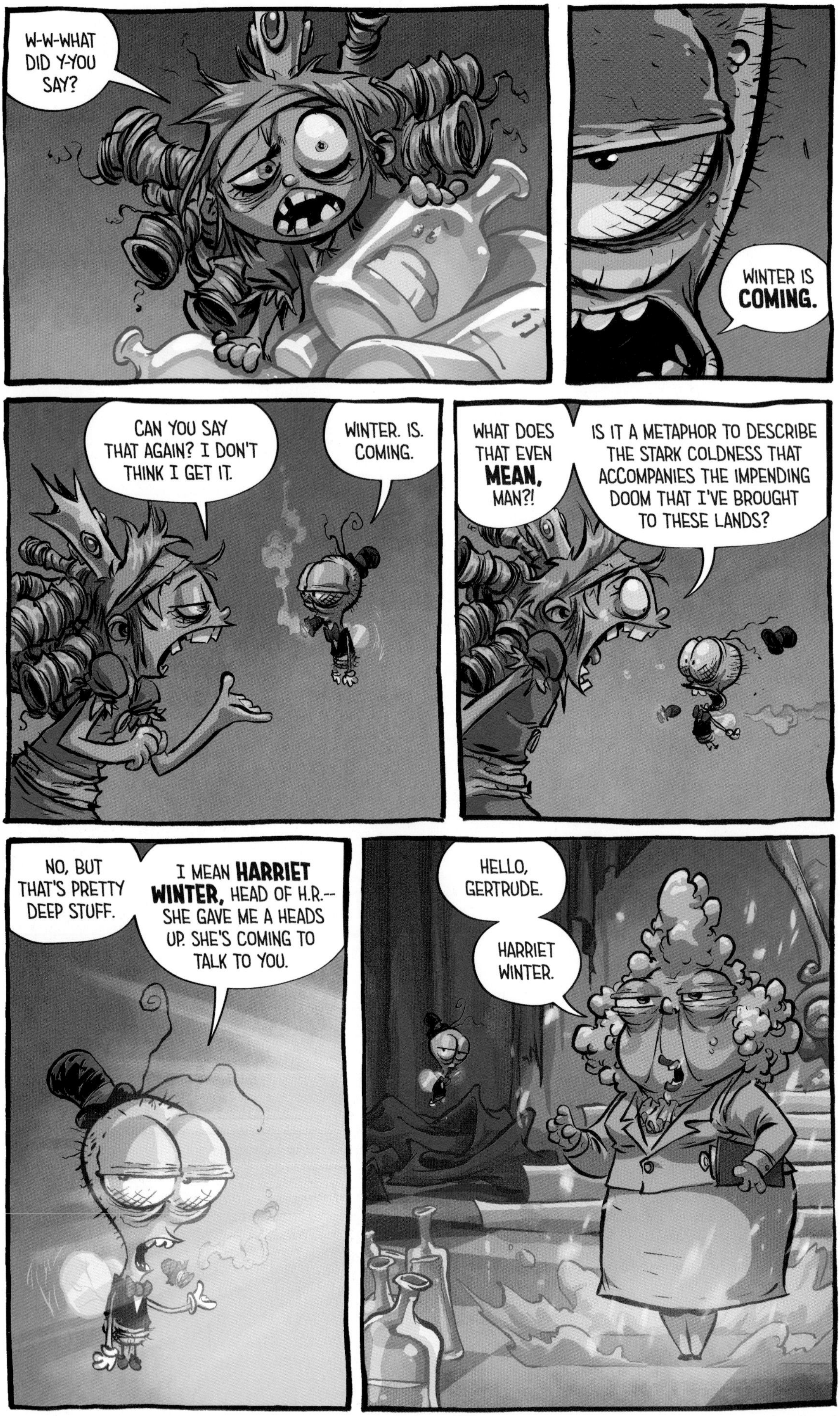

W-W-WHAT DID Y-YOU SAY?
WINTER IS COMING.
CAN YOU SAY THAT AGAIN? I DON'T THINK I GET IT.
WINTER. IS. COMING.
WHAT DOES THAT EVEN MEAN, MAN?!
IS IT A METAPHOR TO DESCRIBE THE STARK COLDNESS THAT ACCOMPANIES THE IMPENDING DOOM THAT I'VE BROUGHT TO THESE LANDS?
NO, BUT THAT'S PRETTY DEEP STUFF.
I MEAN HARRIET WINTER, HEAD OF H.R.-- SHE GAVE ME A HEADS UP. SHE'S COMING TO TALK TO YOU.
HELLO, GERTRUDE.
HARRIET WINTER.

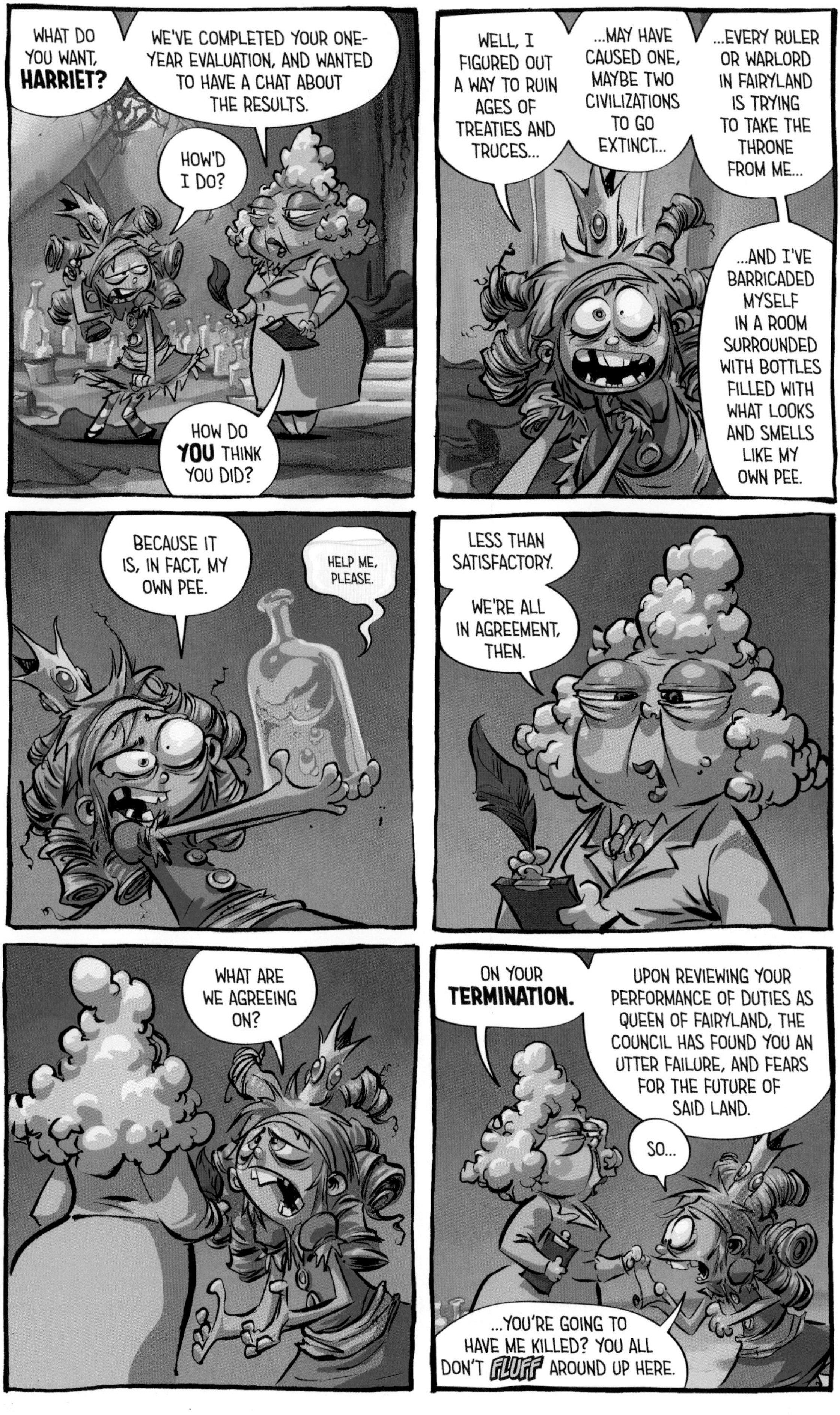
WHAT DO YOU WANT, HARRIET?
WE'VE COMPLETED YOUR ONE-YEAR EVALUATION, AND WANTED TO HAVE A CHAT ABOUT THE RESULTS.
HOW'D I DO?
HOW DO YOU THINK YOU DID?
WELL, I FIGURED OUT A WAY TO RUIN AGES OF TREATIES AND TRUCES...
...MAY HAVE CAUSED ONE, MAYBE TWO CIVILIZATIONS TO GO EXTINCT...
...EVERY RULER OR WARLORD IN FAIRYLAND IS TRYING TO TAKE THE THRONE FROM ME...
...AND I'VE BARRICADED MYSELF IN A ROOM SURROUNDED WITH BOTTLES FILLED WITH WHAT LOOKS AND SMELLS LIKE MY OWN PEE.
BECAUSE IT IS, IN FACT, MY OWN PEE.
HELP ME, PLEASE.
LESS THAN SATISFACTORY.
WE'RE ALL IN AGREEMENT, THEN.
WHAT ARE WE AGREEING ON?
ON YOUR TERMINATION.
UPON REVIEWING YOUR PERFORMANCE OF DUTIES AS QUEEN OF FAIRYLAND, THE COUNCIL HAS FOUND YOU AN UTTER FAILURE, AND FEARS FOR THE FUTURE OF SAID LAND.
SO...
...YOU'RE GOING TO HAVE ME KILLED? YOU ALL DON'T FLUFF AROUND UP HERE.

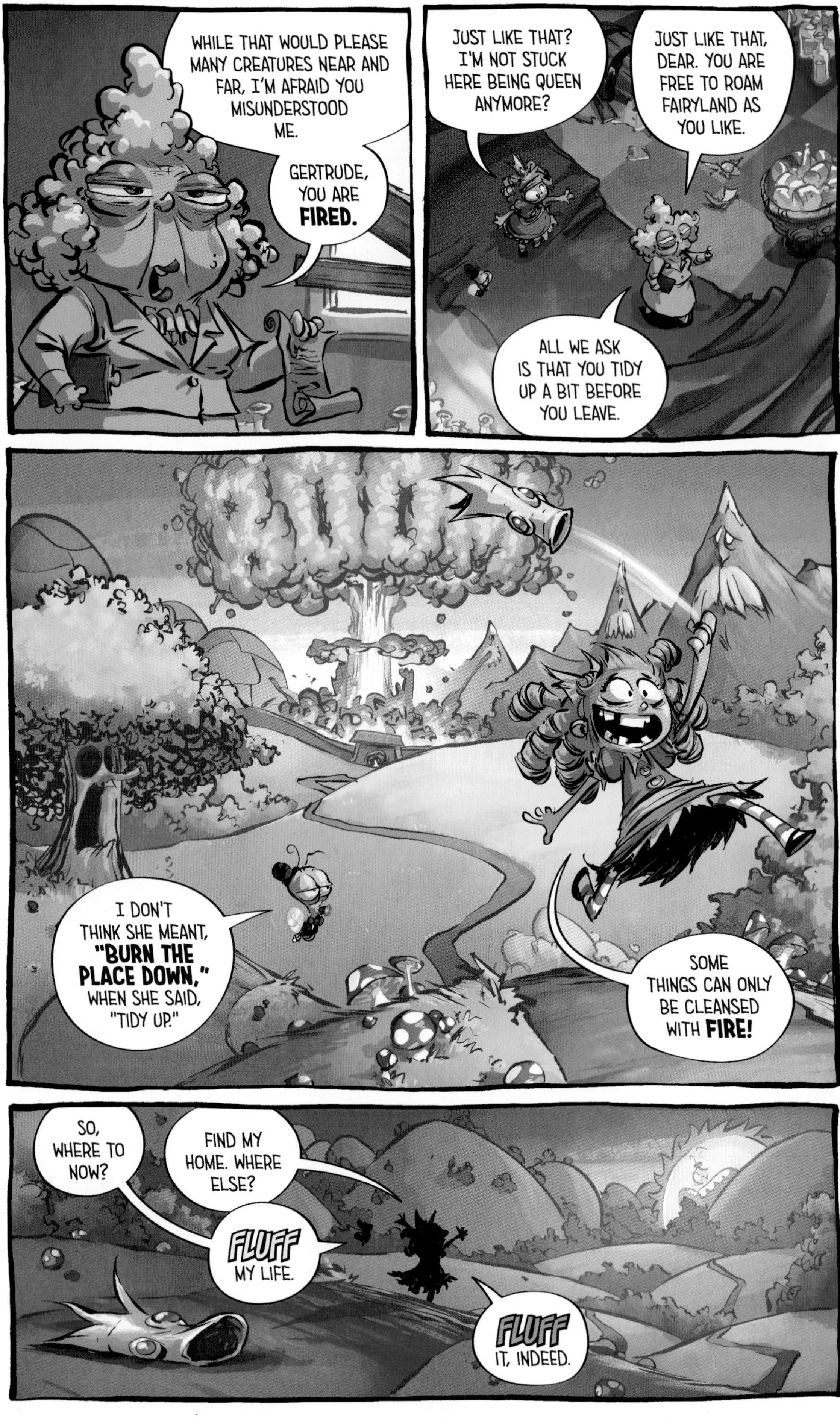
WHILE THAT WOULD PLEASE MANY CREATURES NEAR AND FAR, I'M AFRAID YOU MISUNDERSTOOD ME.
GERTRUDE, YOU ARE **FIRED.**
JUST LIKE THAT? I'M NOT STUCK HERE BEING QUEEN ANYMORE?
JUST LIKE THAT, DEAR. YOU ARE FREE TO ROAM FAIRYLAND AS YOU LIKE.
ALL WE ASK IS THAT YOU TIDY UP A BIT BEFORE YOU LEAVE.
I DON'T THINK SHE MEANT, **"BURN THE PLACE DOWN,"** WHEN SHE SAID, "TIDY UP."
SOME THINGS CAN ONLY BE CLEANSED WITH **FIRE!**
SO, WHERE TO NOW?
FIND MY HOME. WHERE ELSE?
FLUFF MY LIFE.
FLUFF IT, INDEED.

SEVEN

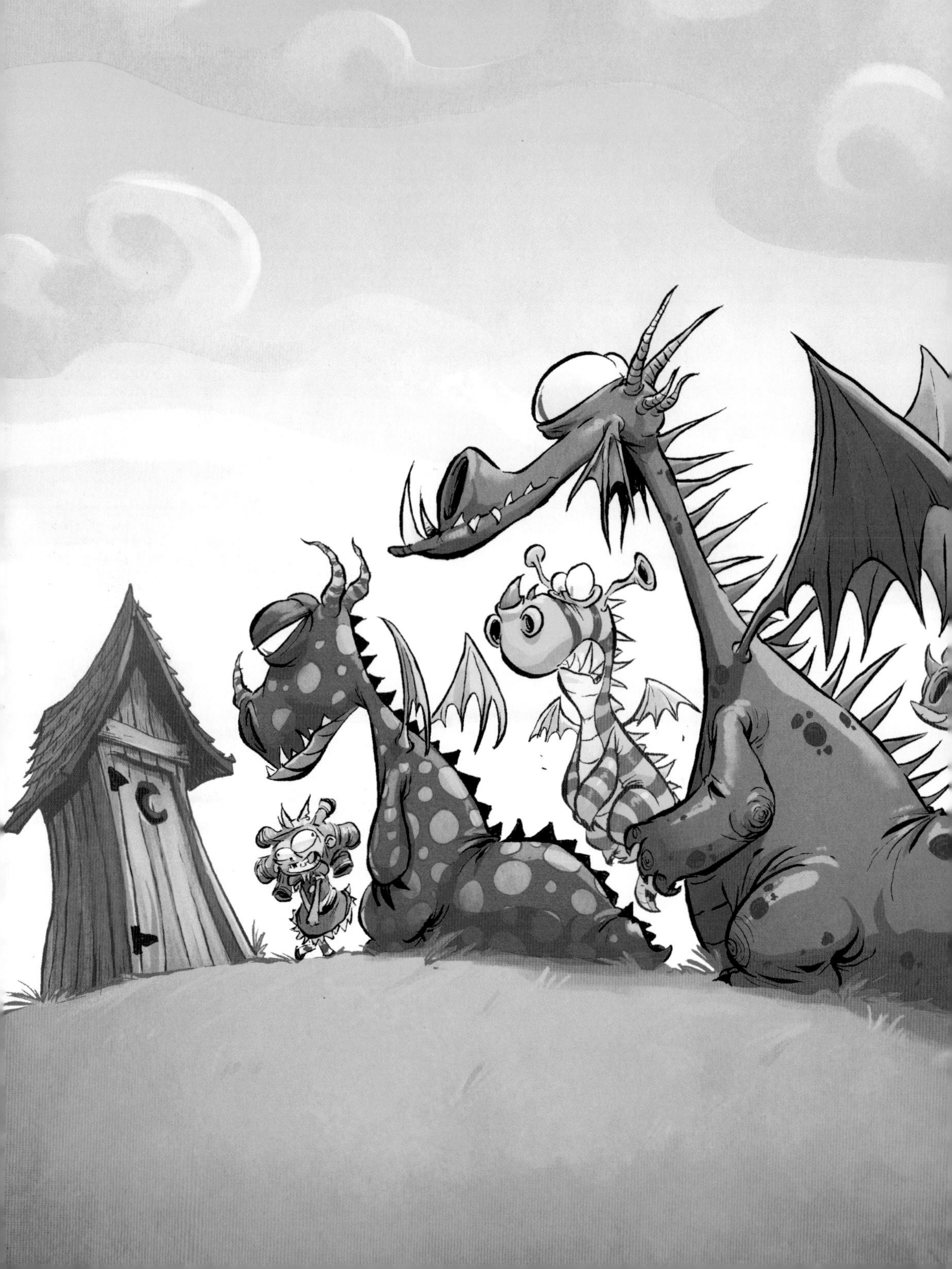

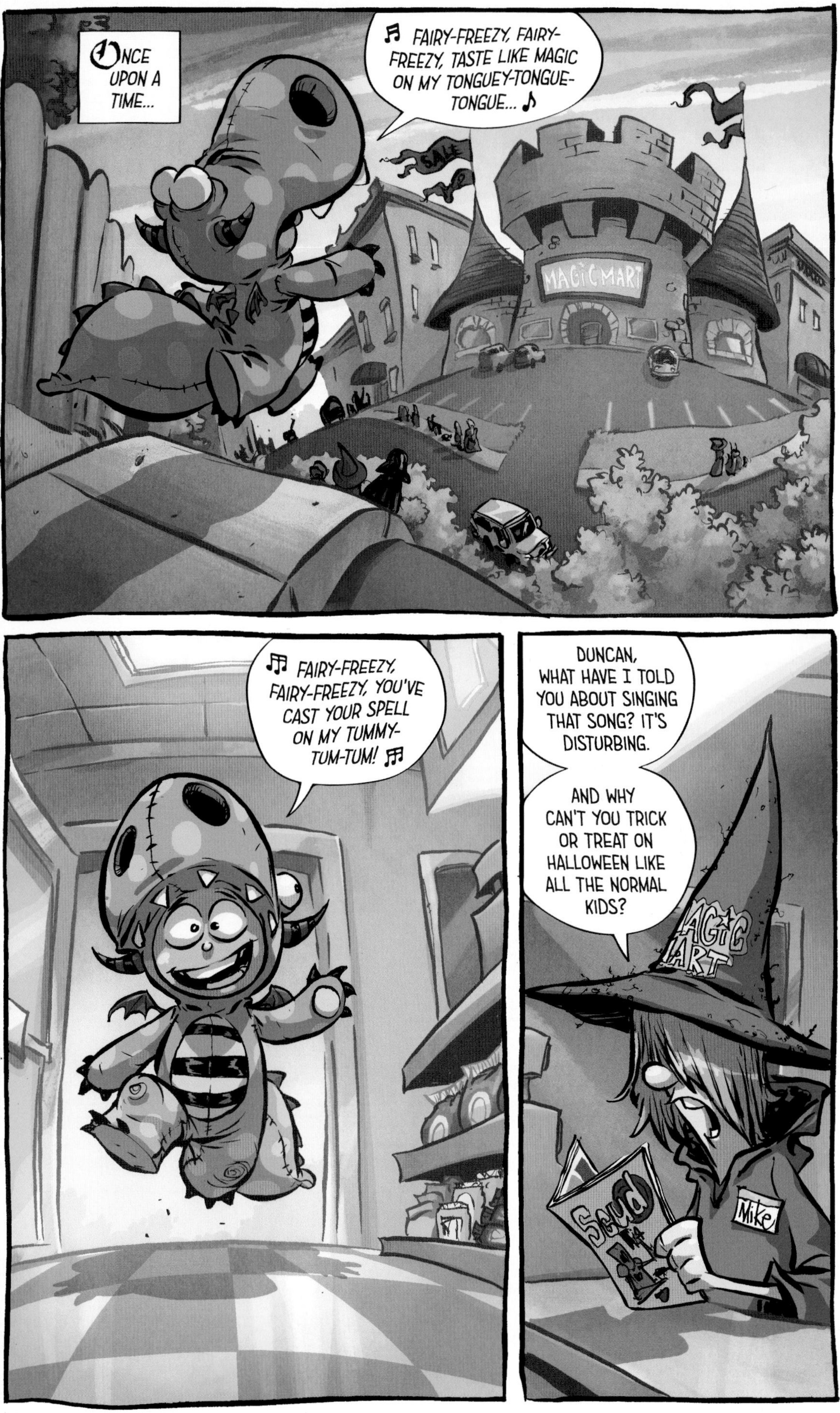
ONCE UPON A TIME...
♬ FAIRY-FREEZY, FAIRY-FREEZY, TASTE LIKE MAGIC ON MY TONGUEY-TONGUE-TONGUE... ♪
SALE
MAGIC MART
♬ FAIRY-FREEZY, FAIRY-FREEZY, YOU'VE CAST YOUR SPELL ON MY TUMMY-TUM-TUM! ♬
DUNCAN, WHAT HAVE I TOLD YOU ABOUT SINGING THAT SONG? IT'S DISTURBING.
AND WHY CAN'T YOU TRICK OR TREAT ON HALLOWEEN LIKE ALL THE NORMAL KIDS?
MAGIC MART
Mike

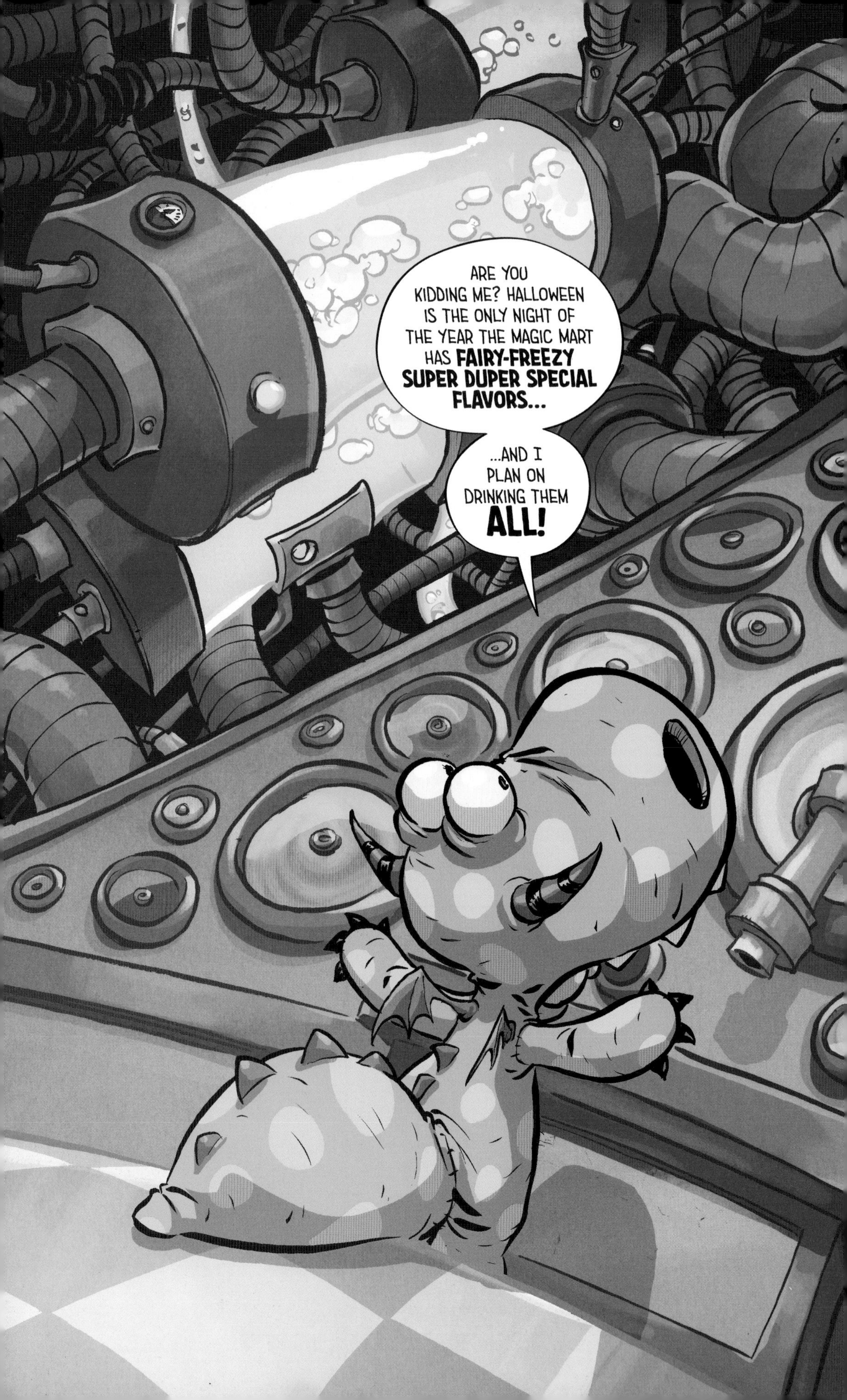
ARE YOU KIDDING ME? HALLOWEEN IS THE ONLY NIGHT OF THE YEAR THE MAGIC MART HAS **FAIRY-FREEZY SUPER DUPER SPECIAL FLAVORS...**
...AND I PLAN ON DRINKING THEM **ALL!**

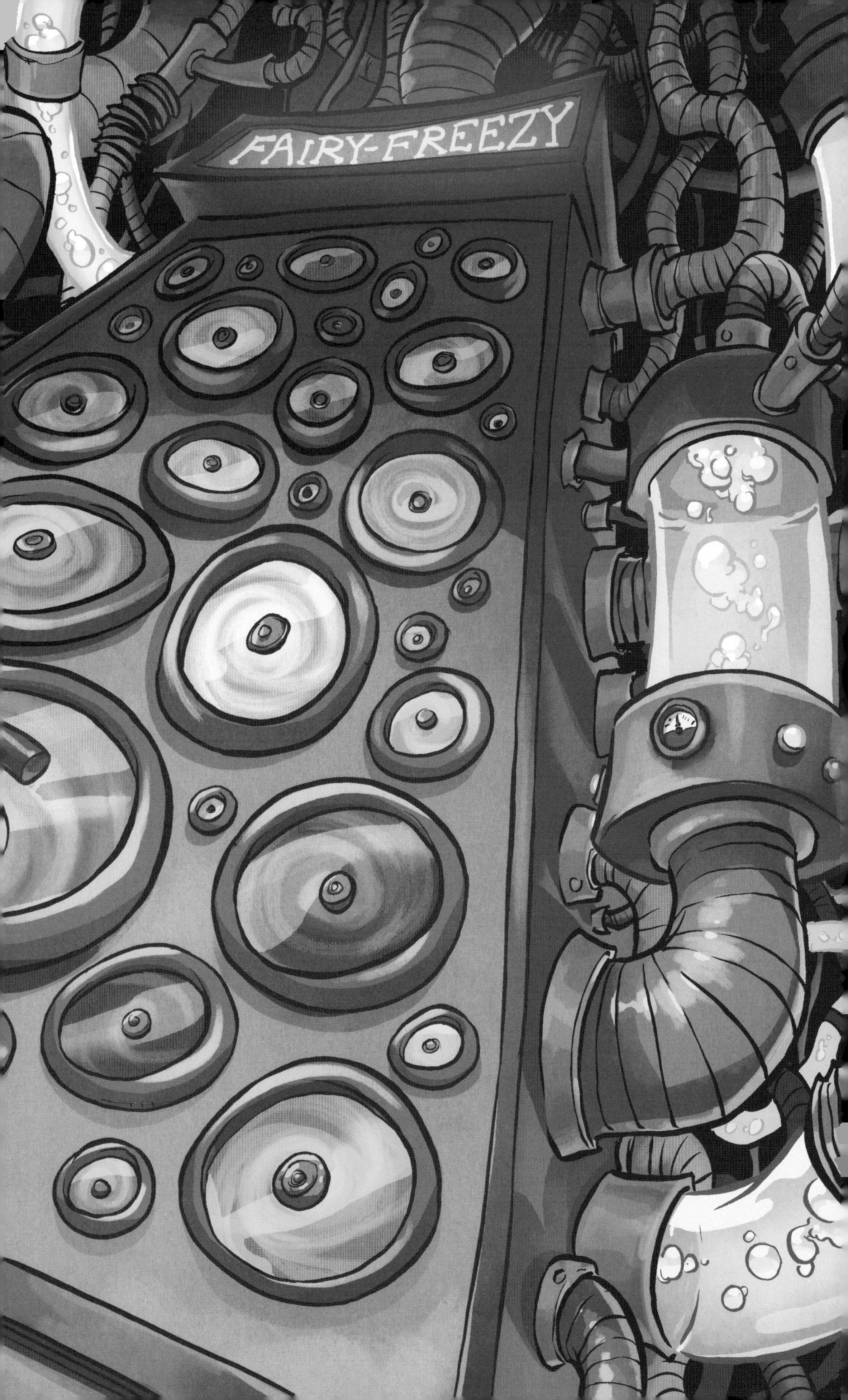
FAIRY-FREEZY

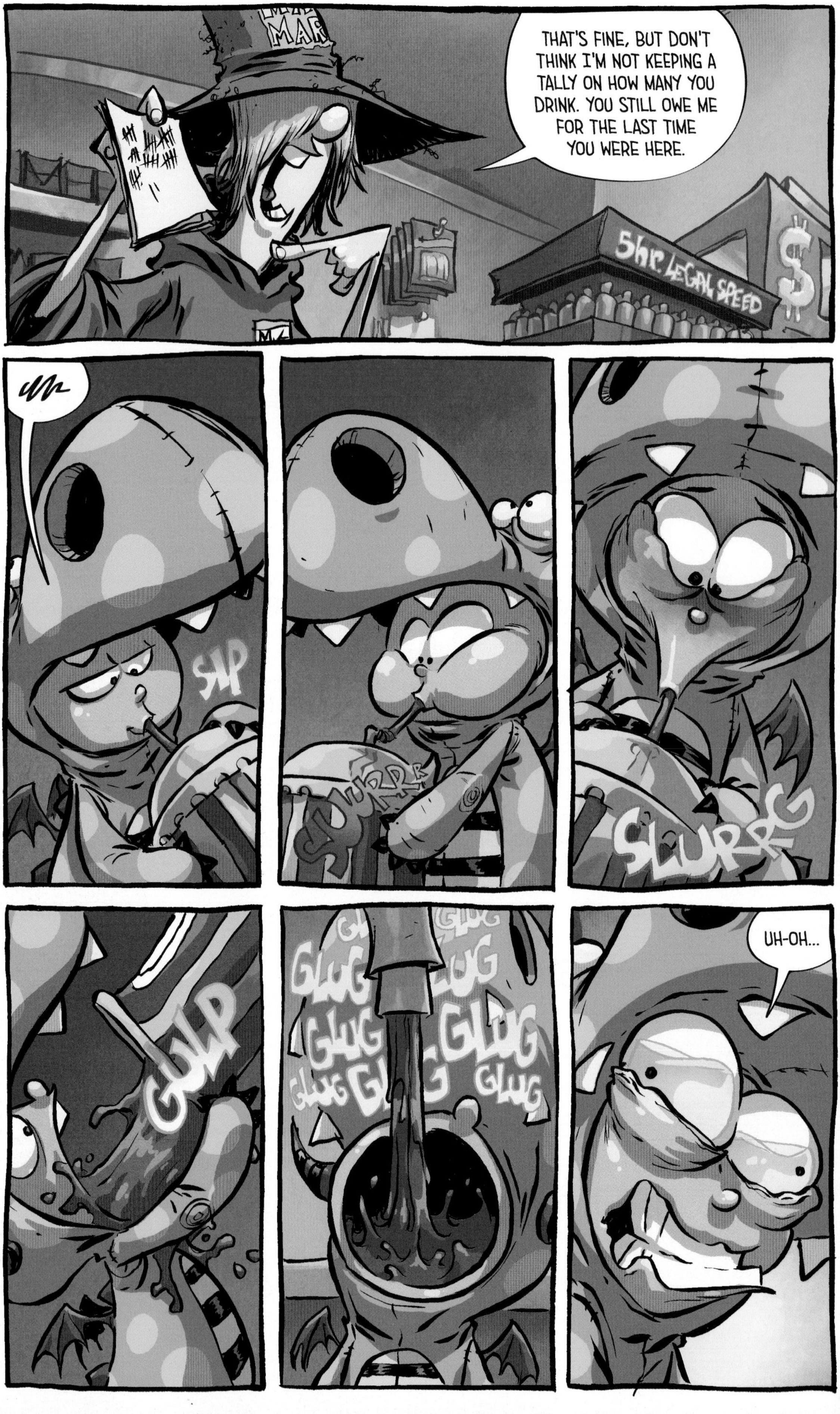
THAT'S FINE, BUT DON'T THINK I'M NOT KEEPING A TALLY ON HOW MANY YOU DRINK. YOU STILL OWE ME FOR THE LAST TIME YOU WERE HERE.
5hr LEGAL SPEED
SIP
SLURRG
GULP
GLUG GLUG GLUG GLUG GLUG GLUG
UH-OH...

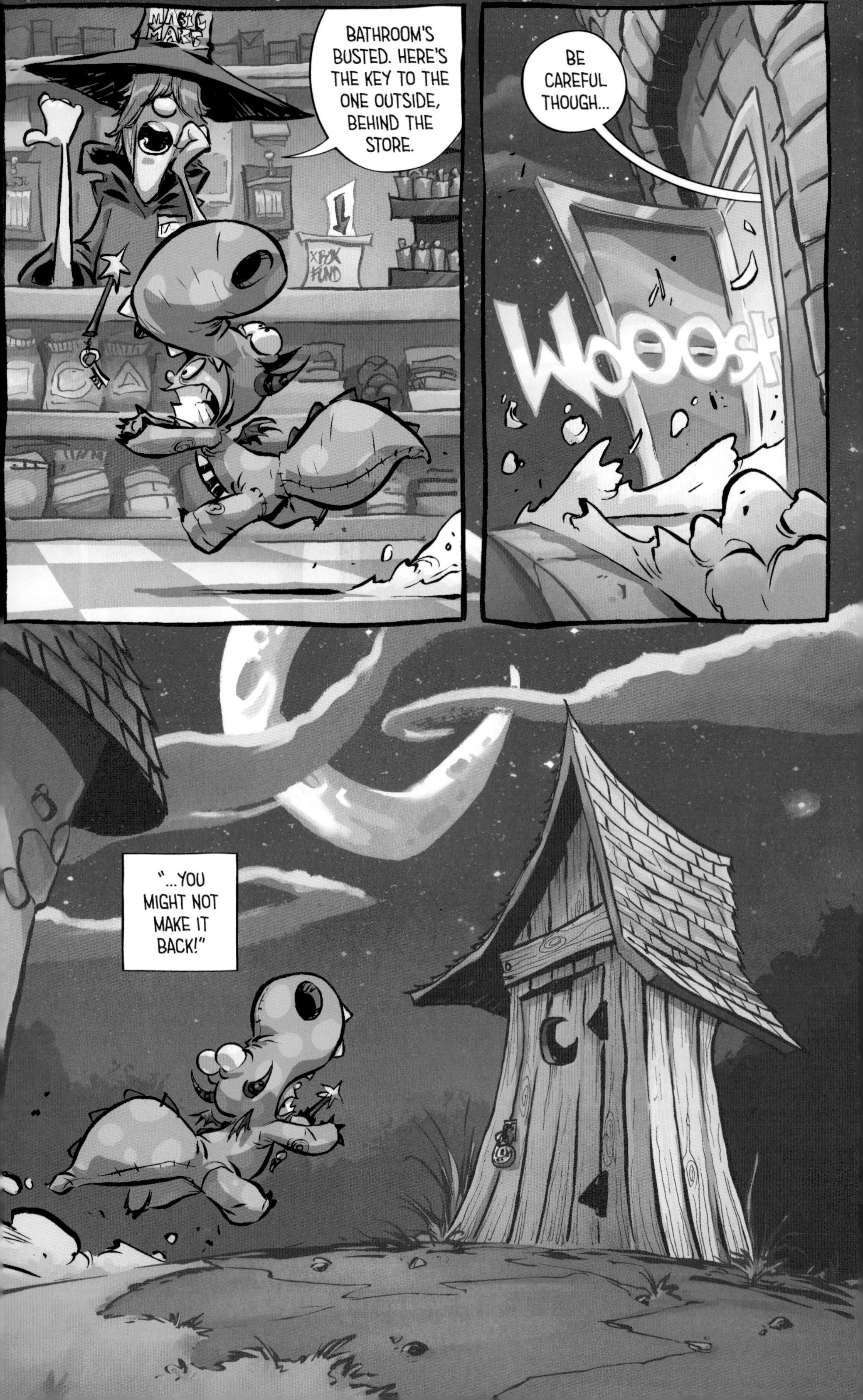
MAGIC MART
BATHROOM'S BUSTED. HERE'S THE KEY TO THE ONE OUTSIDE, BEHIND THE STORE.
BE CAREFUL THOUGH...
WOOOSH
"...YOU MIGHT NOT MAKE IT BACK!"

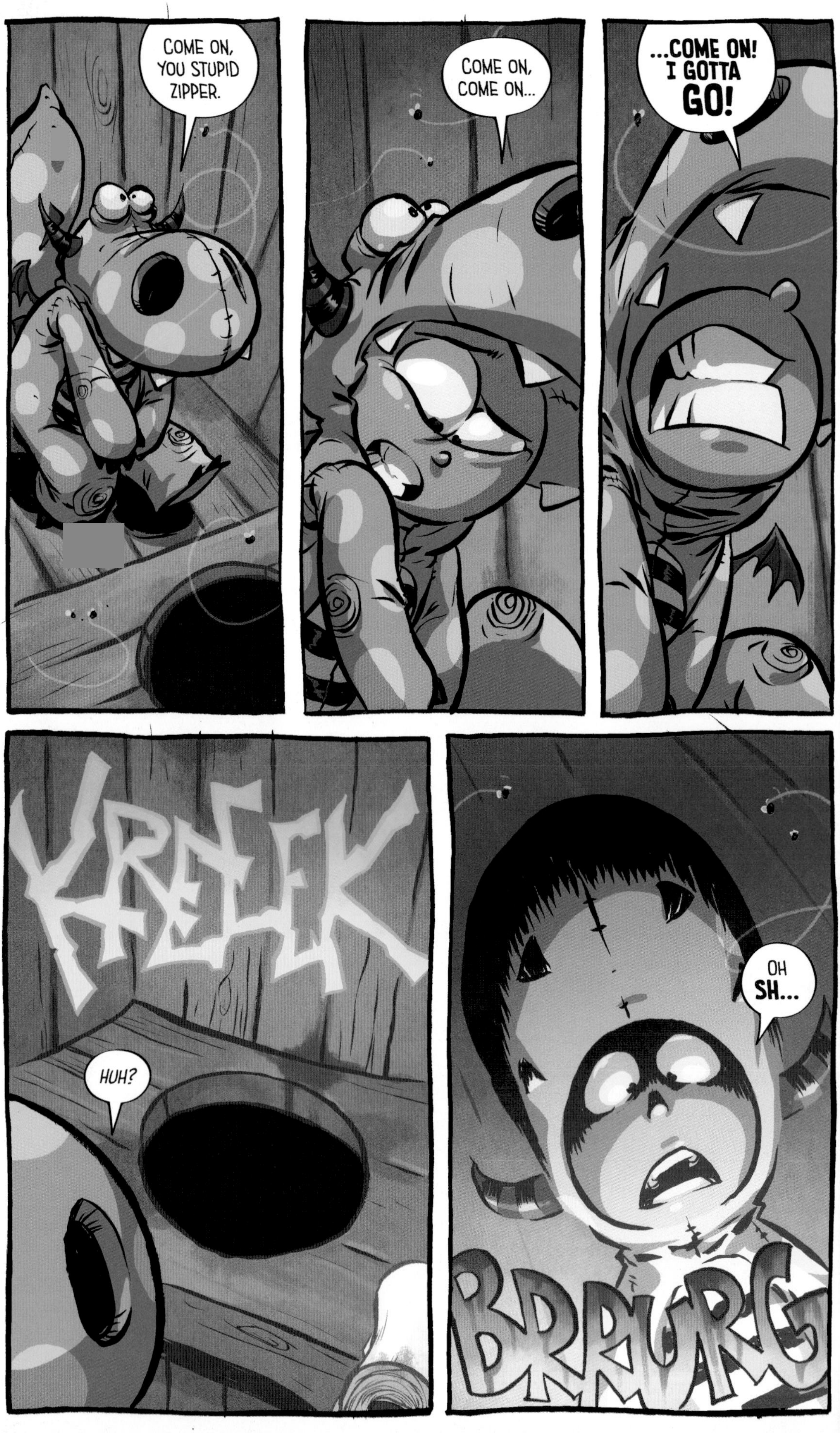
COME ON, YOU STUPID ZIPPER.
COME ON, COME ON...
...COME ON! I GOTTA GO!
KREEEK
HUH?
OH SH...
BRRURG

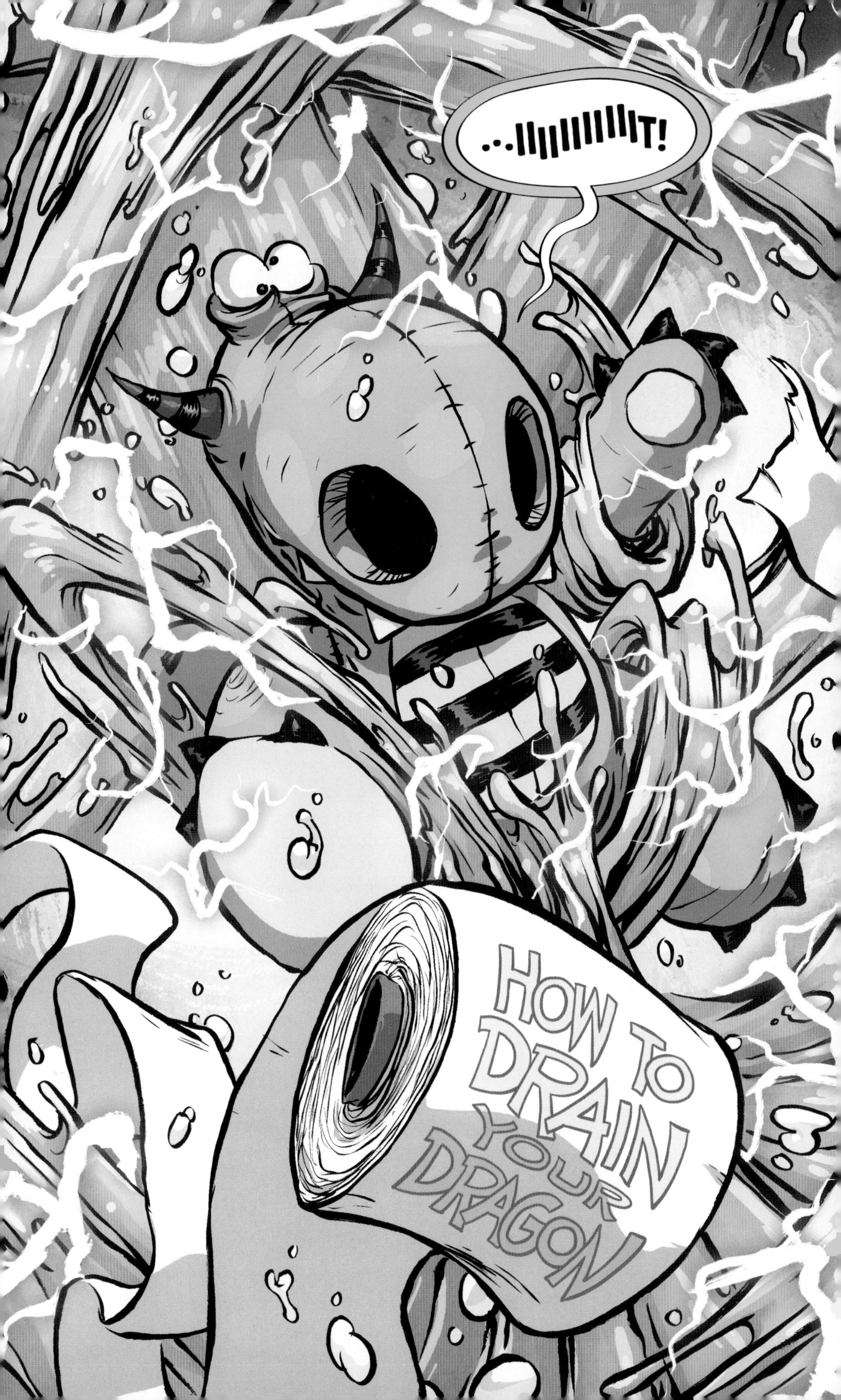
...IIIIIIIIIIIT!
HOW TO DRAIN YOUR DRAGON

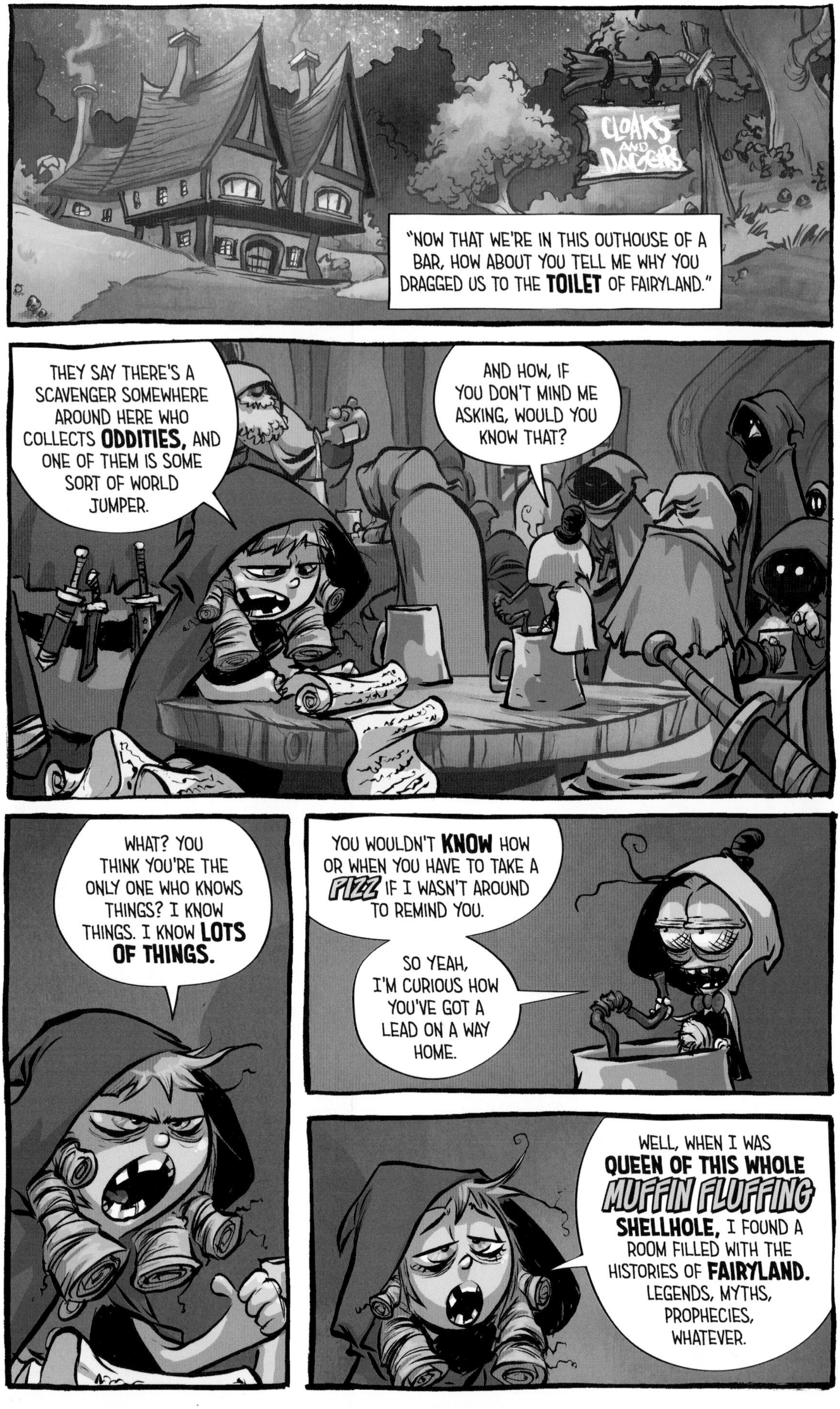
CLOAKS AND DAGGERS
"NOW THAT WE'RE IN THIS OUTHOUSE OF A BAR, HOW ABOUT YOU TELL ME WHY YOU DRAGGED US TO THE TOILET OF FAIRYLAND."
THEY SAY THERE'S A SCAVENGER SOMEWHERE AROUND HERE WHO COLLECTS ODDITIES, AND ONE OF THEM IS SOME SORT OF WORLD JUMPER.
AND HOW, IF YOU DON'T MIND ME ASKING, WOULD YOU KNOW THAT?
WHAT? YOU THINK YOU'RE THE ONLY ONE WHO KNOWS THINGS? I KNOW THINGS. I KNOW LOTS OF THINGS.
YOU WOULDN'T KNOW HOW OR WHEN YOU HAVE TO TAKE A PIZZ IF I WASN'T AROUND TO REMIND YOU.
SO YEAH, I'M CURIOUS HOW YOU'VE GOT A LEAD ON A WAY HOME.
WELL, WHEN I WAS QUEEN OF THIS WHOLE MUFFIN FLUFFING SHELLHOLE, I FOUND A ROOM FILLED WITH THE HISTORIES OF FAIRYLAND. LEGENDS, MYTHS, PROPHECIES, WHATEVER.

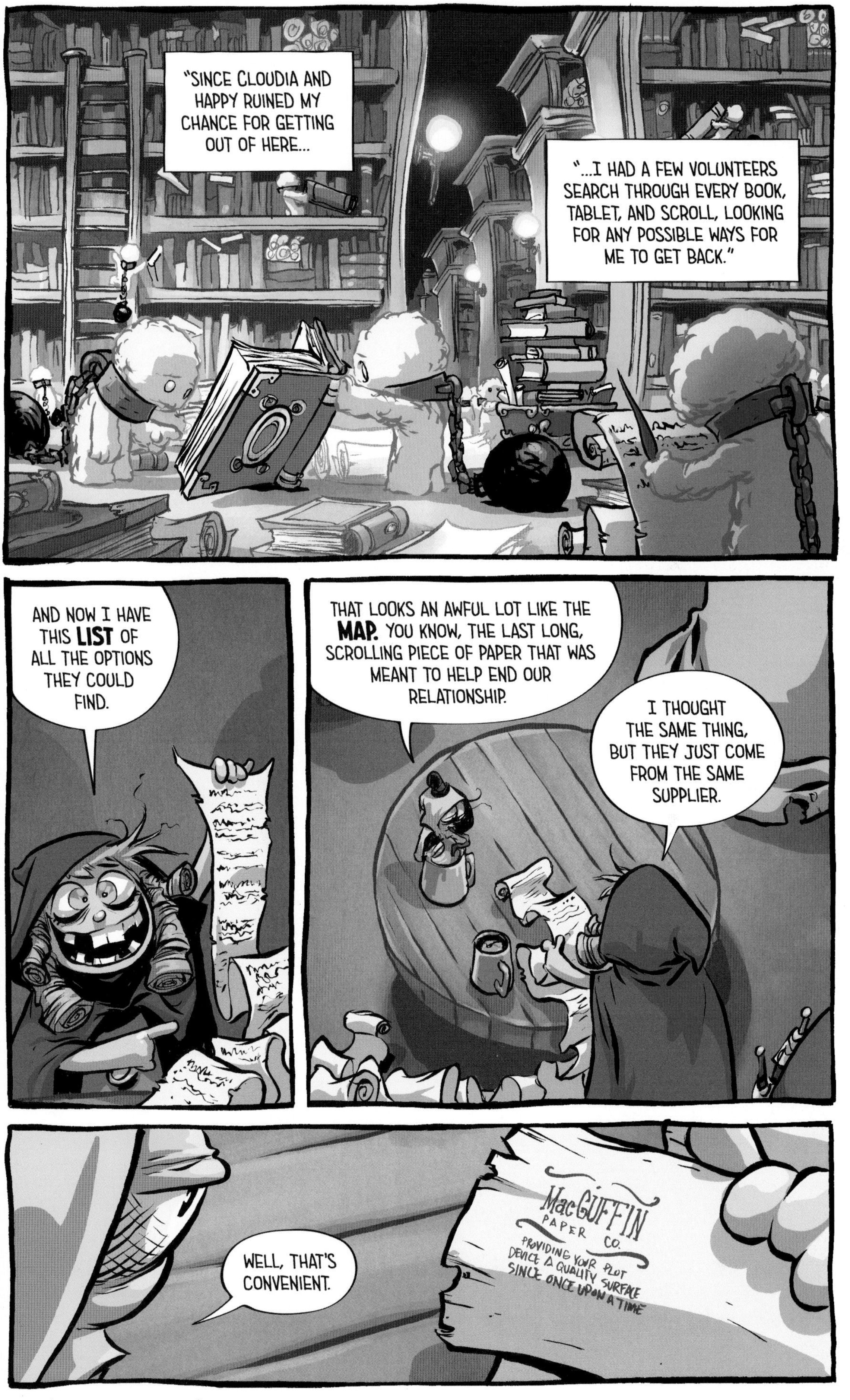
"SINCE CLOUDIA AND HAPPY RUINED MY CHANCE FOR GETTING OUT OF HERE...
"...I HAD A FEW VOLUNTEERS SEARCH THROUGH EVERY BOOK, TABLET, AND SCROLL, LOOKING FOR ANY POSSIBLE WAYS FOR ME TO GET BACK."
AND NOW I HAVE THIS LIST OF ALL THE OPTIONS THEY COULD FIND.
THAT LOOKS AN AWFUL LOT LIKE THE MAP. YOU KNOW, THE LAST LONG, SCROLLING PIECE OF PAPER THAT WAS MEANT TO HELP END OUR RELATIONSHIP.
I THOUGHT THE SAME THING, BUT THEY JUST COME FROM THE SAME SUPPLIER.
WELL, THAT'S CONVENIENT.
MacGUFFIN PAPER CO.
PROVIDING YOUR PLOT DEVICE A QUALITY SURFACE SINCE ONCE UPON A TIME

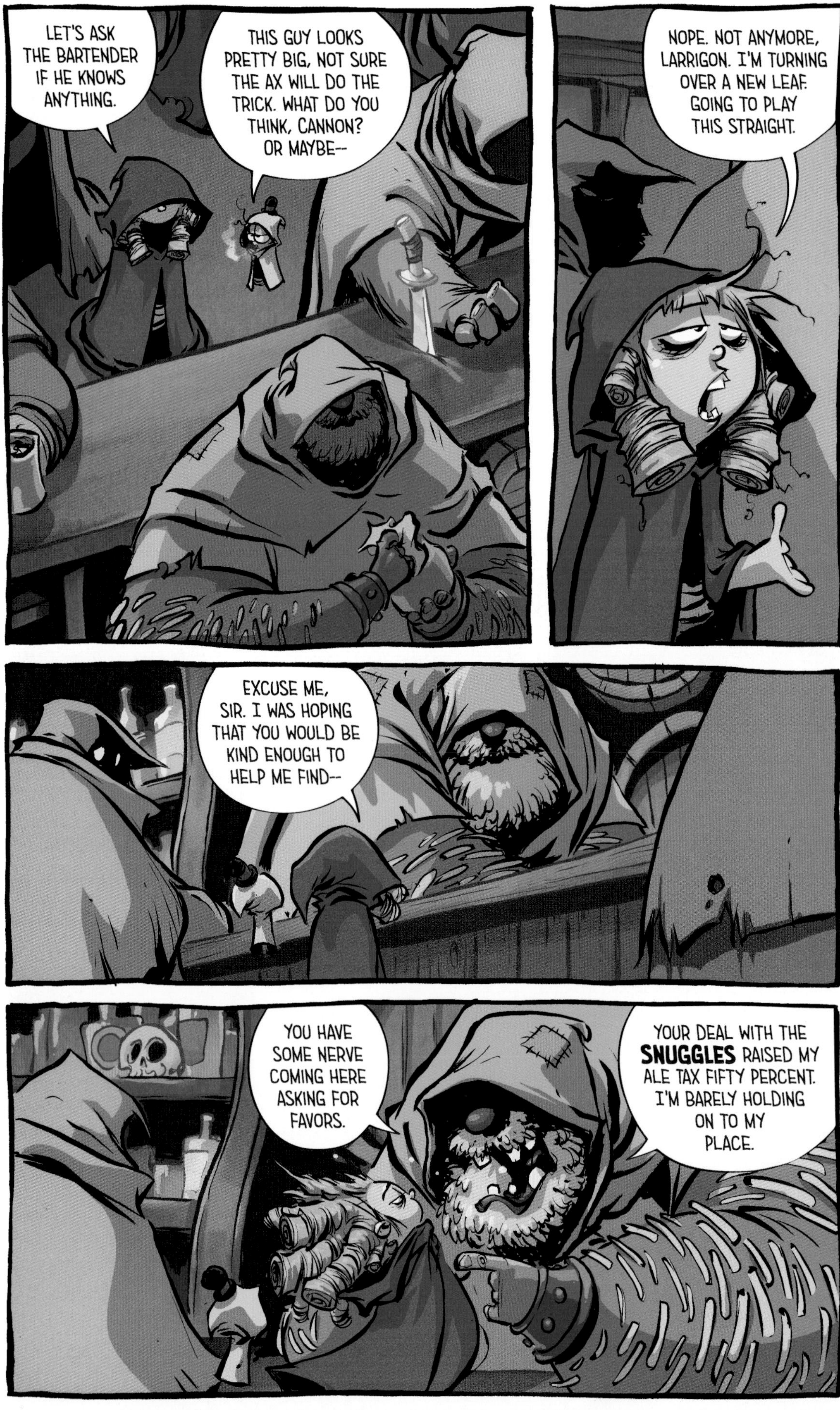
LET'S ASK THE BARTENDER IF HE KNOWS ANYTHING.
THIS GUY LOOKS PRETTY BIG, NOT SURE THE AX WILL DO THE TRICK. WHAT DO YOU THINK, CANNON? OR MAYBE--
NOPE. NOT ANYMORE, LARRIGON. I'M TURNING OVER A NEW LEAF. GOING TO PLAY THIS STRAIGHT.
EXCUSE ME, SIR. I WAS HOPING THAT YOU WOULD BE KIND ENOUGH TO HELP ME FIND--
YOU HAVE SOME NERVE COMING HERE ASKING FOR FAVORS.
YOUR DEAL WITH THE **SNUGGLES** RAISED MY ALE TAX FIFTY PERCENT. I'M BARELY HOLDING ON TO MY PLACE.

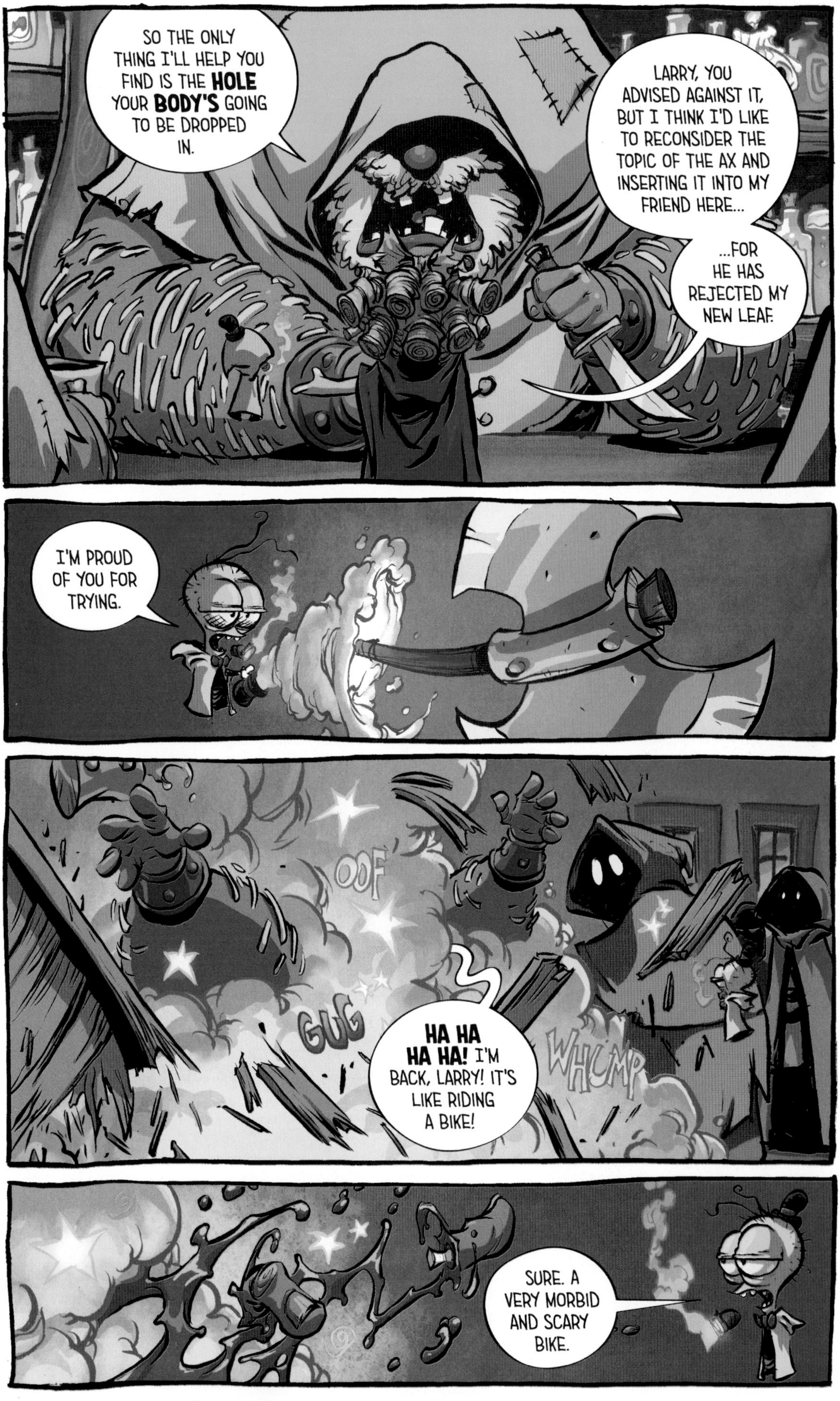

SO THE ONLY THING I'LL HELP YOU FIND IS THE **HOLE** YOUR **BODY'S** GOING TO BE DROPPED IN.
LARRY, YOU ADVISED AGAINST IT, BUT I THINK I'D LIKE TO RECONSIDER THE TOPIC OF THE AX AND INSERTING IT INTO MY FRIEND HERE...
...FOR HE HAS REJECTED MY NEW LEAF.
I'M PROUD OF YOU FOR TRYING.
OOF
GUG
WHUMP
HA HA HA HA! I'M BACK, LARRY! IT'S LIKE RIDING A BIKE!
SURE. A VERY MORBID AND SCARY BIKE.

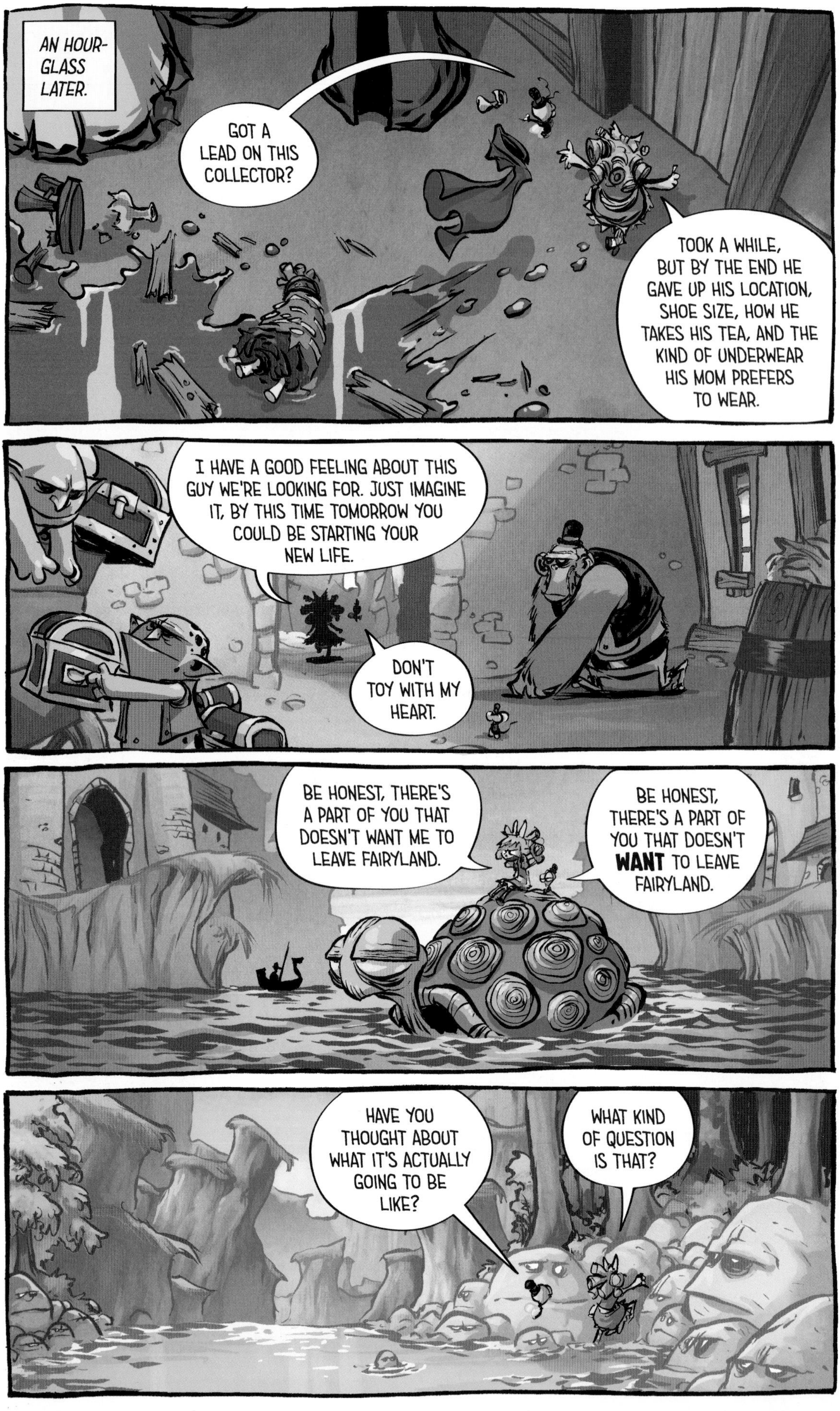
AN HOUR-GLASS LATER.
GOT A LEAD ON THIS COLLECTOR?
TOOK A WHILE, BUT BY THE END HE GAVE UP HIS LOCATION, SHOE SIZE, HOW HE TAKES HIS TEA, AND THE KIND OF UNDERWEAR HIS MOM PREFERS TO WEAR.
I HAVE A GOOD FEELING ABOUT THIS GUY WE'RE LOOKING FOR. JUST IMAGINE IT, BY THIS TIME TOMORROW YOU COULD BE STARTING YOUR NEW LIFE.
DON'T TOY WITH MY HEART.
BE HONEST, THERE'S A PART OF YOU THAT DOESN'T WANT ME TO LEAVE FAIRYLAND.
BE HONEST, THERE'S A PART OF YOU THAT DOESN'T **WANT** TO LEAVE FAIRYLAND.
HAVE YOU THOUGHT ABOUT WHAT IT'S ACTUALLY GOING TO BE LIKE?
WHAT KIND OF QUESTION IS THAT?

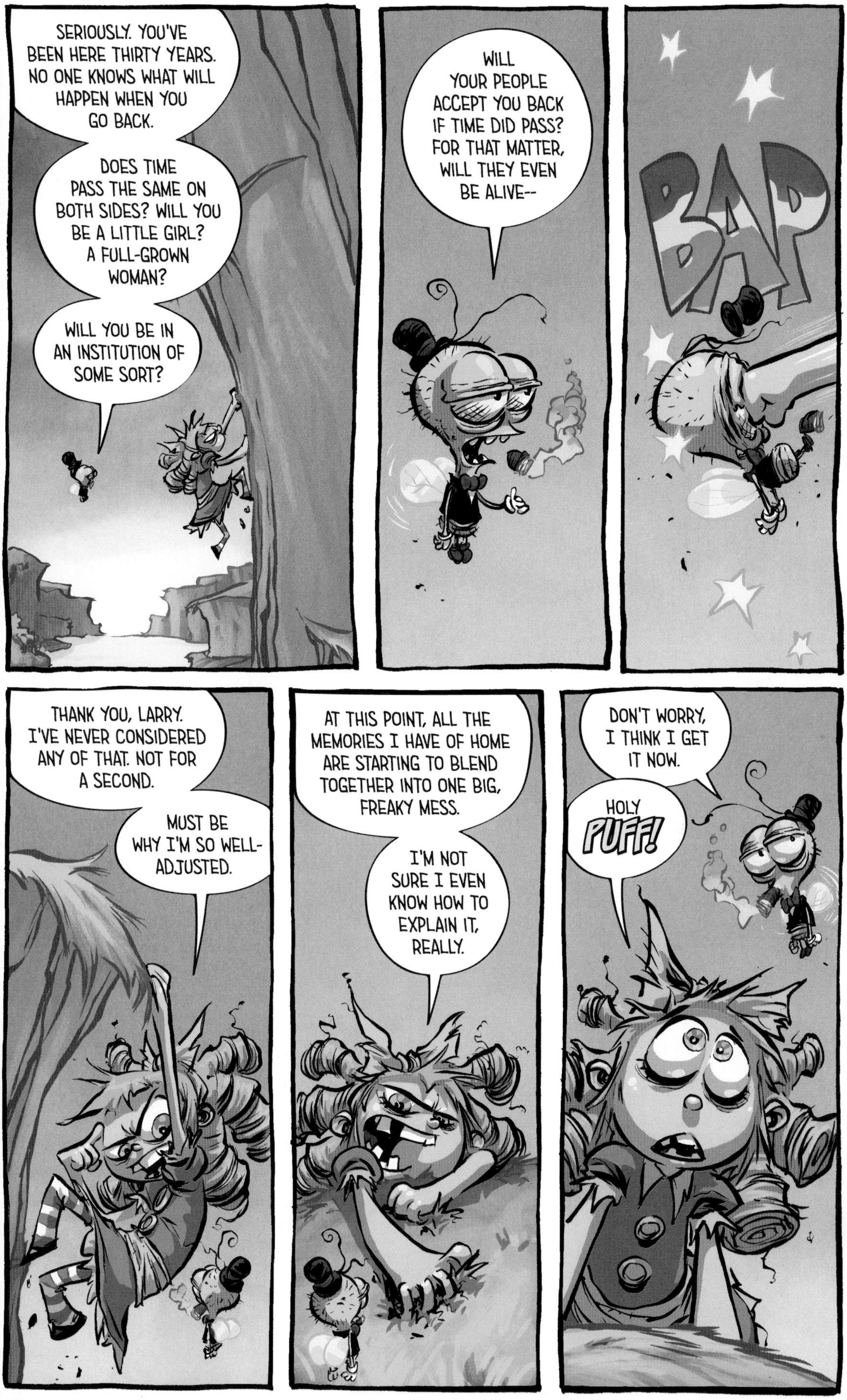
SERIOUSLY. YOU'VE BEEN HERE THIRTY YEARS. NO ONE KNOWS WHAT WILL HAPPEN WHEN YOU GO BACK.
DOES TIME PASS THE SAME ON BOTH SIDES? WILL YOU BE A LITTLE GIRL? A FULL-GROWN WOMAN?
WILL YOU BE IN AN INSTITUTION OF SOME SORT?
WILL YOUR PEOPLE ACCEPT YOU BACK IF TIME DID PASS? FOR THAT MATTER, WILL THEY EVEN BE ALIVE--
BAP
THANK YOU, LARRY. I'VE NEVER CONSIDERED ANY OF THAT. NOT FOR A SECOND.
MUST BE WHY I'M SO WELL-ADJUSTED.
AT THIS POINT, ALL THE MEMORIES I HAVE OF HOME ARE STARTING TO BLEND TOGETHER INTO ONE BIG, FREAKY MESS.
I'M NOT SURE I EVEN KNOW HOW TO EXPLAIN IT, REALLY.
DON'T WORRY, I THINK I GET IT NOW.
HOLY PUFF!

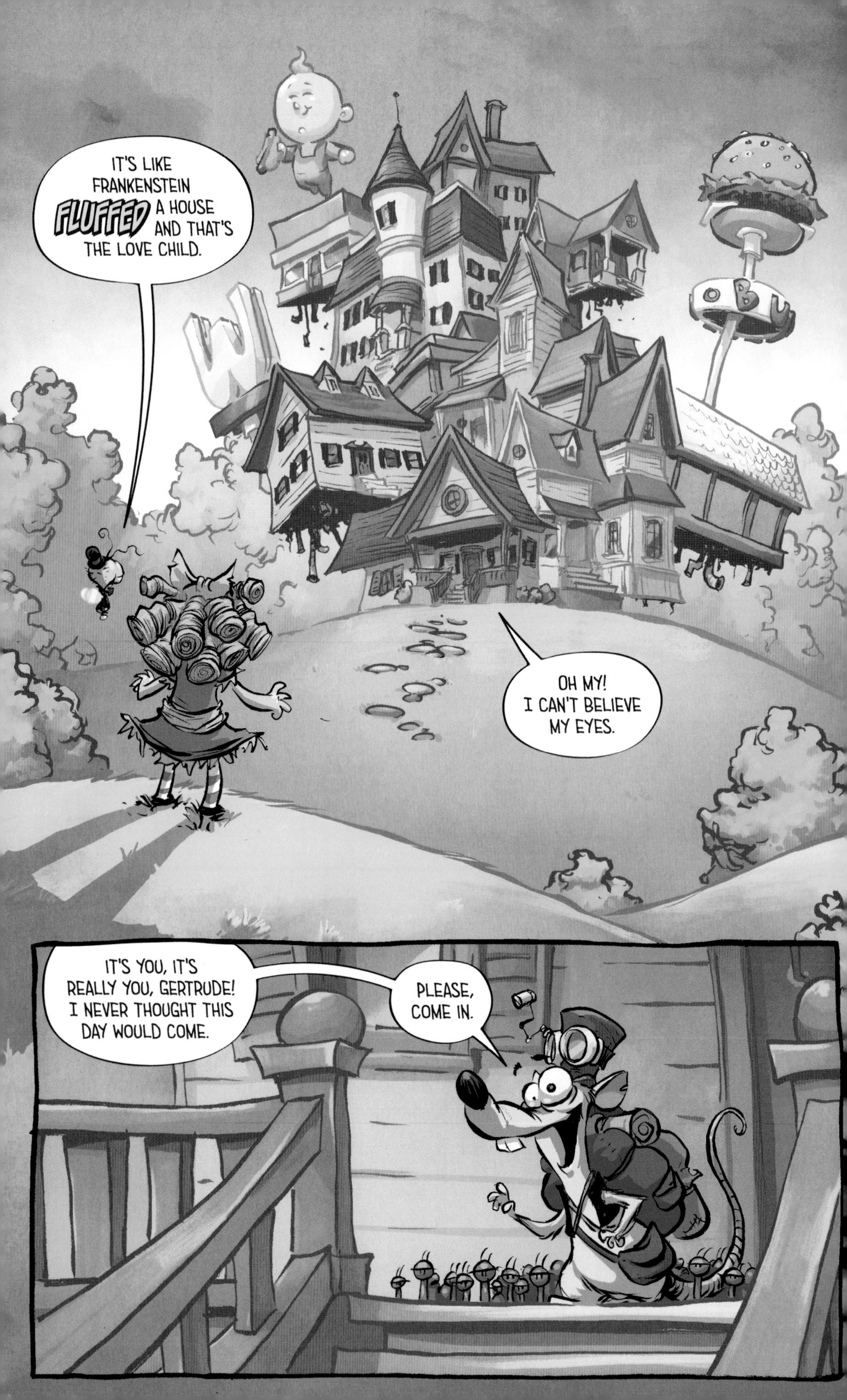
IT'S LIKE FRANKENSTEIN FLUFFED A HOUSE AND THAT'S THE LOVE CHILD.
OH MY! I CAN'T BELIEVE MY EYES.
IT'S YOU, IT'S REALLY YOU, GERTRUDE! I NEVER THOUGHT THIS DAY WOULD COME.
PLEASE, COME IN.

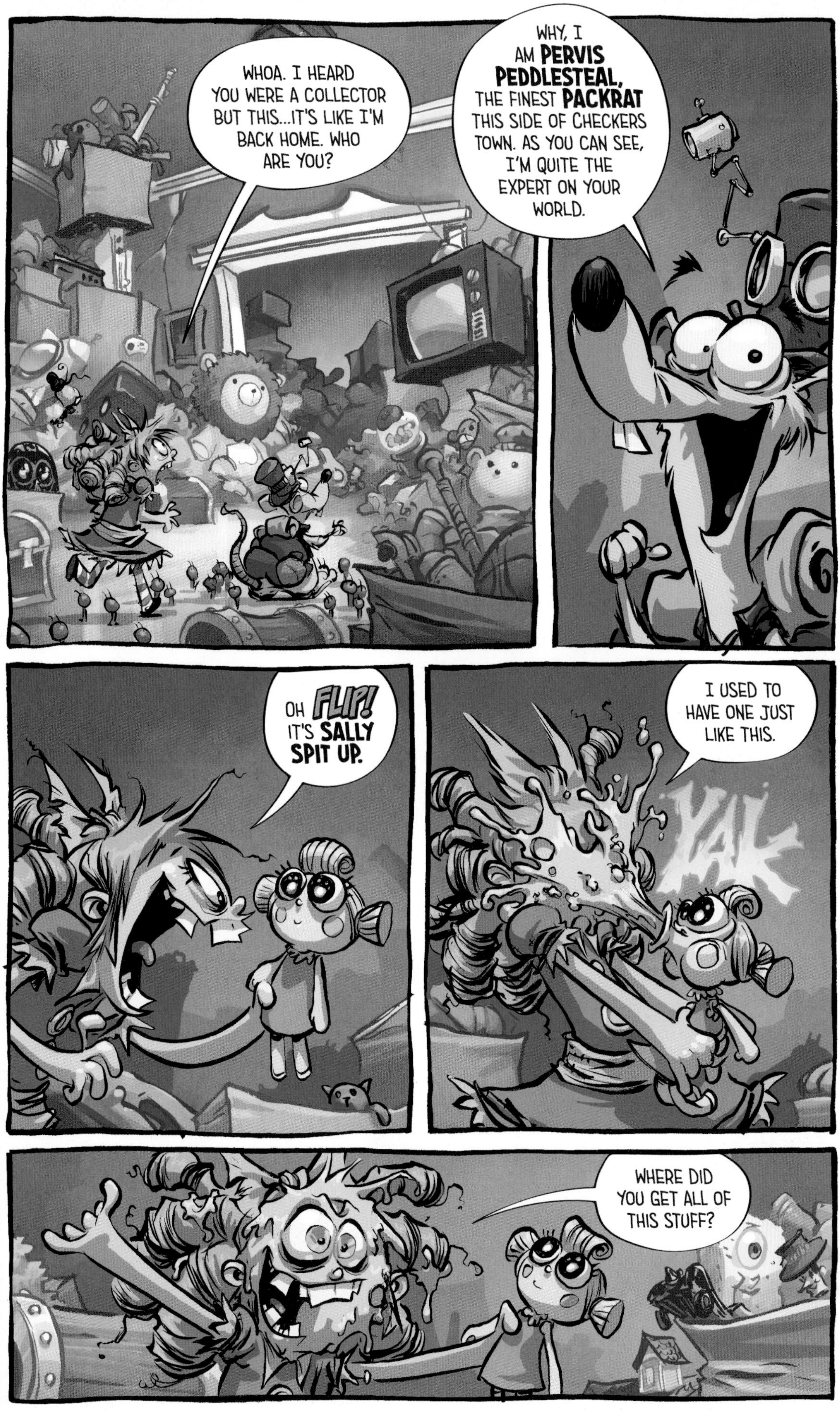
WHOA. I HEARD YOU WERE A COLLECTOR BUT THIS...IT'S LIKE I'M BACK HOME. WHO ARE YOU?
WHY, I AM **PERVIS PEDDLESTEAL,** THE FINEST **PACKRAT** THIS SIDE OF CHECKERS TOWN. AS YOU CAN SEE, I'M QUITE THE EXPERT ON YOUR WORLD.
OH FLIP! IT'S **SALLY SPIT UP.**
I USED TO HAVE ONE JUST LIKE THIS.
YAK
WHERE DID YOU GET ALL OF THIS STUFF?

IT ALL BEGAN AROUND THE TURN OF THE THIRD PRETENDURY. I FOUND THIS SMALL TOY LEFT BEHIND BY A CHILD OF THE REAL WORLD.

AFTER THAT, I BECAME OBSESSED WITH ADDING TO MY COLLECTION.

YOU SEE, EVERY TIME A GUEST ARRIVES, THEY BRING THINGS WITH THEM-- INTENTIONALLY, OR NOT SO INTENTIONALLY--SO ME AND MY LITTLE HELPERS SEEK THOSE THINGS OUT AND BRING THEM HERE.

YOU HAVE A LOT OF STUFF **FROM** MY WORLD. BUT WHAT ABOUT A WAY **TO** MY WORLD? YOU GOT ANYTHING THAT SWINGS BOTH WAYS?

HMMM. I MIGHT HAVE JUST THE THING.

BUT, I'LL WANT SOMETHING FROM YOU IN RETURN.

ᴡᴡᴡ ᴡ ᴡᴡᴡ ᴡᴡᴡᴡ ᴡᴡᴡᴡᴡ ᴡᴡᴡ ᴡᴡ ᴡ

THAT'S PRETTY DARK, PERVIS. BUT YOU HAVE A DEAL.

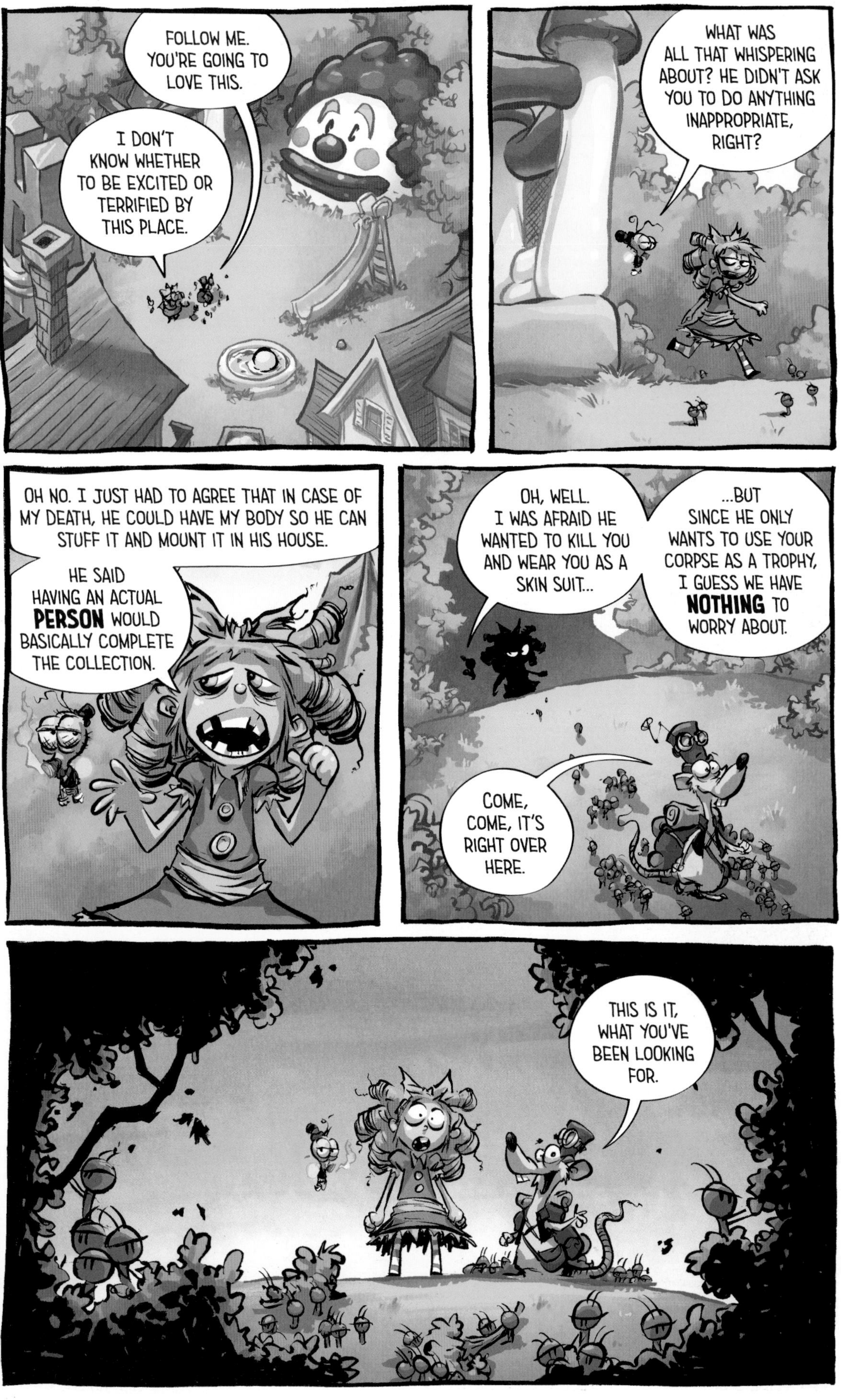
FOLLOW ME. YOU'RE GOING TO LOVE THIS.
I DON'T KNOW WHETHER TO BE EXCITED OR TERRIFIED BY THIS PLACE.
WHAT WAS ALL THAT WHISPERING ABOUT? HE DIDN'T ASK YOU TO DO ANYTHING INAPPROPRIATE, RIGHT?
OH NO. I JUST HAD TO AGREE THAT IN CASE OF MY DEATH, HE COULD HAVE MY BODY SO HE CAN STUFF IT AND MOUNT IT IN HIS HOUSE.
HE SAID HAVING AN ACTUAL **PERSON** WOULD BASICALLY COMPLETE THE COLLECTION.
OH, WELL. I WAS AFRAID HE WANTED TO KILL YOU AND WEAR YOU AS A SKIN SUIT...
...BUT SINCE HE ONLY WANTS TO USE YOUR CORPSE AS A TROPHY, I GUESS WE HAVE **NOTHING** TO WORRY ABOUT.
COME, COME, IT'S RIGHT OVER HERE.
THIS IS IT, WHAT YOU'VE BEEN LOOKING FOR.

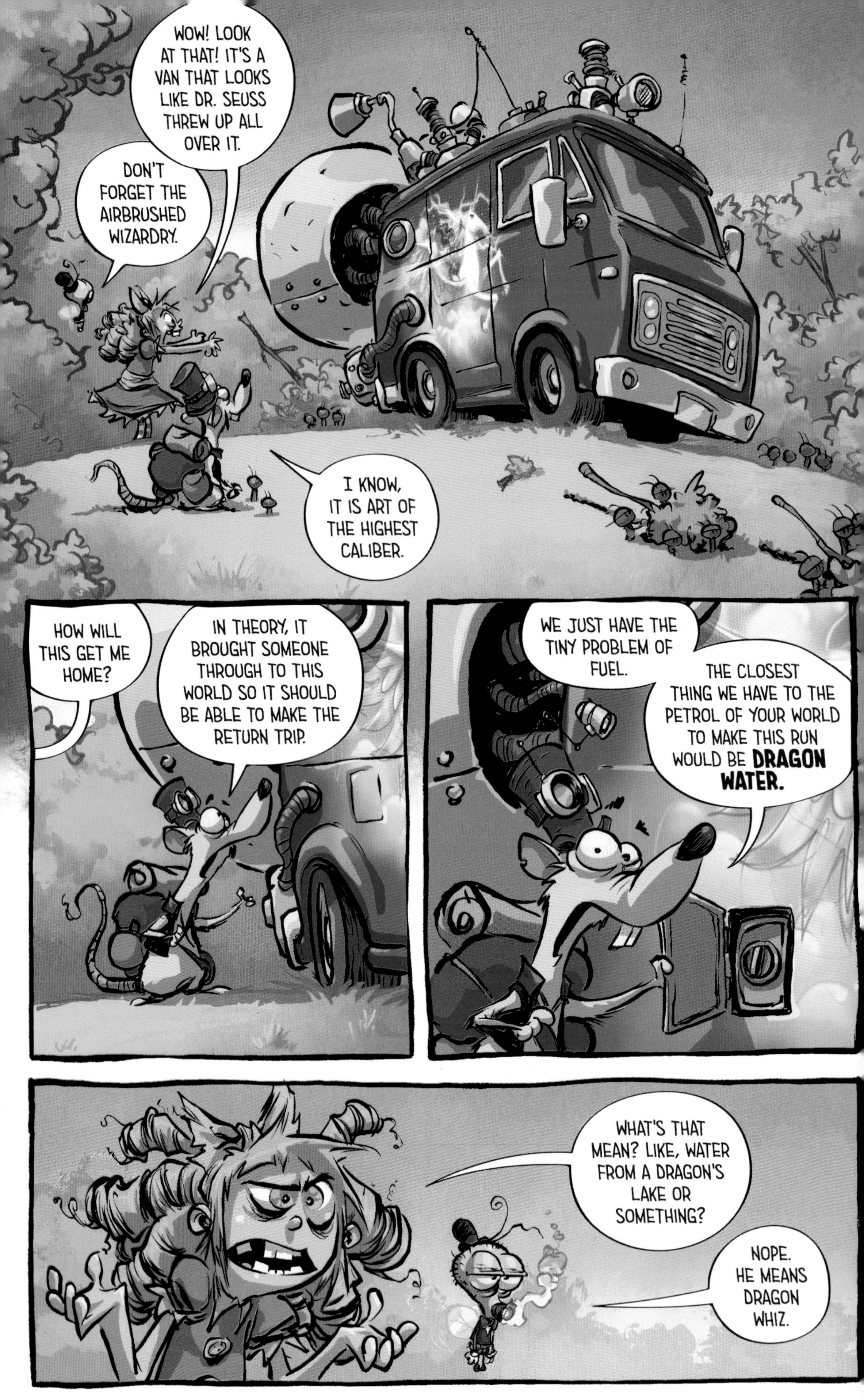
WOW! LOOK AT THAT! IT'S A VAN THAT LOOKS LIKE DR. SEUSS THREW UP ALL OVER IT.
DON'T FORGET THE AIRBRUSHED WIZARDRY.
I KNOW, IT IS ART OF THE HIGHEST CALIBER.
HOW WILL THIS GET ME HOME?
IN THEORY, IT BROUGHT SOMEONE THROUGH TO THIS WORLD SO IT SHOULD BE ABLE TO MAKE THE RETURN TRIP.
WE JUST HAVE THE TINY PROBLEM OF FUEL.
THE CLOSEST THING WE HAVE TO THE PETROL OF YOUR WORLD TO MAKE THIS RUN WOULD BE **DRAGON WATER.**
WHAT'S THAT MEAN? LIKE, WATER FROM A DRAGON'S LAKE OR SOMETHING?
NOPE. HE MEANS DRAGON WHIZ.

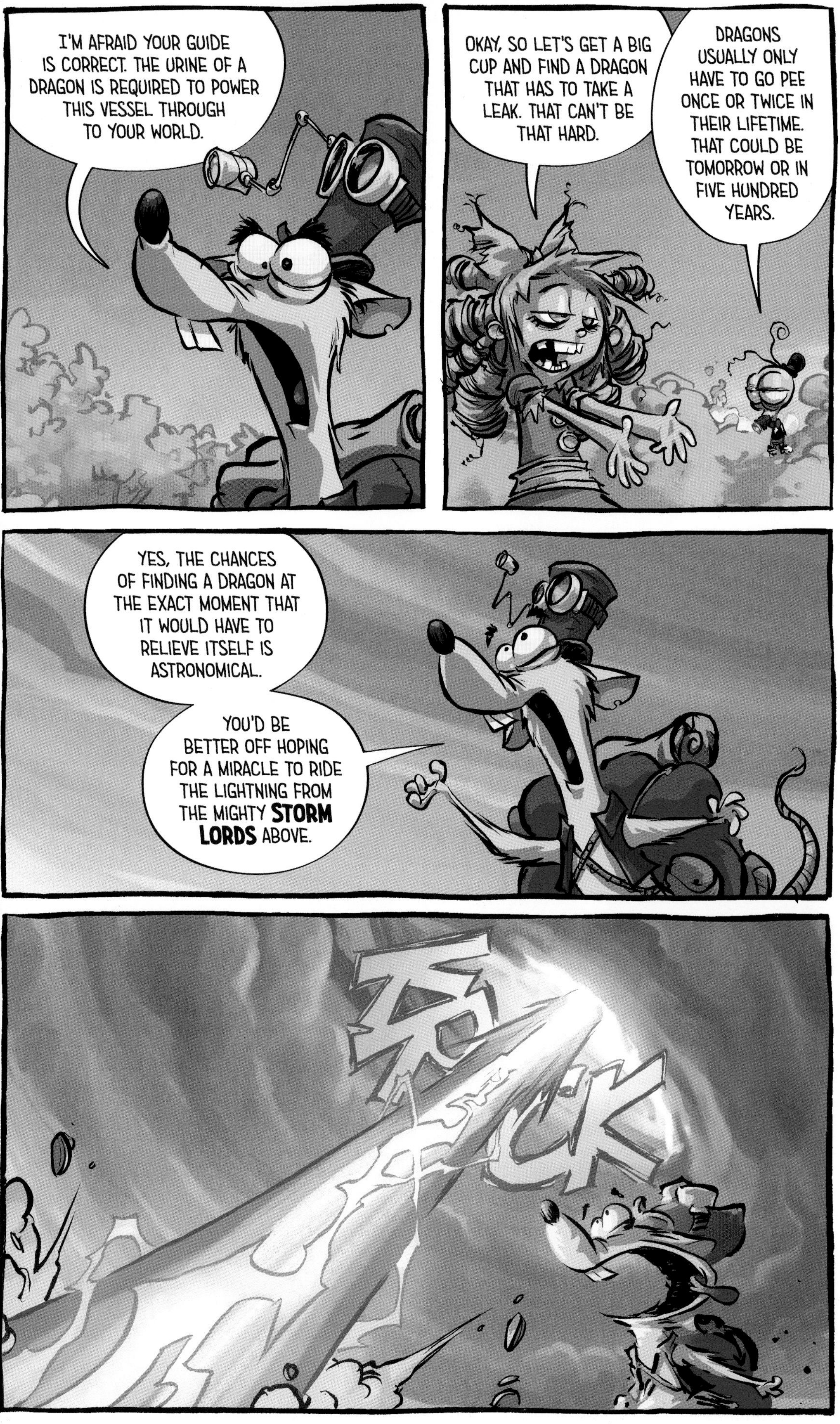
I'M AFRAID YOUR GUIDE IS CORRECT. THE URINE OF A DRAGON IS REQUIRED TO POWER THIS VESSEL THROUGH TO YOUR WORLD.
OKAY, SO LET'S GET A BIG CUP AND FIND A DRAGON THAT HAS TO TAKE A LEAK. THAT CAN'T BE THAT HARD.
DRAGONS USUALLY ONLY HAVE TO GO PEE ONCE OR TWICE IN THEIR LIFETIME. THAT COULD BE TOMORROW OR IN FIVE HUNDRED YEARS.
YES, THE CHANCES OF FINDING A DRAGON AT THE EXACT MOMENT THAT IT WOULD HAVE TO RELIEVE ITSELF IS ASTRONOMICAL.
YOU'D BE BETTER OFF HOPING FOR A MIRACLE TO RIDE THE LIGHTNING FROM THE MIGHTY **STORM LORDS** ABOVE.

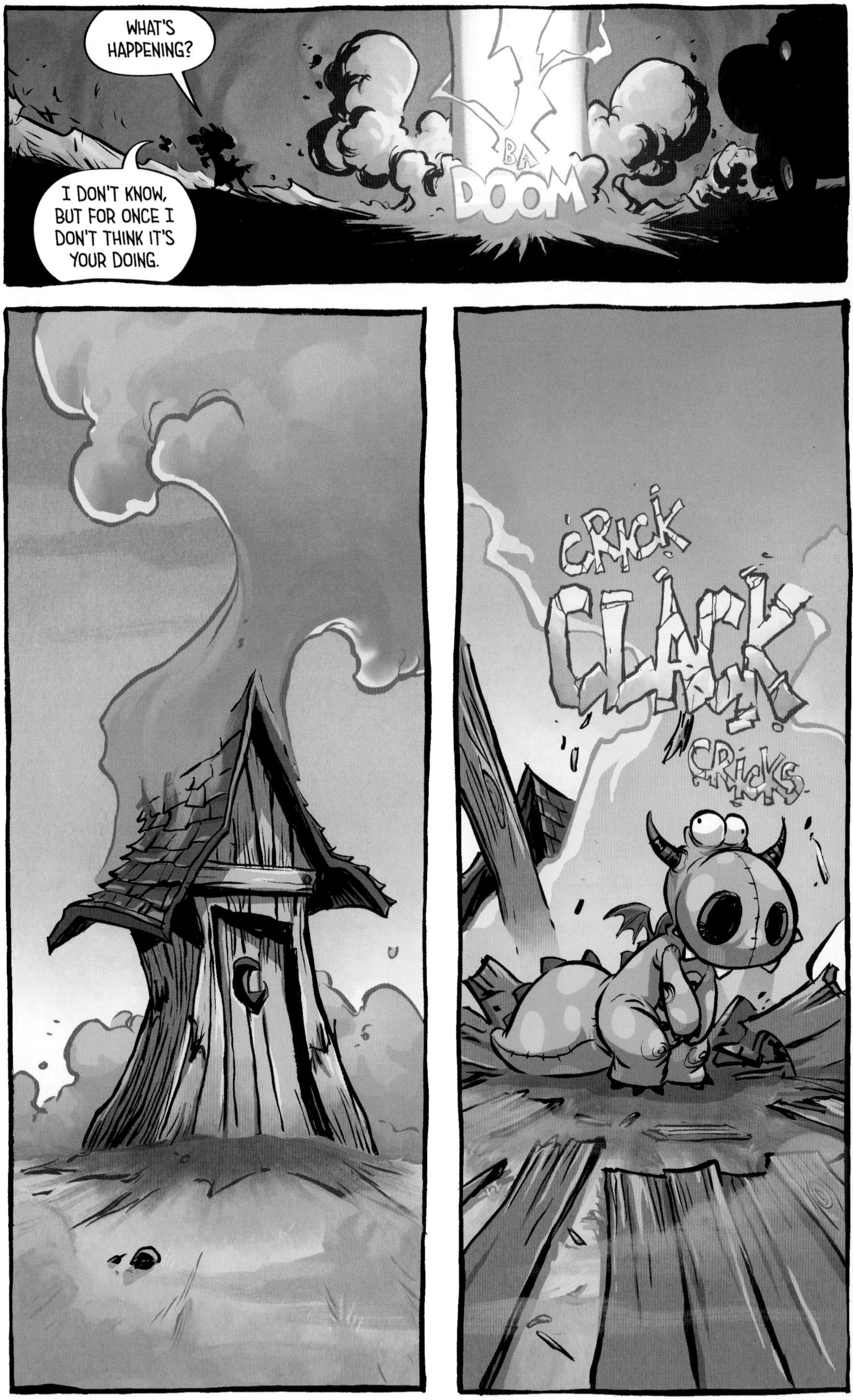
WHAT'S HAPPENING?
I DON'T KNOW, BUT FOR ONCE I DON'T THINK IT'S YOUR DOING.
BA
DOOM
CRICK
CLACK
CRICKS

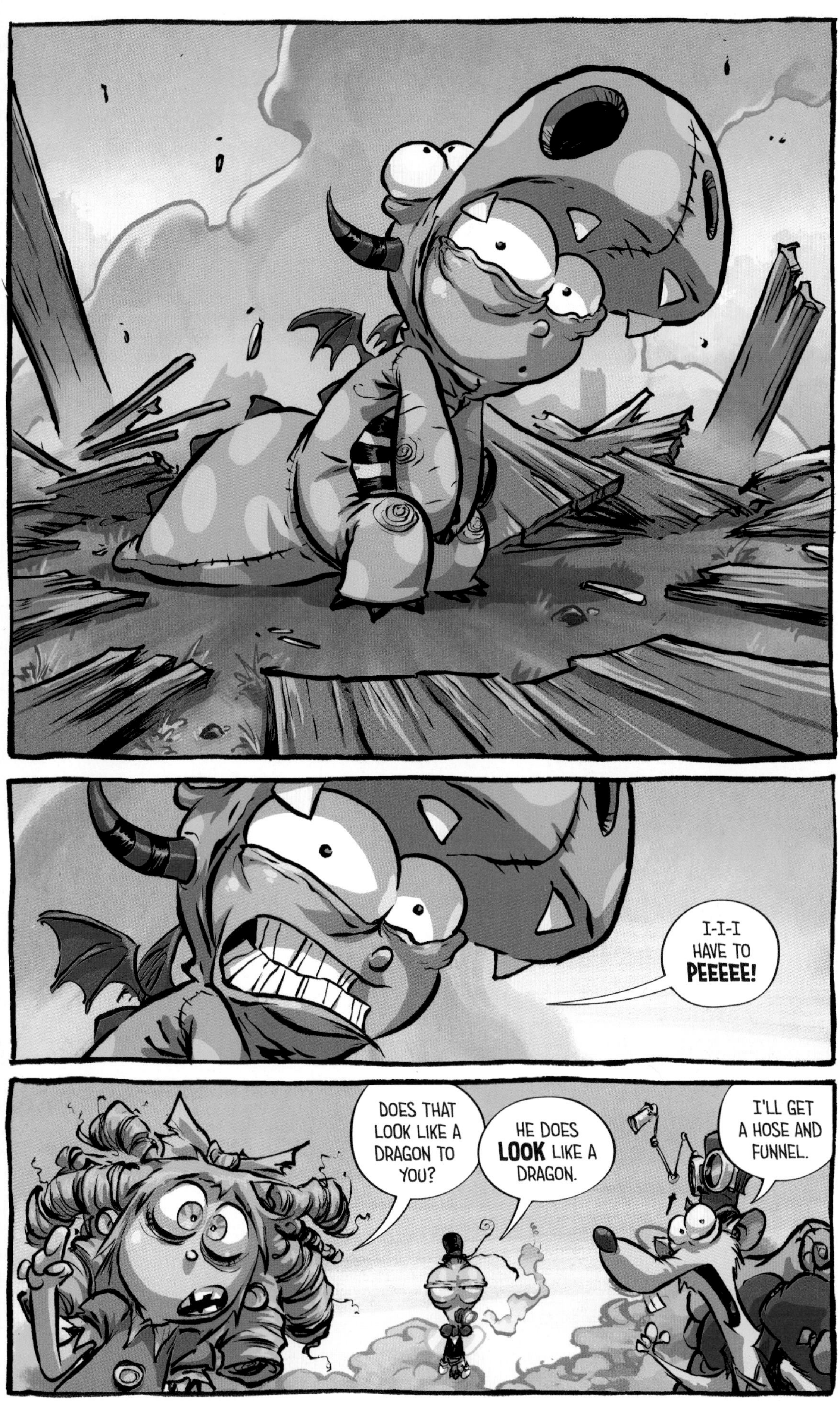
I-I-I HAVE TO PEEEEE!
DOES THAT LOOK LIKE A DRAGON TO YOU?
HE DOES LOOK LIKE A DRAGON.
I'LL GET A HOSE AND FUNNEL.

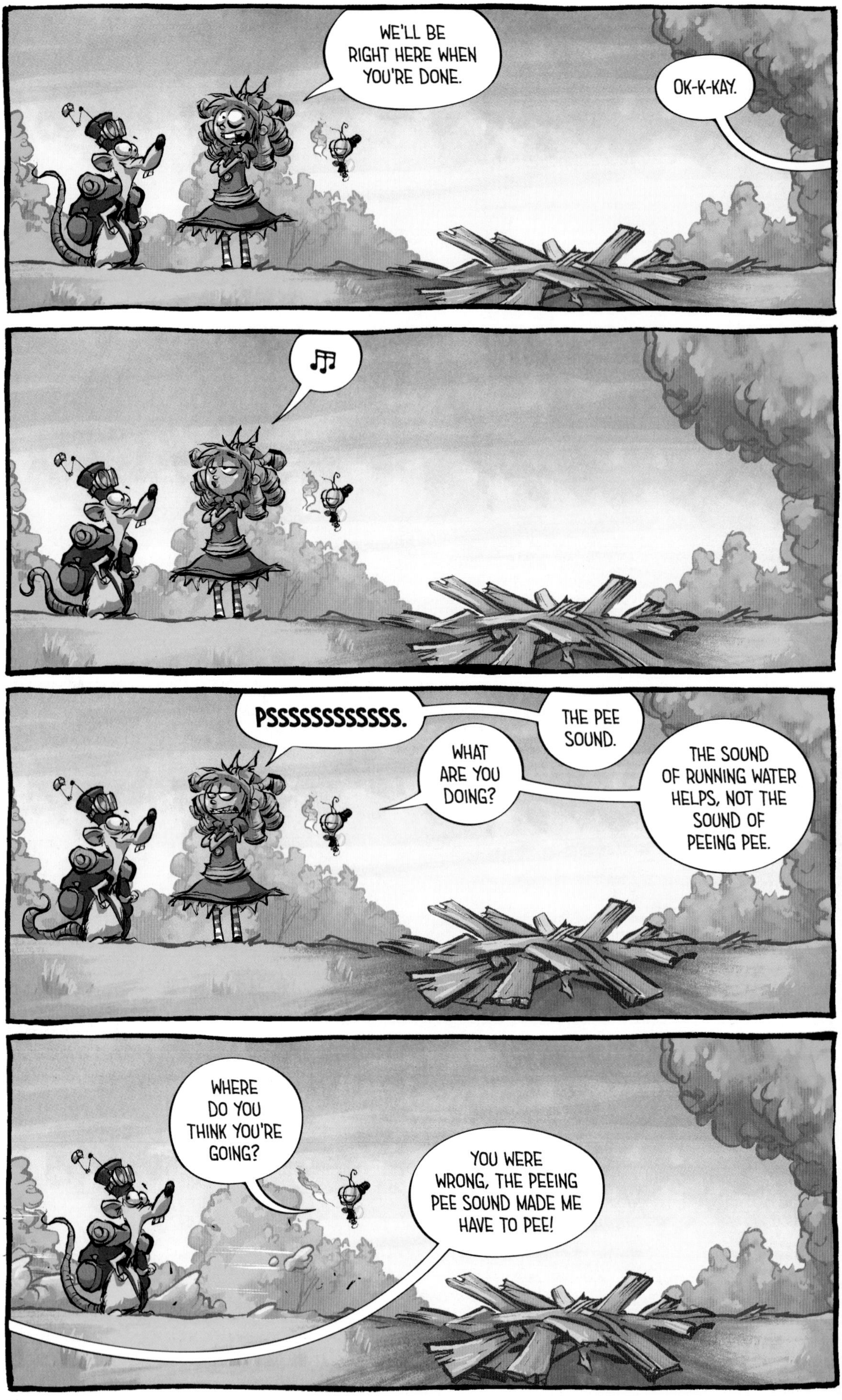
WE'LL BE RIGHT HERE WHEN YOU'RE DONE.
OK-K-KAY.
♬
PSSSSSSSSSSSS.
THE PEE SOUND.
WHAT ARE YOU DOING?
THE SOUND OF RUNNING WATER HELPS, NOT THE SOUND OF PEEING PEE.
WHERE DO YOU THINK YOU'RE GOING?
YOU WERE WRONG, THE PEEING PEE SOUND MADE ME HAVE TO PEE!

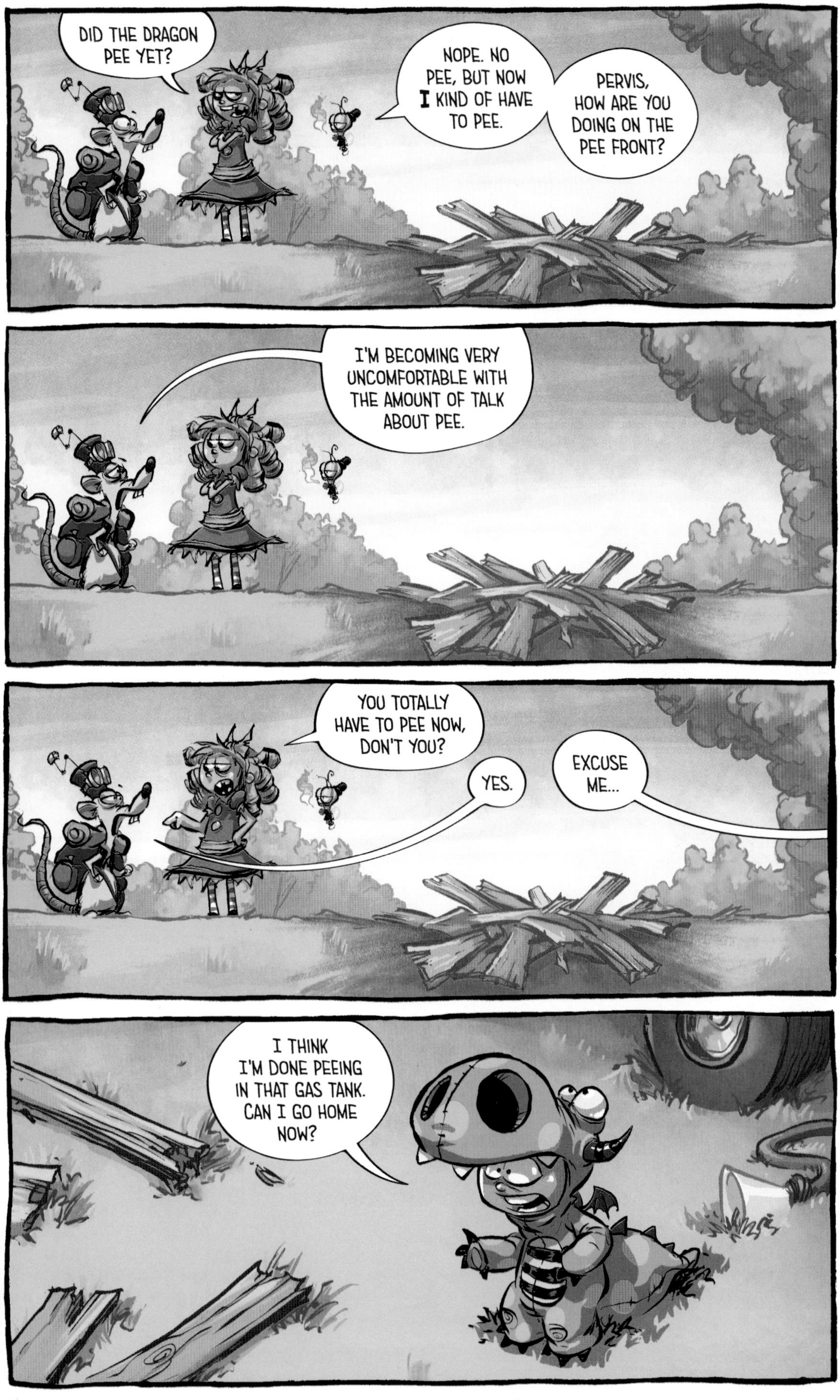
DID THE DRAGON PEE YET?
NOPE. NO PEE, BUT NOW I KIND OF HAVE TO PEE.
PERVIS, HOW ARE YOU DOING ON THE PEE FRONT?
I'M BECOMING VERY UNCOMFORTABLE WITH THE AMOUNT OF TALK ABOUT PEE.
YOU TOTALLY HAVE TO PEE NOW, DON'T YOU?
YES.
EXCUSE ME...
I THINK I'M DONE PEEING IN THAT GAS TANK. CAN I GO HOME NOW?

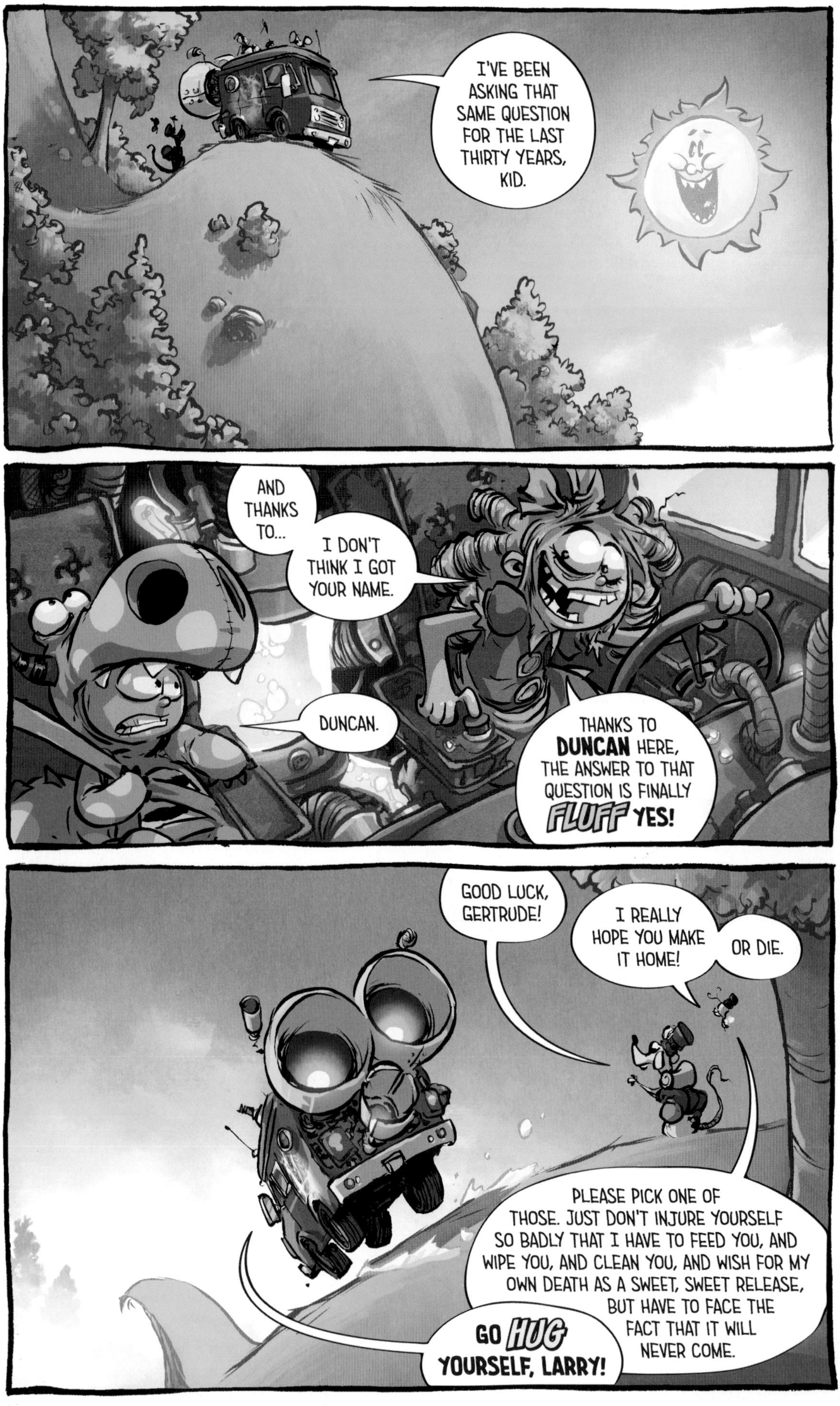
I'VE BEEN ASKING THAT SAME QUESTION FOR THE LAST THIRTY YEARS, KID.
AND THANKS TO...
I DON'T THINK I GOT YOUR NAME.
DUNCAN.
THANKS TO DUNCAN HERE, THE ANSWER TO THAT QUESTION IS FINALLY FLUFF YES!
GOOD LUCK, GERTRUDE!
I REALLY HOPE YOU MAKE IT HOME!
OR DIE.
PLEASE PICK ONE OF THOSE. JUST DON'T INJURE YOURSELF SO BADLY THAT I HAVE TO FEED YOU, AND WIPE YOU, AND CLEAN YOU, AND WISH FOR MY OWN DEATH AS A SWEET, SWEET RELEASE, BUT HAVE TO FACE THE FACT THAT IT WILL NEVER COME.
GO HUG YOURSELF, LARRY!

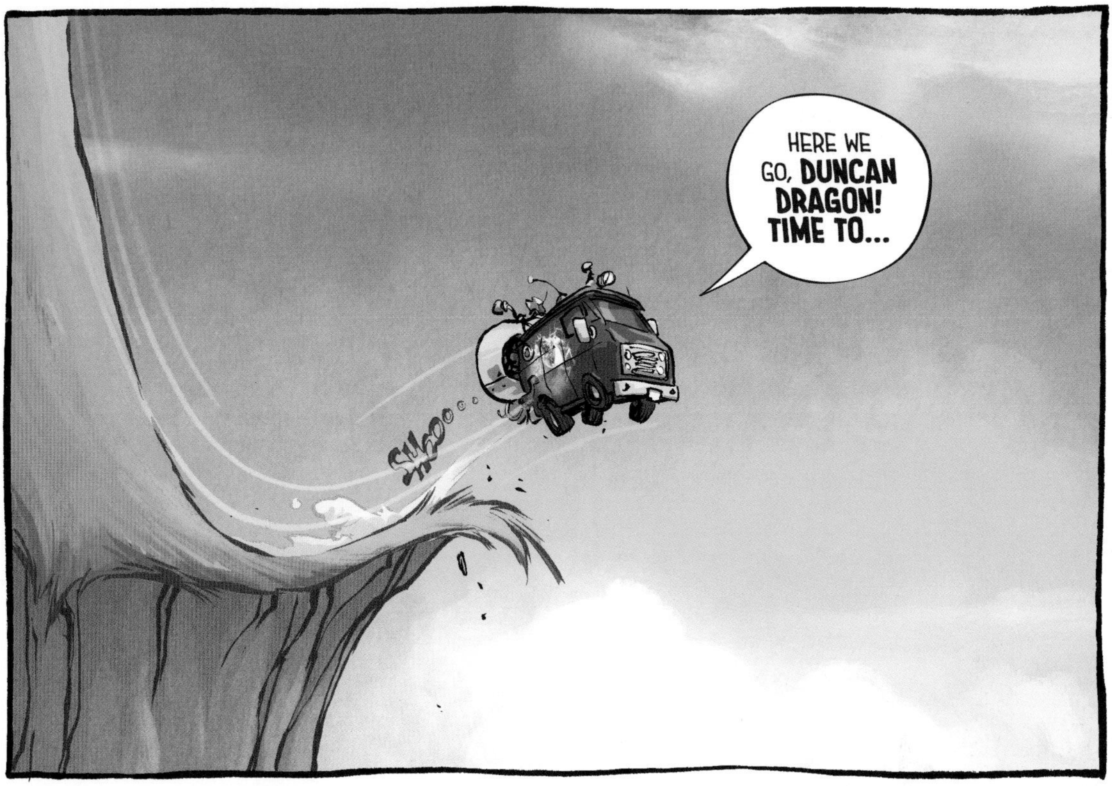
HERE WE GO, **DUNCAN DRAGON!** **TIME TO...**
SHOOooo

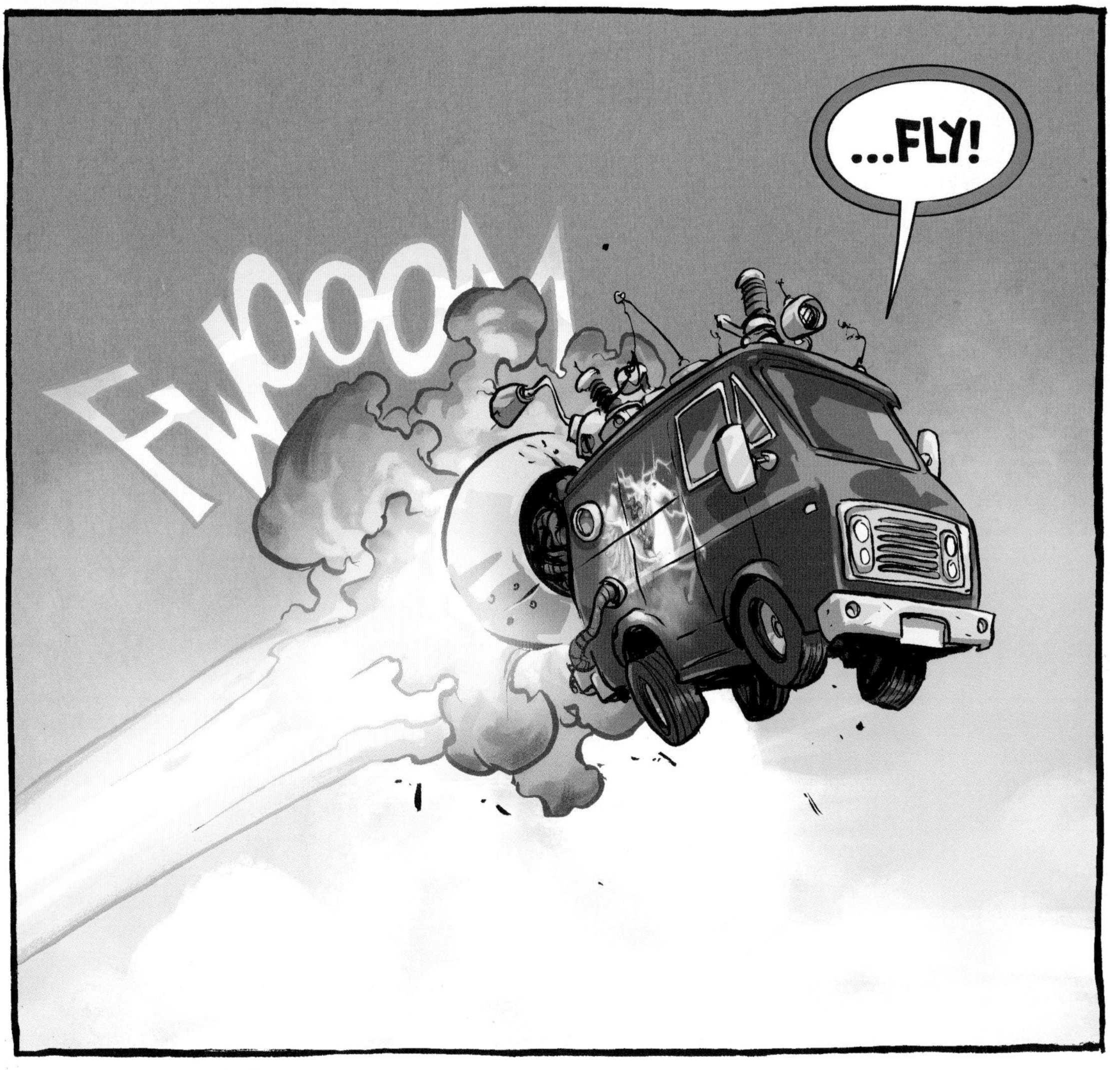
...FLY!
FWOOOM

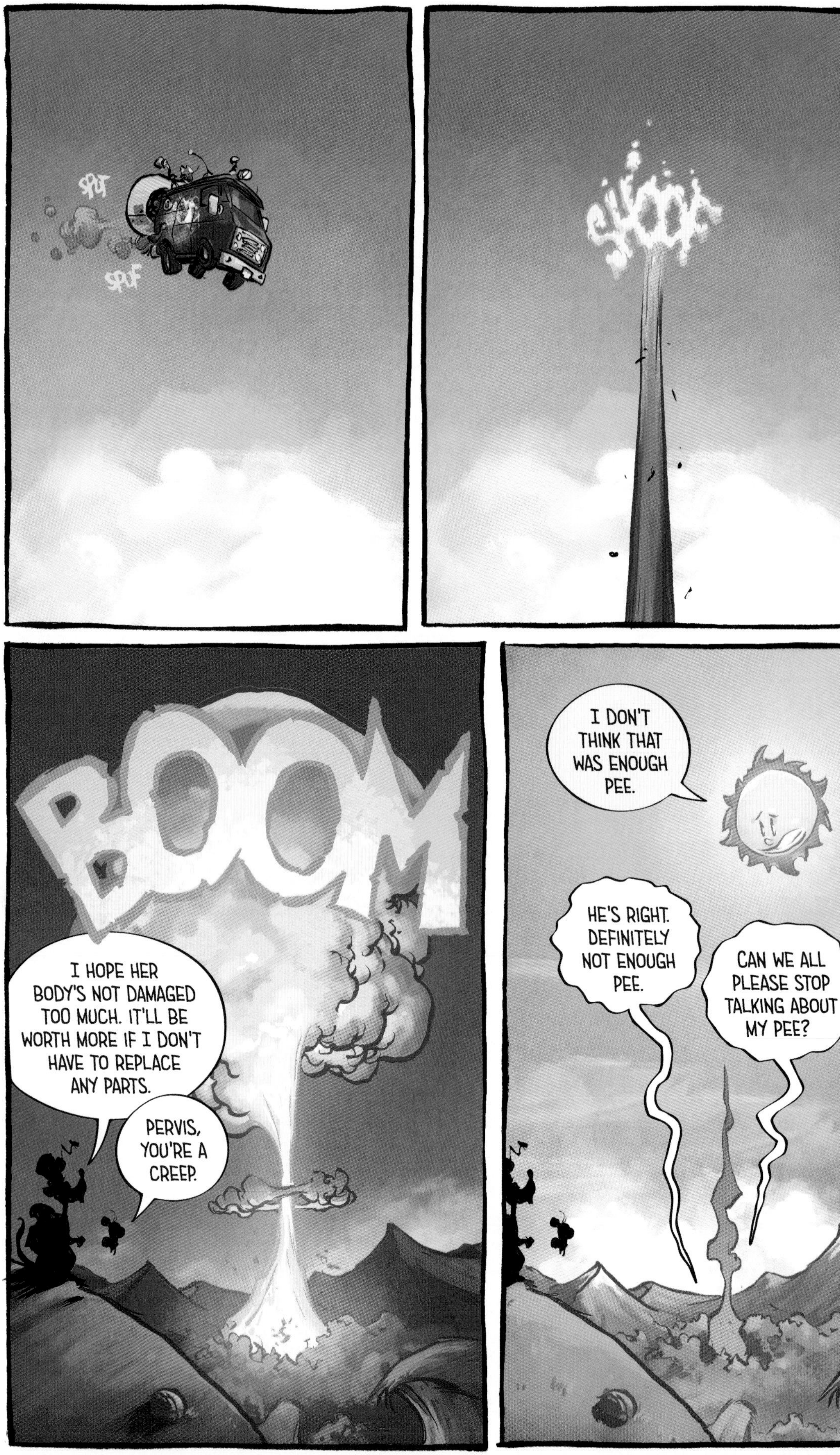
SPUT
SPUF
SHOOF
BOOM
I HOPE HER BODY'S NOT DAMAGED TOO MUCH. IT'LL BE WORTH MORE IF I DON'T HAVE TO REPLACE ANY PARTS.
PERVIS, YOU'RE A CREEP.
I DON'T THINK THAT WAS ENOUGH PEE.
HE'S RIGHT. DEFINITELY NOT ENOUGH PEE.
CAN WE ALL PLEASE STOP TALKING ABOUT MY PEE?

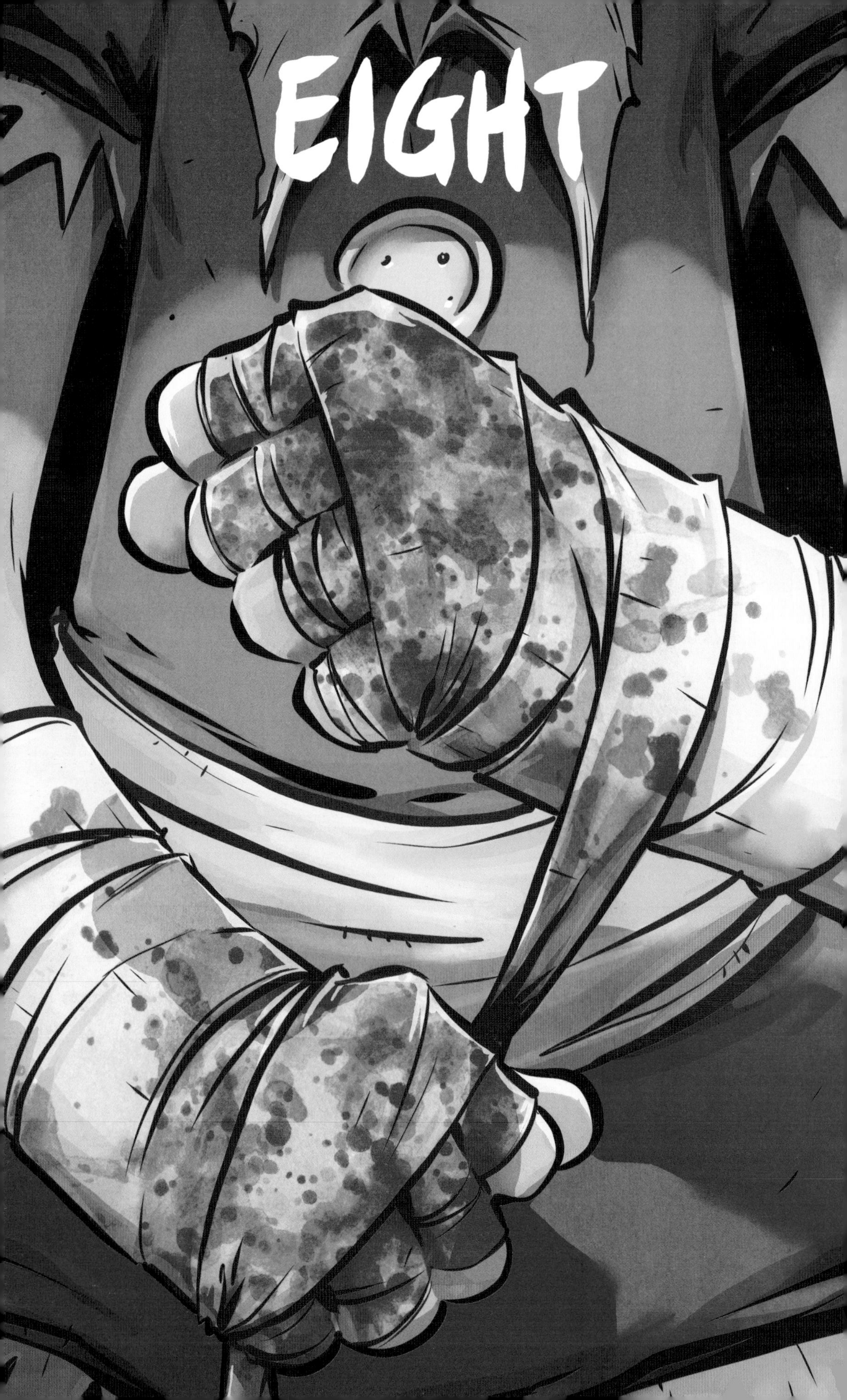
EIGHT

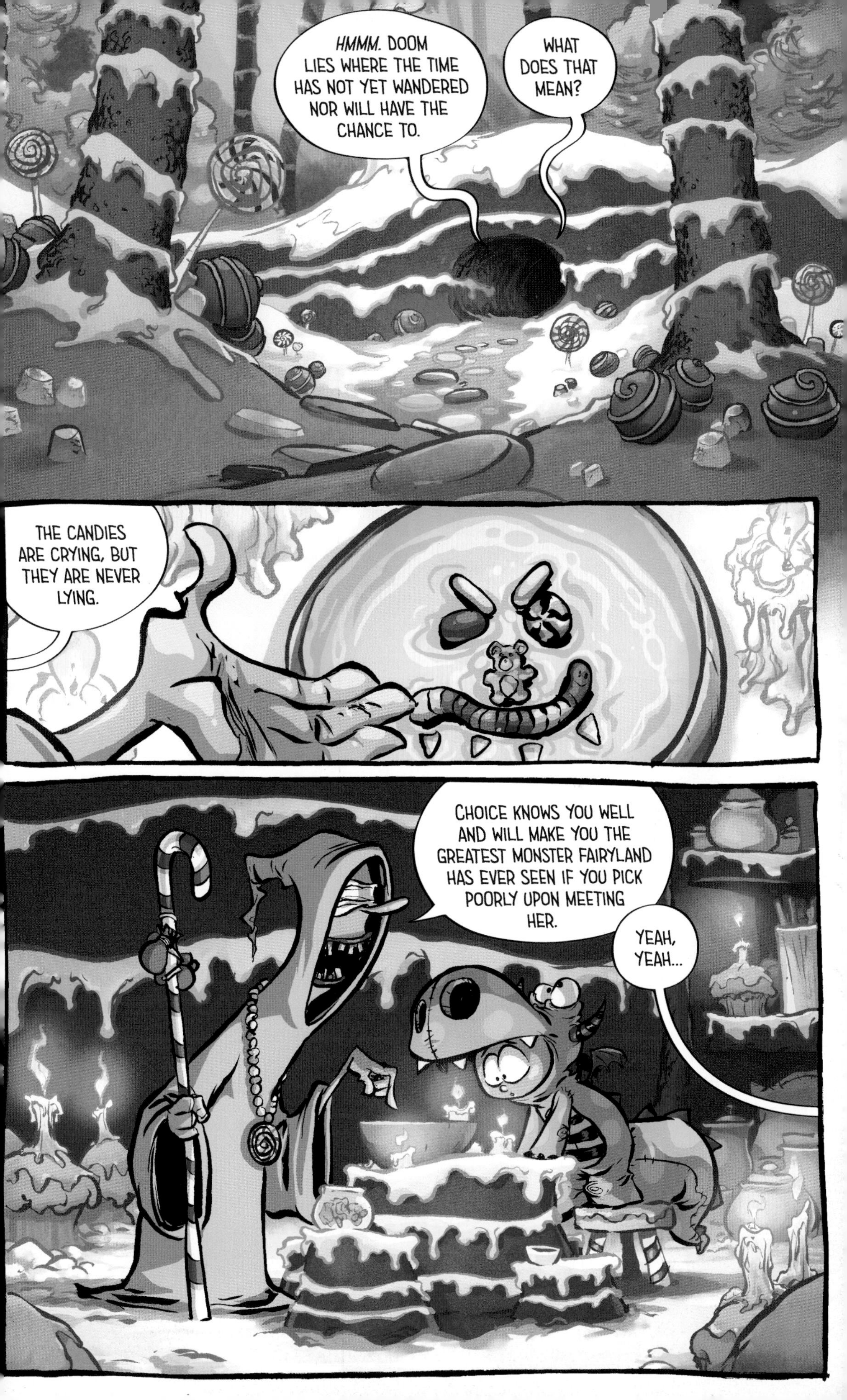
HMMM. DOOM LIES WHERE THE TIME HAS NOT YET WANDERED NOR WILL HAVE THE CHANCE TO.
WHAT DOES THAT MEAN?
THE CANDIES ARE CRYING, BUT THEY ARE NEVER LYING.
CHOICE KNOWS YOU WELL AND WILL MAKE YOU THE GREATEST MONSTER FAIRYLAND HAS EVER SEEN IF YOU PICK POORLY UPON MEETING HER.
YEAH, YEAH...

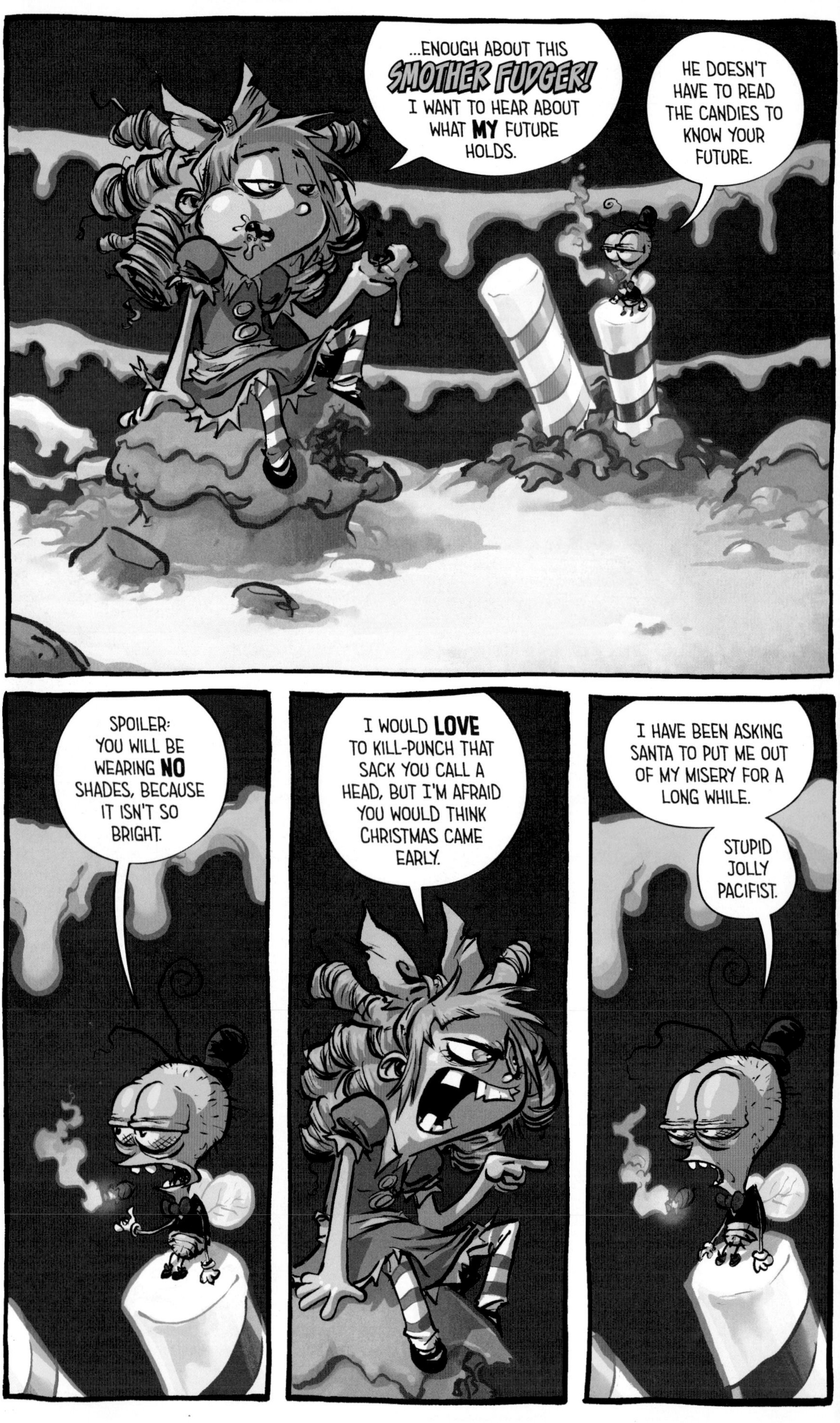
...ENOUGH ABOUT THIS SMOTHER FUDGER! I WANT TO HEAR ABOUT WHAT MY FUTURE HOLDS.
HE DOESN'T HAVE TO READ THE CANDIES TO KNOW YOUR FUTURE.
SPOILER: YOU WILL BE WEARING NO SHADES, BECAUSE IT ISN'T SO BRIGHT.
I WOULD LOVE TO KILL-PUNCH THAT SACK YOU CALL A HEAD, BUT I'M AFRAID YOU WOULD THINK CHRISTMAS CAME EARLY.
I HAVE BEEN ASKING SANTA TO PUT ME OUT OF MY MISERY FOR A LONG WHILE.
STUPID JOLLY PACIFIST.

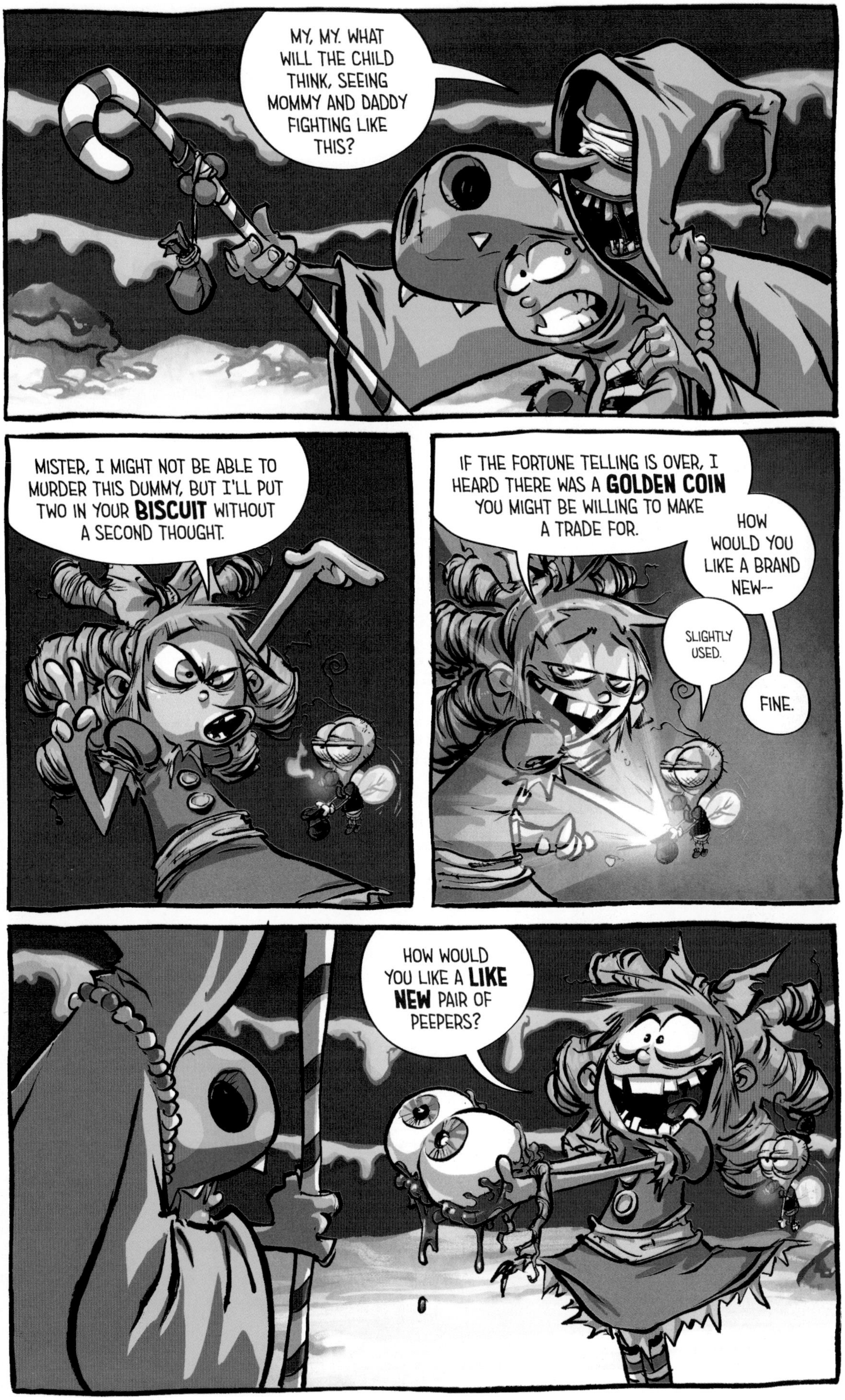
MY, MY. WHAT WILL THE CHILD THINK, SEEING MOMMY AND DADDY FIGHTING LIKE THIS?
MISTER, I MIGHT NOT BE ABLE TO MURDER THIS DUMMY, BUT I'LL PUT TWO IN YOUR **BISCUIT** WITHOUT A SECOND THOUGHT.
IF THE FORTUNE TELLING IS OVER, I HEARD THERE WAS A **GOLDEN COIN** YOU MIGHT BE WILLING TO MAKE A TRADE FOR.
HOW WOULD YOU LIKE A BRAND NEW--
SLIGHTLY USED.
FINE.
HOW WOULD YOU LIKE A **LIKE NEW** PAIR OF PEEPERS?

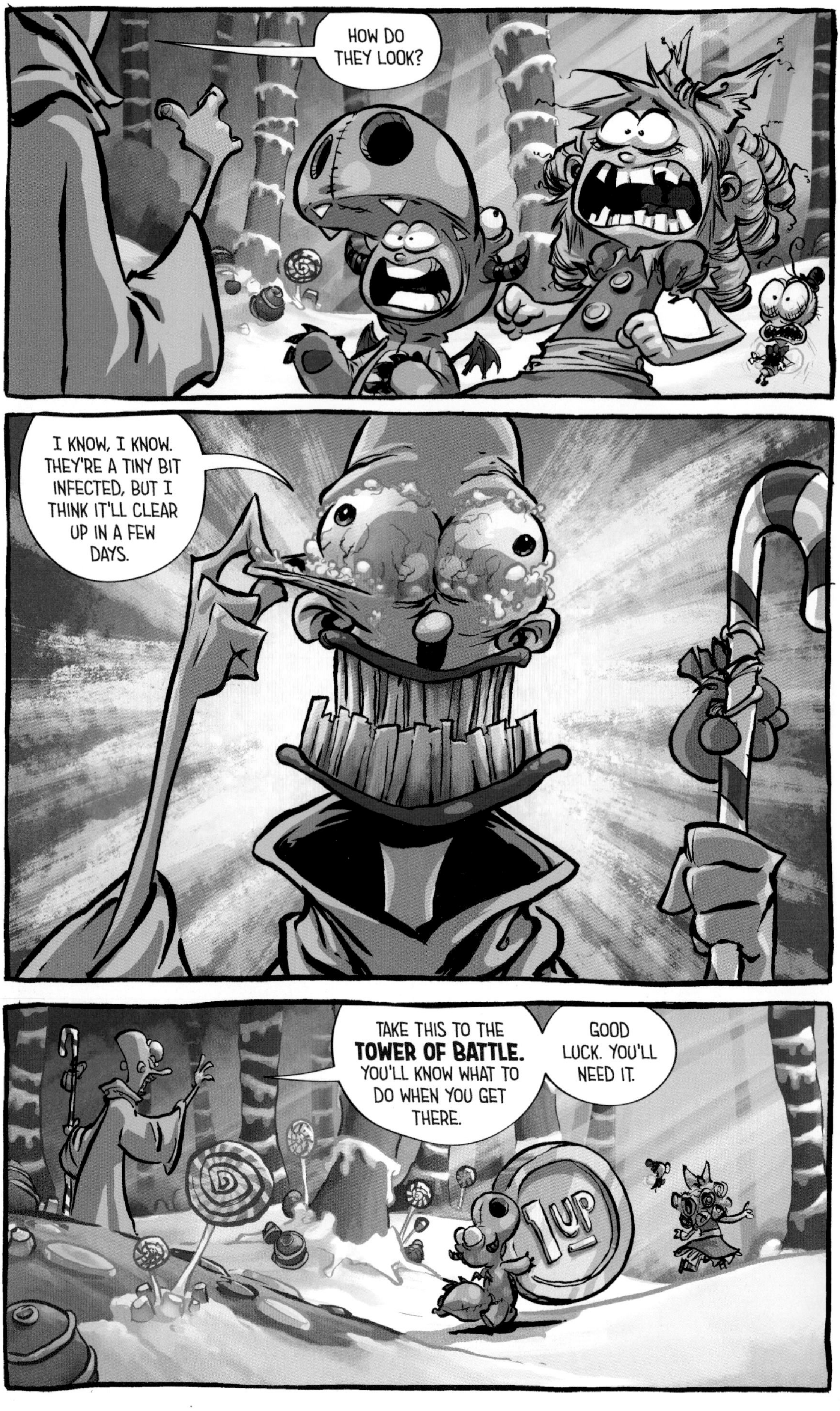
HOW DO THEY LOOK?
I KNOW, I KNOW. THEY'RE A TINY BIT INFECTED, BUT I THINK IT'LL CLEAR UP IN A FEW DAYS.
TAKE THIS TO THE **TOWER OF BATTLE.** YOU'LL KNOW WHAT TO DO WHEN YOU GET THERE.
GOOD LUCK. YOU'LL NEED IT.
1UP

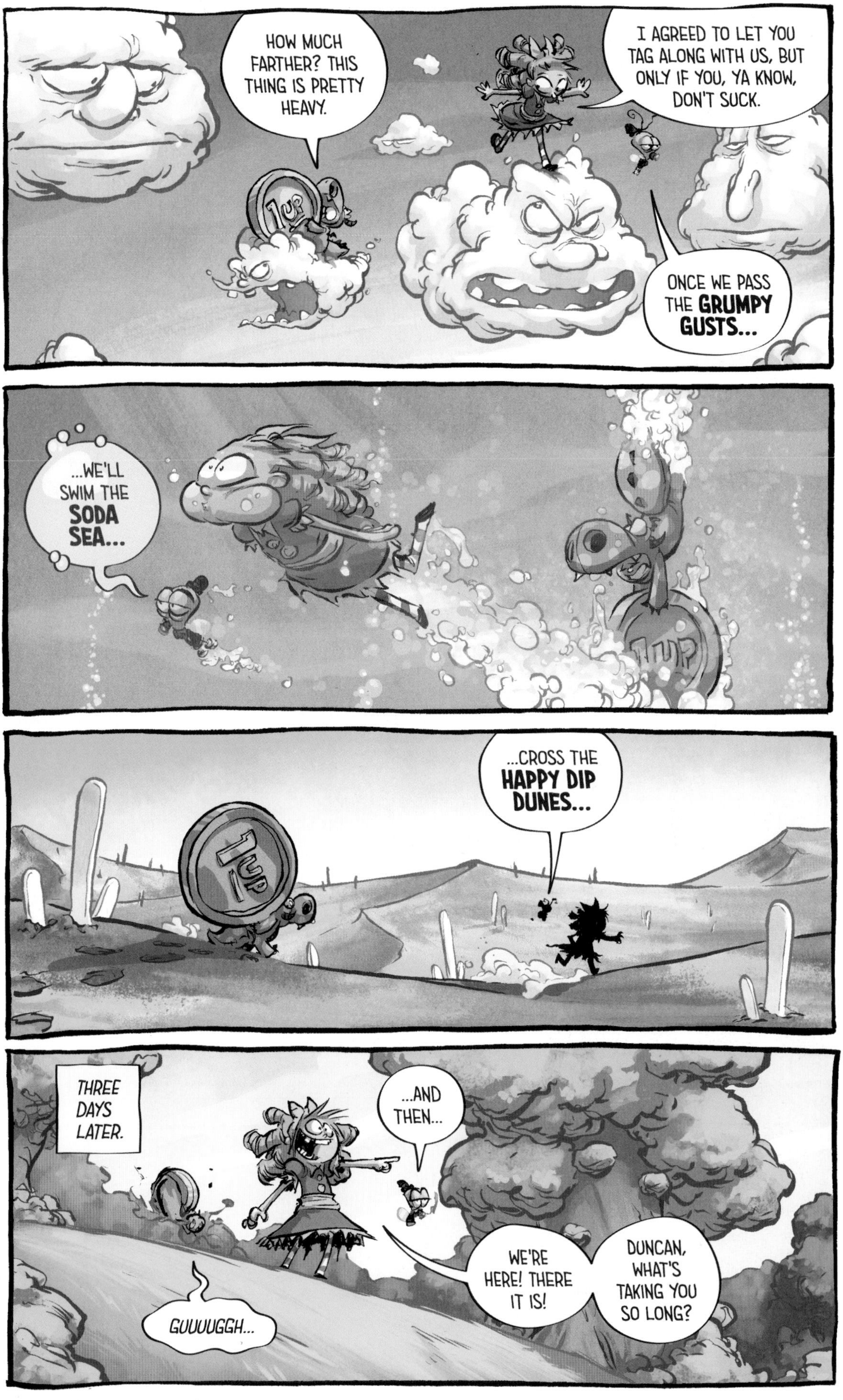
HOW MUCH FARTHER? THIS THING IS PRETTY HEAVY.
I AGREED TO LET YOU TAG ALONG WITH US, BUT ONLY IF YOU, YA KNOW, DON'T SUCK.
ONCE WE PASS THE GRUMPY GUSTS...
...WE'LL SWIM THE SODA SEA...
...CROSS THE HAPPY DIP DUNES...
THREE DAYS LATER.
...AND THEN...
WE'RE HERE! THERE IT IS!
DUNCAN, WHAT'S TAKING YOU SO LONG?
GUUUUGGH...

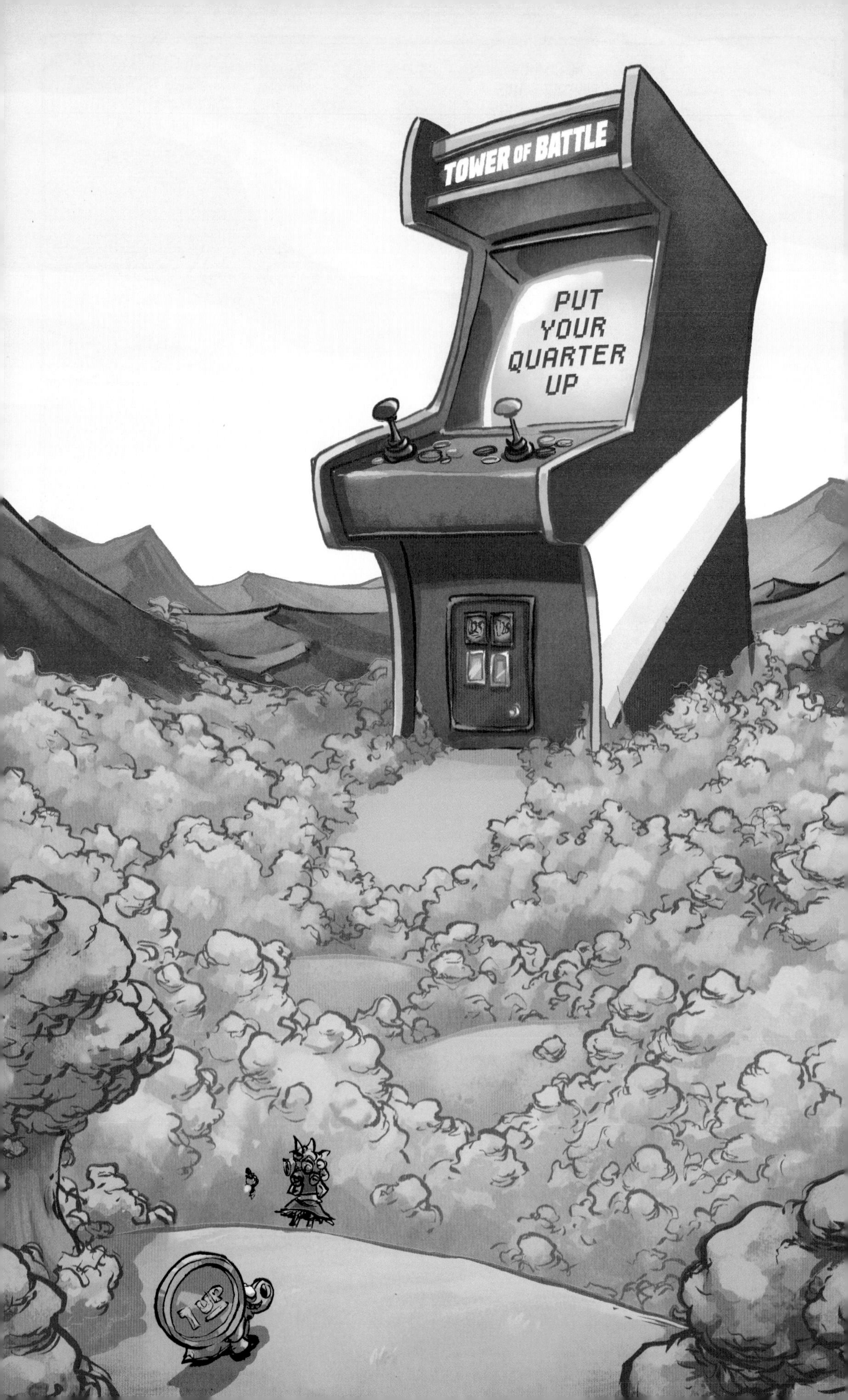
TOWER OF BATTLE
PUT YOUR QUARTER UP
1UP

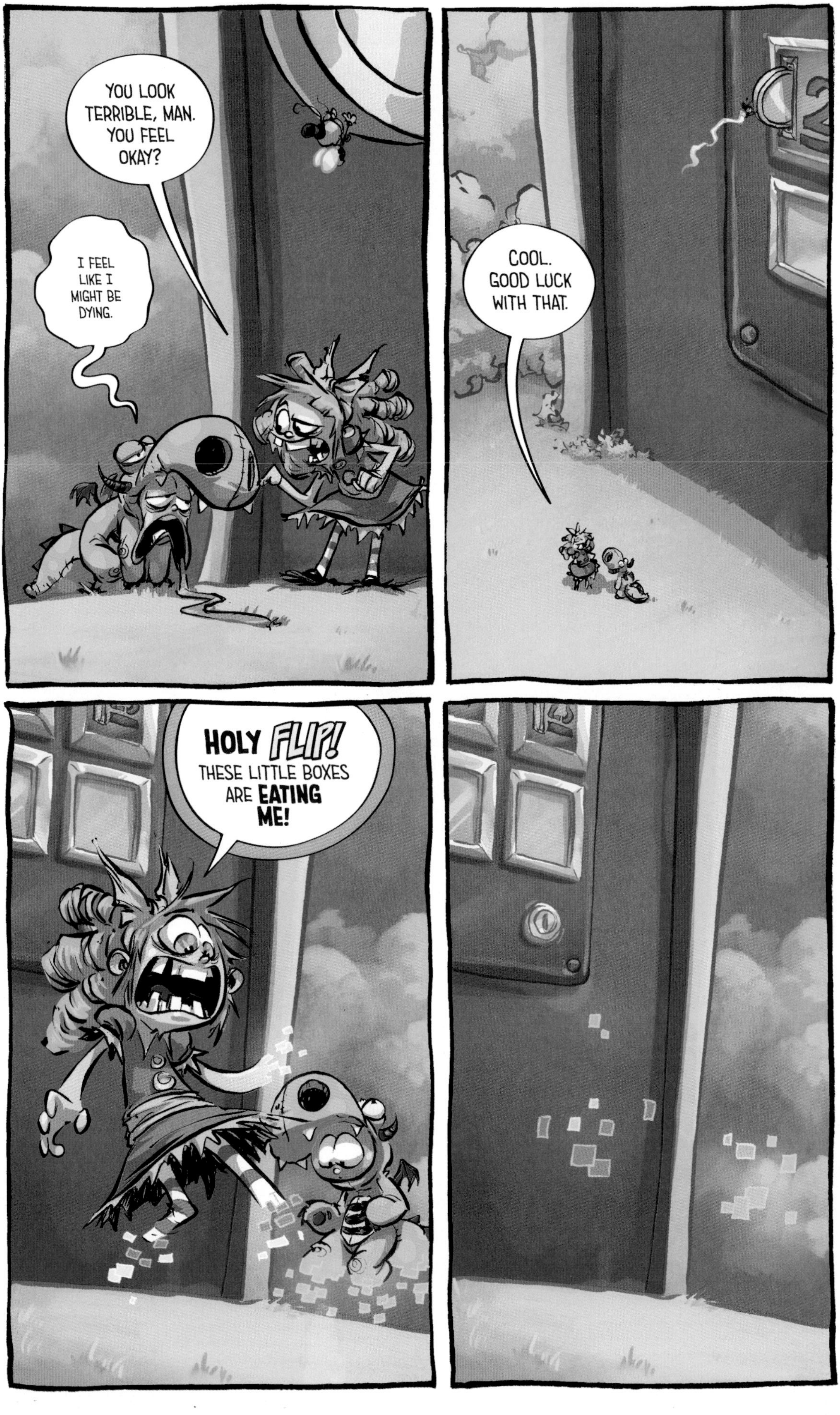
YOU LOOK TERRIBLE, MAN. YOU FEEL OKAY?
I FEEL LIKE I MIGHT BE DYING.
COOL. GOOD LUCK WITH THAT.
HOLY FLIP! THESE LITTLE BOXES ARE EATING ME!

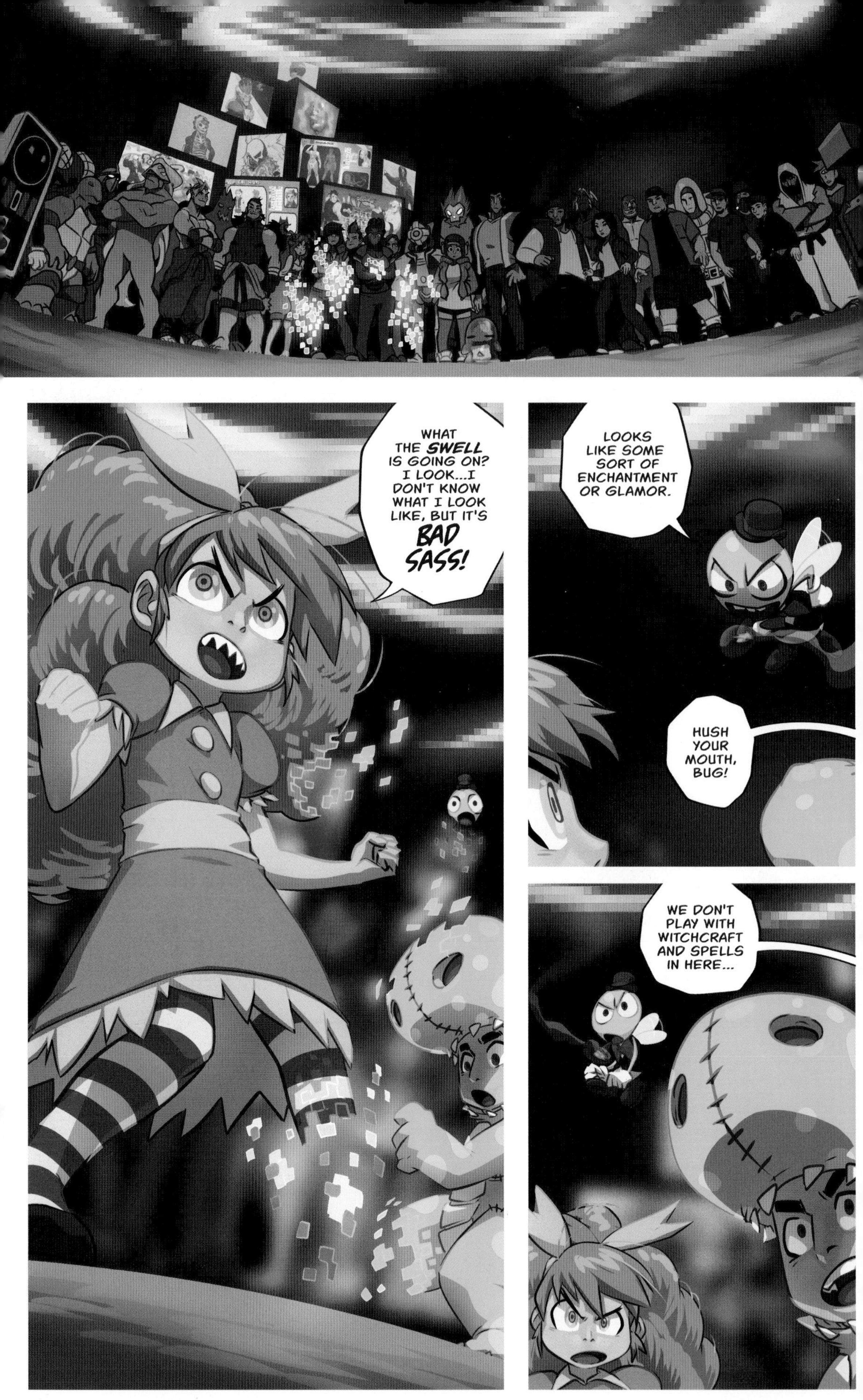
WHAT THE SWELL IS GOING ON? I LOOK...I DON'T KNOW WHAT I LOOK LIKE, BUT IT'S BAD SASS!
LOOKS LIKE SOME SORT OF ENCHANTMENT OR GLAMOR.
HUSH YOUR MOUTH, BUG!
WE DON'T PLAY WITH WITCHCRAFT AND SPELLS IN HERE...

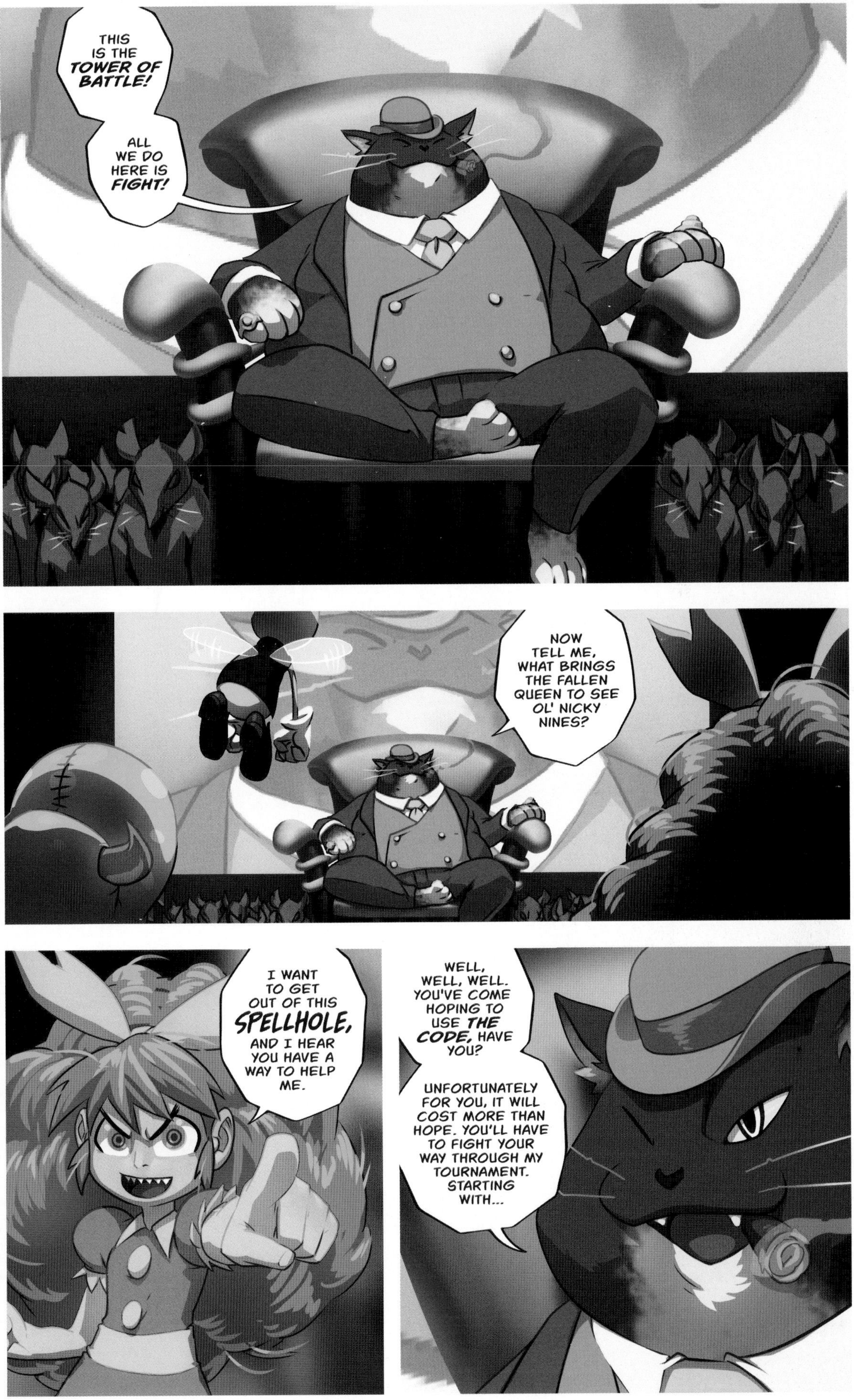
THIS IS THE TOWER OF BATTLE!
ALL WE DO HERE IS FIGHT!
NOW TELL ME, WHAT BRINGS THE FALLEN QUEEN TO SEE OL' NICKY NINES?
I WANT TO GET OUT OF THIS SPELLHOLE, AND I HEAR YOU HAVE A WAY TO HELP ME.
WELL, WELL, WELL. YOU'VE COME HOPING TO USE THE CODE, HAVE YOU?
UNFORTUNATELY FOR YOU, IT WILL COST MORE THAN HOPE. YOU'LL HAVE TO FIGHT YOUR WAY THROUGH MY TOURNAMENT. STARTING WITH...

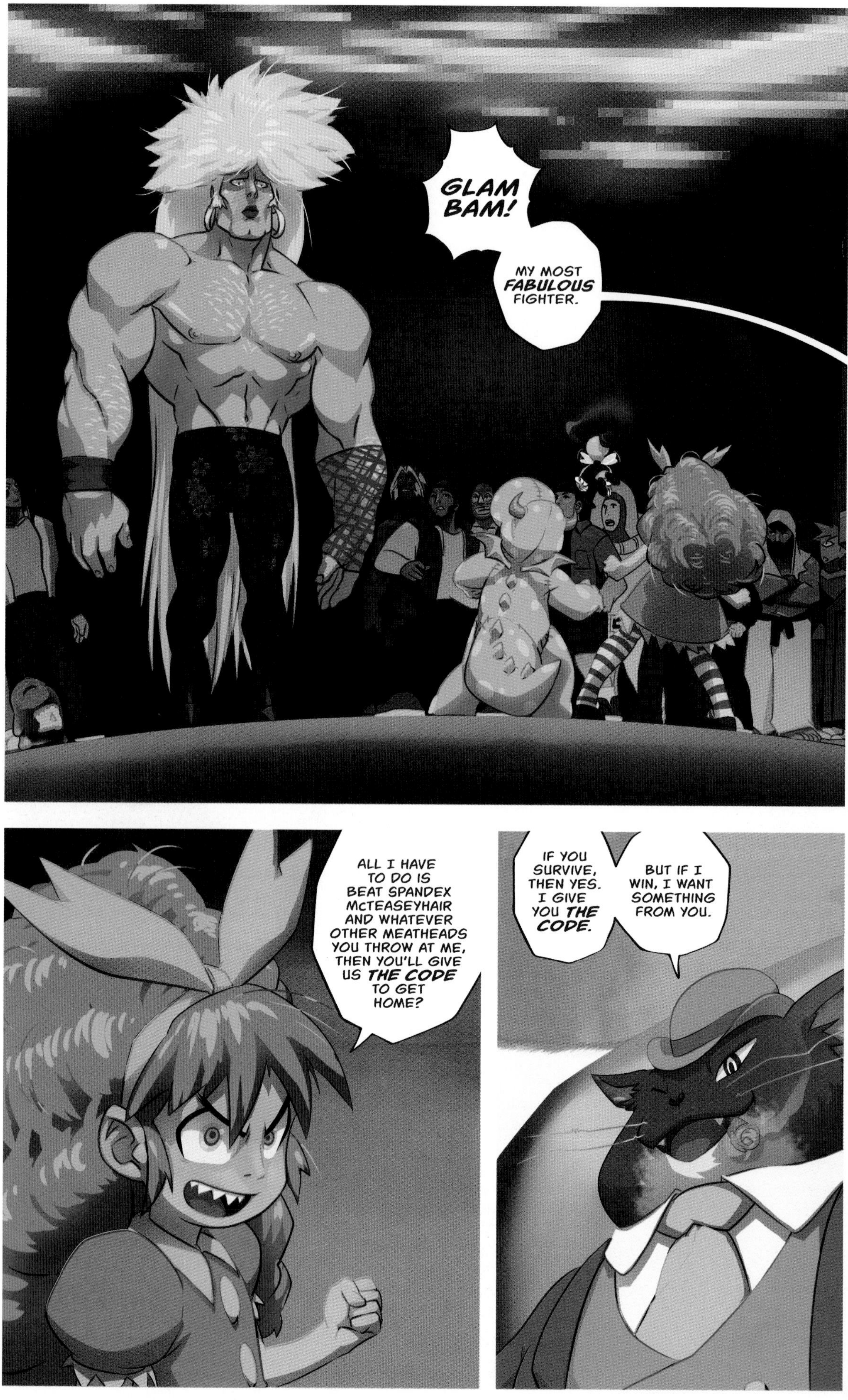

GLAM BAM!
MY MOST FABULOUS FIGHTER.
ALL I HAVE TO DO IS BEAT SPANDEX McTEASEYHAIR AND WHATEVER OTHER MEATHEADS YOU THROW AT ME, THEN YOU'LL GIVE US THE CODE TO GET HOME?
IF YOU SURVIVE, THEN YES. I GIVE YOU THE CODE.
BUT IF I WIN, I WANT SOMETHING FROM YOU.

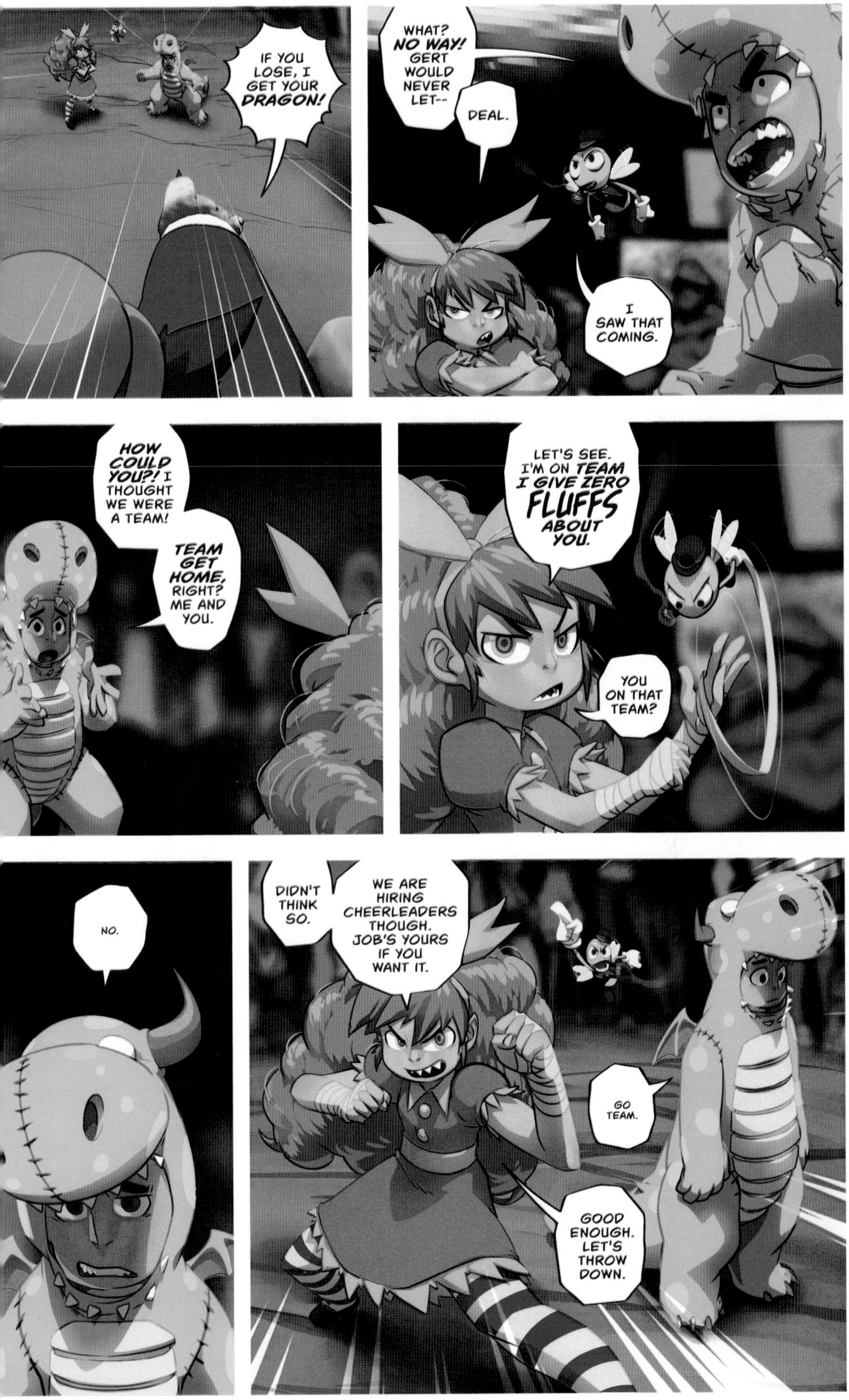
IF YOU LOSE, I GET YOUR *DRAGON!*
WHAT? ***NO WAY!*** GERT WOULD NEVER LET--
DEAL.
I SAW THAT COMING.
HOW COULD YOU?! I THOUGHT WE WERE A TEAM!
TEAM GET HOME, RIGHT? ME AND YOU.
LET'S SEE. I'M ON ***TEAM I GIVE ZERO FLUFFS ABOUT YOU.***
YOU ON THAT TEAM?
NO.
DIDN'T THINK SO.
WE ARE HIRING CHEERLEADERS THOUGH. JOB'S YOURS IF YOU WANT IT.
GO TEAM.
GOOD ENOUGH. LET'S THROW DOWN.

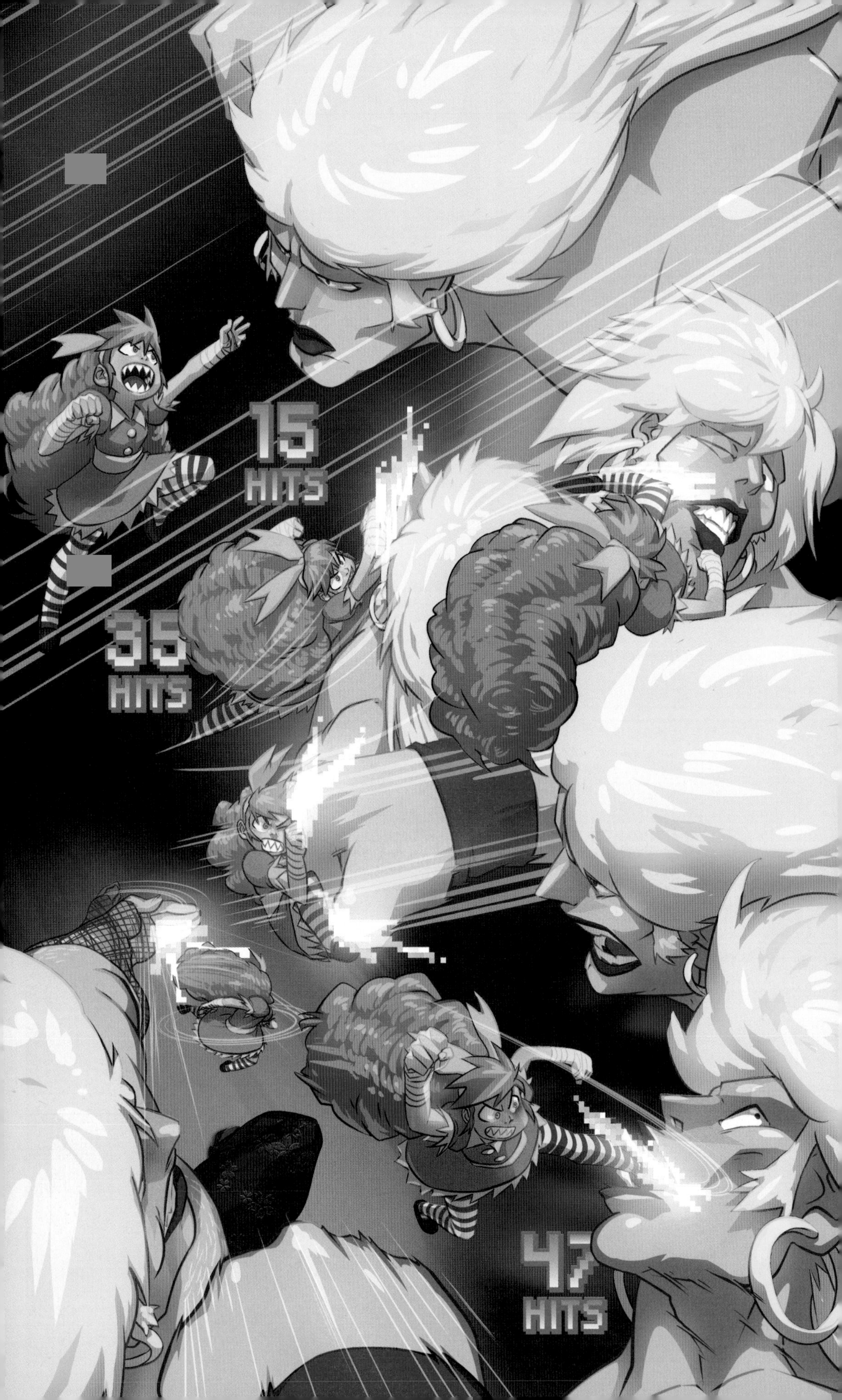
15
HITS
35
HITS
47
HITS

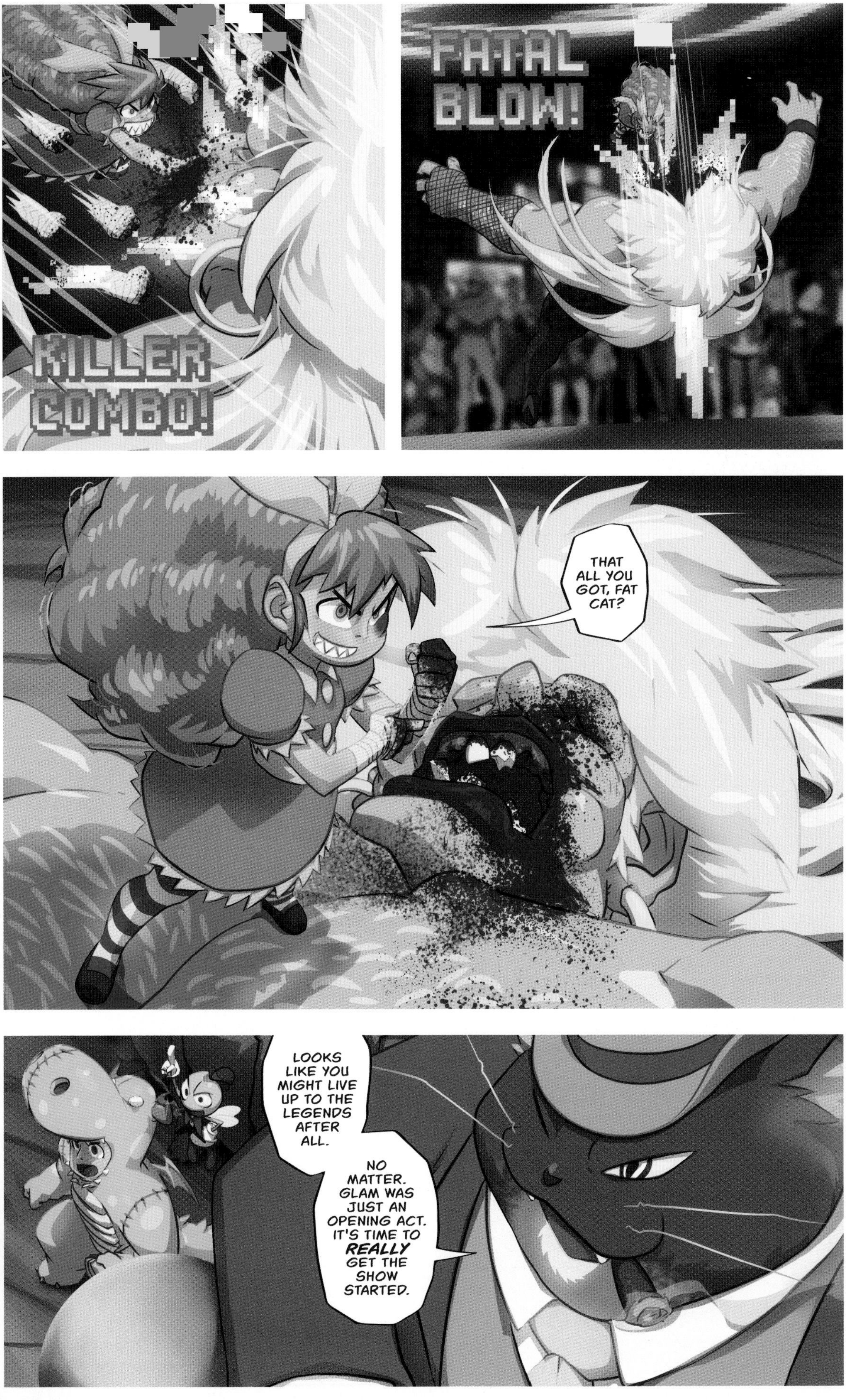
KILLER COMBO!
FATAL BLOW!
THAT ALL YOU GOT, FAT CAT?
LOOKS LIKE YOU MIGHT LIVE UP TO THE LEGENDS AFTER ALL.
NO MATTER. GLAM WAS JUST AN OPENING ACT. IT'S TIME TO ***REALLY*** GET THE SHOW STARTED.

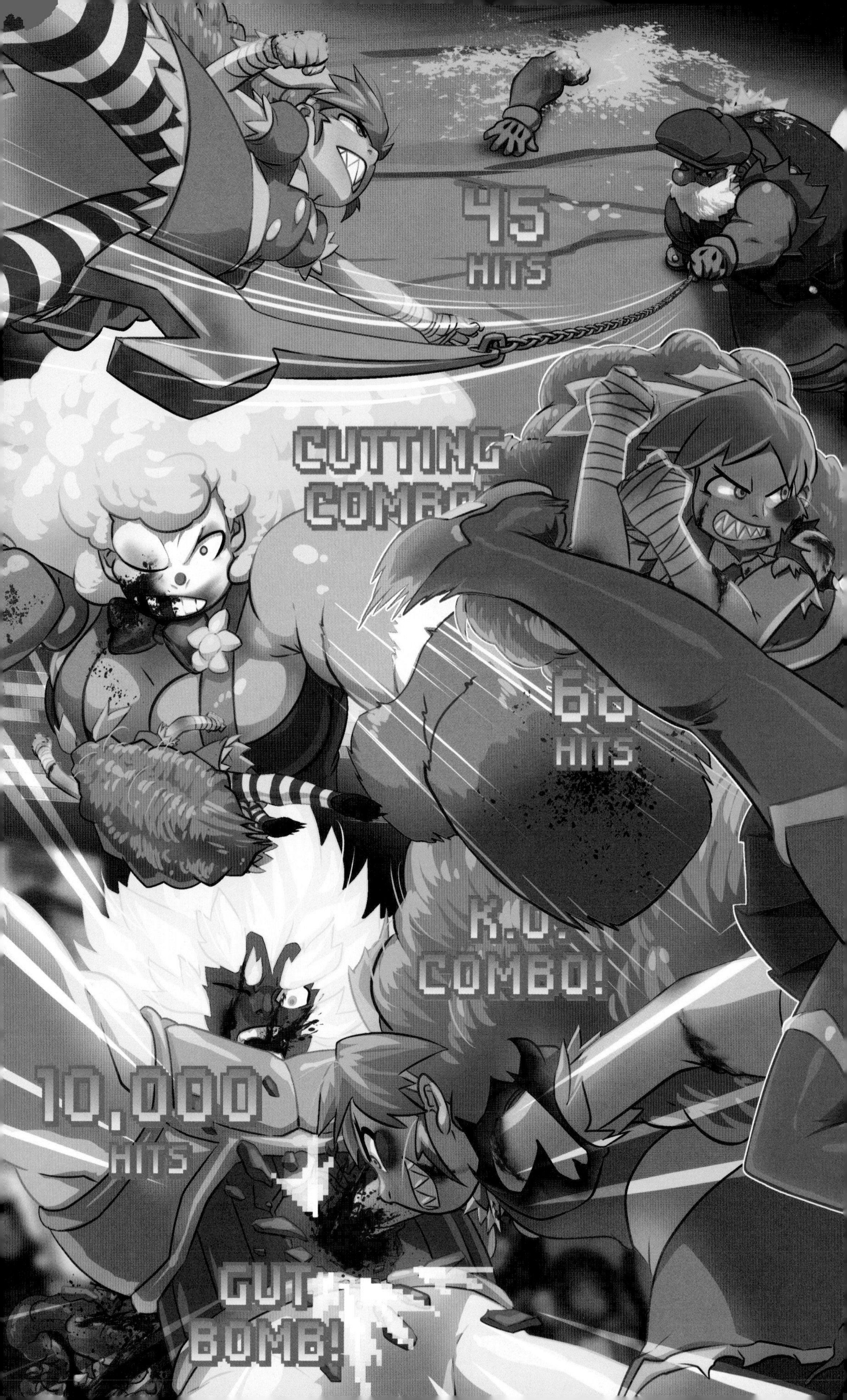

45
HITS
CUTTING
HITS
COMBO!
10,000
HITS
GUT
BOMB!

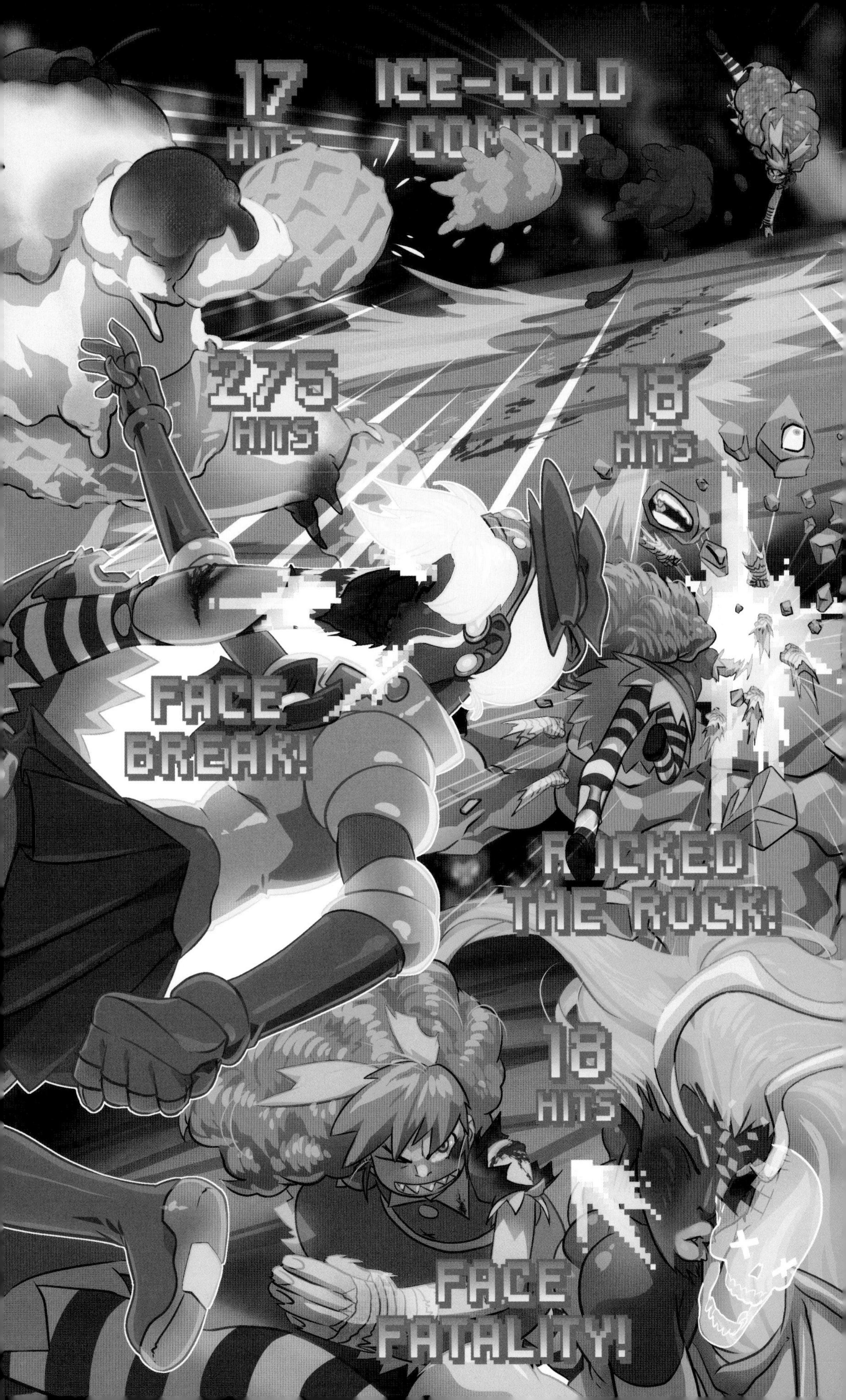

17 HITS
ICE-COLD COMBO!
275 HITS
18 HITS
FACE BREAK!
ROCKED THE ROCK!
18 HITS
FACE FATALITY!

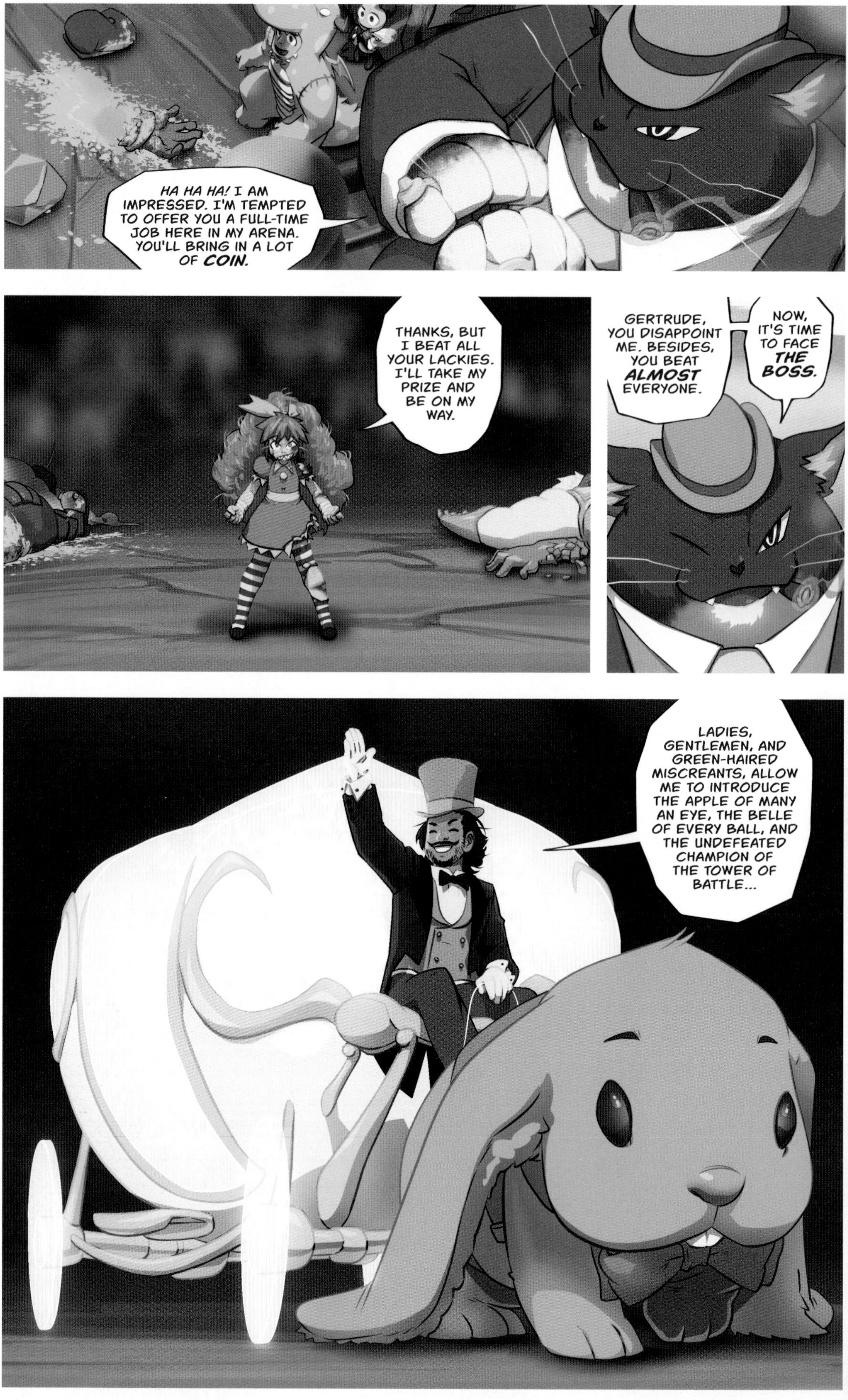
HA HA HA! I AM IMPRESSED. I'M TEMPTED TO OFFER YOU A FULL-TIME JOB HERE IN MY ARENA. YOU'LL BRING IN A LOT OF COIN.
THANKS, BUT I BEAT ALL YOUR LACKIES. I'LL TAKE MY PRIZE AND BE ON MY WAY.
GERTRUDE, YOU DISAPPOINT ME. BESIDES, YOU BEAT ALMOST EVERYONE.
NOW, IT'S TIME TO FACE THE BOSS.
LADIES, GENTLEMEN, AND GREEN-HAIRED MISCREANTS, ALLOW ME TO INTRODUCE THE APPLE OF MANY AN EYE, THE BELLE OF EVERY BALL, AND THE UNDEFEATED CHAMPION OF THE TOWER OF BATTLE...

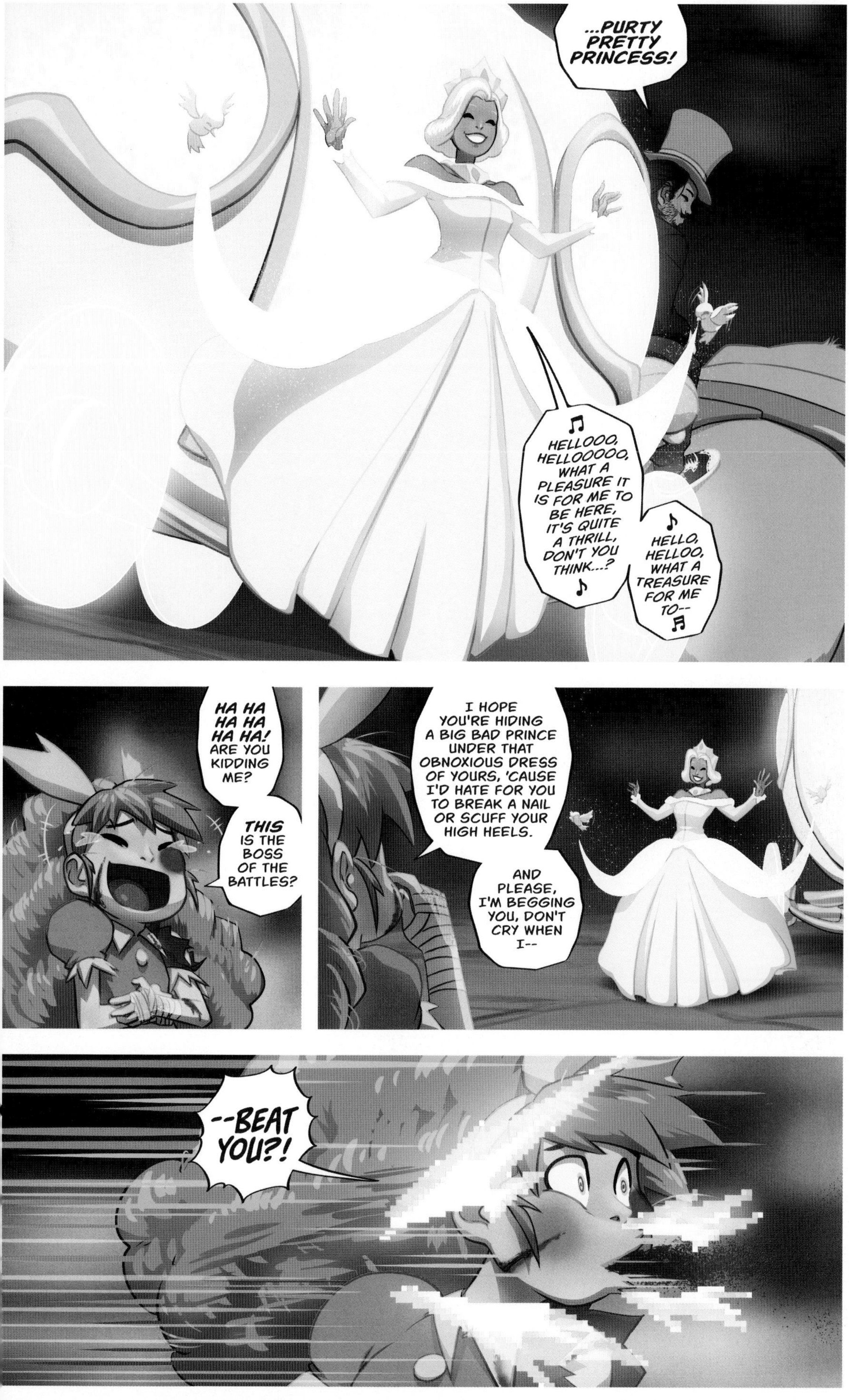
...PURTY PRETTY PRINCESS!
♫ HELLOOO, HELLOOOOO, WHAT A PLEASURE IT IS FOR ME TO BE HERE, IT'S QUITE A THRILL, DON'T YOU THINK...? ♪
♪ HELLO, HELLOO, WHAT A TREASURE FOR ME TO-- ♬
HA HA HA HA HA HA! ARE YOU KIDDING ME?
THIS IS THE BOSS OF THE BATTLES?
I HOPE YOU'RE HIDING A BIG BAD PRINCE UNDER THAT OBNOXIOUS DRESS OF YOURS, 'CAUSE I'D HATE FOR YOU TO BREAK A NAIL OR SCUFF YOUR HIGH HEELS.
AND PLEASE, I'M BEGGING YOU, DON'T CRY WHEN I--
--BEAT YOU?!

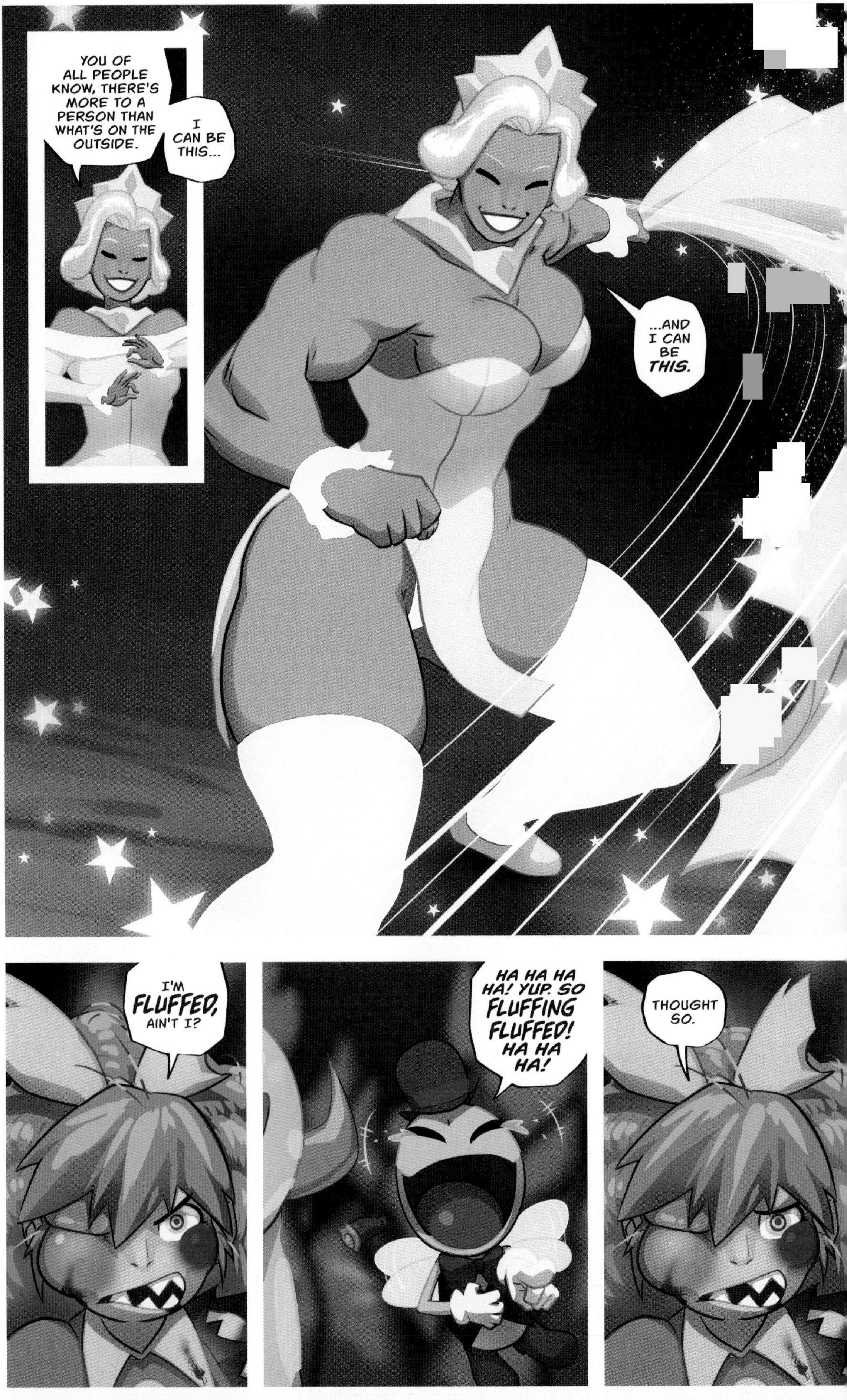
YOU OF ALL PEOPLE KNOW, THERE'S MORE TO A PERSON THAN WHAT'S ON THE OUTSIDE.
I CAN BE THIS...
...AND I CAN BE THIS.
I'M FLUFFED, AIN'T I?
HA HA HA HA! YUP. SO FLUFFING FLUFFED! HA HA HA!
THOUGHT SO.

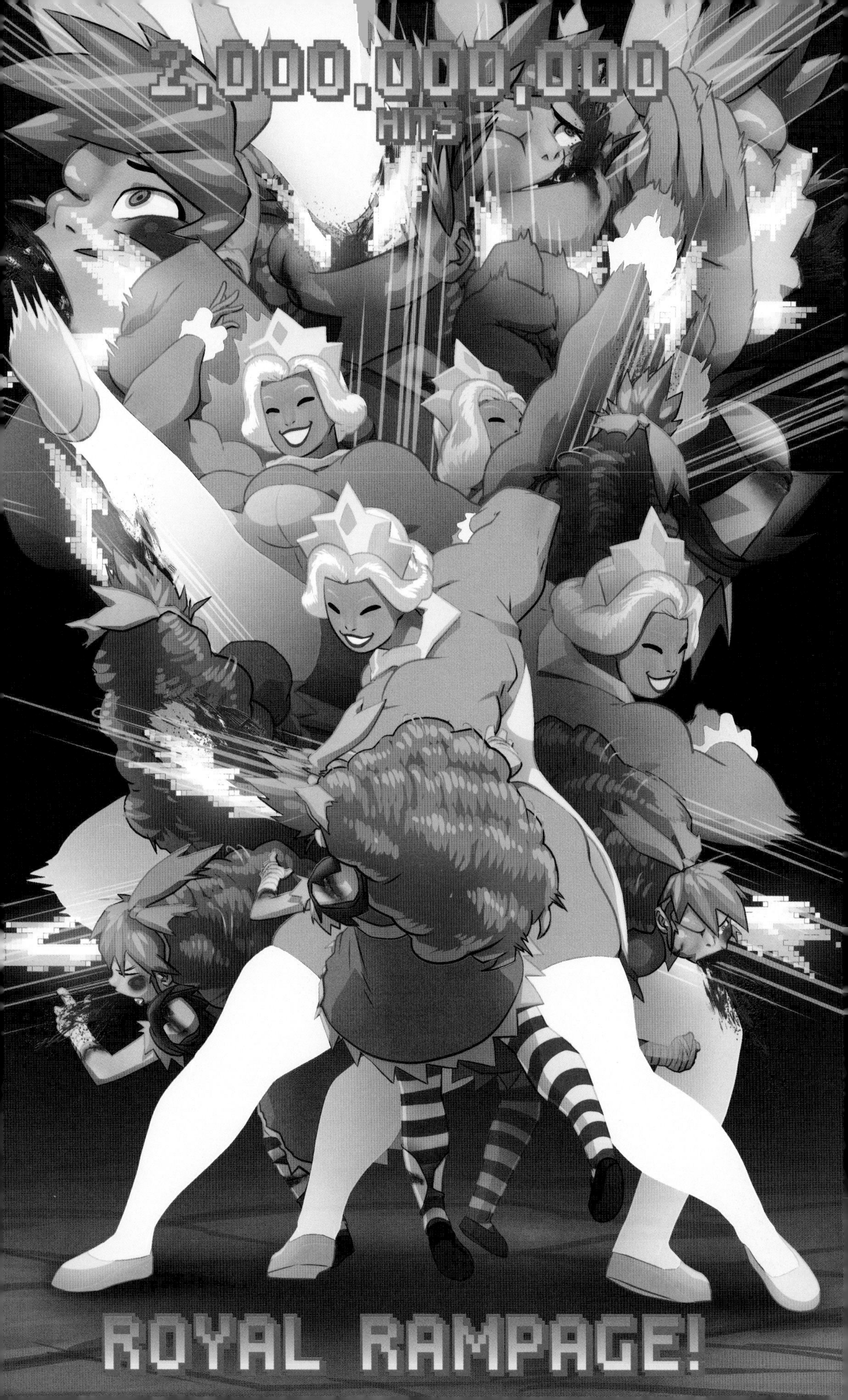
2,000,000,000
HITS
ROYAL RAMPAGE!

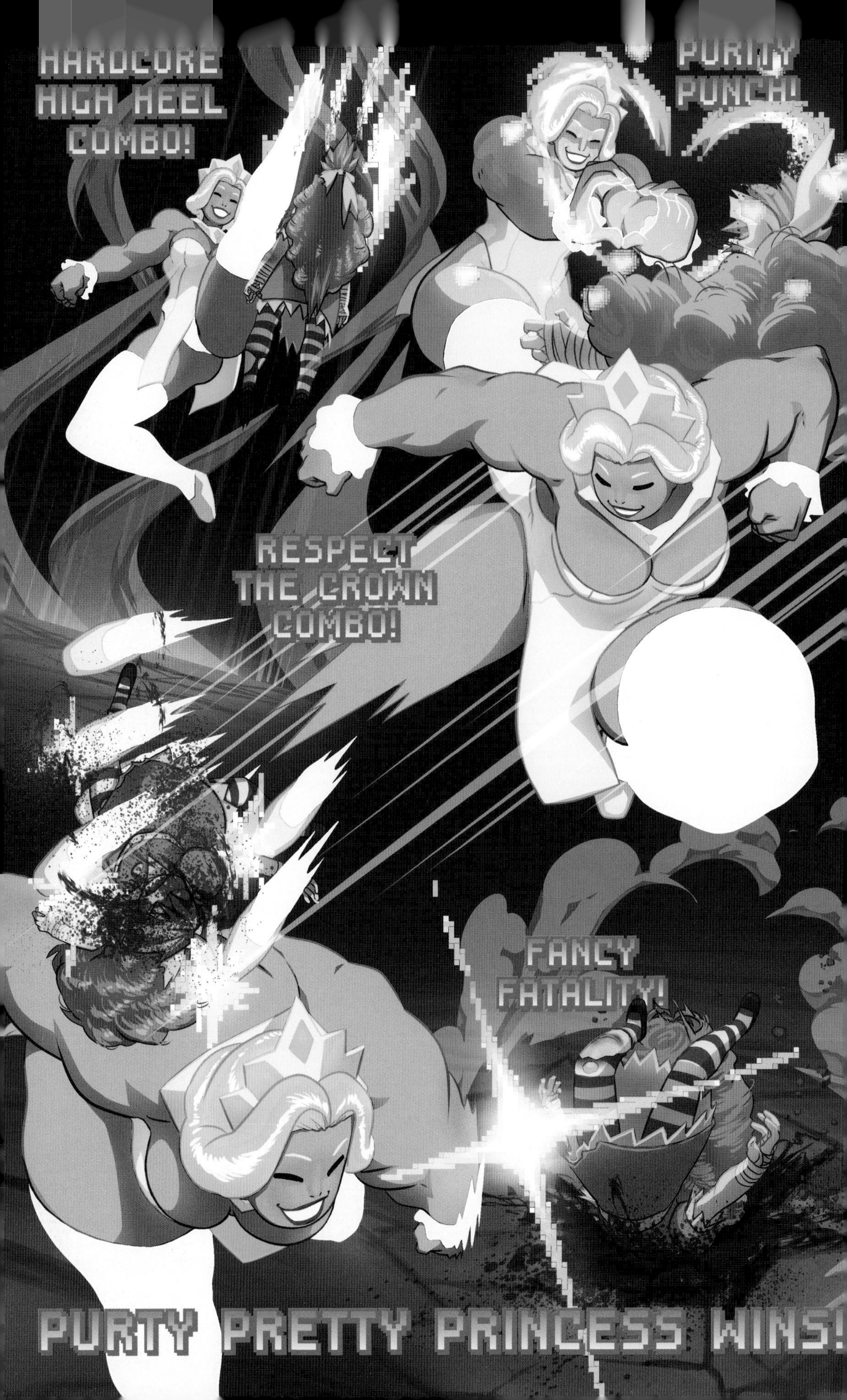
HARDCORE
HIGH HEEL
COMBO!
PURITY
PUNCH!
RESPECT
THE CROWN
COMBO!
FANCY
FATALITY!
PURTY PRETTY PRINCESS WINS!

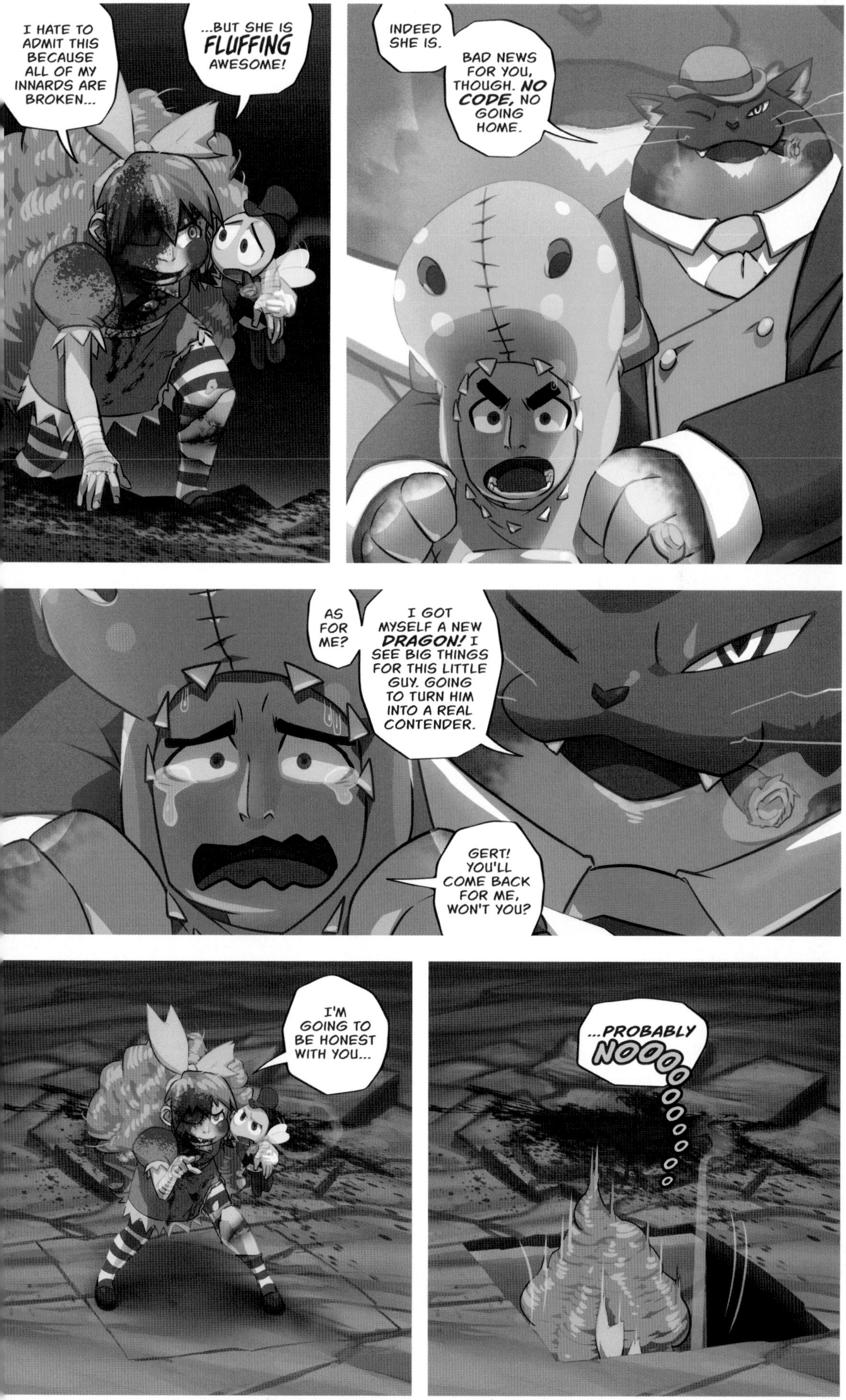

I HATE TO ADMIT THIS BECAUSE ALL OF MY INNARDS ARE BROKEN...
...BUT SHE IS FLUFFING AWESOME!
INDEED SHE IS.
BAD NEWS FOR YOU, THOUGH. NO CODE, NO GOING HOME.
AS FOR ME?
I GOT MYSELF A NEW DRAGON! I SEE BIG THINGS FOR THIS LITTLE GUY. GOING TO TURN HIM INTO A REAL CONTENDER.
GERT! YOU'LL COME BACK FOR ME, WON'T YOU?
I'M GOING TO BE HONEST WITH YOU...
...PROBABLY NOOOOOOOOOOO

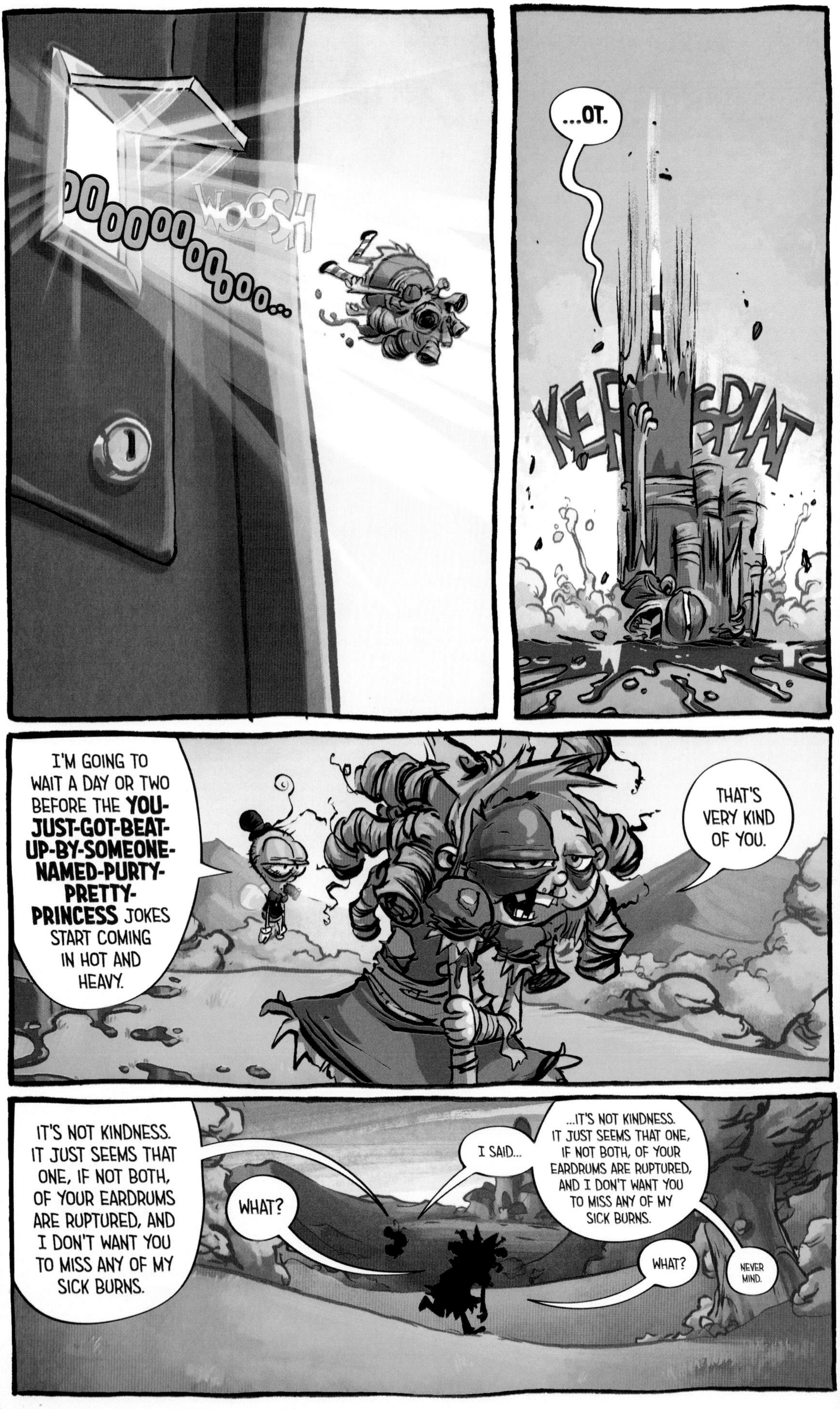
OOOOOOOOOOooo...
WOOSH
...OT.
KER-SPLAT
I'M GOING TO WAIT A DAY OR TWO BEFORE THE **YOU-JUST-GOT-BEAT-UP-BY-SOMEONE-NAMED-PURTY-PRETTY-PRINCESS** JOKES START COMING IN HOT AND HEAVY.
THAT'S VERY KIND OF YOU.
IT'S NOT KINDNESS. IT JUST SEEMS THAT ONE, IF NOT BOTH, OF YOUR EARDRUMS ARE RUPTURED, AND I DON'T WANT YOU TO MISS ANY OF MY SICK BURNS.
WHAT?
I SAID...
...IT'S NOT KINDNESS. IT JUST SEEMS THAT ONE, IF NOT BOTH, OF YOUR EARDRUMS ARE RUPTURED, AND I DON'T WANT YOU TO MISS ANY OF MY SICK BURNS.
WHAT?
NEVER MIND.

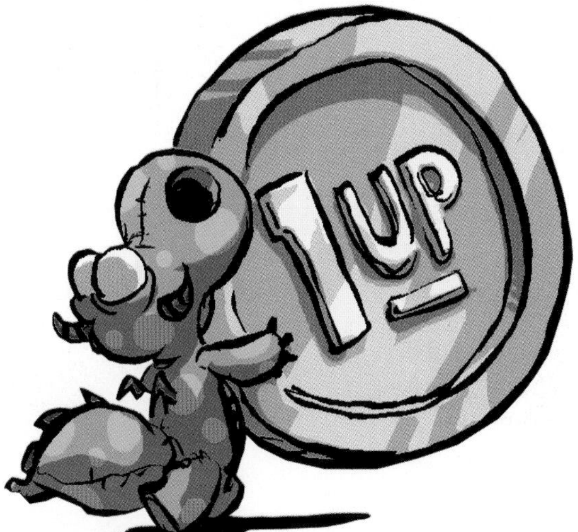
1UP

NINE

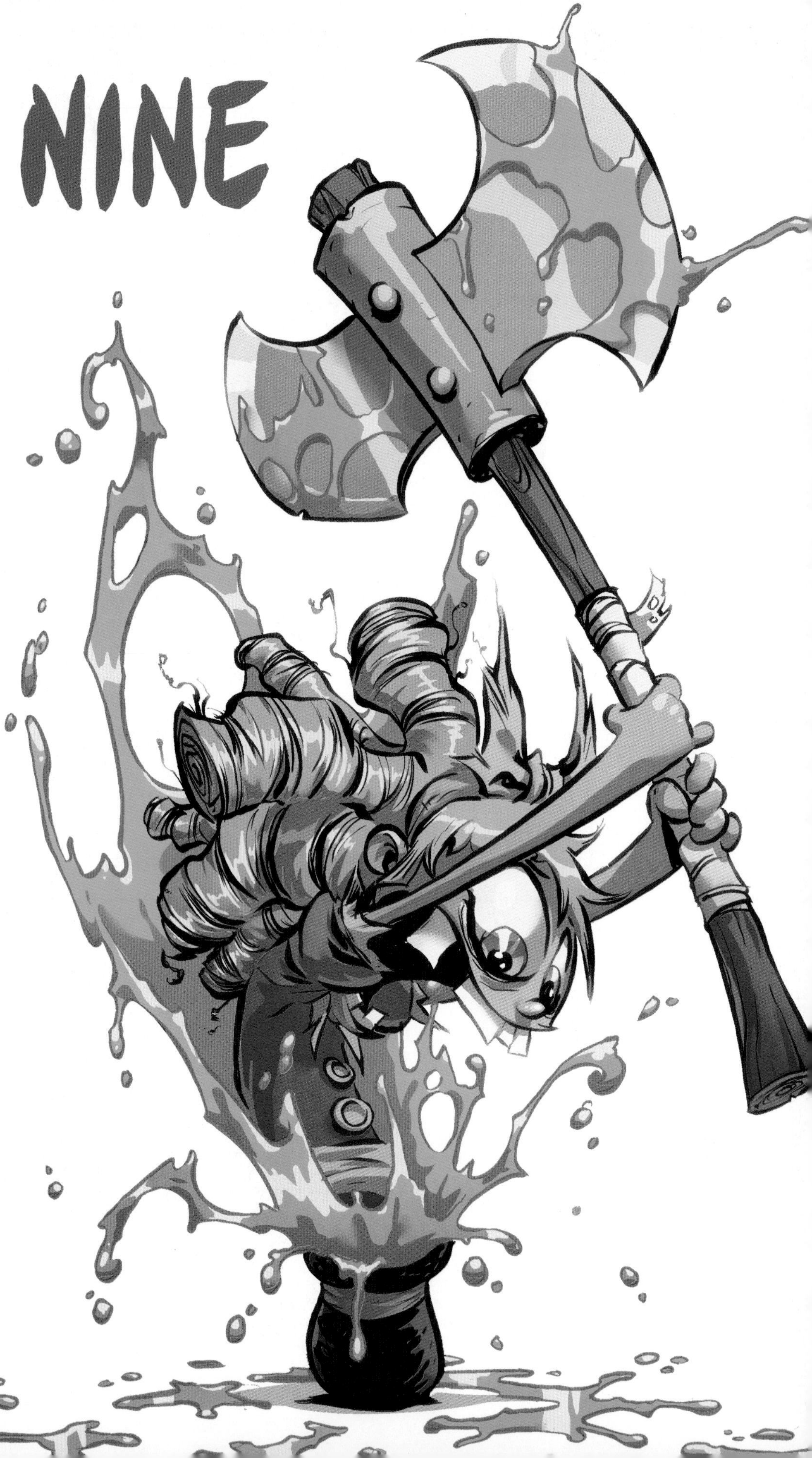

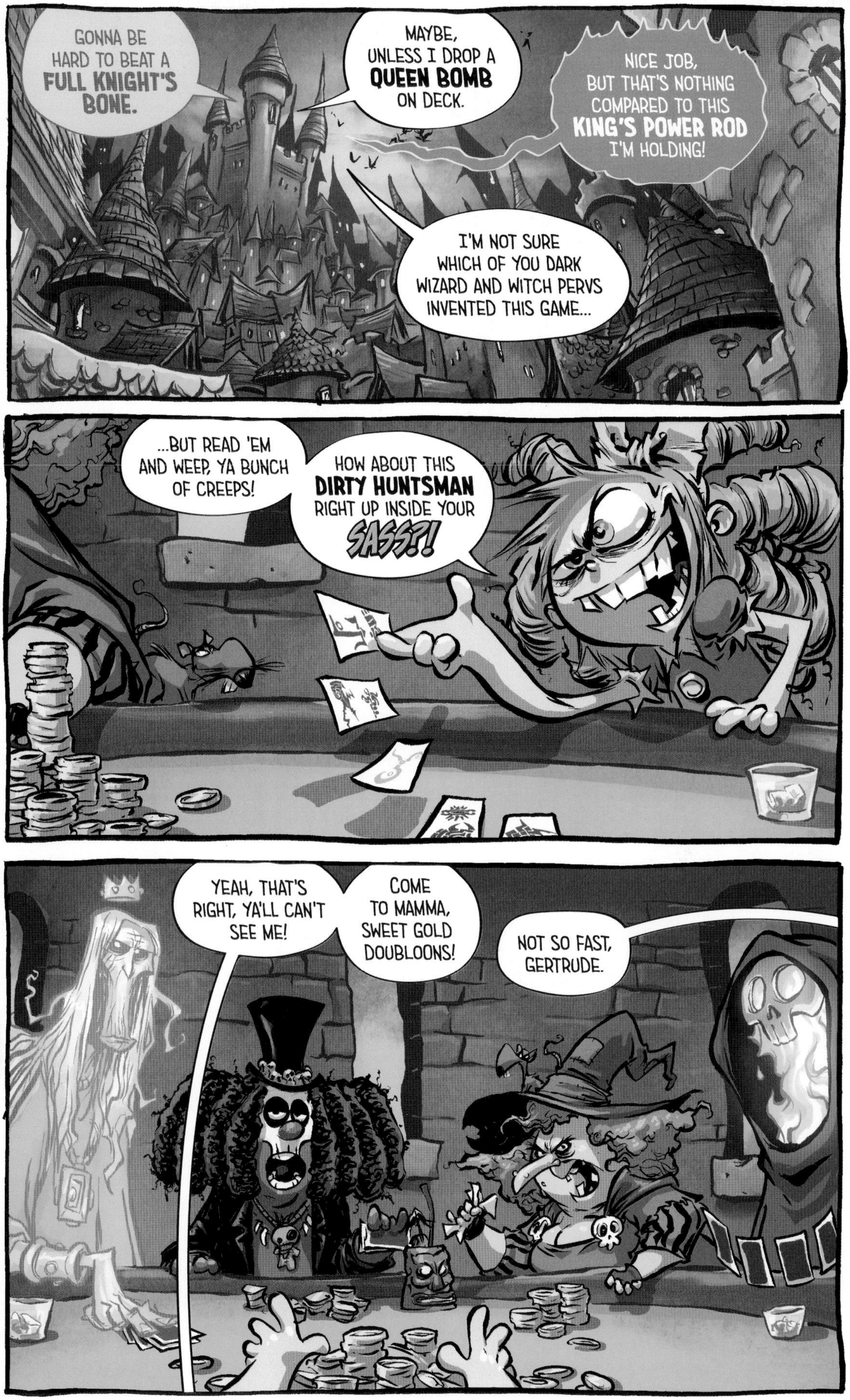

GONNA BE HARD TO BEAT A FULL KNIGHT'S BONE.
MAYBE, UNLESS I DROP A QUEEN BOMB ON DECK.
NICE JOB, BUT THAT'S NOTHING COMPARED TO THIS KING'S POWER ROD I'M HOLDING!
I'M NOT SURE WHICH OF YOU DARK WIZARD AND WITCH PERVS INVENTED THIS GAME...
...BUT READ 'EM AND WEEP, YA BUNCH OF CREEPS!
HOW ABOUT THIS DIRTY HUNTSMAN RIGHT UP INSIDE YOUR SASS?!
YEAH, THAT'S RIGHT, YA'LL CAN'T SEE ME!
COME TO MAMMA, SWEET GOLD DOUBLOONS!
NOT SO FAST, GERTRUDE.

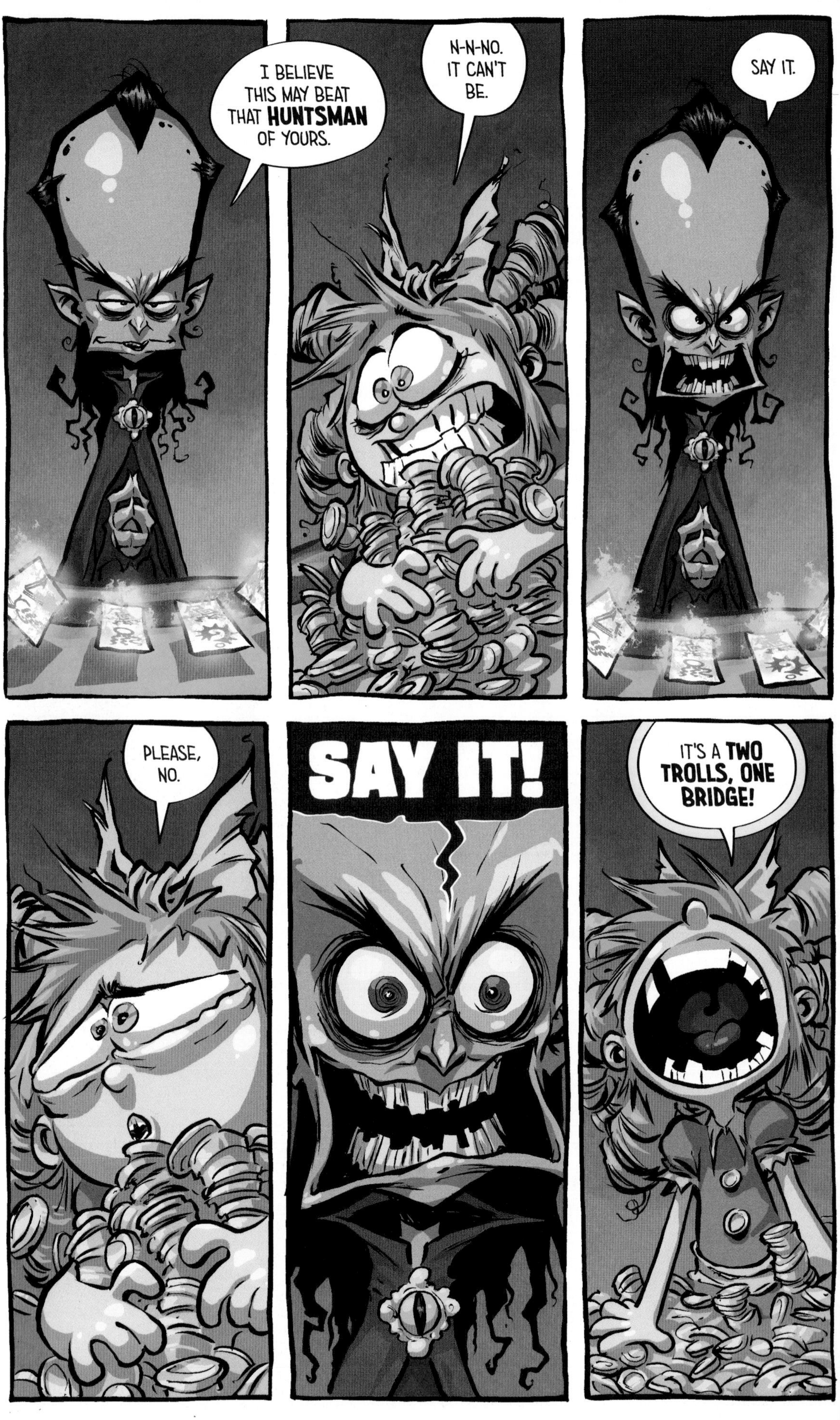
I BELIEVE THIS MAY BEAT THAT **HUNTSMAN** OF YOURS.
N-N-NO. IT CAN'T BE.
SAY IT.
PLEASE, NO.
SAY IT!
IT'S A **TWO TROLLS, ONE BRIDGE!**

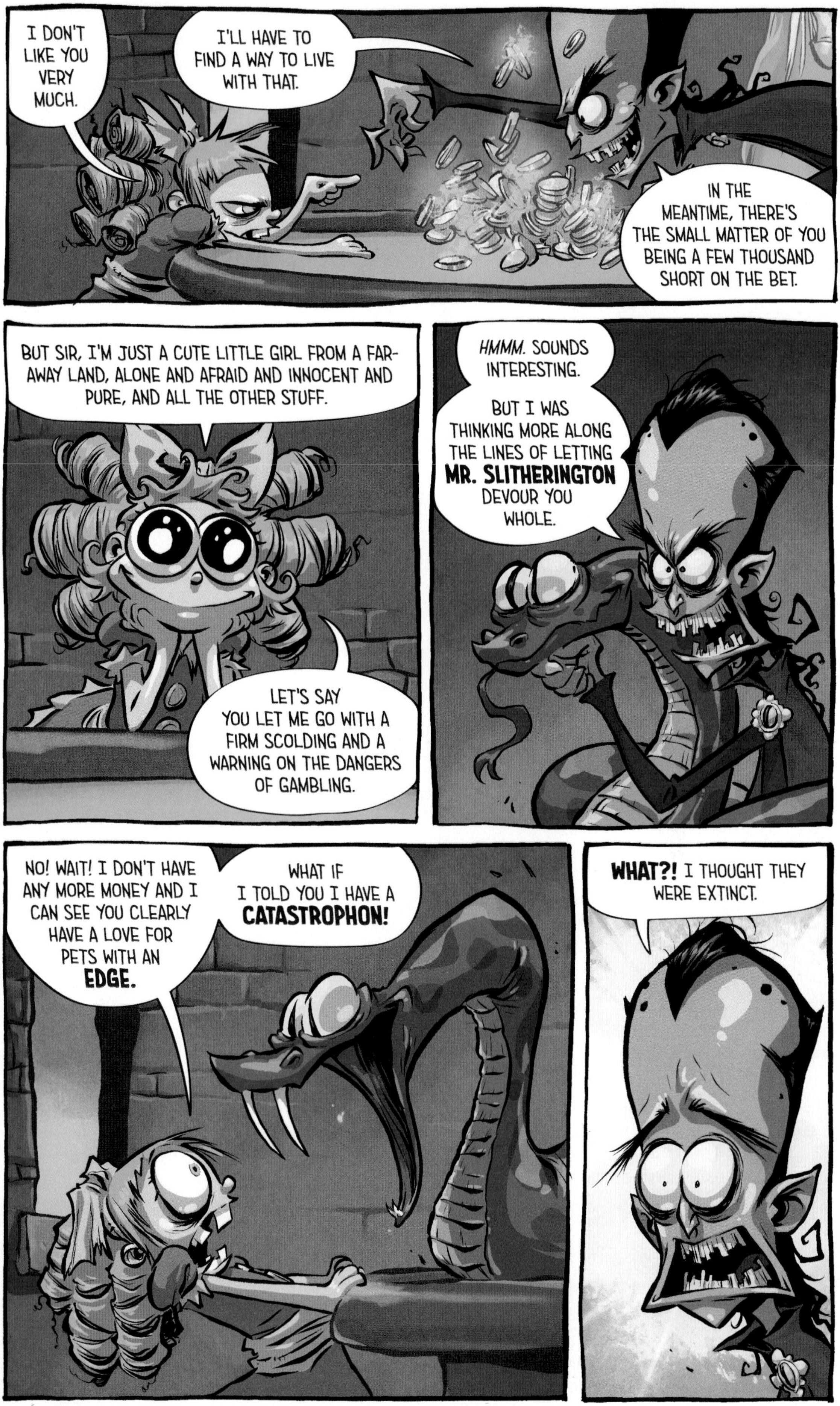
I DON'T LIKE YOU VERY MUCH.
I'LL HAVE TO FIND A WAY TO LIVE WITH THAT.
IN THE MEANTIME, THERE'S THE SMALL MATTER OF YOU BEING A FEW THOUSAND SHORT ON THE BET.
BUT SIR, I'M JUST A CUTE LITTLE GIRL FROM A FAR-AWAY LAND, ALONE AND AFRAID AND INNOCENT AND PURE, AND ALL THE OTHER STUFF.
LET'S SAY YOU LET ME GO WITH A FIRM SCOLDING AND A WARNING ON THE DANGERS OF GAMBLING.
HMMM. SOUNDS INTERESTING.
BUT I WAS THINKING MORE ALONG THE LINES OF LETTING **MR. SLITHERINGTON** DEVOUR YOU WHOLE.
NO! WAIT! I DON'T HAVE ANY MORE MONEY AND I CAN SEE YOU CLEARLY HAVE A LOVE FOR PETS WITH AN **EDGE.**
WHAT IF I TOLD YOU I HAVE A **CATASTROPHON!**
WHAT?! I THOUGHT THEY WERE EXTINCT.

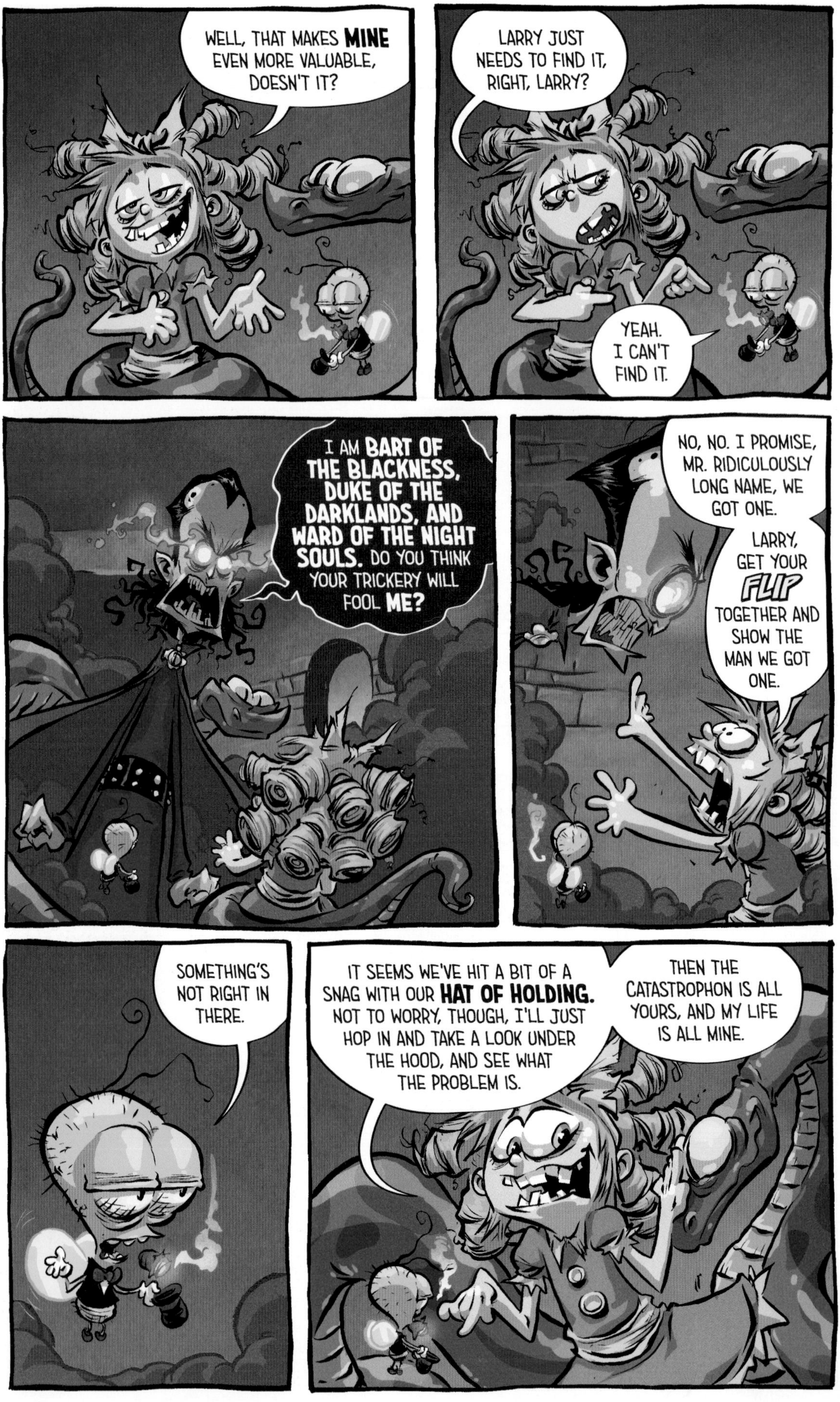
WELL, THAT MAKES **MINE** EVEN MORE VALUABLE, DOESN'T IT?
LARRY JUST NEEDS TO FIND IT, RIGHT, LARRY?
YEAH. I CAN'T FIND IT.
I AM **BART OF THE BLACKNESS, DUKE OF THE DARKLANDS, AND WARD OF THE NIGHT SOULS.** DO YOU THINK YOUR TRICKERY WILL FOOL **ME?**
NO, NO. I PROMISE, MR. RIDICULOUSLY LONG NAME, WE GOT ONE.
LARRY, GET YOUR FLIP TOGETHER AND SHOW THE MAN WE GOT ONE.
SOMETHING'S NOT RIGHT IN THERE.
IT SEEMS WE'VE HIT A BIT OF A SNAG WITH OUR **HAT OF HOLDING.** NOT TO WORRY, THOUGH, I'LL JUST HOP IN AND TAKE A LOOK UNDER THE HOOD, AND SEE WHAT THE PROBLEM IS.
THEN THE CATASTROPHON IS ALL YOURS, AND MY LIFE IS ALL MINE.

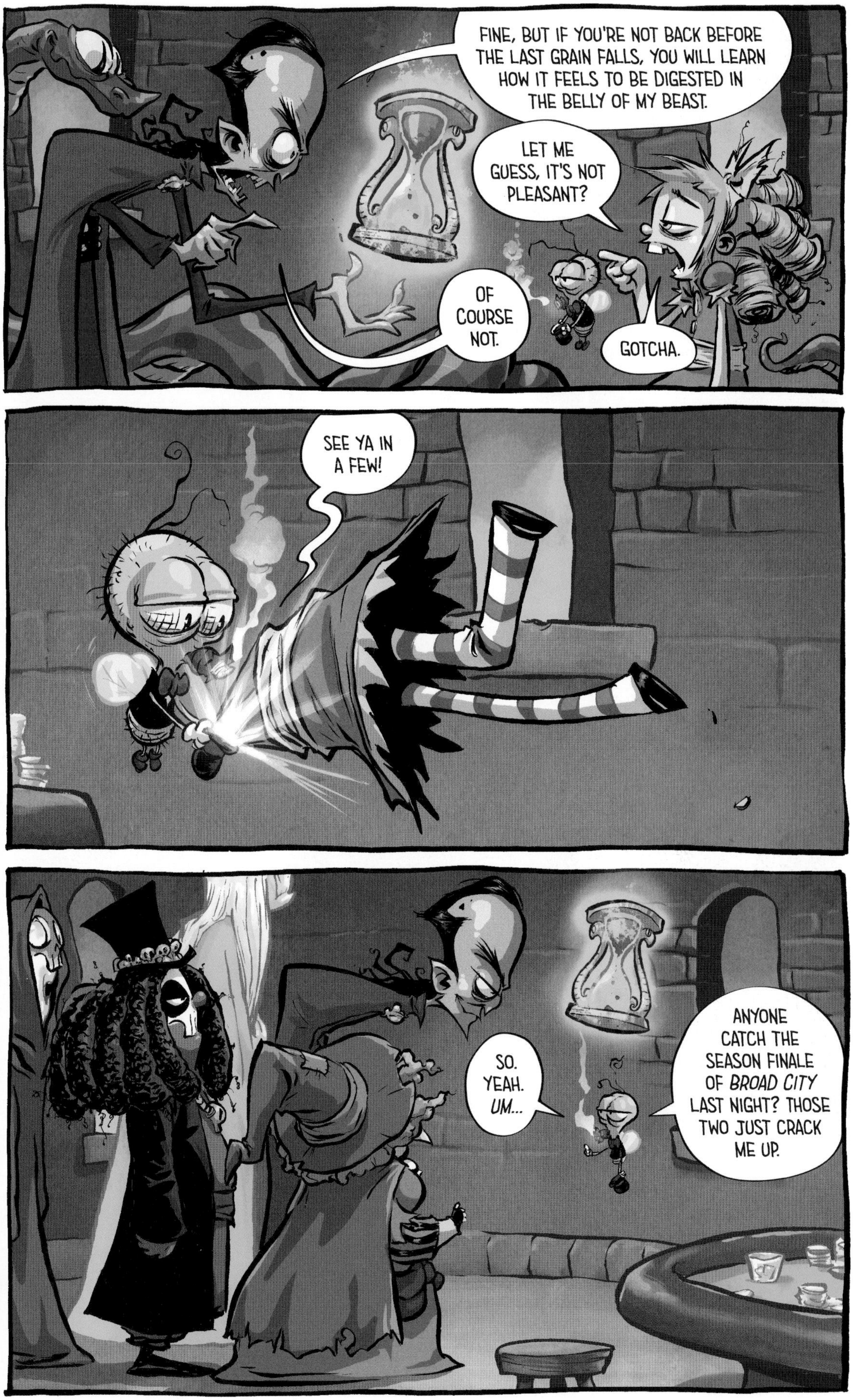
FINE, BUT IF YOU'RE NOT BACK BEFORE THE LAST GRAIN FALLS, YOU WILL LEARN HOW IT FEELS TO BE DIGESTED IN THE BELLY OF MY BEAST.
LET ME GUESS, IT'S NOT PLEASANT?
OF COURSE NOT.
GOTCHA.
SEE YA IN A FEW!
SO. YEAH. *UM...*
ANYONE CATCH THE SEASON FINALE OF *BROAD CITY* LAST NIGHT? THOSE TWO JUST CRACK ME UP.

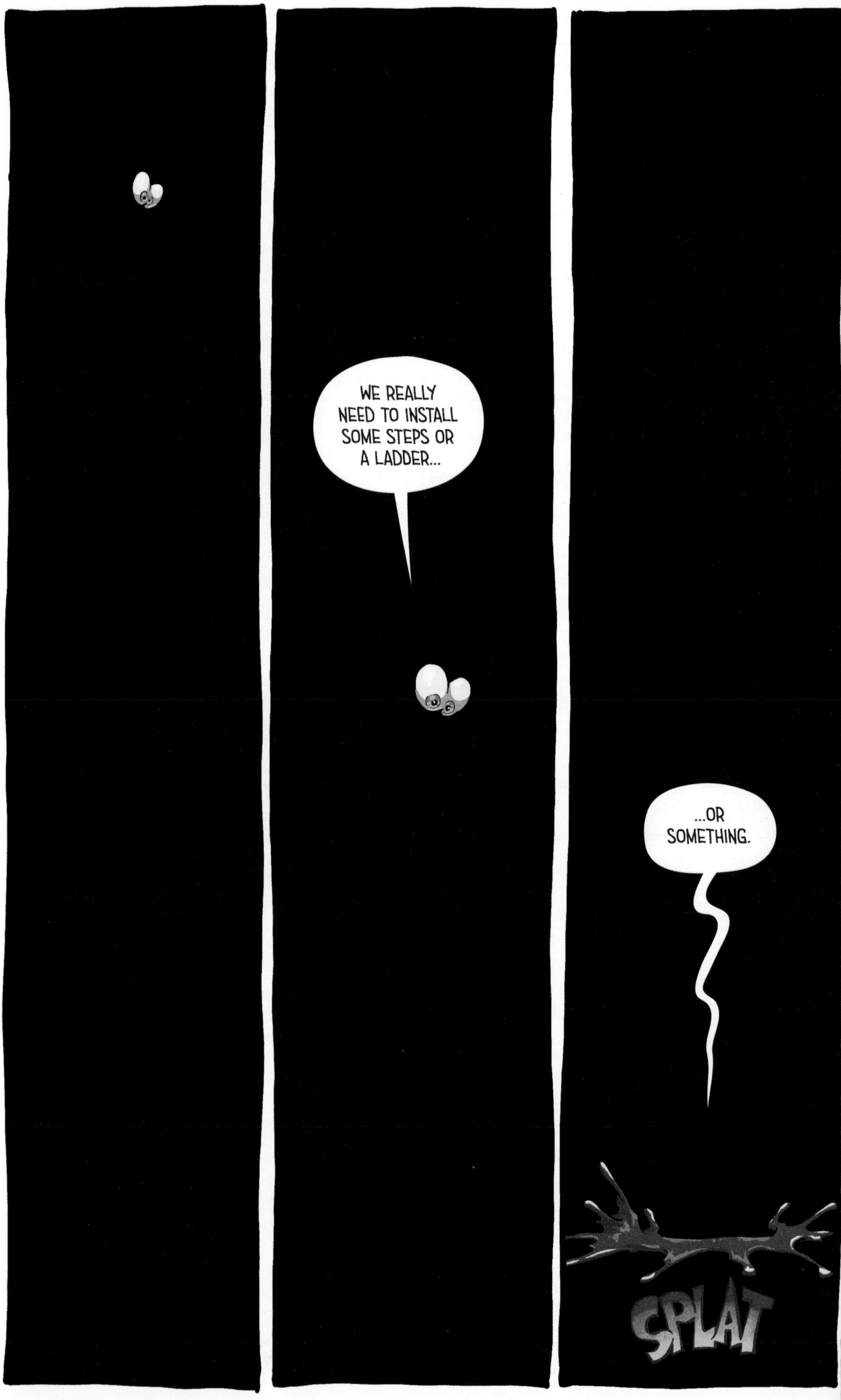
WE REALLY NEED TO INSTALL SOME STEPS OR A LADDER...
...OR SOMETHING.
SPLAT

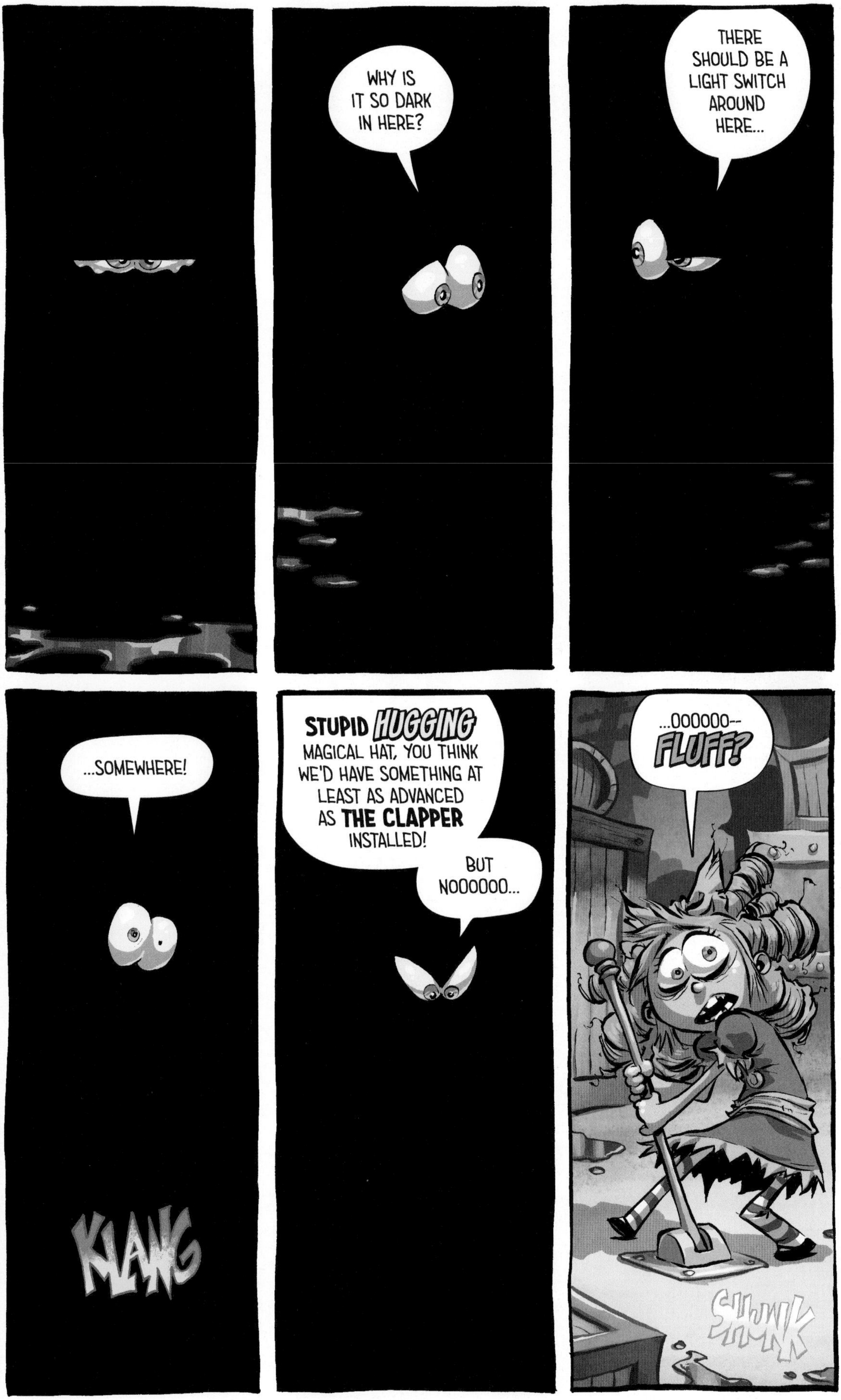

WHY IS IT SO DARK IN HERE?
THERE SHOULD BE A LIGHT SWITCH AROUND HERE...
...SOMEWHERE!
KLANG
STUPID HUGGING MAGICAL HAT, YOU THINK WE'D HAVE SOMETHING AT LEAST AS ADVANCED AS THE CLAPPER INSTALLED!
BUT NOOOOOO...
...OOOOOO--FLUFF?
SHUNK

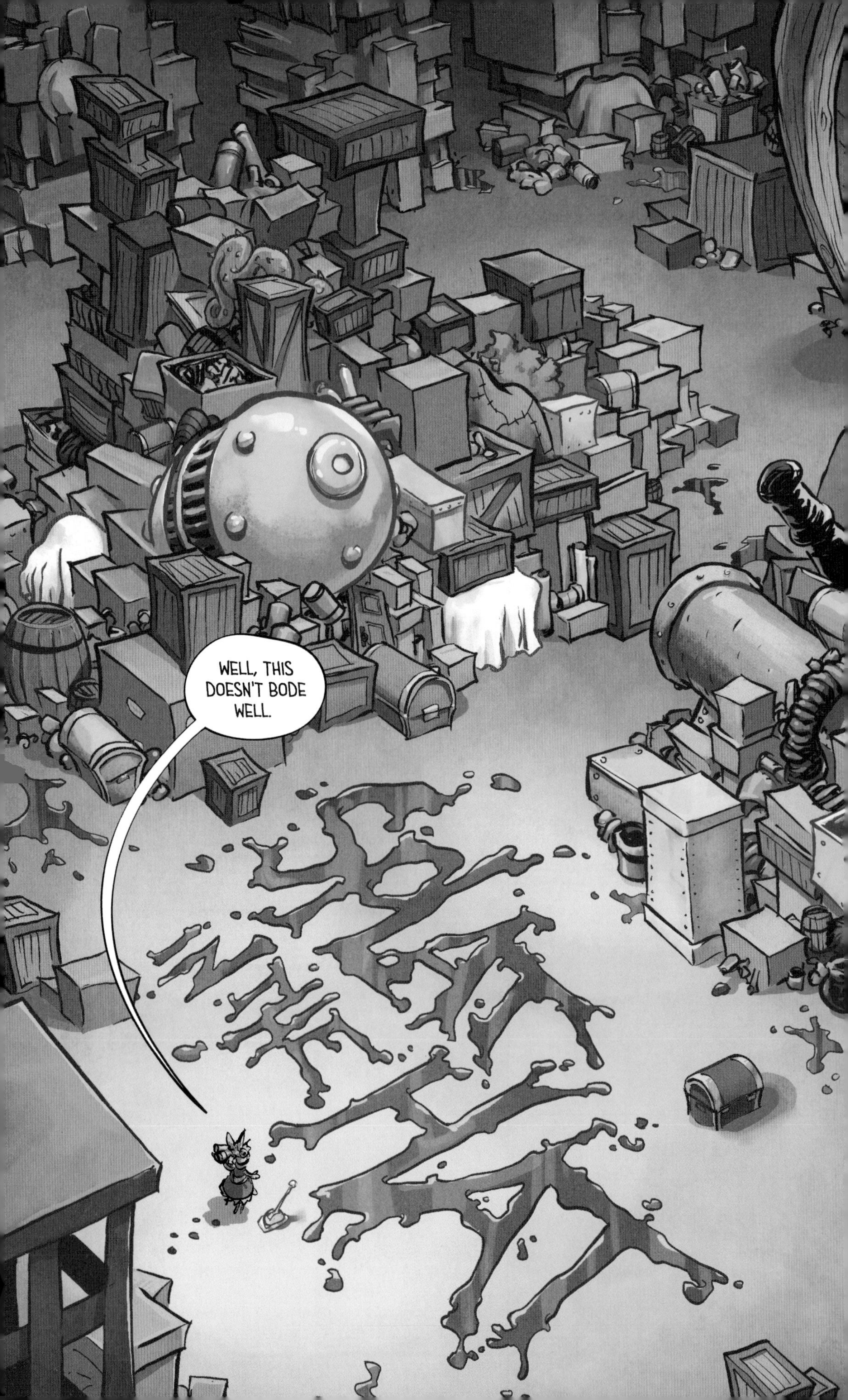
WELL, THIS DOESN'T BODE WELL.

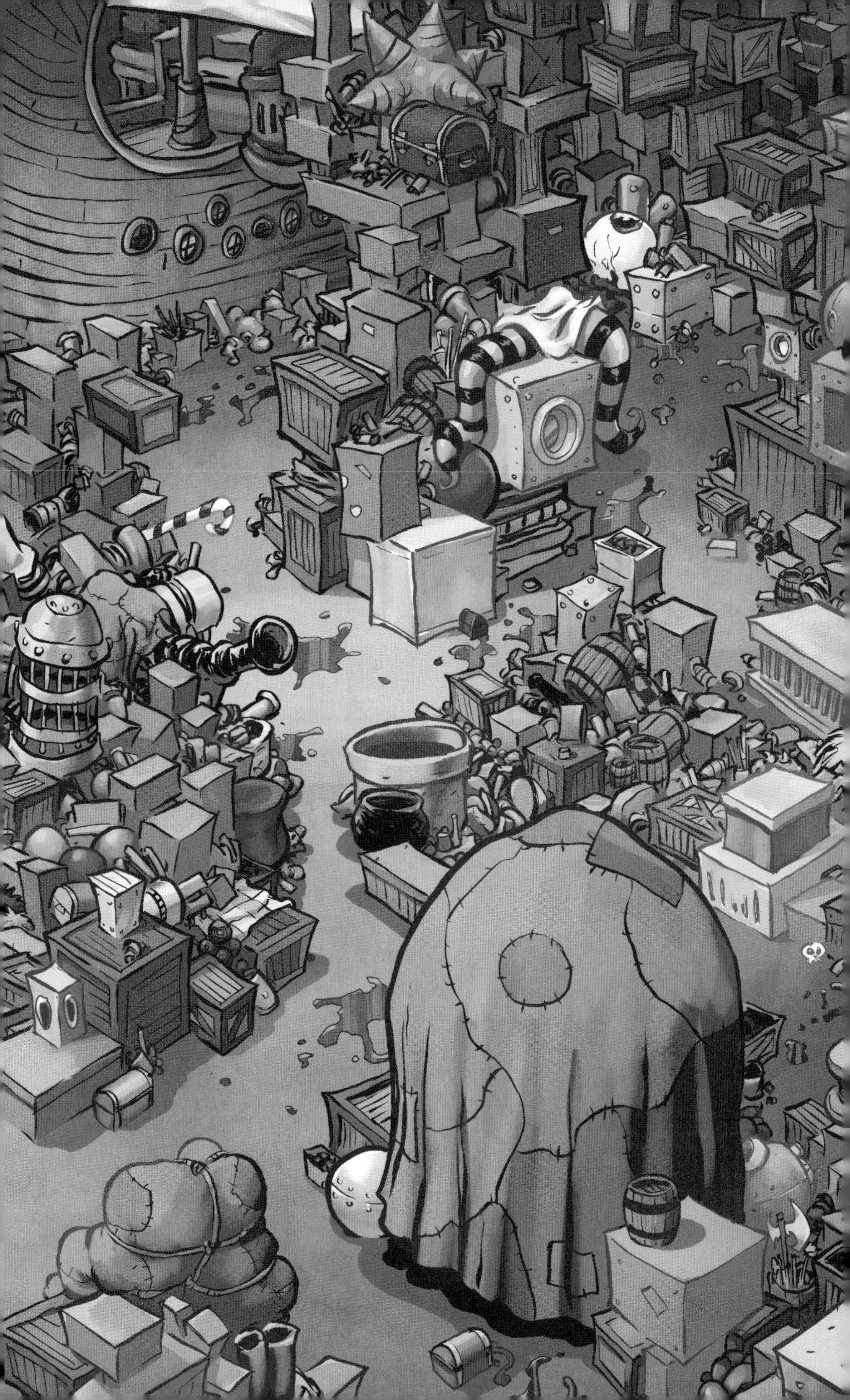

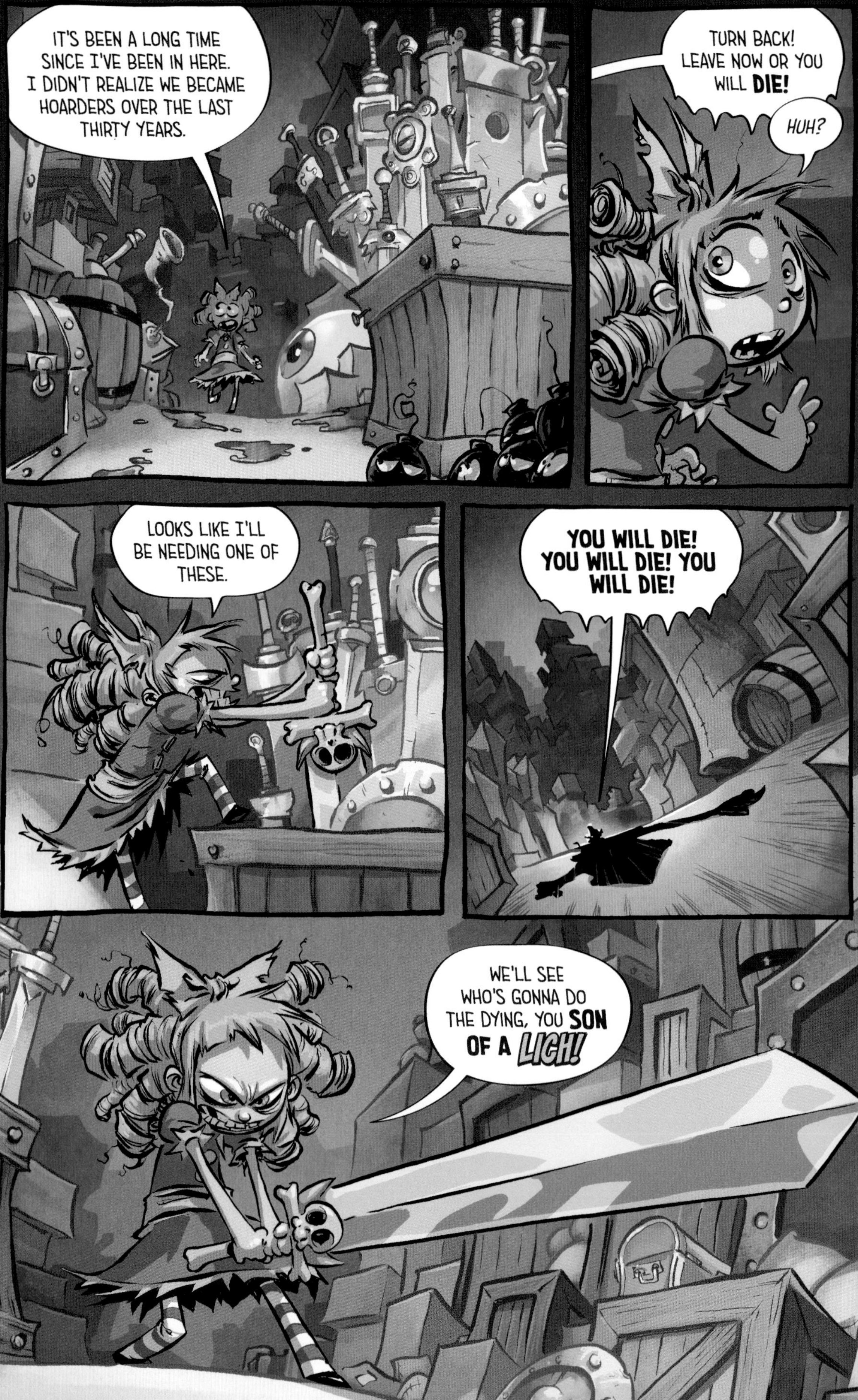
IT'S BEEN A LONG TIME SINCE I'VE BEEN IN HERE. I DIDN'T REALIZE WE BECAME HOARDERS OVER THE LAST THIRTY YEARS.
TURN BACK! LEAVE NOW OR YOU WILL DIE!
HUH?
LOOKS LIKE I'LL BE NEEDING ONE OF THESE.
YOU WILL DIE! YOU WILL DIE! YOU WILL DIE!
WE'LL SEE WHO'S GONNA DO THE DYING, YOU SON OF A LICH!

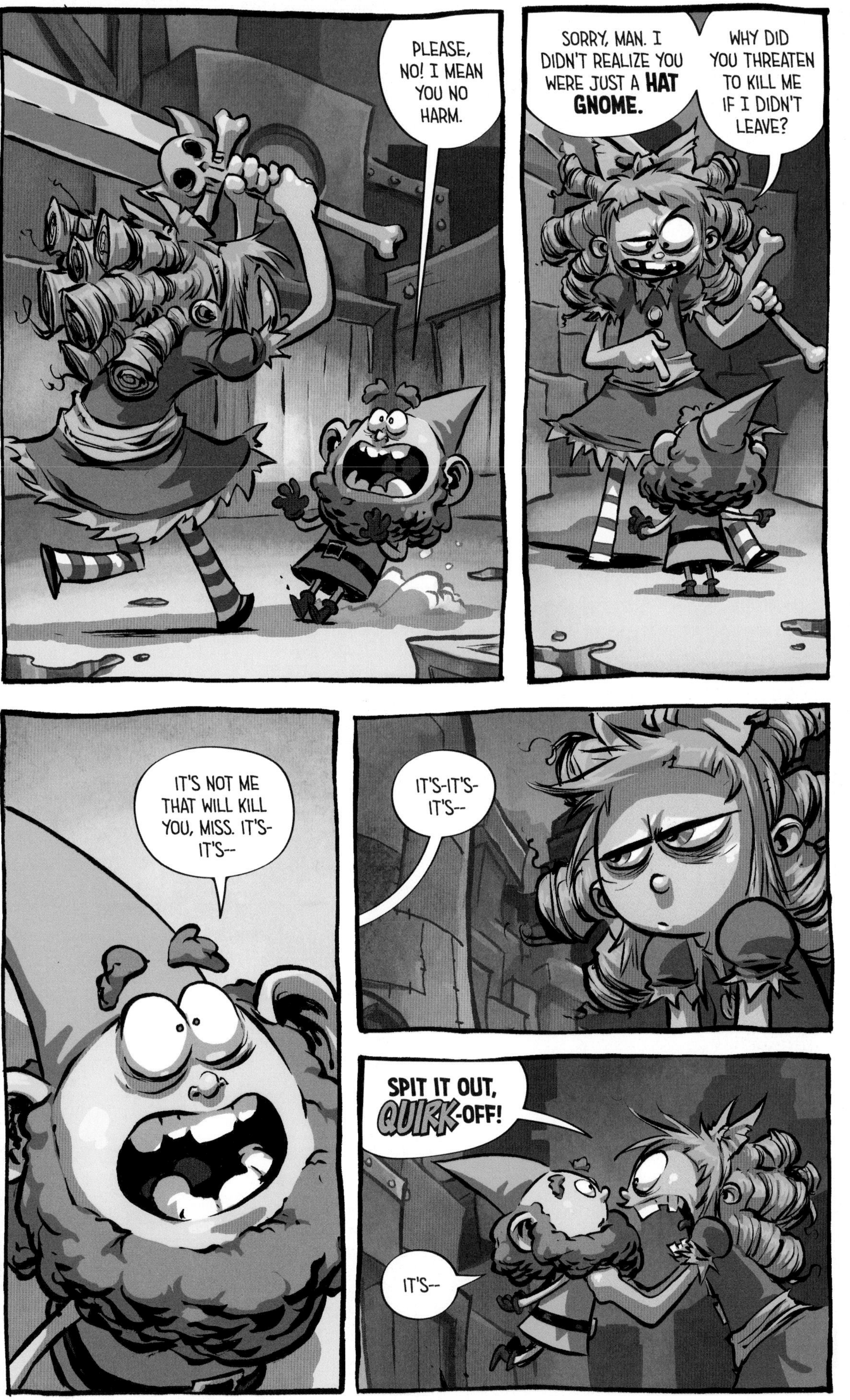
PLEASE, NO! I MEAN YOU NO HARM.
SORRY, MAN. I DIDN'T REALIZE YOU WERE JUST A **HAT GNOME.**
WHY DID YOU THREATEN TO KILL ME IF I DIDN'T LEAVE?
IT'S NOT ME THAT WILL KILL YOU, MISS. IT'S- IT'S--
IT'S-IT'S- IT'S--
SPIT IT OUT, QUIRK-OFF!
IT'S--

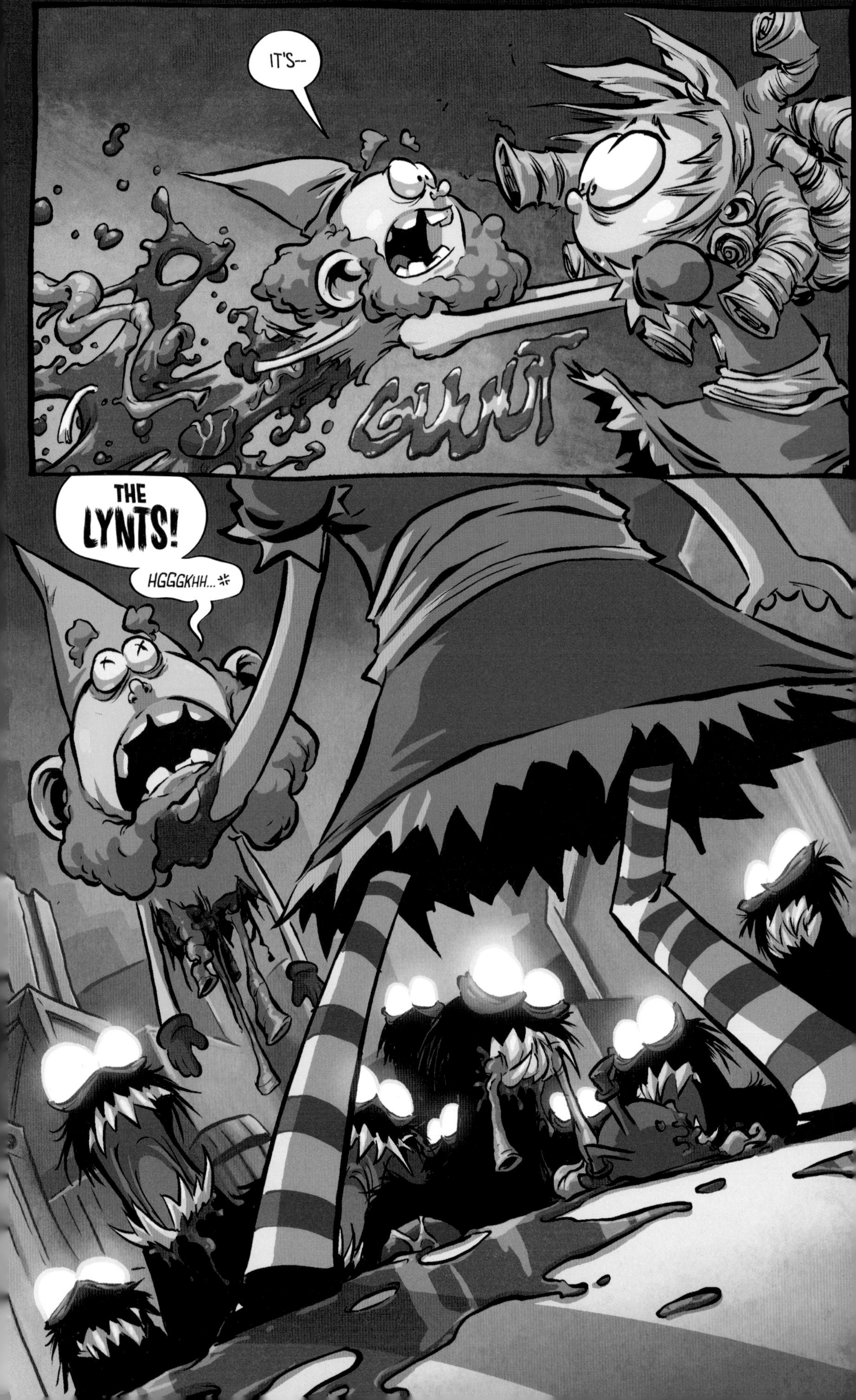
IT'S--
GUNT
THE LYNTS!
HGGGKHH...

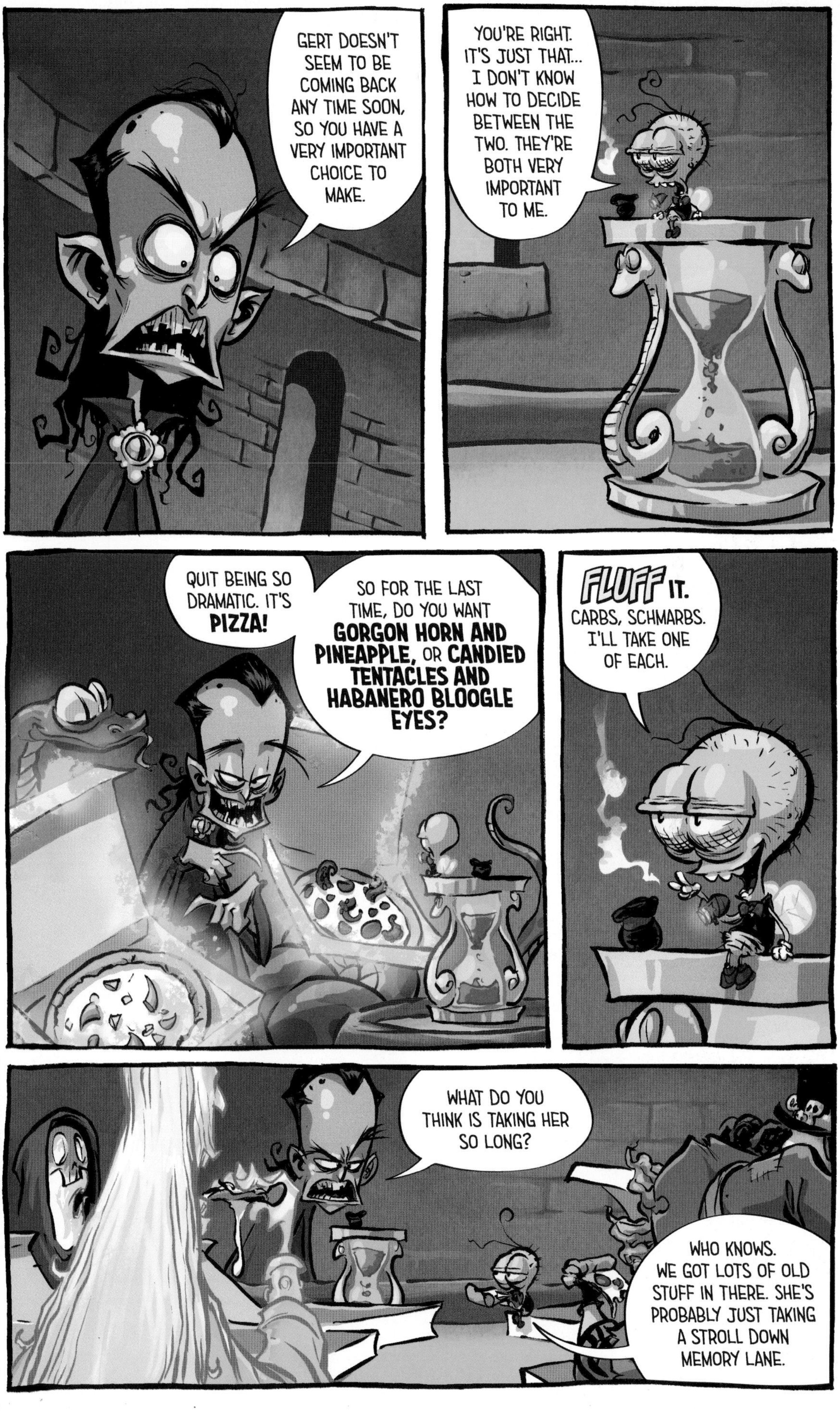
GERT DOESN'T SEEM TO BE COMING BACK ANY TIME SOON, SO YOU HAVE A VERY IMPORTANT CHOICE TO MAKE.
YOU'RE RIGHT. IT'S JUST THAT... I DON'T KNOW HOW TO DECIDE BETWEEN THE TWO. THEY'RE BOTH VERY IMPORTANT TO ME.
QUIT BEING SO DRAMATIC. IT'S PIZZA!
SO FOR THE LAST TIME, DO YOU WANT GORGON HORN AND PINEAPPLE, OR CANDIED TENTACLES AND HABANERO BLOOGLE EYES?
FLUFF IT. CARBS, SCHMARBS. I'LL TAKE ONE OF EACH.
WHAT DO YOU THINK IS TAKING HER SO LONG?
WHO KNOWS. WE GOT LOTS OF OLD STUFF IN THERE. SHE'S PROBABLY JUST TAKING A STROLL DOWN MEMORY LANE.

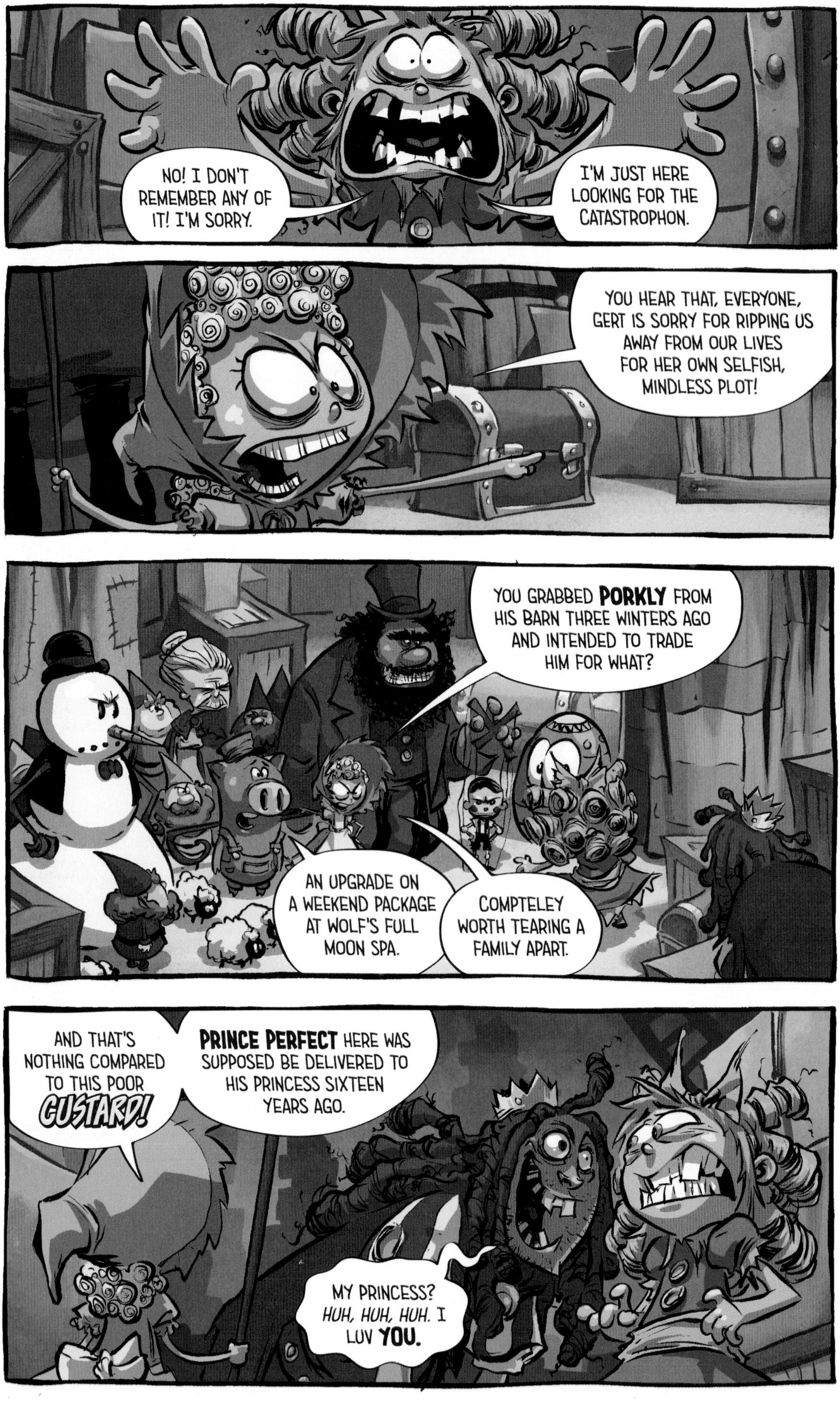

NO! I DON'T REMEMBER ANY OF IT! I'M SORRY.
I'M JUST HERE LOOKING FOR THE CATASTROPHON.
YOU HEAR THAT, EVERYONE, GERT IS SORRY FOR RIPPING US AWAY FROM OUR LIVES FOR HER OWN SELFISH, MINDLESS PLOT!
YOU GRABBED **PORKLY** FROM HIS BARN THREE WINTERS AGO AND INTENDED TO TRADE HIM FOR WHAT?
AN UPGRADE ON A WEEKEND PACKAGE AT WOLF'S FULL MOON SPA.
COMPTELEY WORTH TEARING A FAMILY APART.
AND THAT'S NOTHING COMPARED TO THIS POOR **CUSTARD!**
PRINCE PERFECT HERE WAS SUPPOSED BE DELIVERED TO HIS PRINCESS SIXTEEN YEARS AGO.
MY PRINCESS? *HUH, HUH, HUH.* I LUV **YOU.**

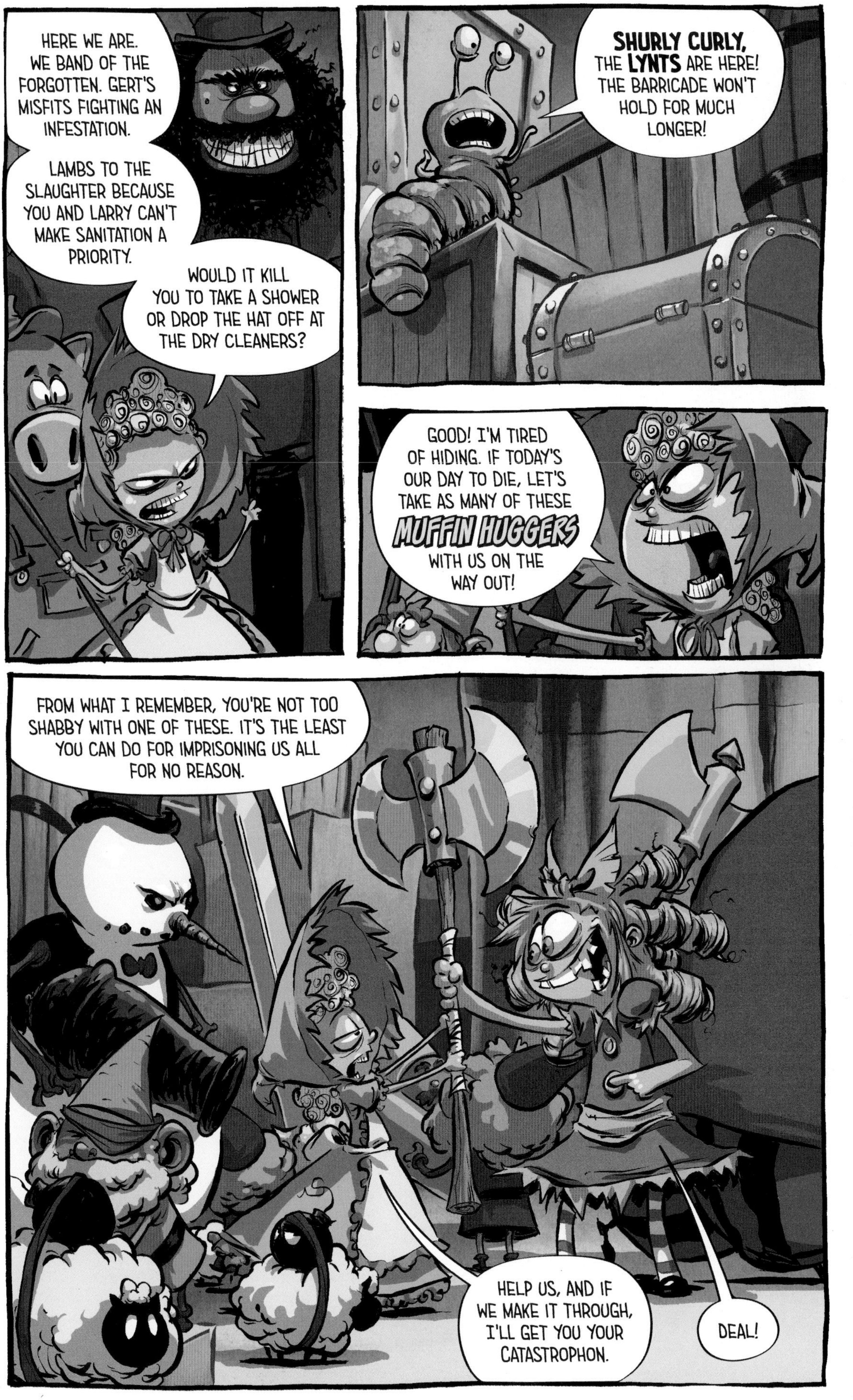
HERE WE ARE. WE BAND OF THE FORGOTTEN. GERT'S MISFITS FIGHTING AN INFESTATION.
LAMBS TO THE SLAUGHTER BECAUSE YOU AND LARRY CAN'T MAKE SANITATION A PRIORITY.
WOULD IT KILL YOU TO TAKE A SHOWER OR DROP THE HAT OFF AT THE DRY CLEANERS?
SHURLY CURLY, THE LYNTS ARE HERE! THE BARRICADE WON'T HOLD FOR MUCH LONGER!
GOOD! I'M TIRED OF HIDING. IF TODAY'S OUR DAY TO DIE, LET'S TAKE AS MANY OF THESE MUFFIN HUGGERS WITH US ON THE WAY OUT!
FROM WHAT I REMEMBER, YOU'RE NOT TOO SHABBY WITH ONE OF THESE. IT'S THE LEAST YOU CAN DO FOR IMPRISONING US ALL FOR NO REASON.
HELP US, AND IF WE MAKE IT THROUGH, I'LL GET YOU YOUR CATASTROPHON.
DEAL!

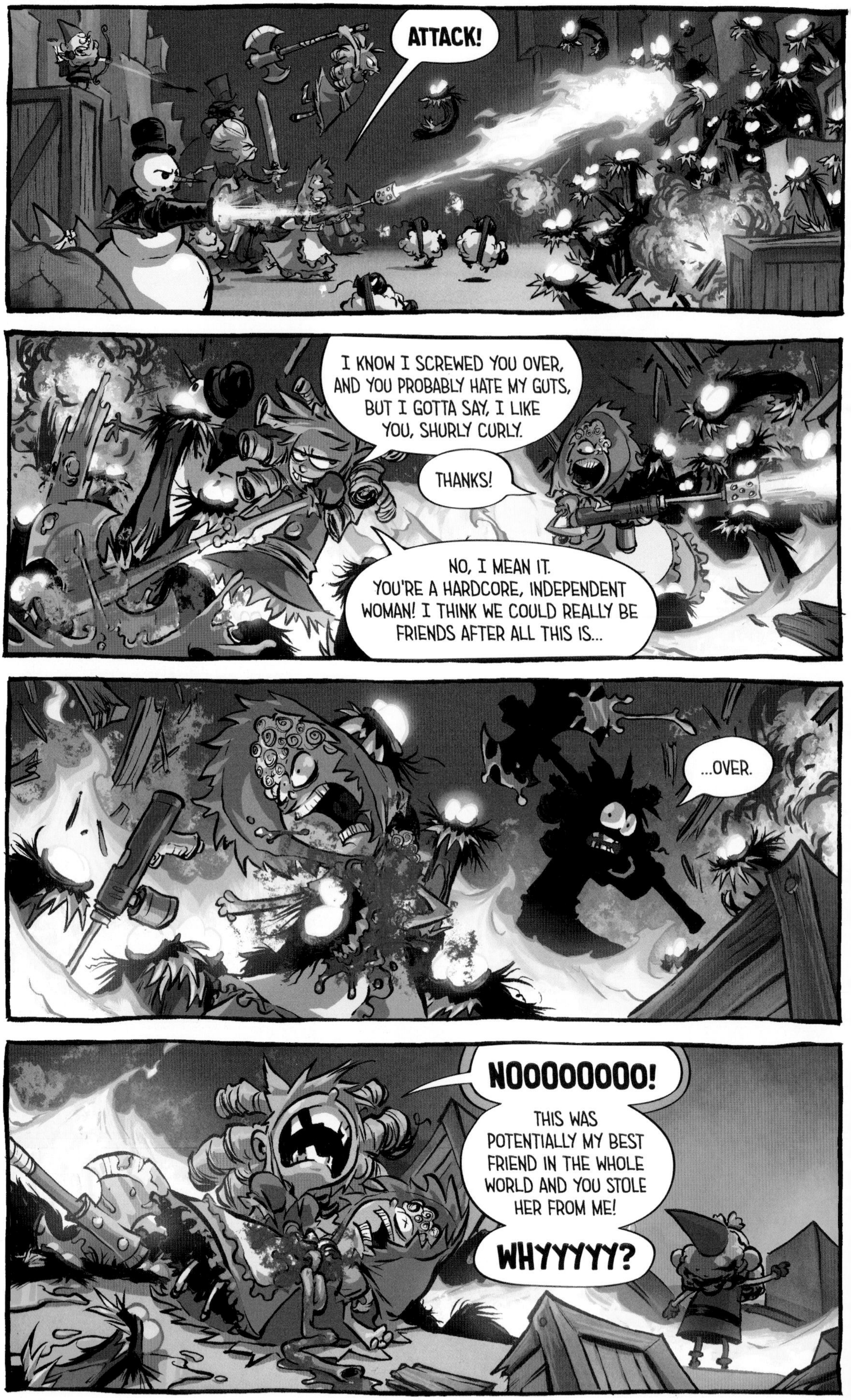
ATTACK!
I KNOW I SCREWED YOU OVER, AND YOU PROBABLY HATE MY GUTS, BUT I GOTTA SAY, I LIKE YOU, SHURLY CURLY.
THANKS!
NO, I MEAN IT. YOU'RE A HARDCORE, INDEPENDENT WOMAN! I THINK WE COULD REALLY BE FRIENDS AFTER ALL THIS IS...
...OVER.
NOOOOOOOO!
THIS WAS POTENTIALLY MY BEST FRIEND IN THE WHOLE WORLD AND YOU STOLE HER FROM ME!
WHYYYYY?

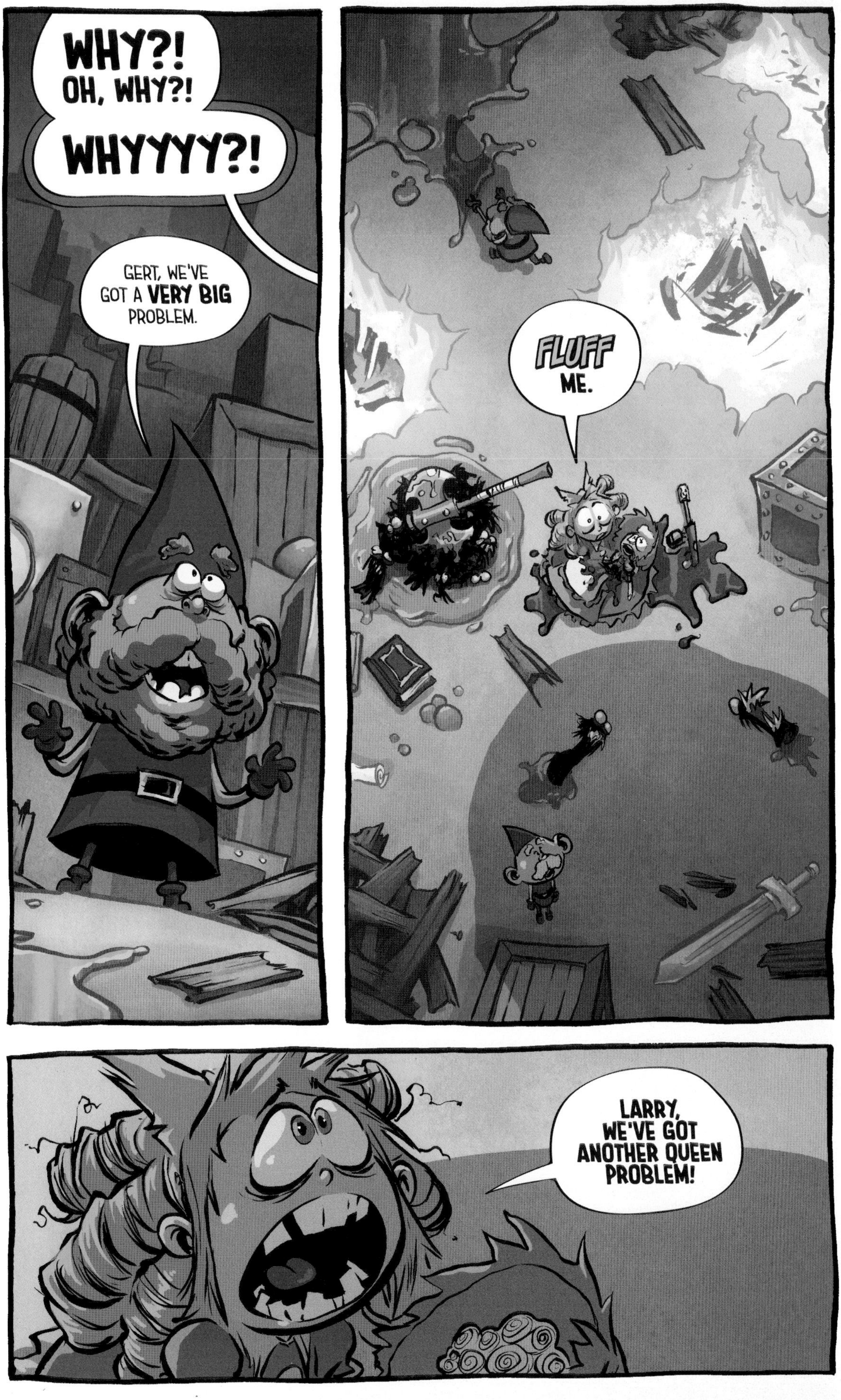
WHY?! OH, WHY?!
WHYYYY?!
GERT, WE'VE GOT A VERY BIG PROBLEM.
FLUFF ME.
LARRY, WE'VE GOT ANOTHER QUEEN PROBLEM!

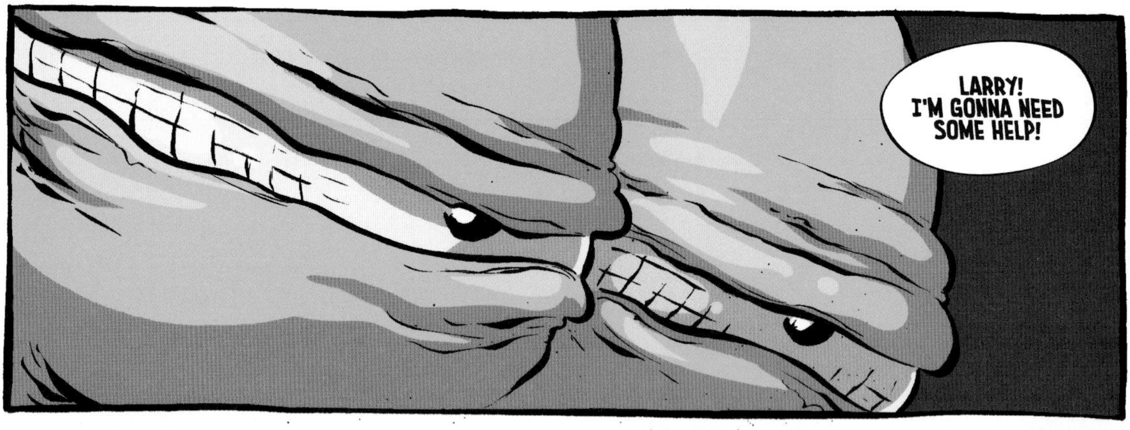
LARRY!
I'M GONNA NEED
SOME HELP!

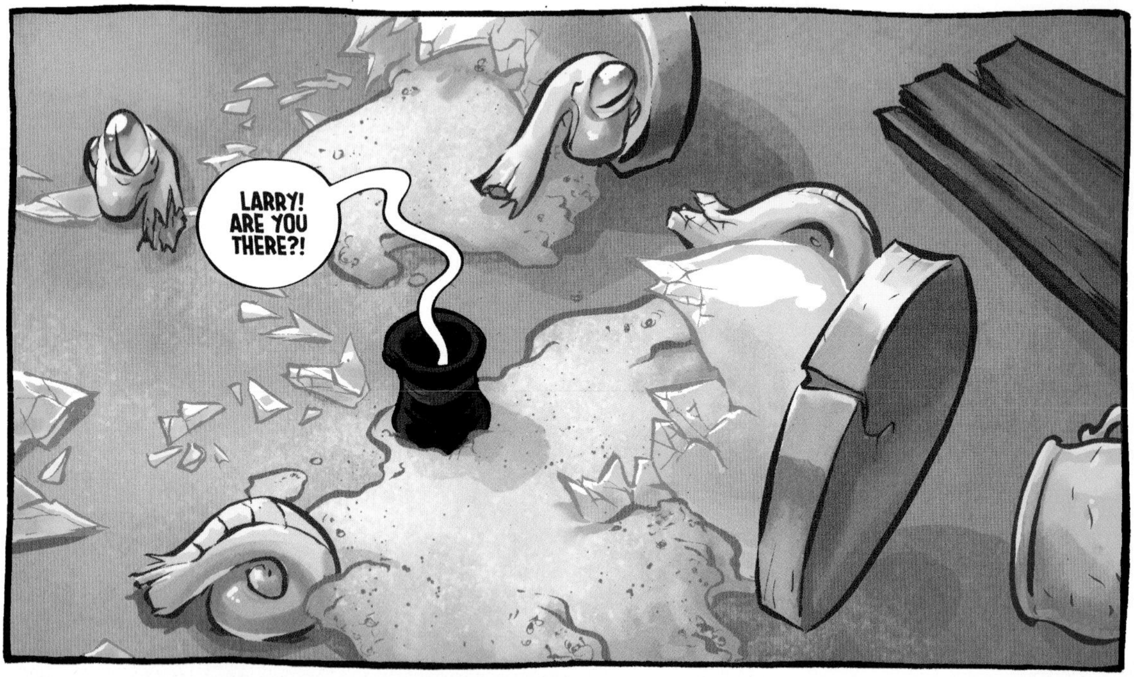
LARRY!
ARE YOU
THERE?!

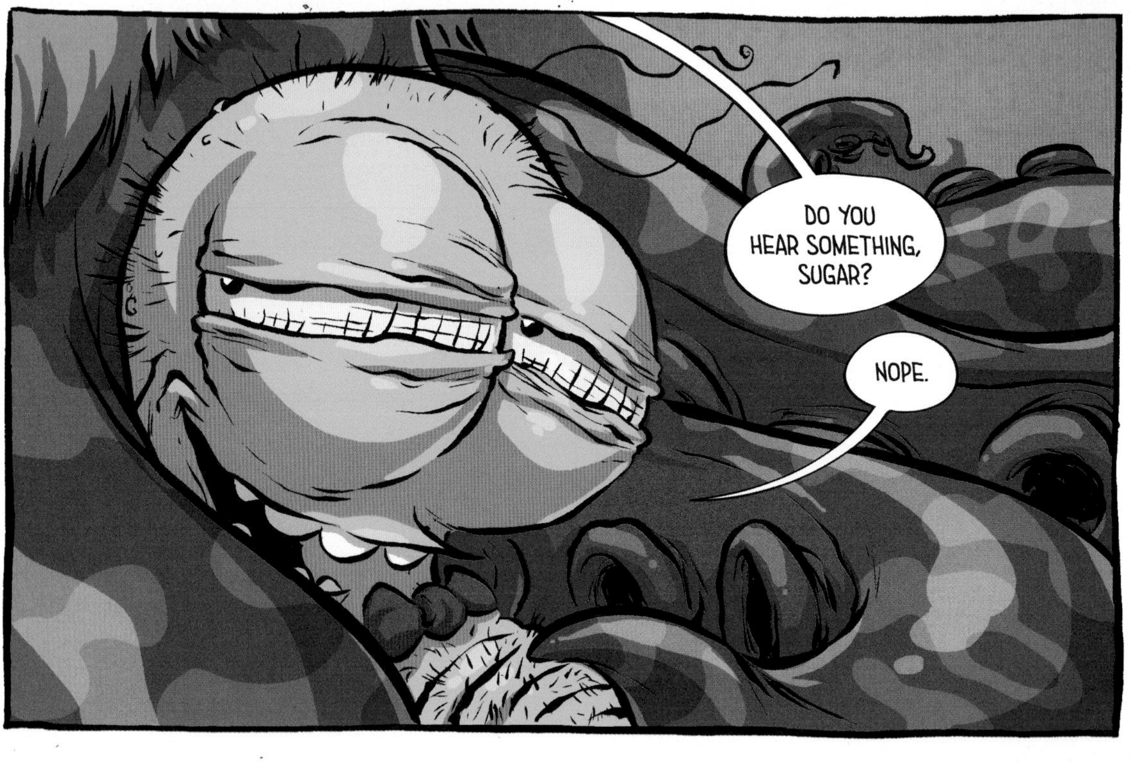
DO YOU
HEAR SOMETHING,
SUGAR?
NOPE.

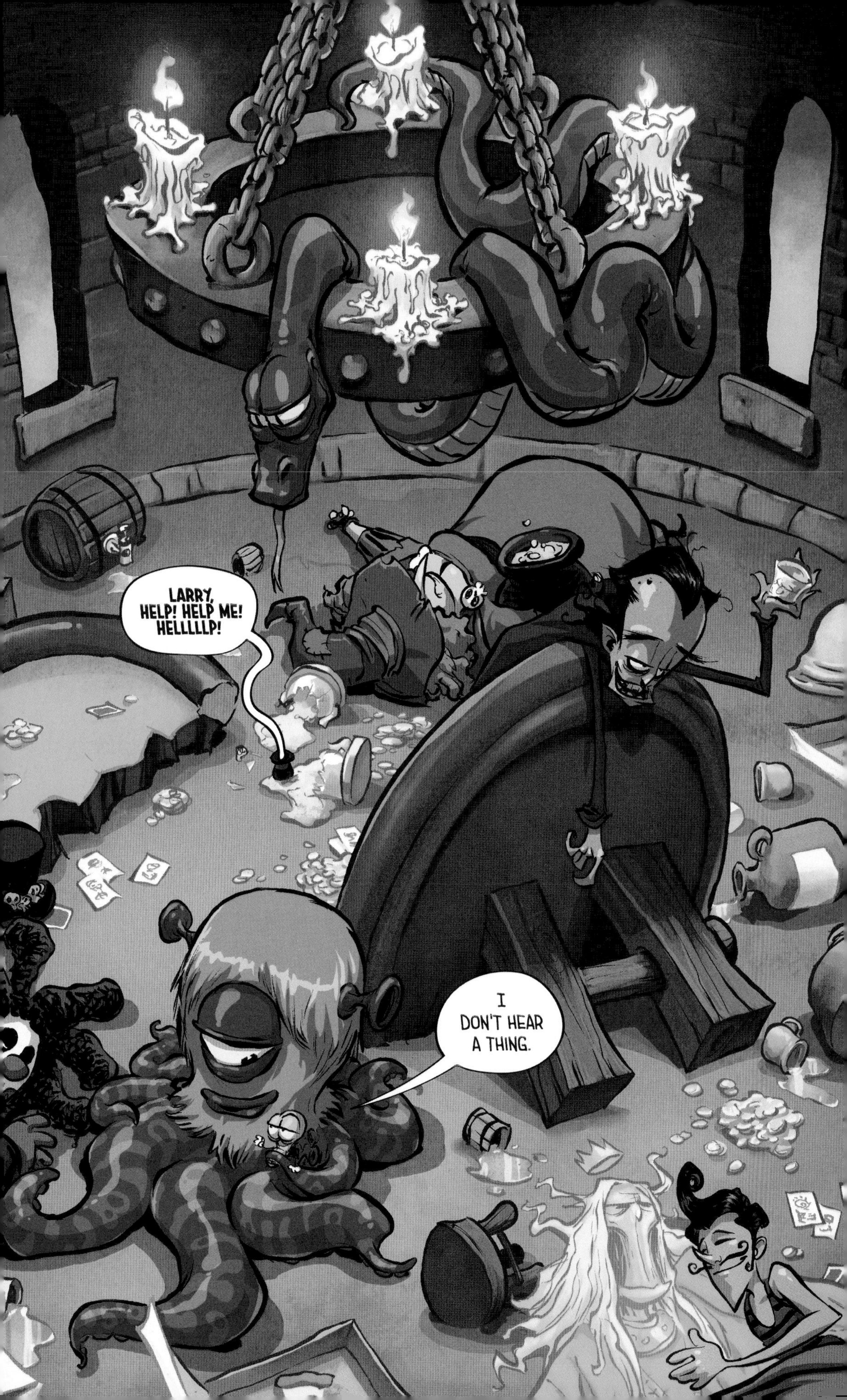
LARRY, HELP! HELP ME! HELLLLLP!
I DON'T HEAR A THING.

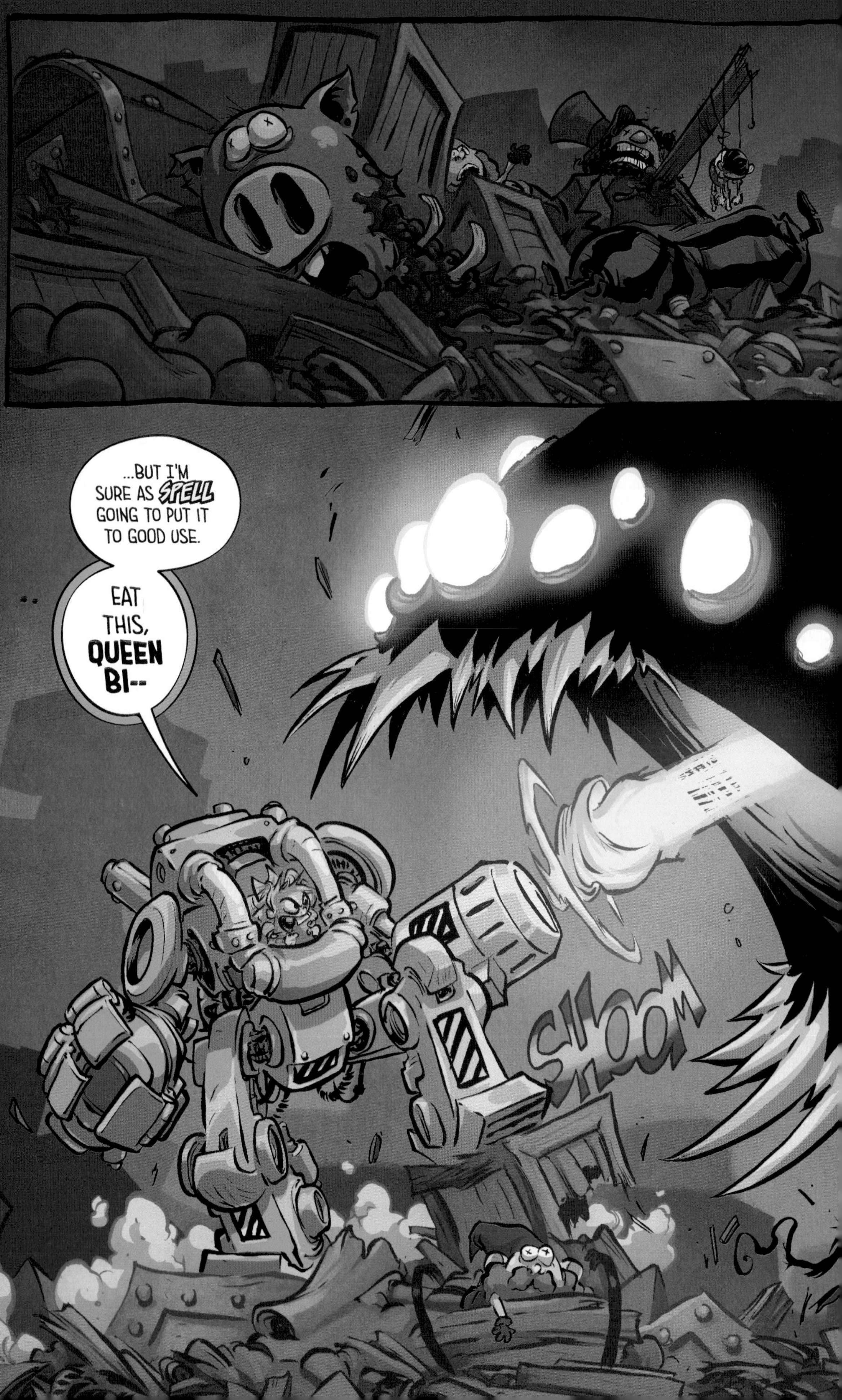
...BUT I'M SURE AS SPELL GOING TO PUT IT TO GOOD USE.
EAT THIS, QUEEN BI--
SHOOM

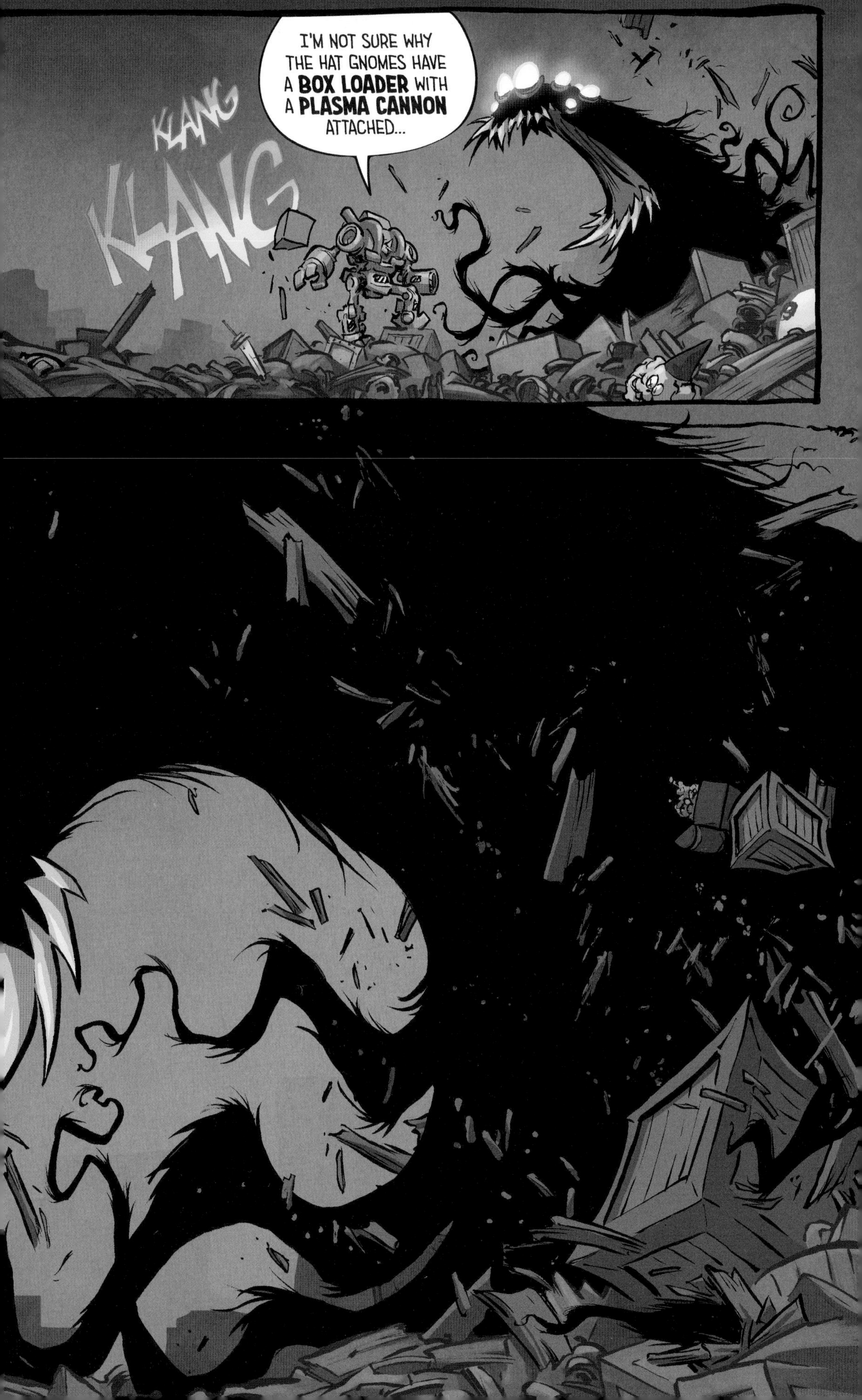
KLANG
KLANG
I'M NOT SURE WHY THE HAT GNOMES HAVE A **BOX LOADER** WITH A **PLASMA CANNON** ATTACHED...

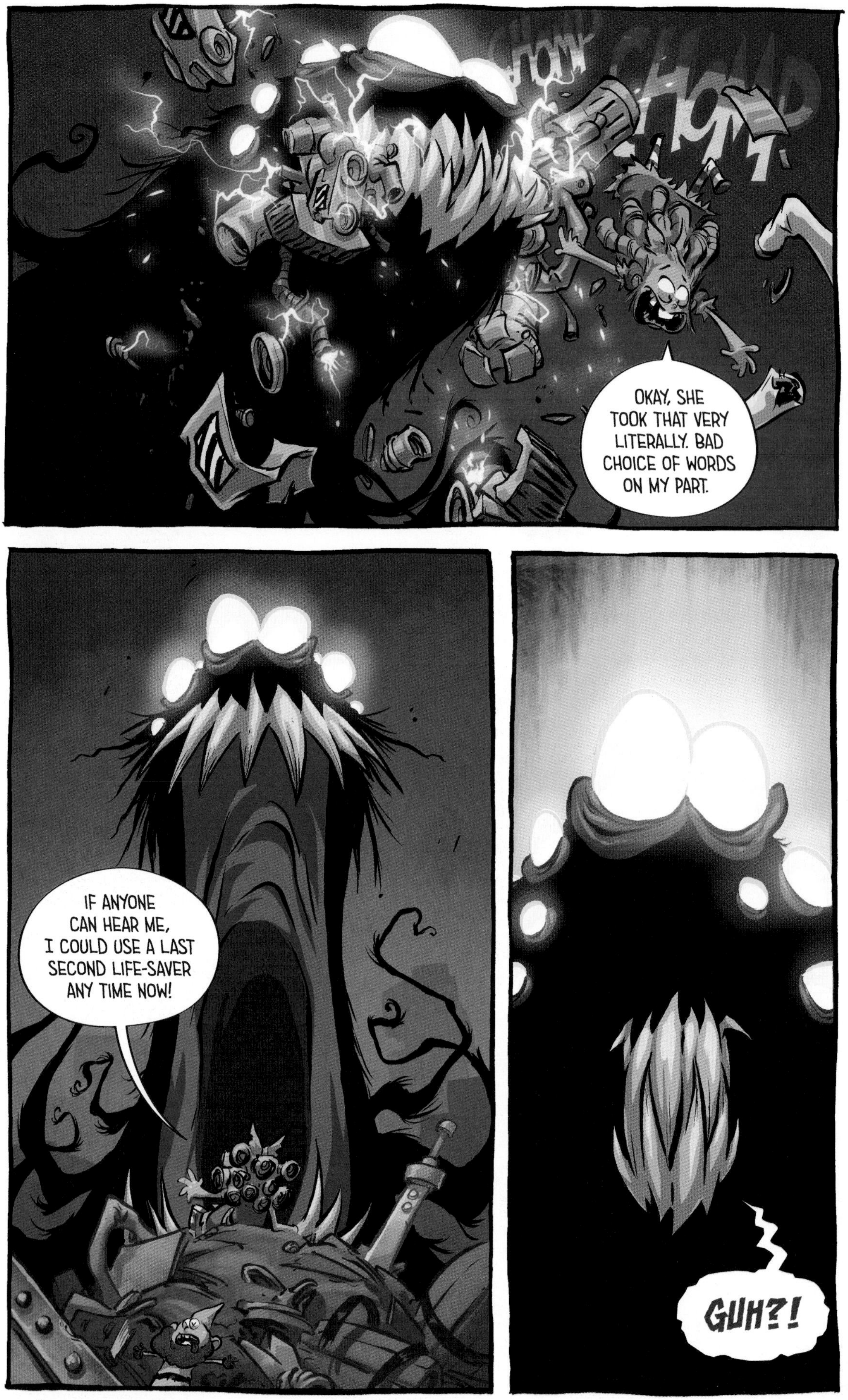
CHOMP CHOMP CHOMP
OKAY, SHE TOOK THAT VERY LITERALLY. BAD CHOICE OF WORDS ON MY PART.
IF ANYONE CAN HEAR ME, I COULD USE A LAST SECOND LIFE-SAVER ANY TIME NOW!
GUH?!

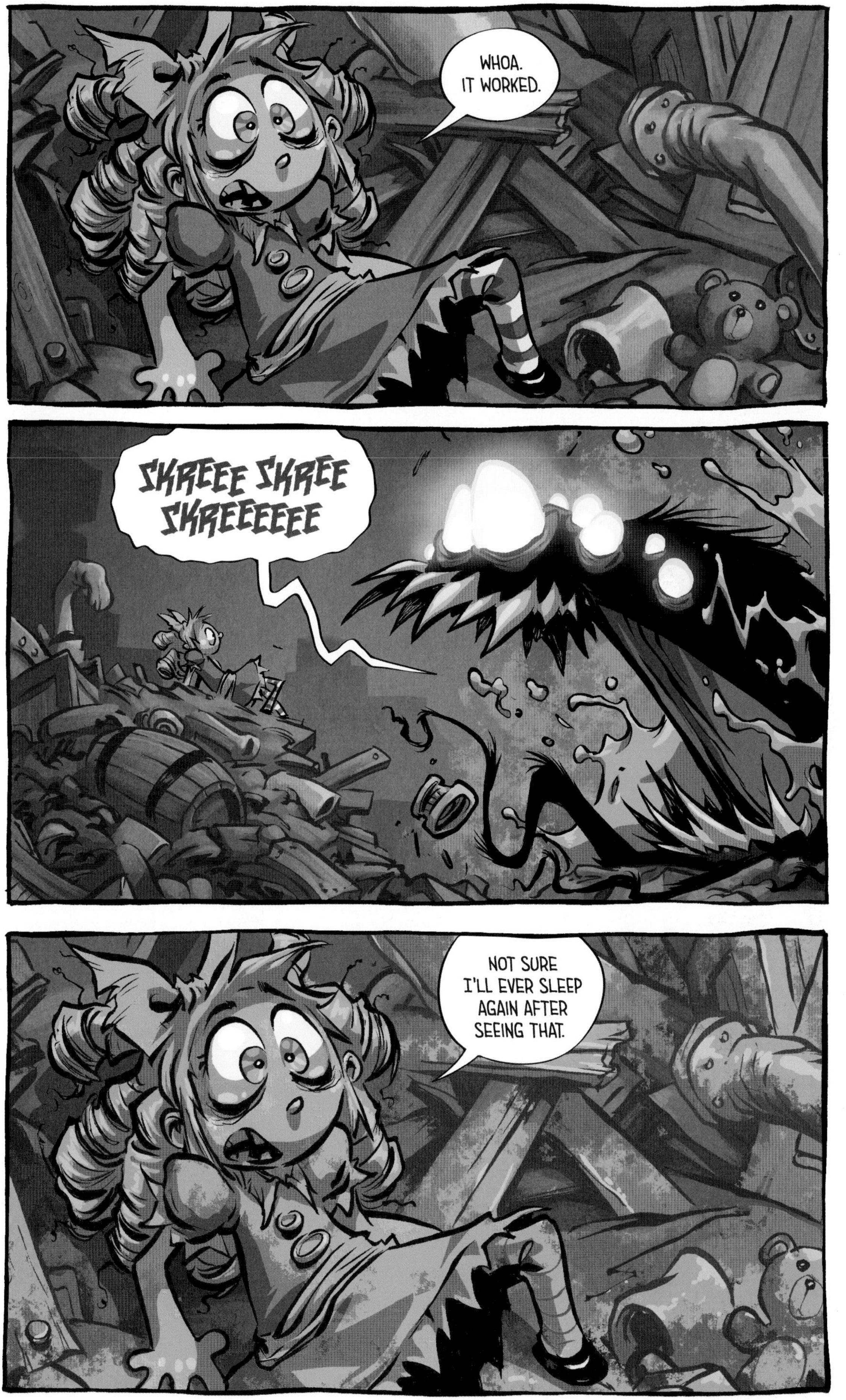
WHOA.
IT WORKED.
SKREEE SKREE SKREEEEEE
NOT SURE I'LL EVER SLEEP AGAIN AFTER SEEING THAT.

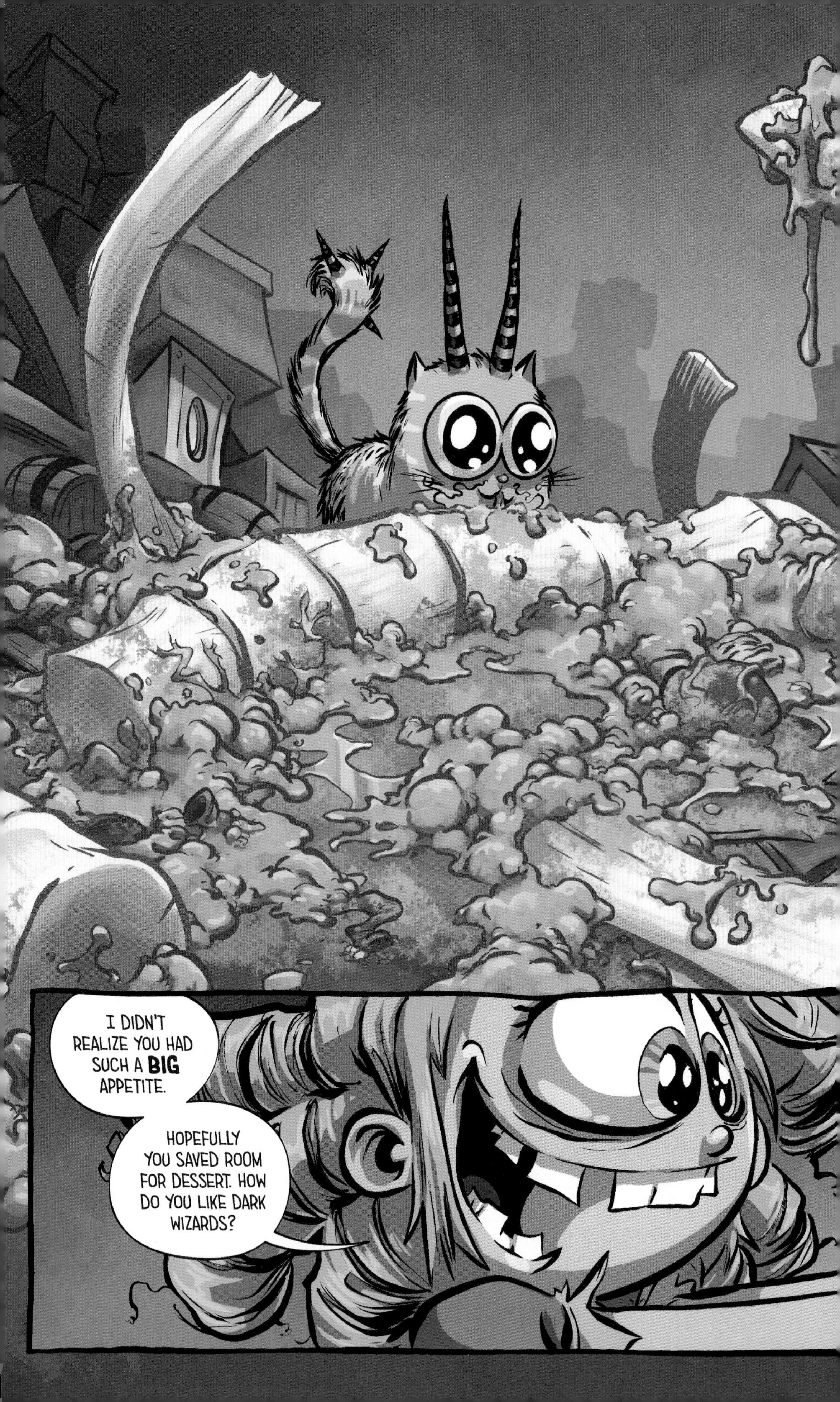
I DIDN'T REALIZE YOU HAD SUCH A **BIG** APPETITE.
HOPEFULLY YOU SAVED ROOM FOR DESSERT. HOW DO YOU LIKE DARK WIZARDS?

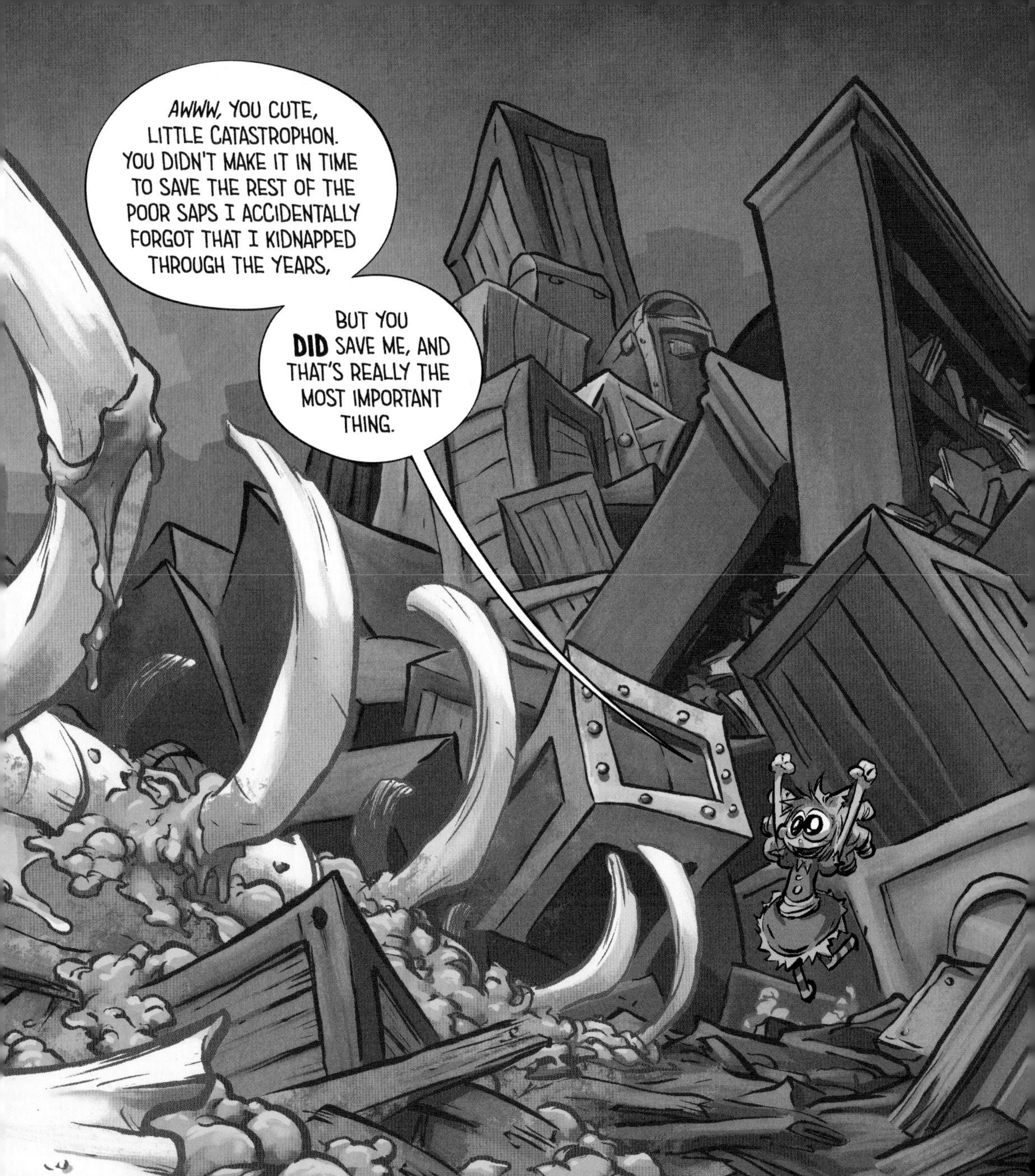
AWWW, YOU CUTE, LITTLE CATASTROPHON. YOU DIDN'T MAKE IT IN TIME TO SAVE THE REST OF THE POOR SAPS I ACCIDENTALLY FORGOT THAT I KIDNAPPED THROUGH THE YEARS,
BUT YOU **DID** SAVE ME, AND THAT'S REALLY THE MOST IMPORTANT THING.

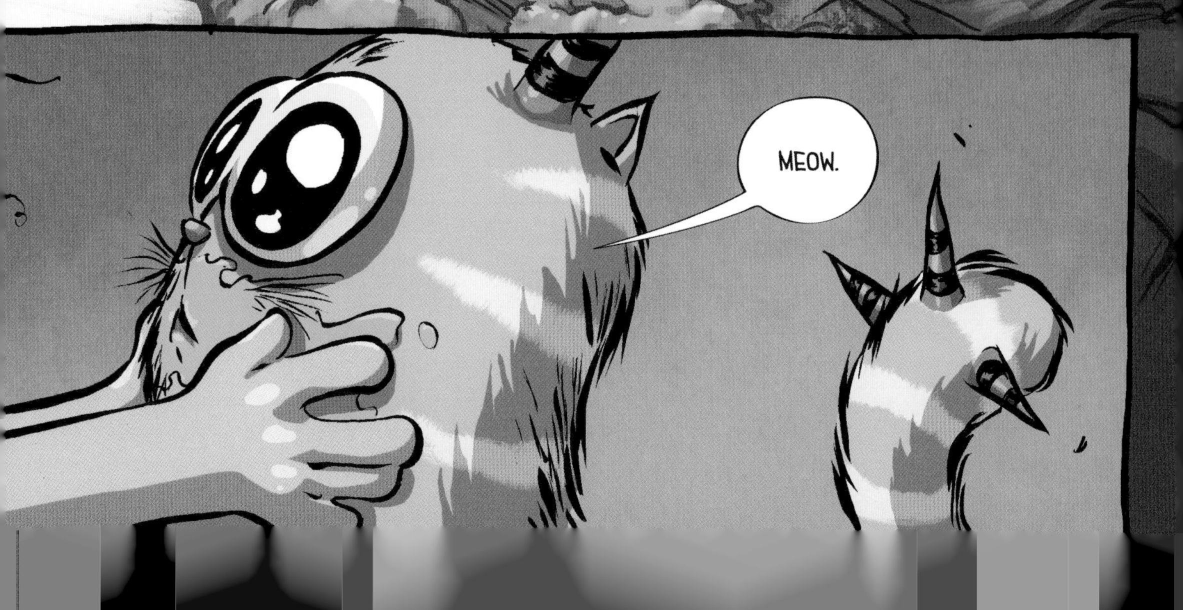
MEOW.

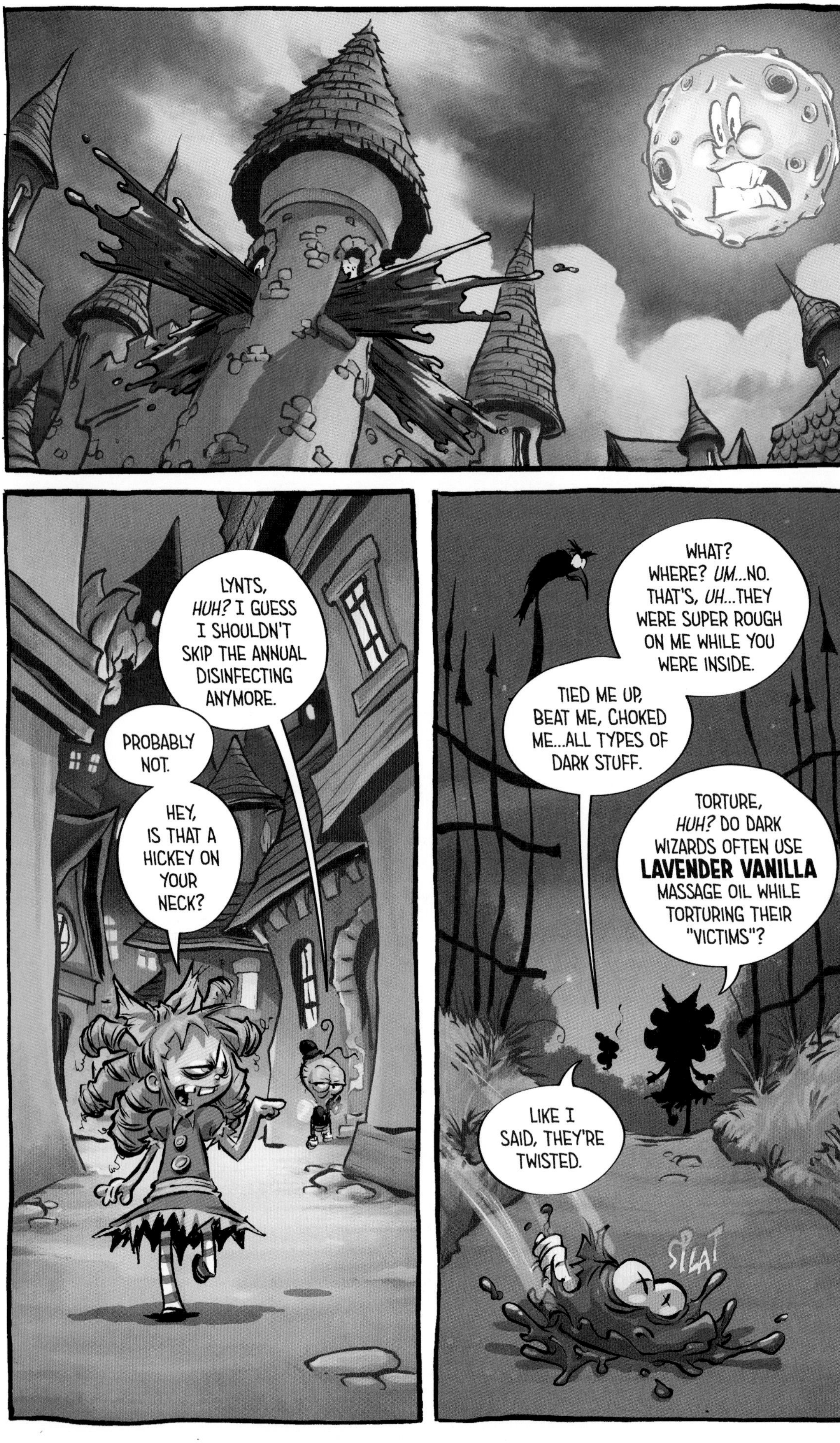
LYNTS, HUH? I GUESS I SHOULDN'T SKIP THE ANNUAL DISINFECTING ANYMORE.
PROBABLY NOT.
HEY, IS THAT A HICKEY ON YOUR NECK?
WHAT? WHERE? UM...NO. THAT'S, UH...THEY WERE SUPER ROUGH ON ME WHILE YOU WERE INSIDE.
TIED ME UP, BEAT ME, CHOKED ME...ALL TYPES OF DARK STUFF.
TORTURE, HUH? DO DARK WIZARDS OFTEN USE LAVENDER VANILLA MASSAGE OIL WHILE TORTURING THEIR "VICTIMS"?
LIKE I SAID, THEY'RE TWISTED.
SPLAT

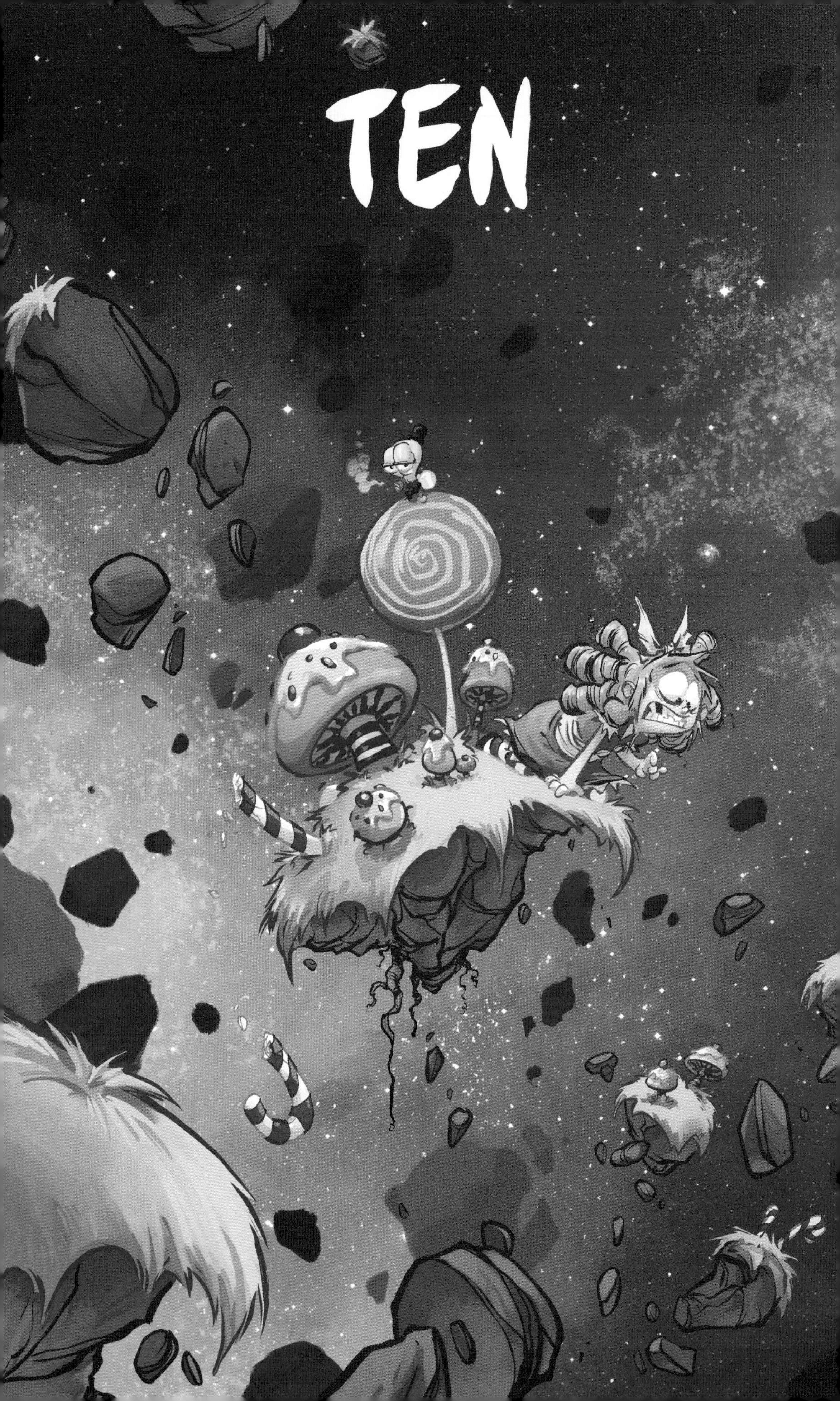
TEN

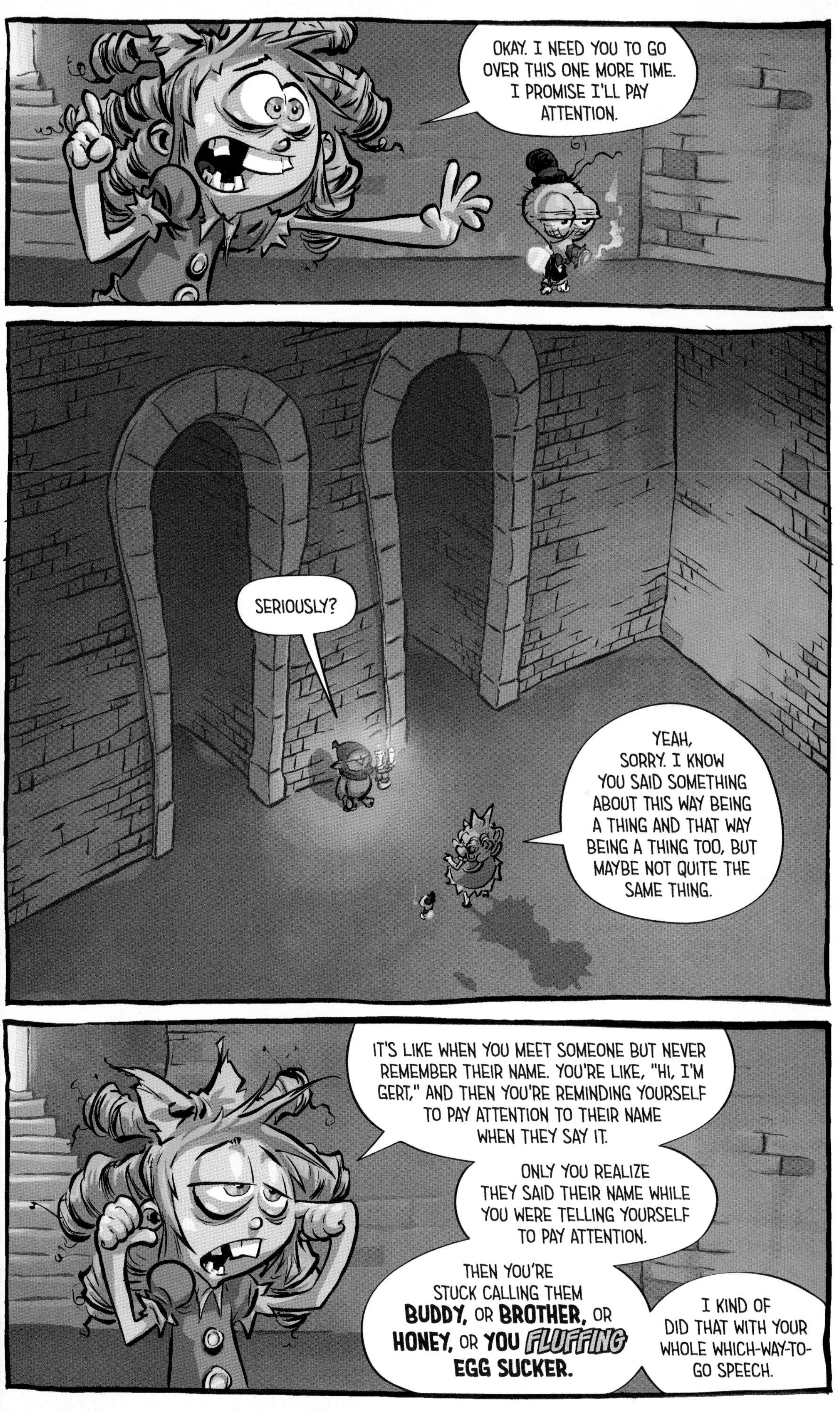
OKAY. I NEED YOU TO GO OVER THIS ONE MORE TIME. I PROMISE I'LL PAY ATTENTION.
SERIOUSLY?
YEAH, SORRY. I KNOW YOU SAID SOMETHING ABOUT THIS WAY BEING A THING AND THAT WAY BEING A THING TOO, BUT MAYBE NOT QUITE THE SAME THING.
IT'S LIKE WHEN YOU MEET SOMEONE BUT NEVER REMEMBER THEIR NAME. YOU'RE LIKE, "HI, I'M GERT," AND THEN YOU'RE REMINDING YOURSELF TO PAY ATTENTION TO THEIR NAME WHEN THEY SAY IT.
ONLY YOU REALIZE THEY SAID THEIR NAME WHILE YOU WERE TELLING YOURSELF TO PAY ATTENTION.
THEN YOU'RE STUCK CALLING THEM **BUDDY,** OR **BROTHER,** OR **HONEY,** OR **YOU** *FLUFFING* **EGG SUCKER.**
I KIND OF DID THAT WITH YOUR WHOLE WHICH-WAY-TO-GO SPEECH.

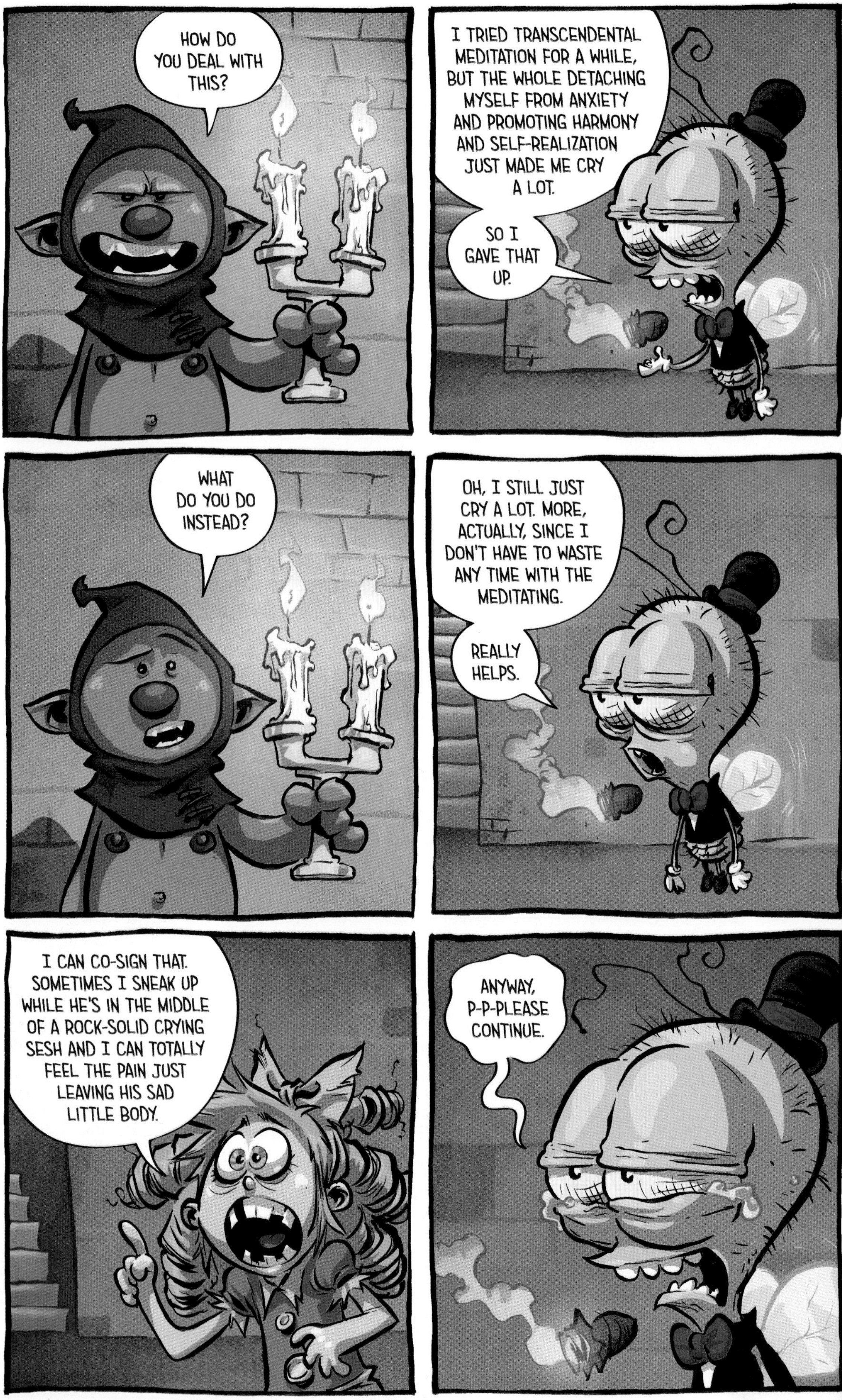
HOW DO YOU DEAL WITH THIS?
I TRIED TRANSCENDENTAL MEDITATION FOR A WHILE, BUT THE WHOLE DETACHING MYSELF FROM ANXIETY AND PROMOTING HARMONY AND SELF-REALIZATION JUST MADE ME CRY A LOT.
SO I GAVE THAT UP.
WHAT DO YOU DO INSTEAD?
OH, I STILL JUST CRY A LOT. MORE, ACTUALLY, SINCE I DON'T HAVE TO WASTE ANY TIME WITH THE MEDITATING.
REALLY HELPS.
I CAN CO-SIGN THAT. SOMETIMES I SNEAK UP WHILE HE'S IN THE MIDDLE OF A ROCK-SOLID CRYING SESH AND I CAN TOTALLY FEEL THE PAIN JUST LEAVING HIS SAD LITTLE BODY.
ANYWAY, P-P-PLEASE CONTINUE.

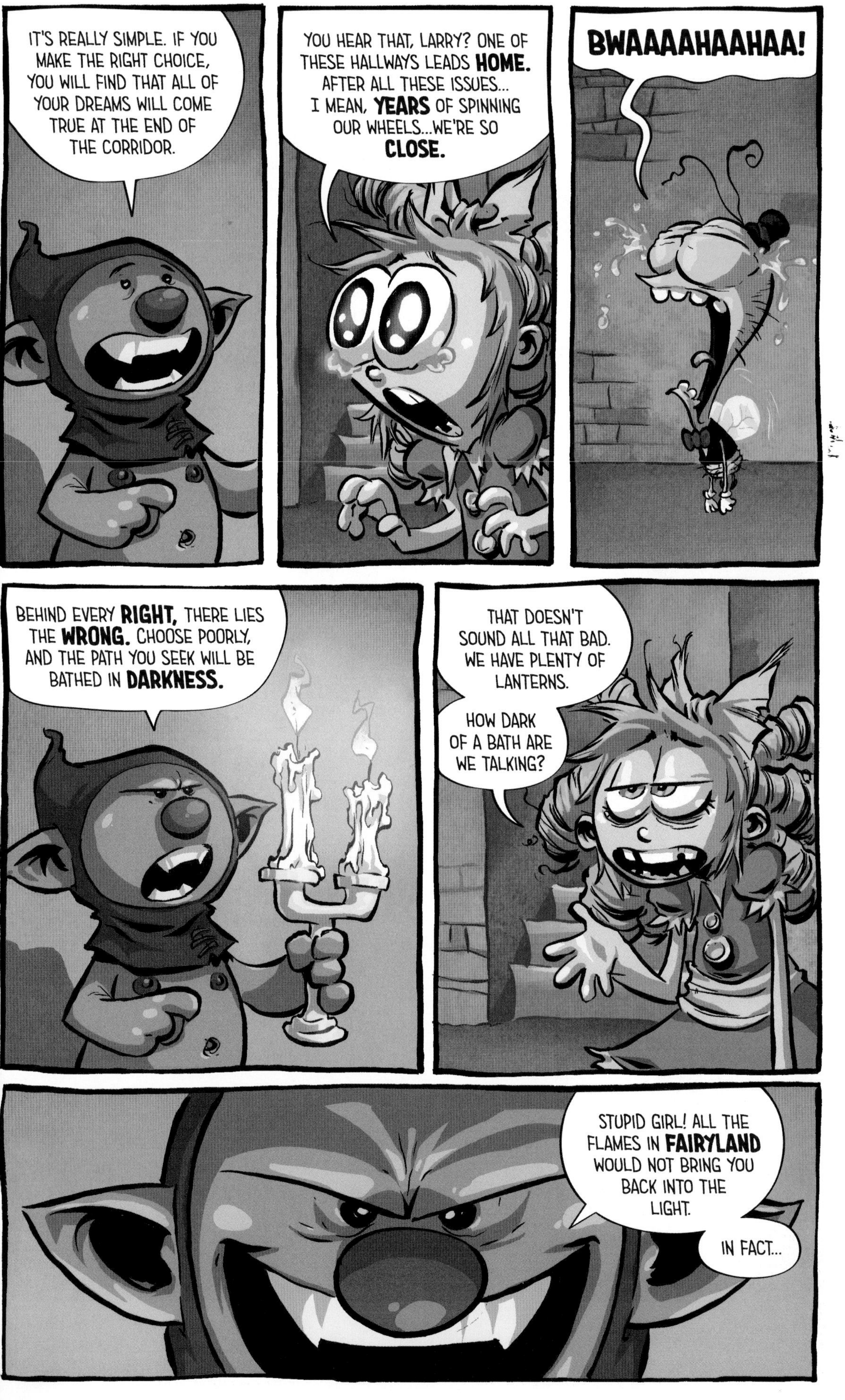
IT'S REALLY SIMPLE. IF YOU MAKE THE RIGHT CHOICE, YOU WILL FIND THAT ALL OF YOUR DREAMS WILL COME TRUE AT THE END OF THE CORRIDOR.
YOU HEAR THAT, LARRY? ONE OF THESE HALLWAYS LEADS **HOME.** AFTER ALL THESE ISSUES... I MEAN, **YEARS** OF SPINNING OUR WHEELS...WE'RE SO **CLOSE.**
BWAAAAHAAHAA!
BEHIND EVERY **RIGHT,** THERE LIES THE **WRONG.** CHOOSE POORLY, AND THE PATH YOU SEEK WILL BE BATHED IN **DARKNESS.**
THAT DOESN'T SOUND ALL THAT BAD. WE HAVE PLENTY OF LANTERNS.
HOW DARK OF A BATH ARE WE TALKING?
STUPID GIRL! ALL THE FLAMES IN **FAIRYLAND** WOULD NOT BRING YOU BACK INTO THE LIGHT.
IN FACT...

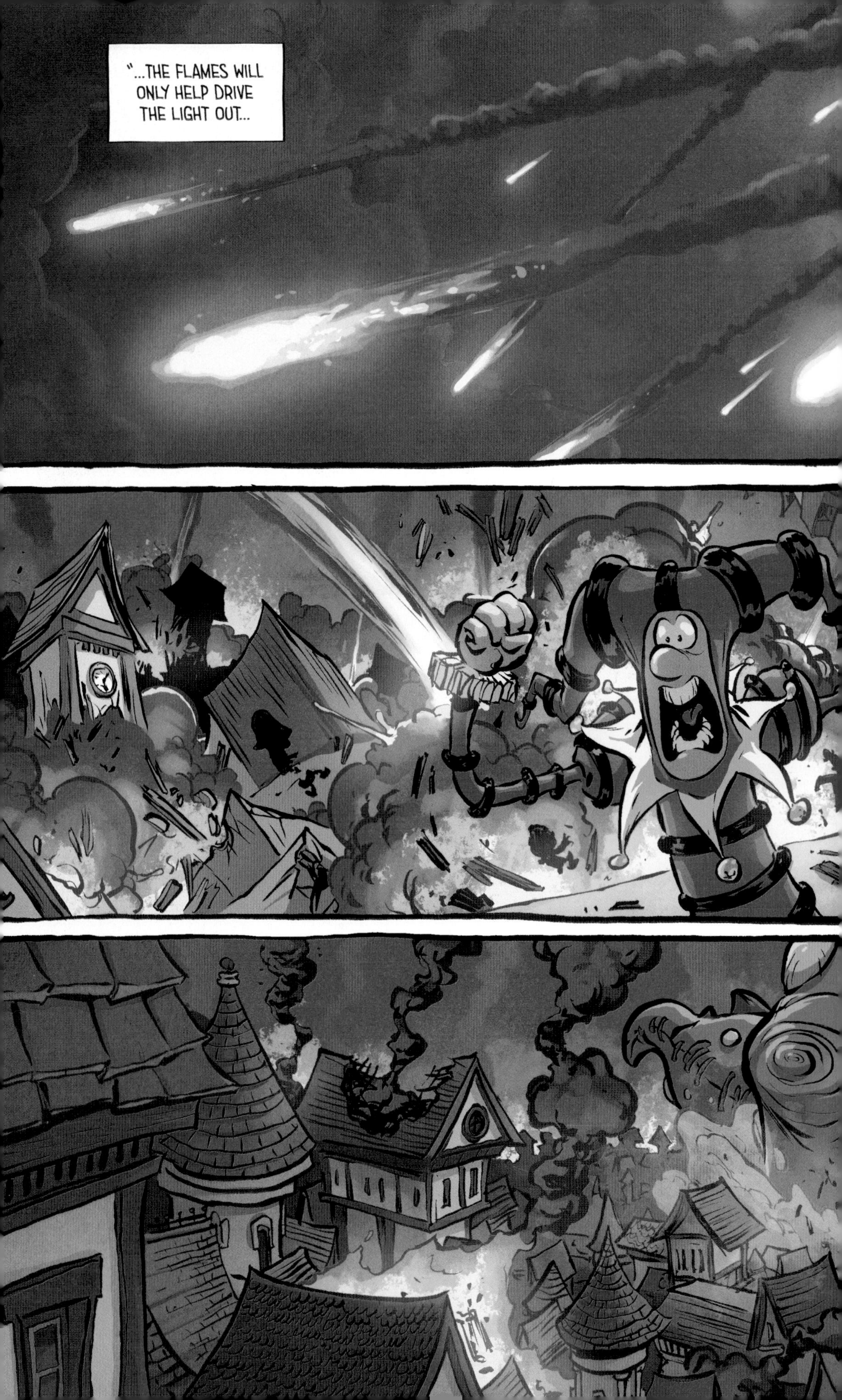
"...THE FLAMES WILL ONLY HELP DRIVE THE LIGHT OUT...

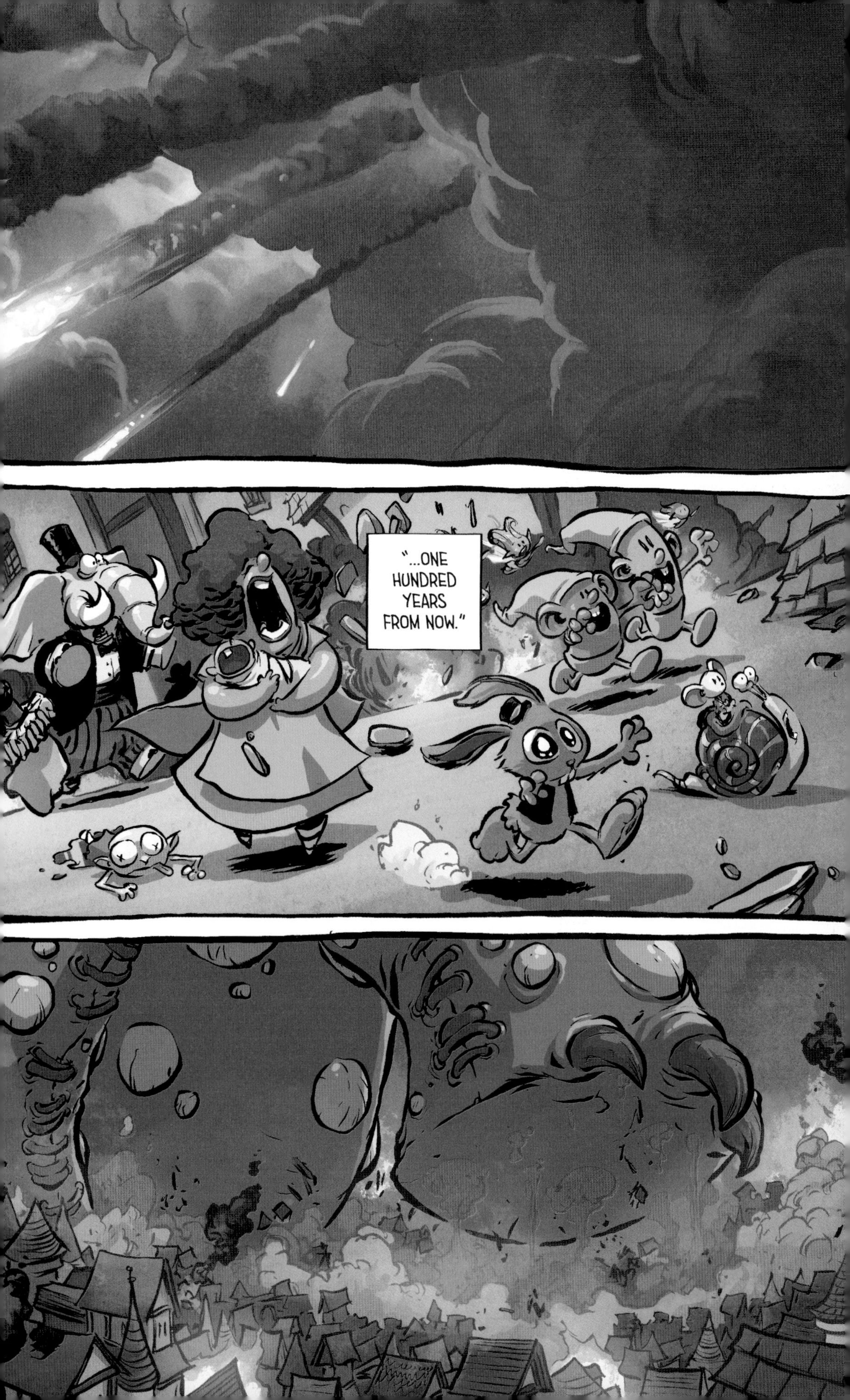
"...ONE HUNDRED YEARS FROM NOW."

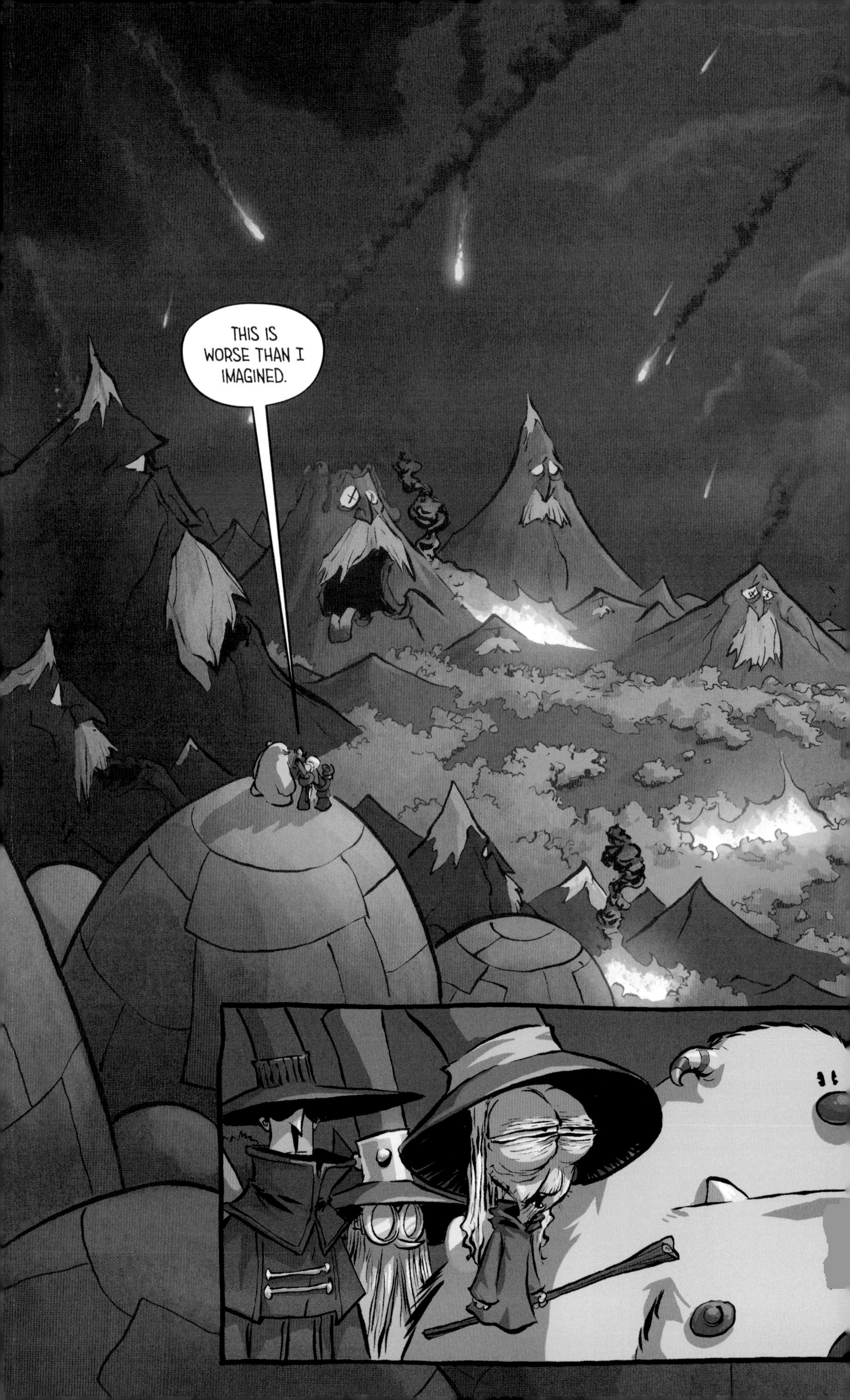
THIS IS WORSE THAN I IMAGINED.

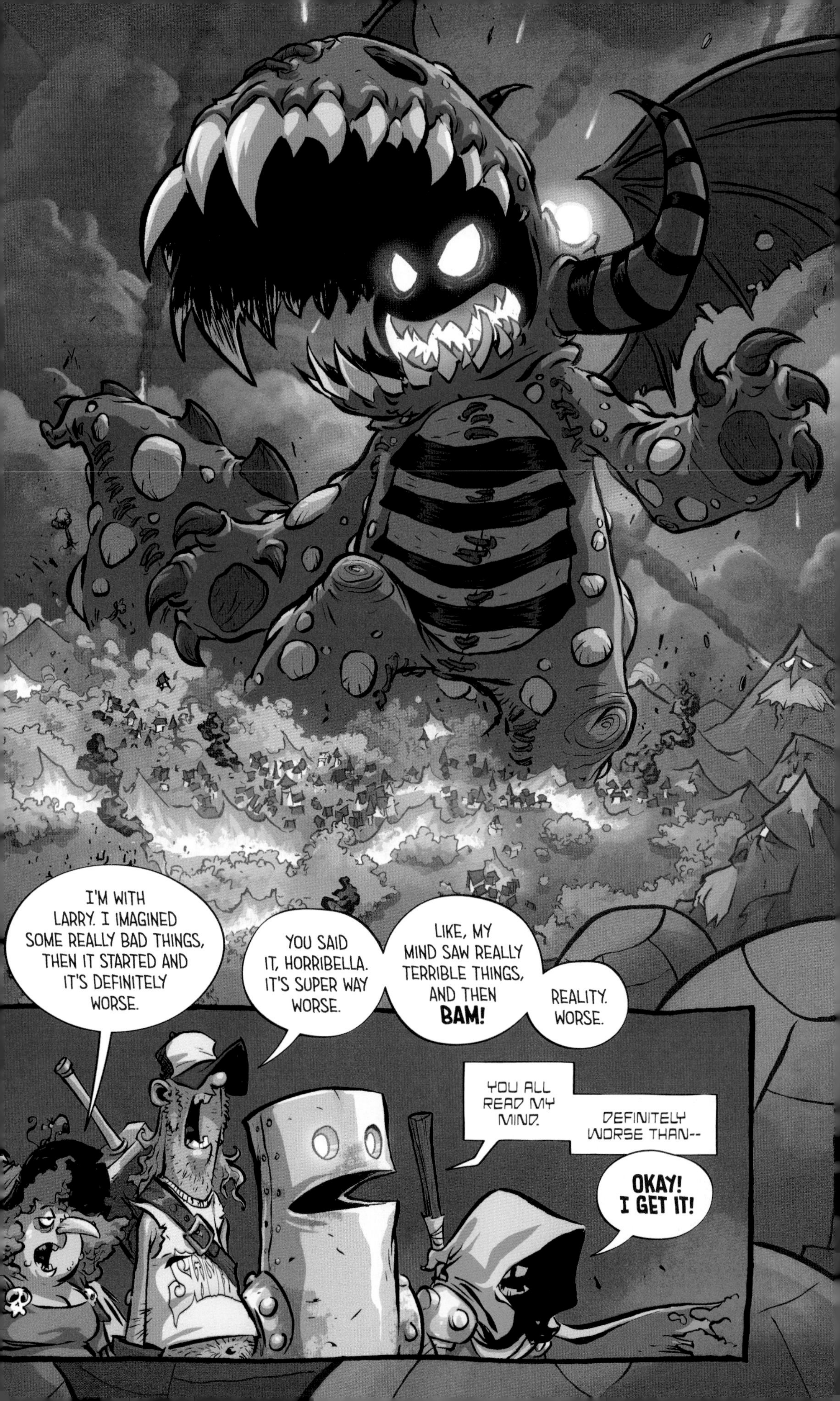

I'M WITH LARRY. I IMAGINED SOME REALLY BAD THINGS, THEN IT STARTED AND IT'S DEFINITELY WORSE.
YOU SAID IT, HORRIBELLA. IT'S SUPER WAY WORSE.
LIKE, MY MIND SAW REALLY TERRIBLE THINGS, AND THEN **BAM!**
REALITY. WORSE.
YOU ALL READ MY MIND.
DEFINITELY WORSE THAN--
OKAY! I GET IT!

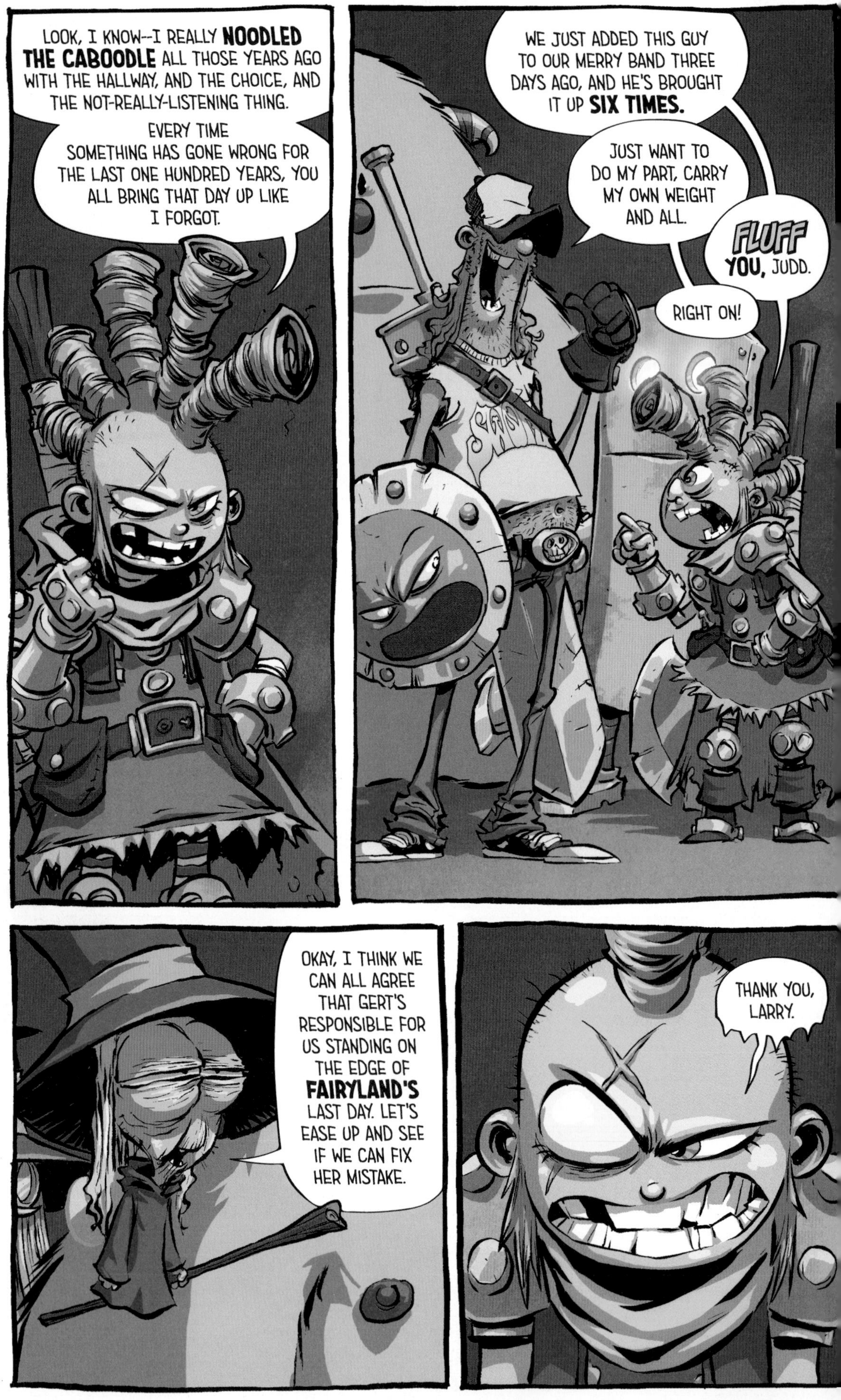

LOOK, I KNOW--I REALLY **NOODLED THE CABOODLE** ALL THOSE YEARS AGO WITH THE HALLWAY, AND THE CHOICE, AND THE NOT-REALLY-LISTENING THING.
EVERY TIME SOMETHING HAS GONE WRONG FOR THE LAST ONE HUNDRED YEARS, YOU ALL BRING THAT DAY UP LIKE I FORGOT.
WE JUST ADDED THIS GUY TO OUR MERRY BAND THREE DAYS AGO, AND HE'S BROUGHT IT UP **SIX TIMES.**
JUST WANT TO DO MY PART, CARRY MY OWN WEIGHT AND ALL.
FLUFF YOU, JUDD.
RIGHT ON!
OKAY, I THINK WE CAN ALL AGREE THAT GERT'S RESPONSIBLE FOR US STANDING ON THE EDGE OF **FAIRYLAND'S** LAST DAY. LET'S EASE UP AND SEE IF WE CAN FIX HER MISTAKE.
THANK YOU, LARRY.

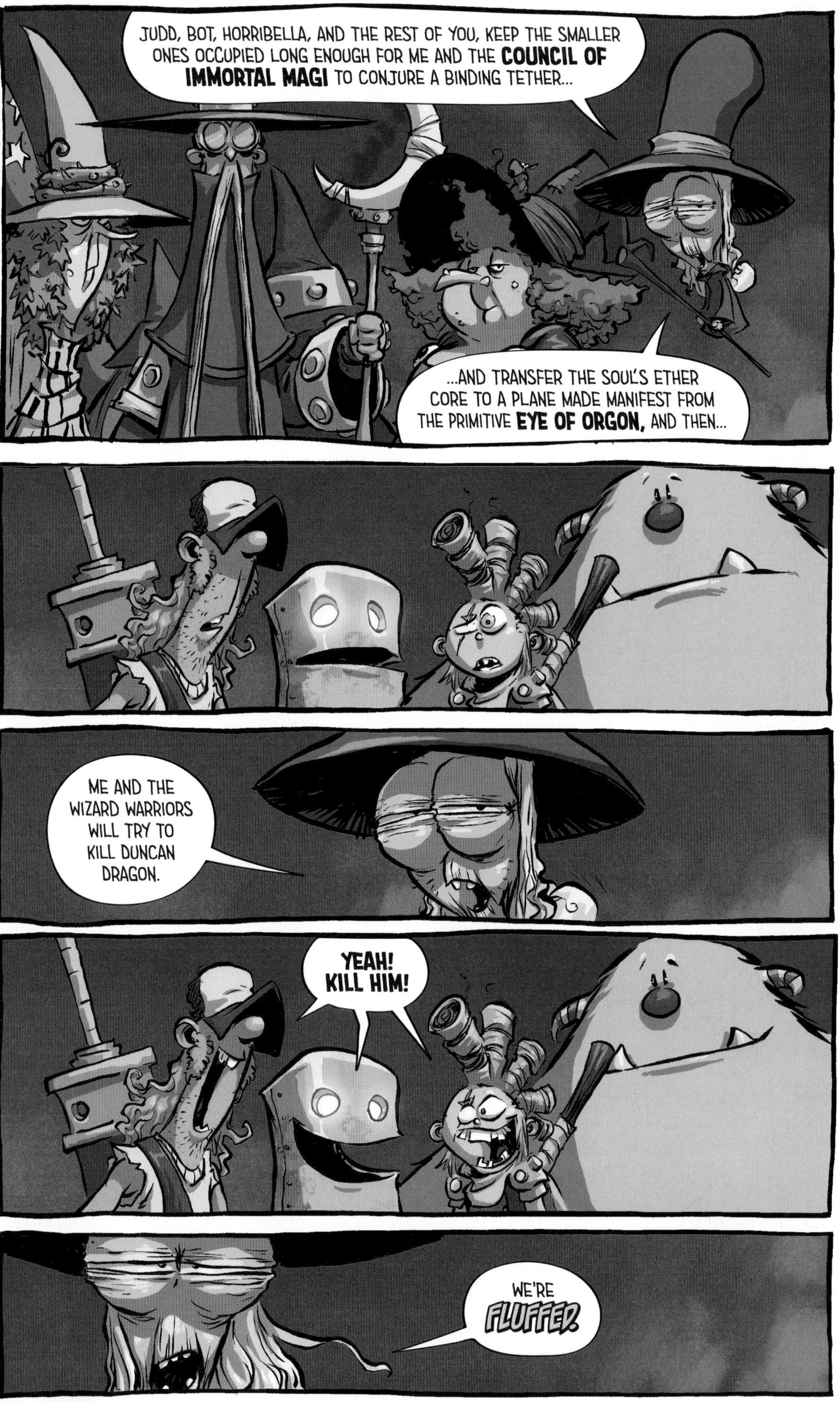
JUDD, BOT, HORRIBELLA, AND THE REST OF YOU, KEEP THE SMALLER ONES OCCUPIED LONG ENOUGH FOR ME AND THE COUNCIL OF IMMORTAL MAGI TO CONJURE A BINDING TETHER...
...AND TRANSFER THE SOUL'S ETHER CORE TO A PLANE MADE MANIFEST FROM THE PRIMITIVE EYE OF ORGON, AND THEN...
ME AND THE WIZARD WARRIORS WILL TRY TO KILL DUNCAN DRAGON.
YEAH! KILL HIM!
WE'RE FLUFFED.

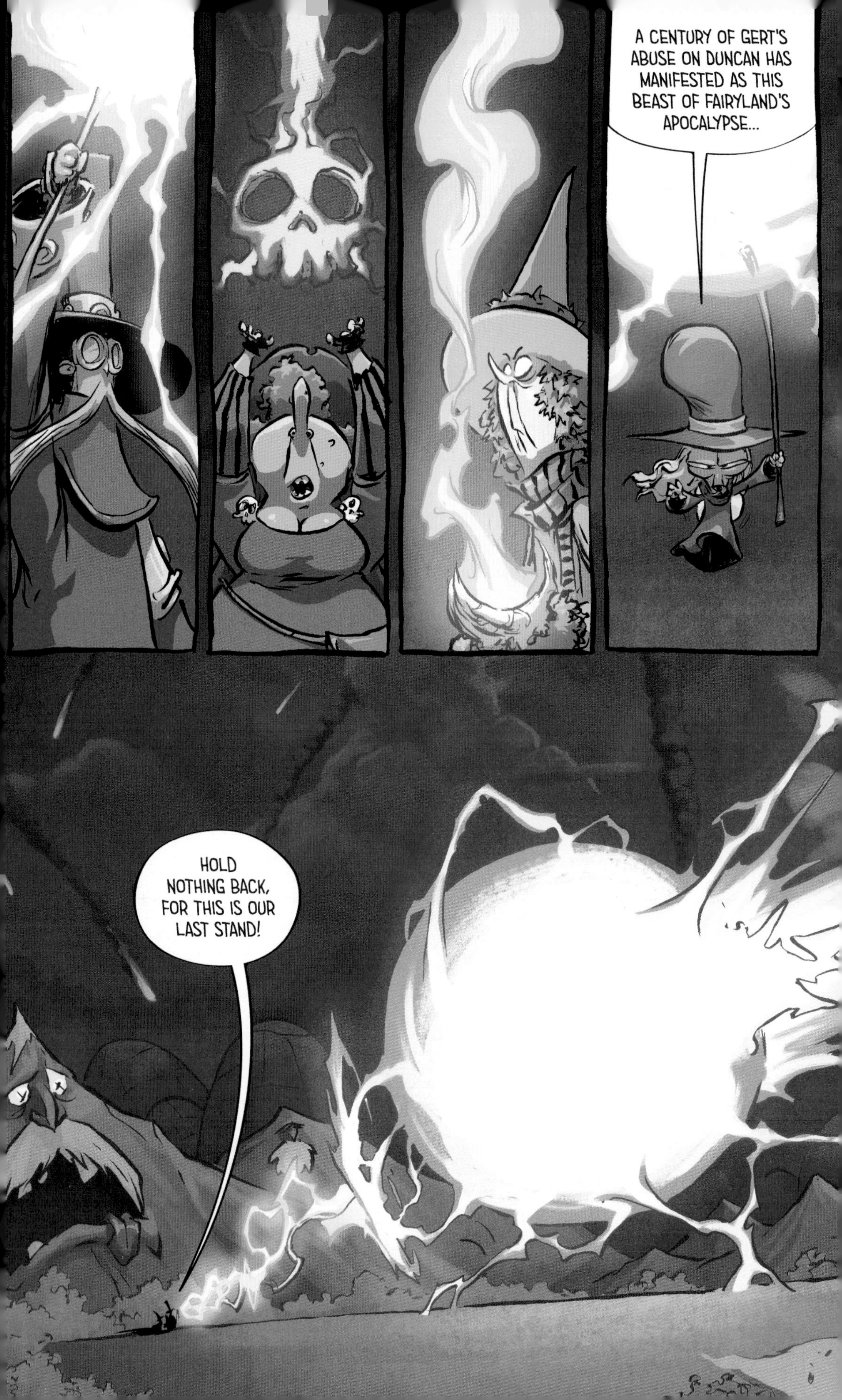
A CENTURY OF GERT'S ABUSE ON DUNCAN HAS MANIFESTED AS THIS BEAST OF FAIRYLAND'S APOCALYPSE...
HOLD NOTHING BACK, FOR THIS IS OUR LAST STAND!

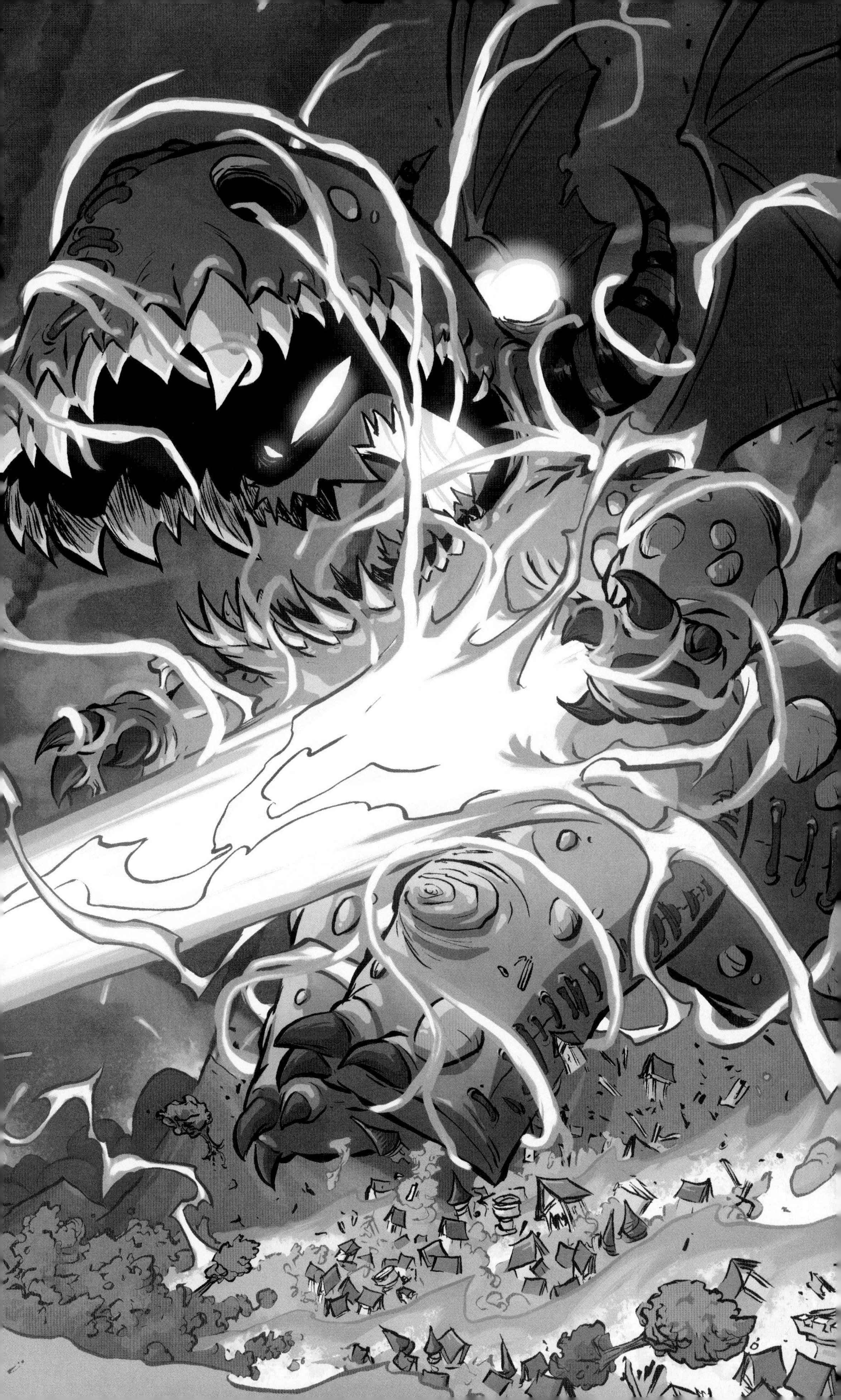

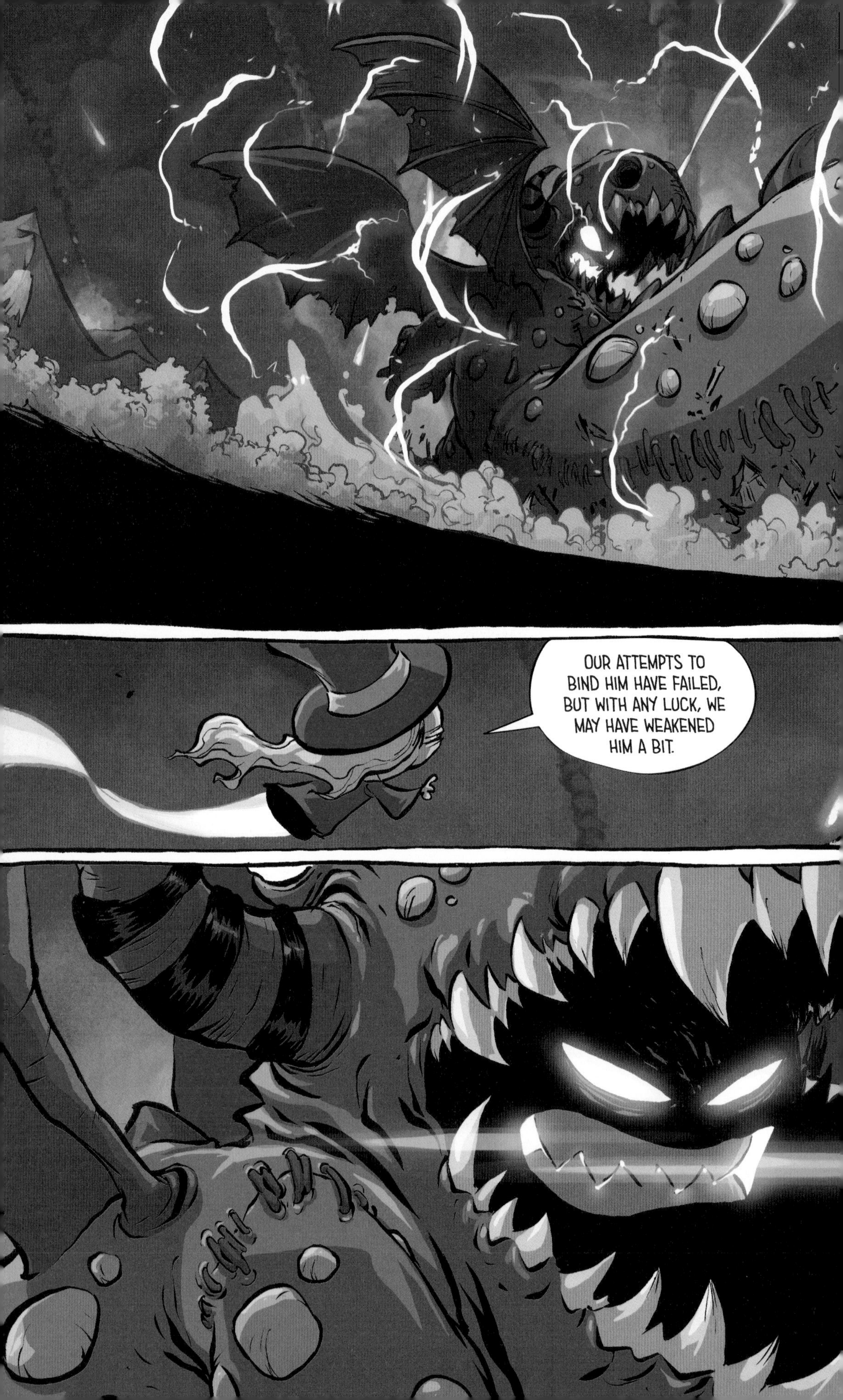
OUR ATTEMPTS TO BIND HIM HAVE FAILED, BUT WITH ANY LUCK, WE MAY HAVE WEAKENED HIM A BIT.

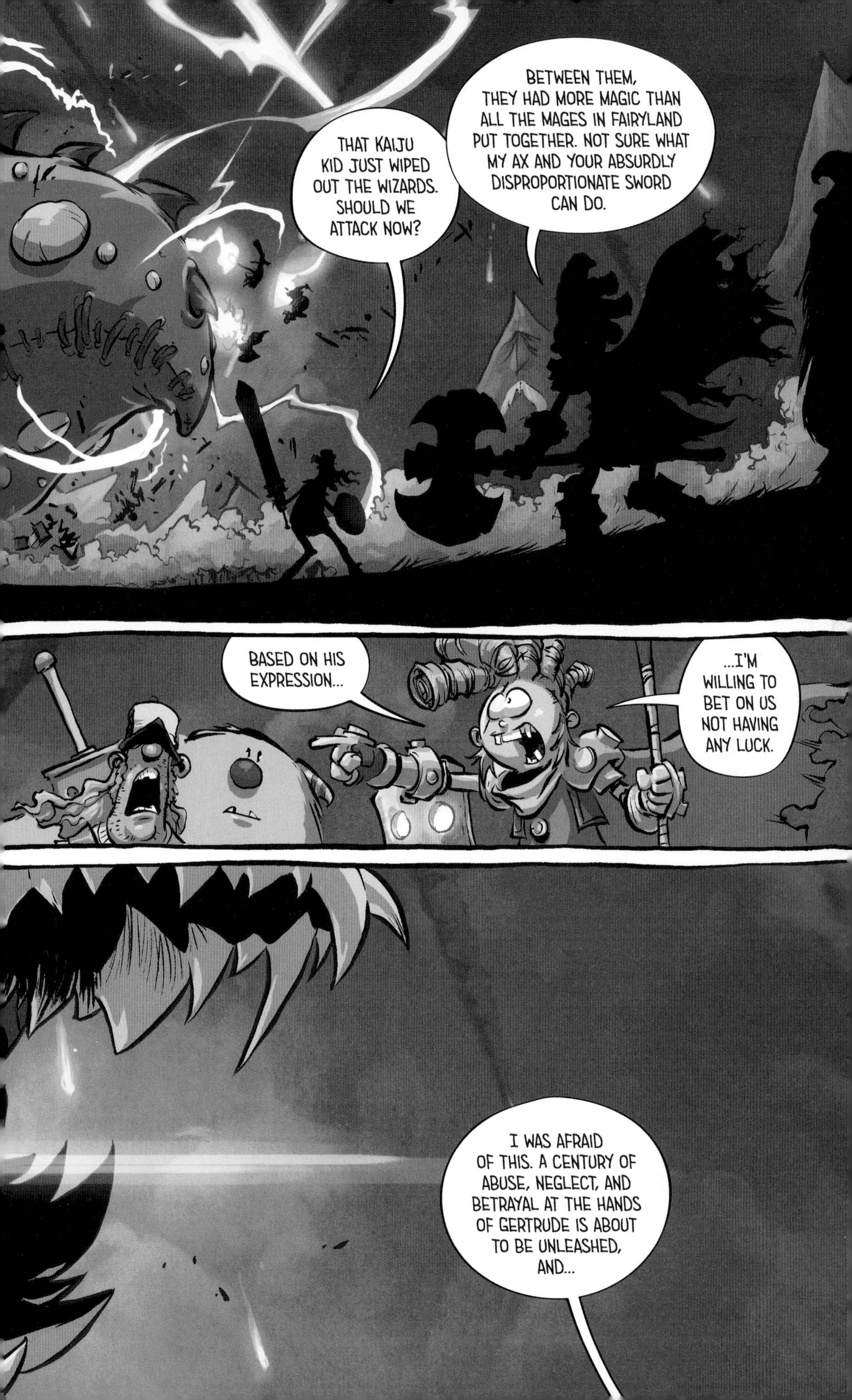
THAT KAIJU KID JUST WIPED OUT THE WIZARDS. SHOULD WE ATTACK NOW?
BETWEEN THEM, THEY HAD MORE MAGIC THAN ALL THE MAGES IN FAIRYLAND PUT TOGETHER. NOT SURE WHAT MY AX AND YOUR ABSURDLY DISPROPORTIONATE SWORD CAN DO.
BASED ON HIS EXPRESSION...
...I'M WILLING TO BET ON US NOT HAVING ANY LUCK.
I WAS AFRAID OF THIS. A CENTURY OF ABUSE, NEGLECT, AND BETRAYAL AT THE HANDS OF GERTRUDE IS ABOUT TO BE UNLEASHED, AND...

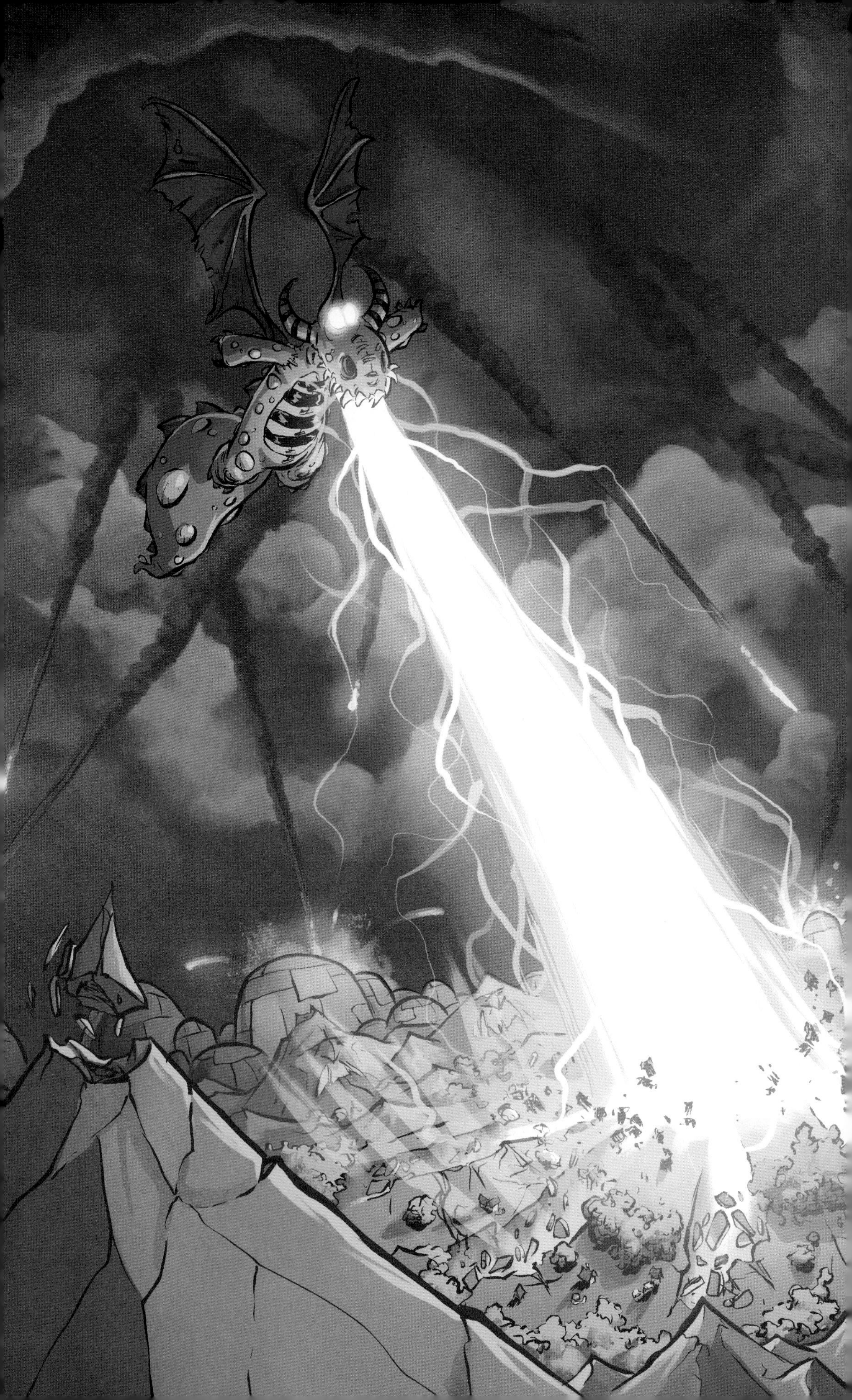

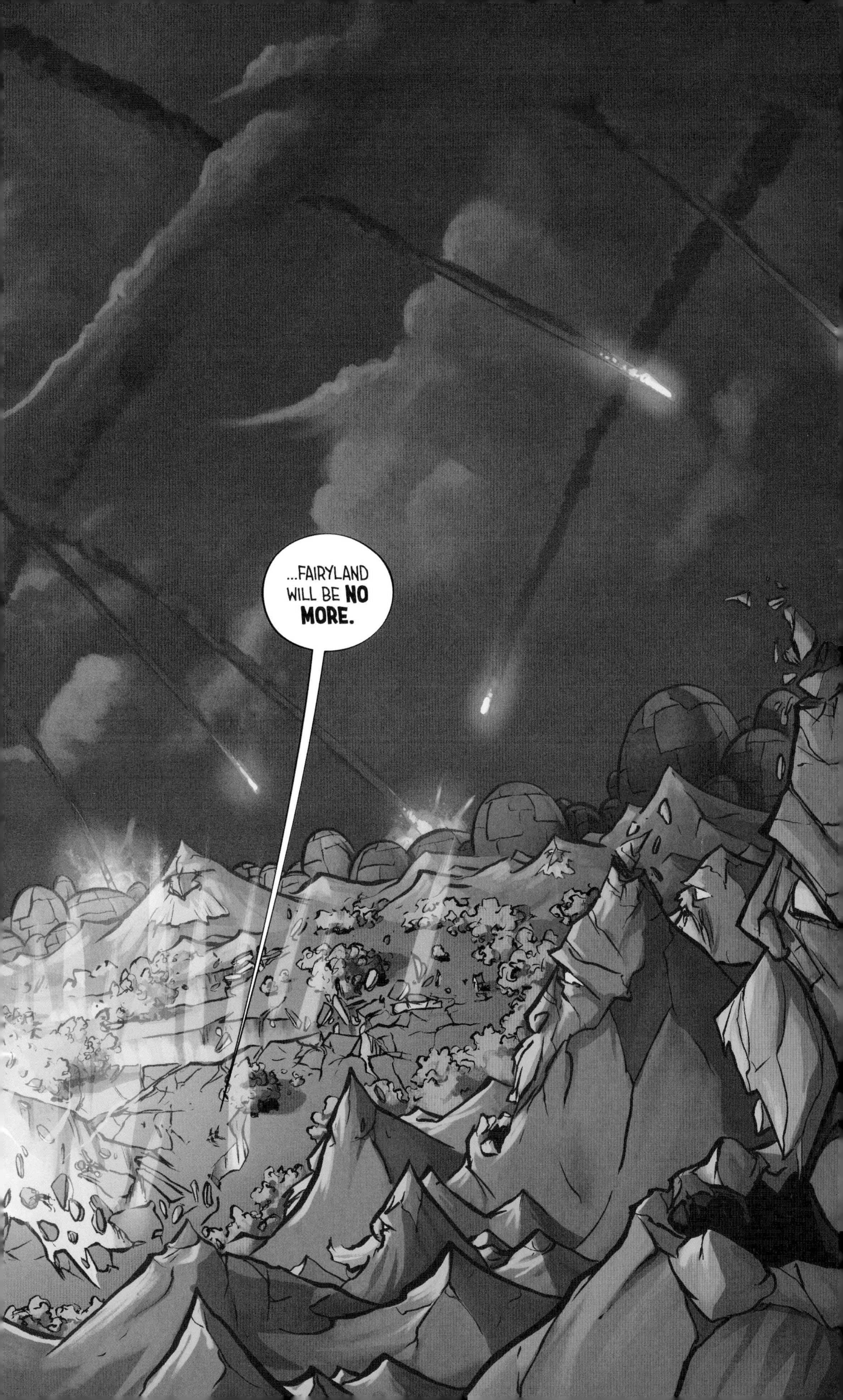
...FAIRYLAND WILL BE NO MORE.

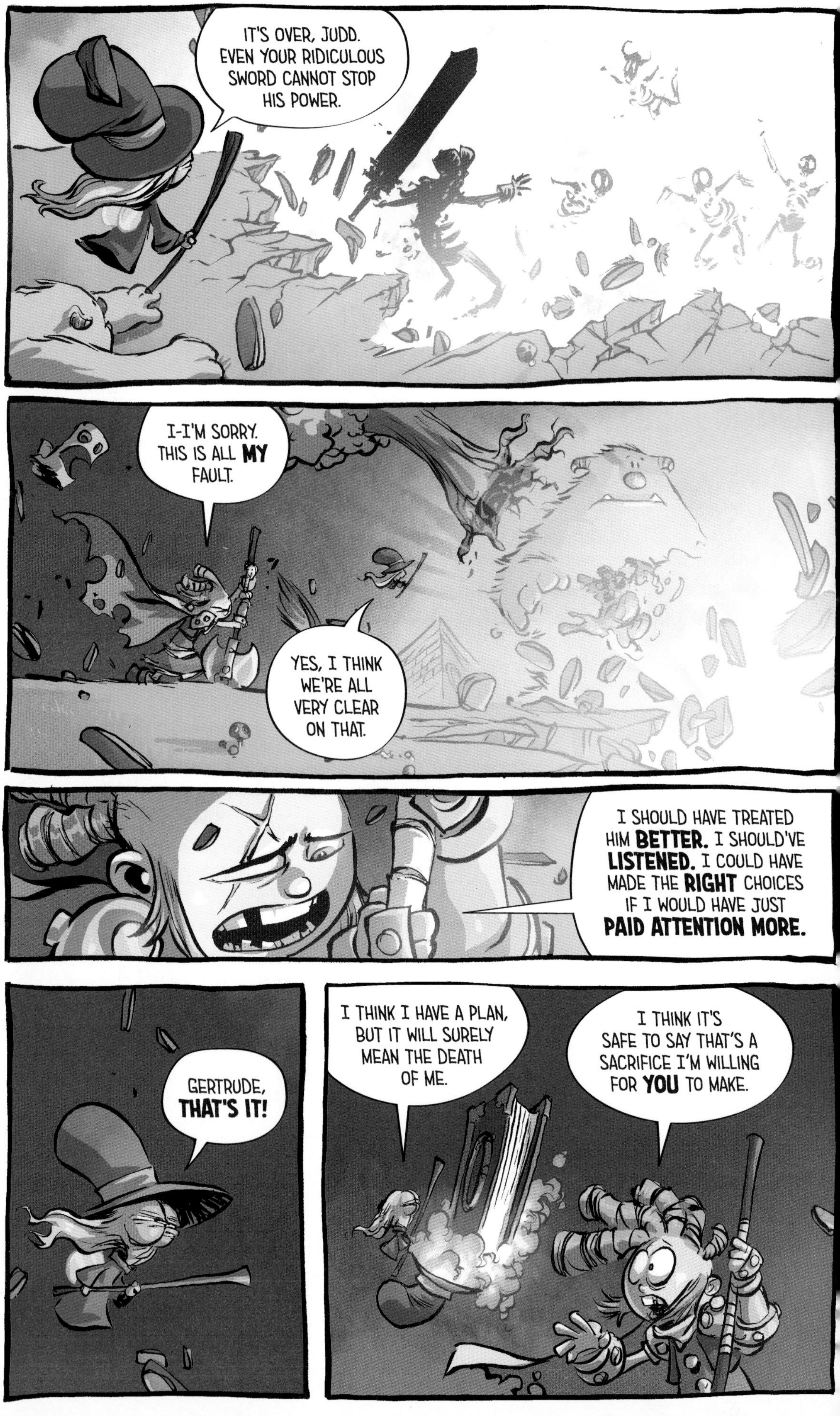
IT'S OVER, JUDD. EVEN YOUR RIDICULOUS SWORD CANNOT STOP HIS POWER.
I-I'M SORRY. THIS IS ALL **MY** FAULT.
YES, I THINK WE'RE ALL VERY CLEAR ON THAT.
I SHOULD HAVE TREATED HIM **BETTER.** I SHOULD'VE **LISTENED.** I COULD HAVE MADE THE **RIGHT** CHOICES IF I WOULD HAVE JUST **PAID ATTENTION MORE.**
GERTRUDE, **THAT'S IT!**
I THINK I HAVE A PLAN, BUT IT WILL SURELY MEAN THE DEATH OF ME.
I THINK IT'S SAFE TO SAY THAT'S A SACRIFICE I'M WILLING FOR **YOU** TO MAKE.

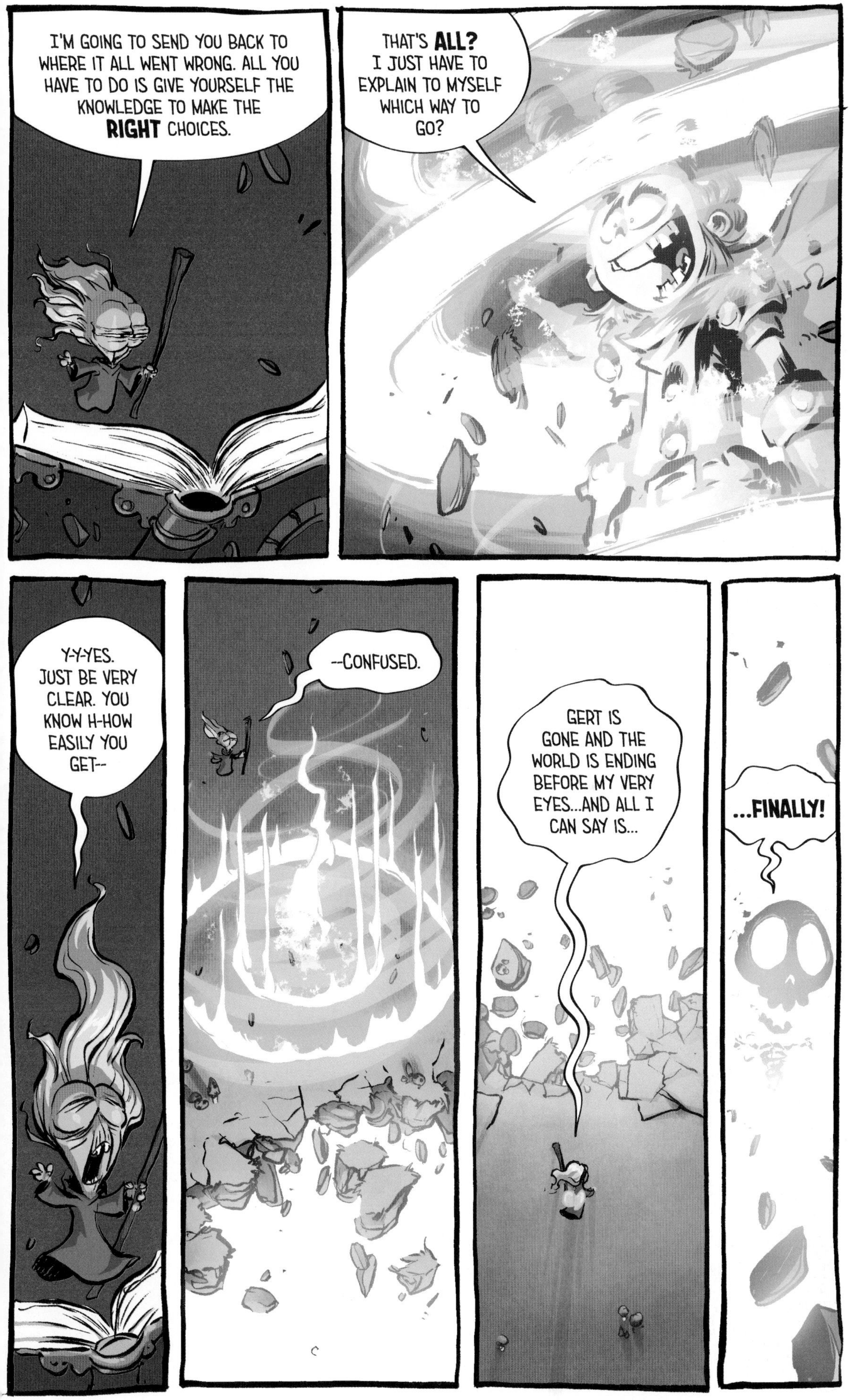
I'M GOING TO SEND YOU BACK TO WHERE IT ALL WENT WRONG. ALL YOU HAVE TO DO IS GIVE YOURSELF THE KNOWLEDGE TO MAKE THE **RIGHT** CHOICES.
THAT'S **ALL?** I JUST HAVE TO EXPLAIN TO MYSELF WHICH WAY TO GO?
Y-Y-YES. JUST BE VERY CLEAR. YOU KNOW H-HOW EASILY YOU GET--
--CONFUSED.
GERT IS GONE AND THE WORLD IS ENDING BEFORE MY VERY EYES...AND ALL I CAN SAY IS...
...FINALLY!

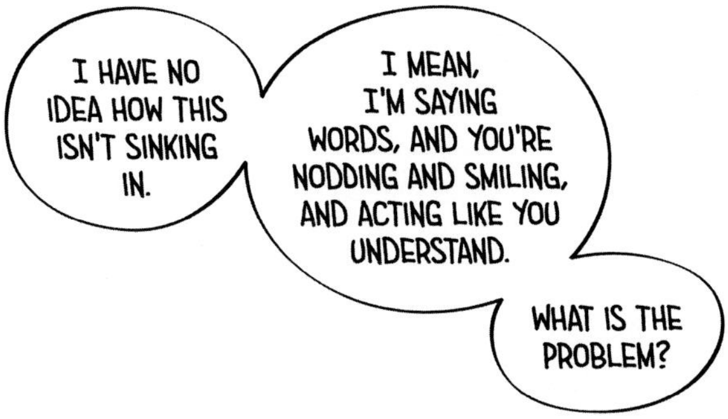
I HAVE NO IDEA HOW THIS ISN'T SINKING IN.
I MEAN, I'M SAYING WORDS, AND YOU'RE NODDING AND SMILING, AND ACTING LIKE YOU UNDERSTAND.
WHAT IS THE PROBLEM?

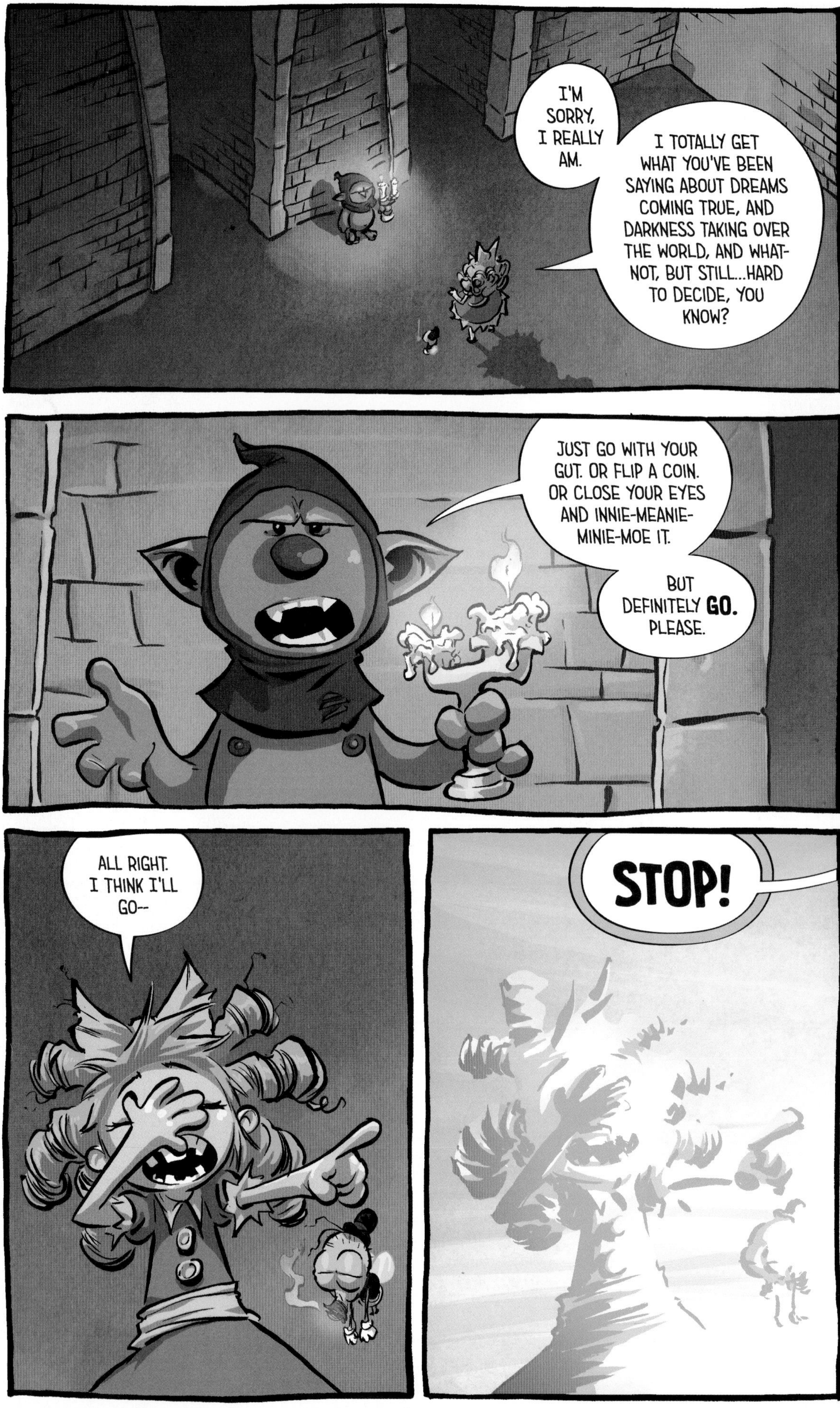
I'M SORRY, I REALLY AM.
I TOTALLY GET WHAT YOU'VE BEEN SAYING ABOUT DREAMS COMING TRUE, AND DARKNESS TAKING OVER THE WORLD, AND WHAT-NOT, BUT STILL...HARD TO DECIDE, YOU KNOW?
JUST GO WITH YOUR GUT. OR FLIP A COIN. OR CLOSE YOUR EYES AND INNIE-MEANIE-MINIE-MOE IT.
BUT DEFINITELY **GO.** PLEASE.
ALL RIGHT. I THINK I'LL GO--
STOP!

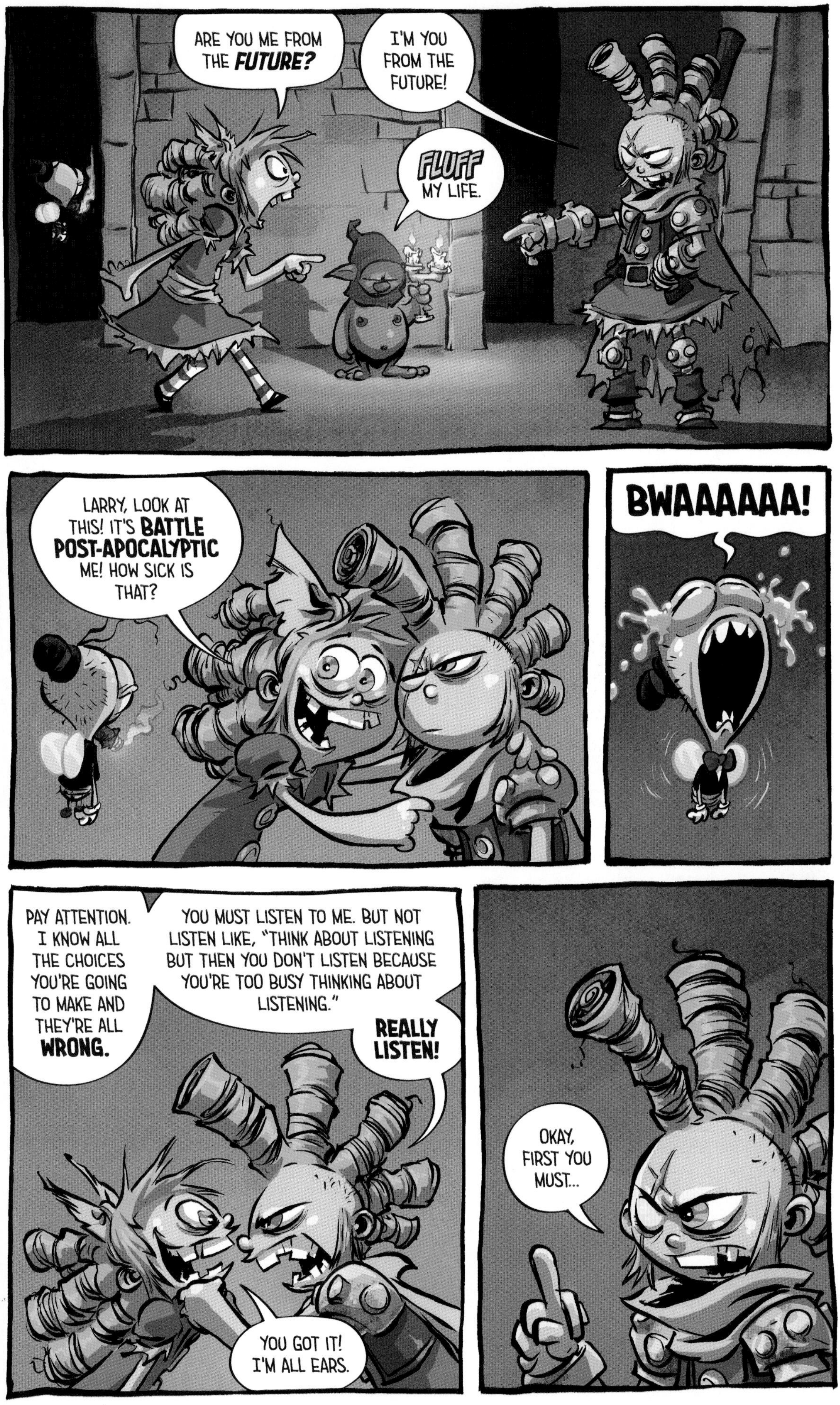
ARE YOU ME FROM THE FUTURE?
I'M YOU FROM THE FUTURE!
FLUFF MY LIFE.
LARRY, LOOK AT THIS! IT'S BATTLE POST-APOCALYPTIC ME! HOW SICK IS THAT?
BWAAAAAA!
PAY ATTENTION. I KNOW ALL THE CHOICES YOU'RE GOING TO MAKE AND THEY'RE ALL WRONG.
YOU MUST LISTEN TO ME. BUT NOT LISTEN LIKE, "THINK ABOUT LISTENING BUT THEN YOU DON'T LISTEN BECAUSE YOU'RE TOO BUSY THINKING ABOUT LISTENING."
REALLY LISTEN!
YOU GOT IT! I'M ALL EARS.
OKAY, FIRST YOU MUST...

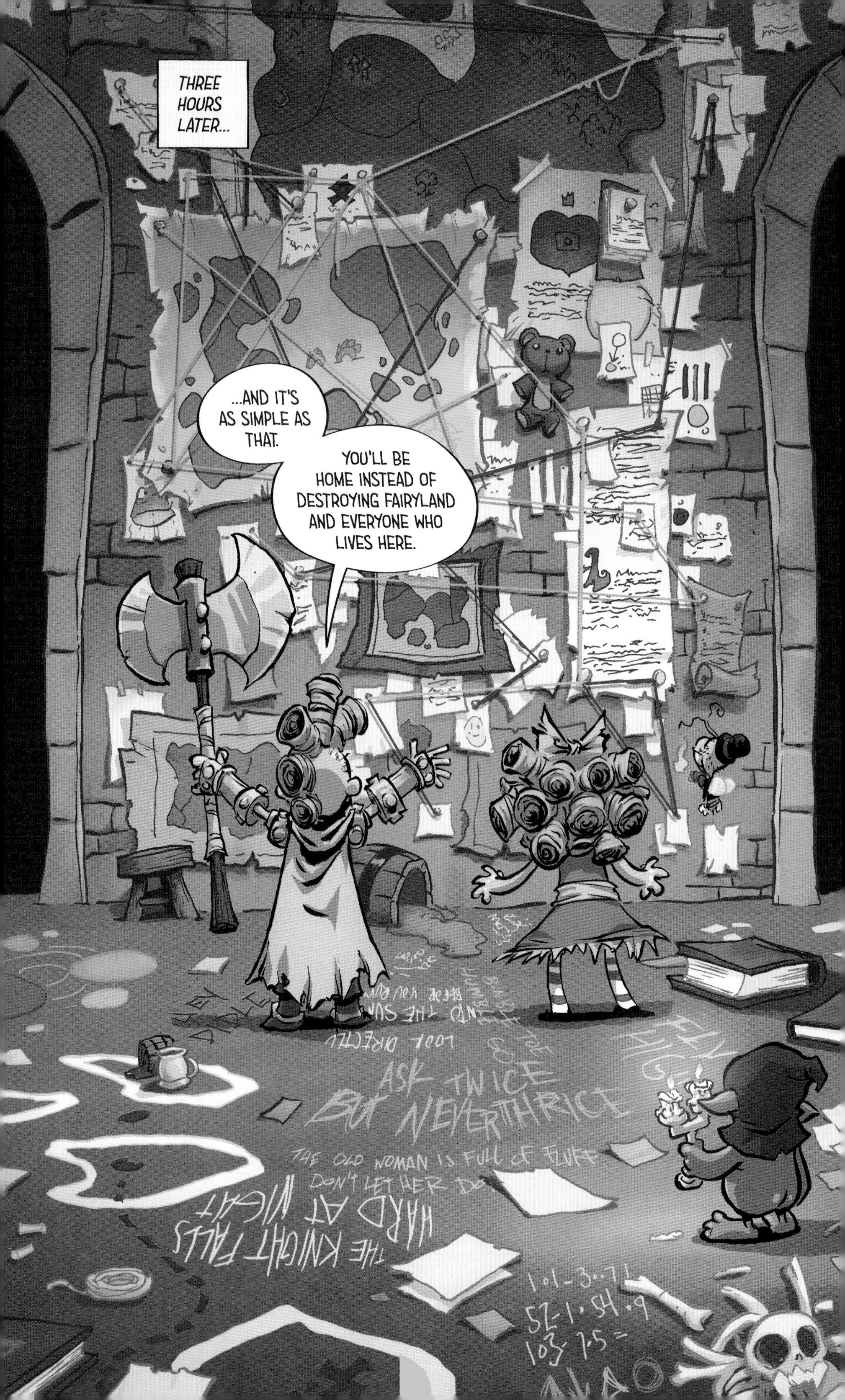
THREE HOURS LATER...
...AND IT'S AS SIMPLE AS THAT.
YOU'LL BE HOME INSTEAD OF DESTROYING FAIRYLAND AND EVERYONE WHO LIVES HERE.
ASK TWICE
BUT NEVER THRICE
THE OLD WOMAN IS FULL OF FLUFF

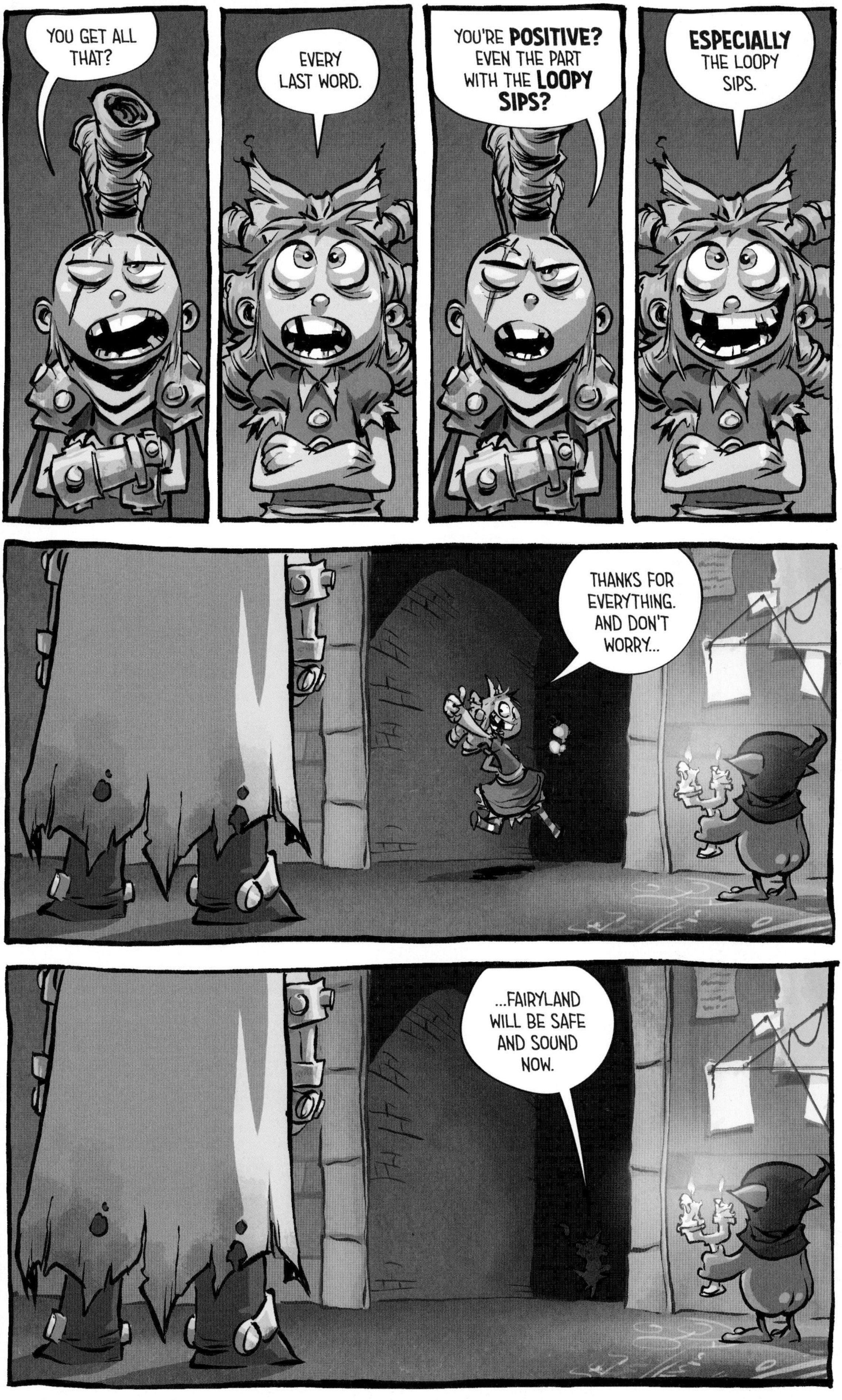
YOU GET ALL THAT?
EVERY LAST WORD.
YOU'RE **POSITIVE?** EVEN THE PART WITH THE **LOOPY SIPS?**
ESPECIALLY THE LOOPY SIPS.
THANKS FOR EVERYTHING. AND DON'T WORRY...
...FAIRYLAND WILL BE SAFE AND SOUND NOW.

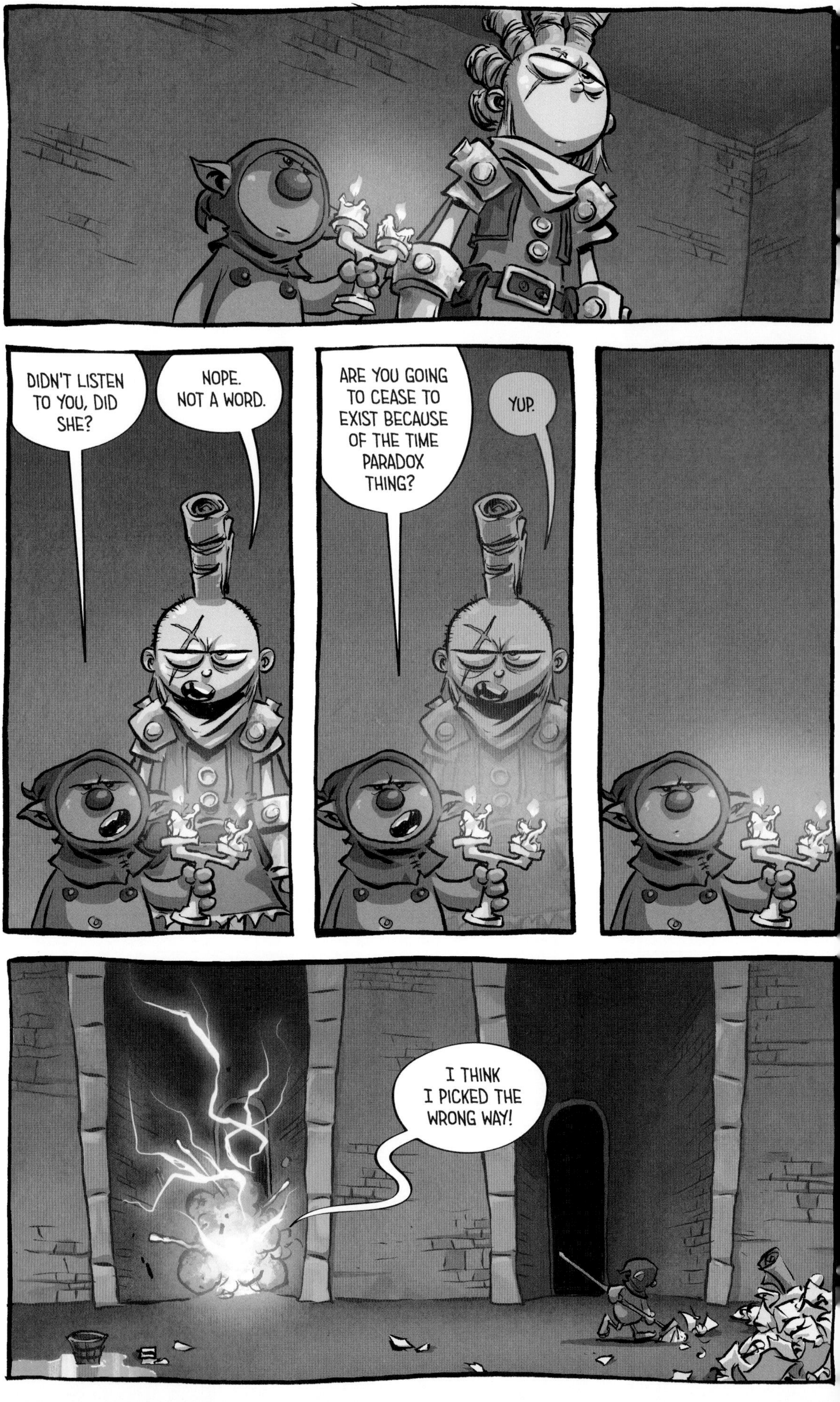
DIDN'T LISTEN TO YOU, DID SHE?
NOPE. NOT A WORD.
ARE YOU GOING TO CEASE TO EXIST BECAUSE OF THE TIME PARADOX THING?
YUP.
I THINK I PICKED THE WRONG WAY!

VARIANT
COVERS

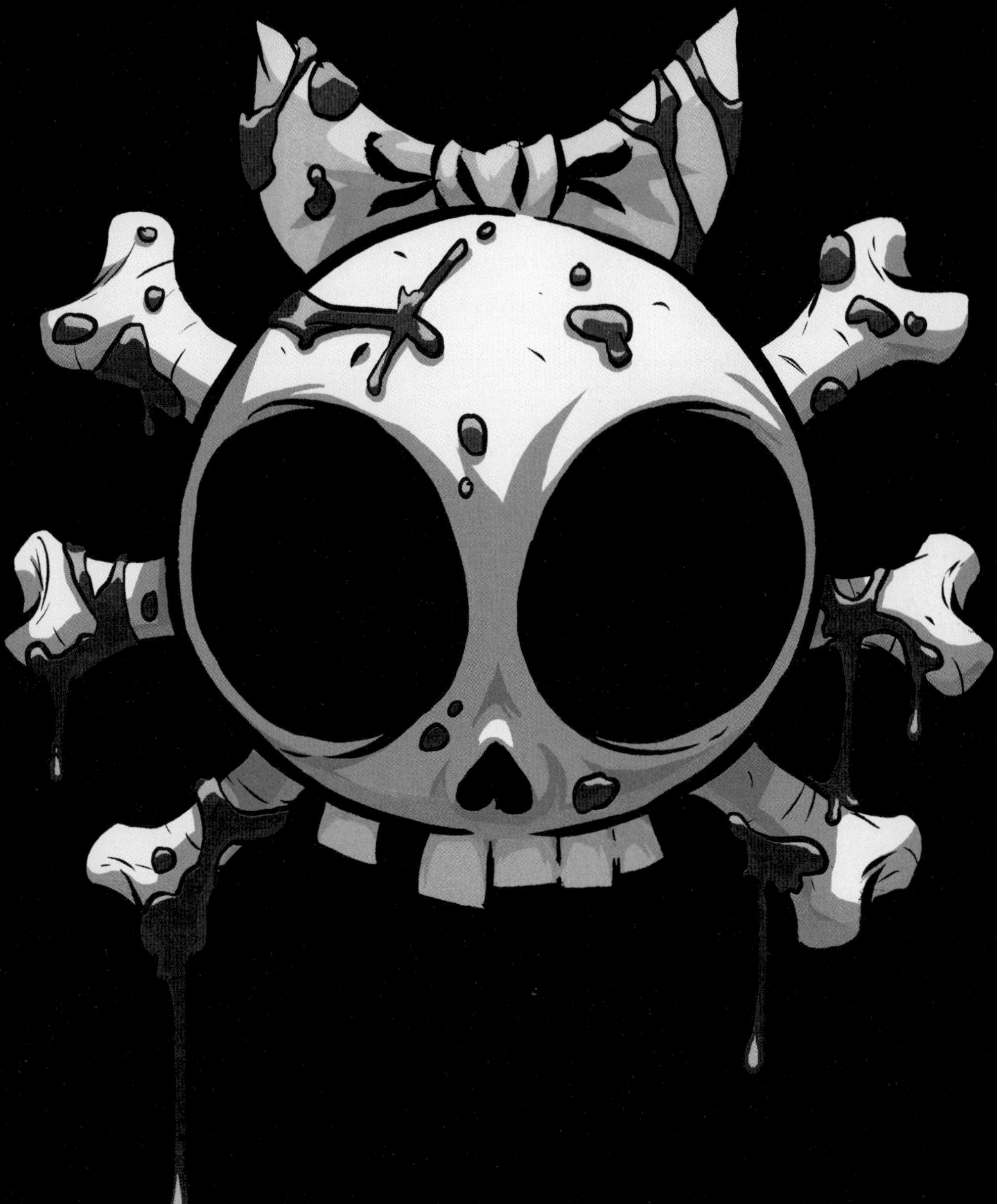

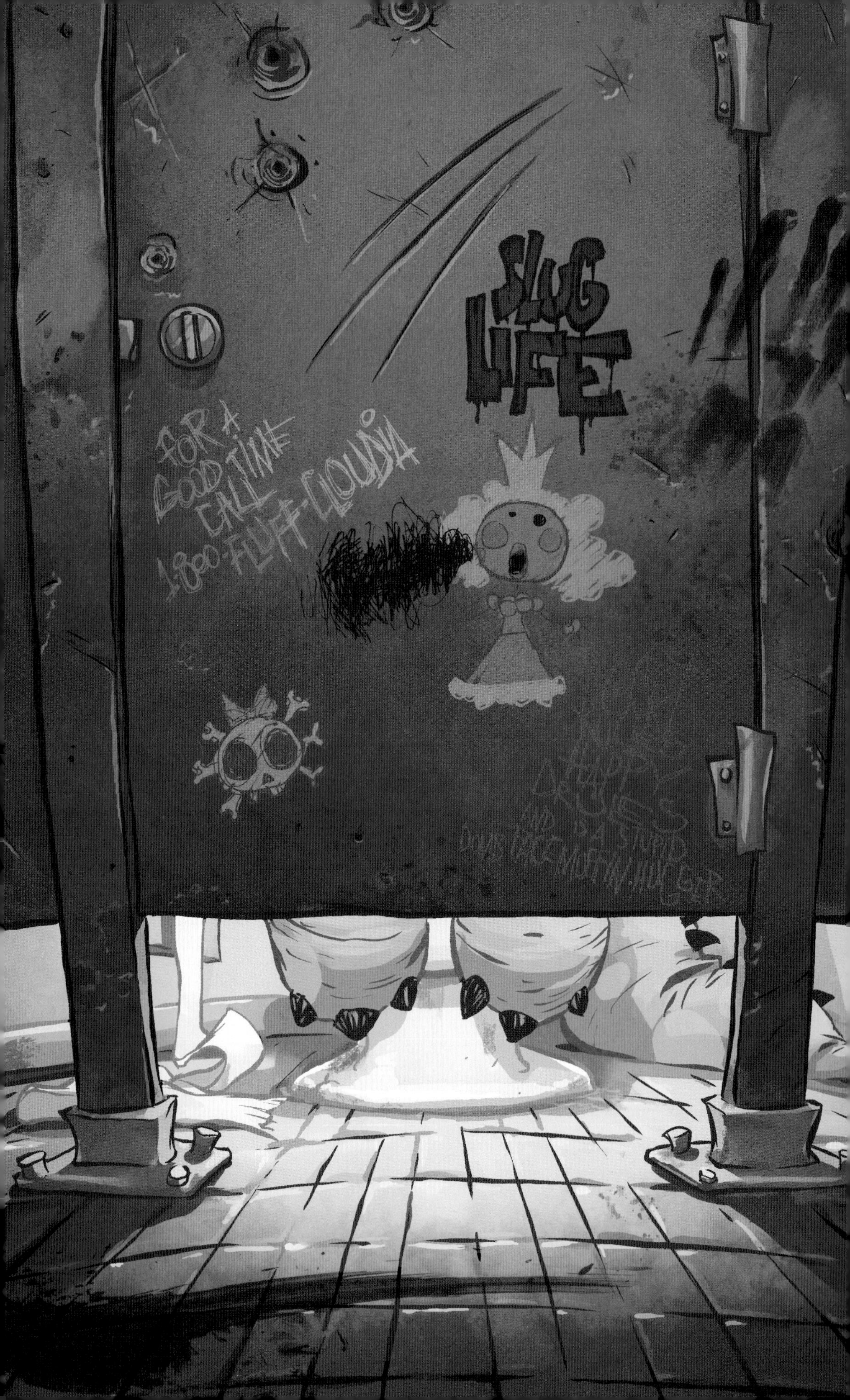
SLUG LIFE
FOR A GOOD TIME CALL 1-800-FLUFF-CLOUDIA
RULES
AND IS A STUPID
DUMB CUPCAKE MUFFIN HUGGER

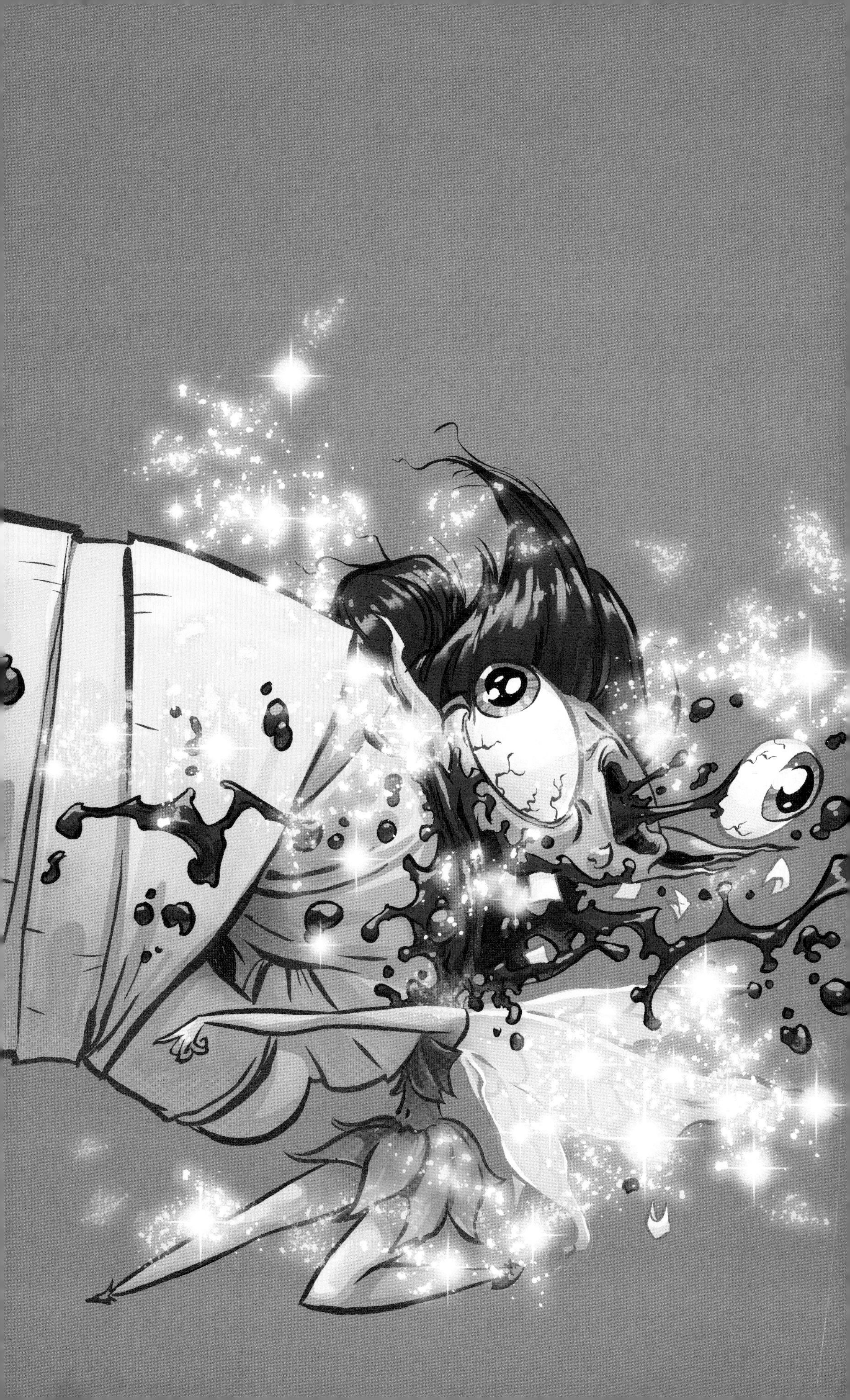

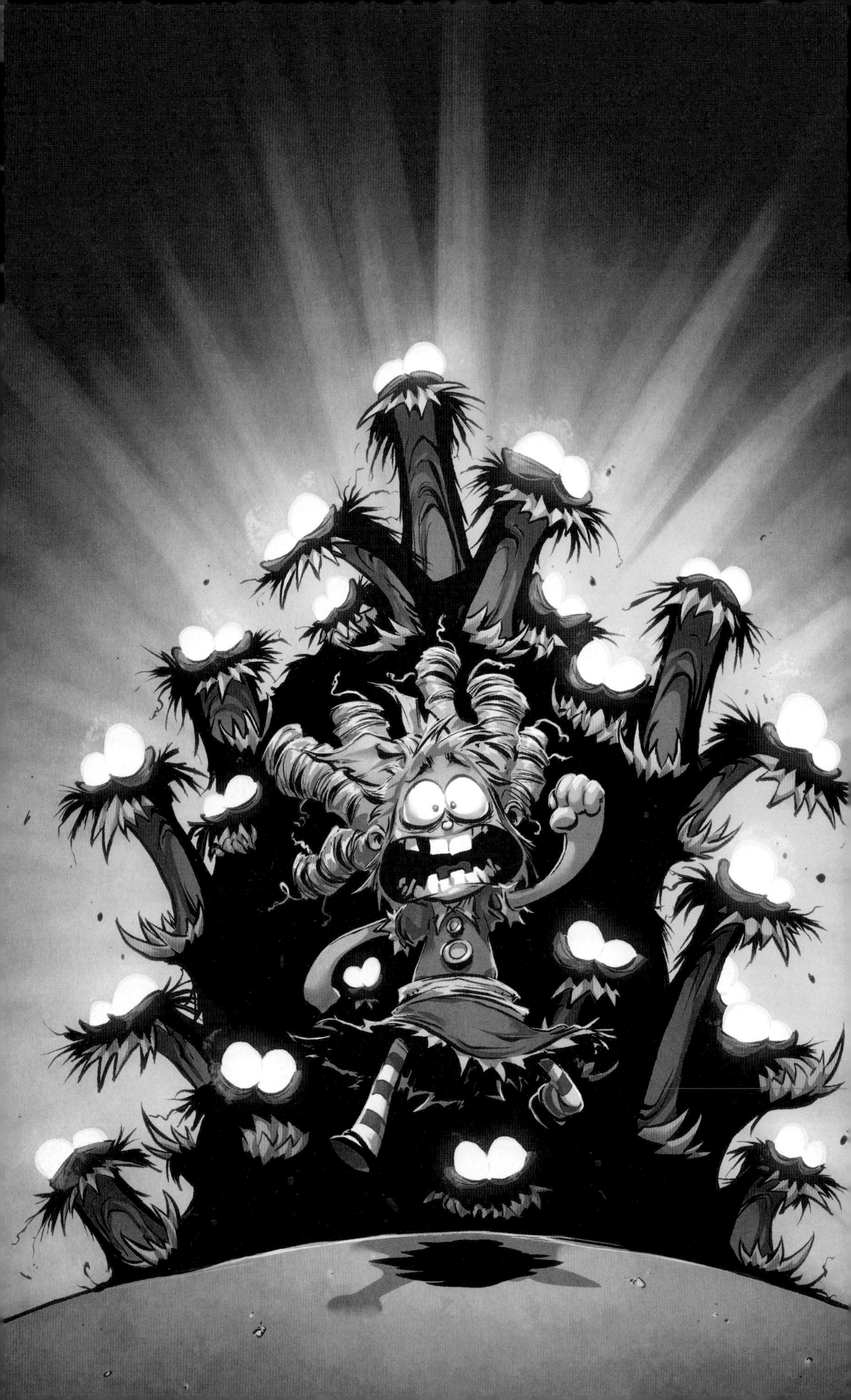

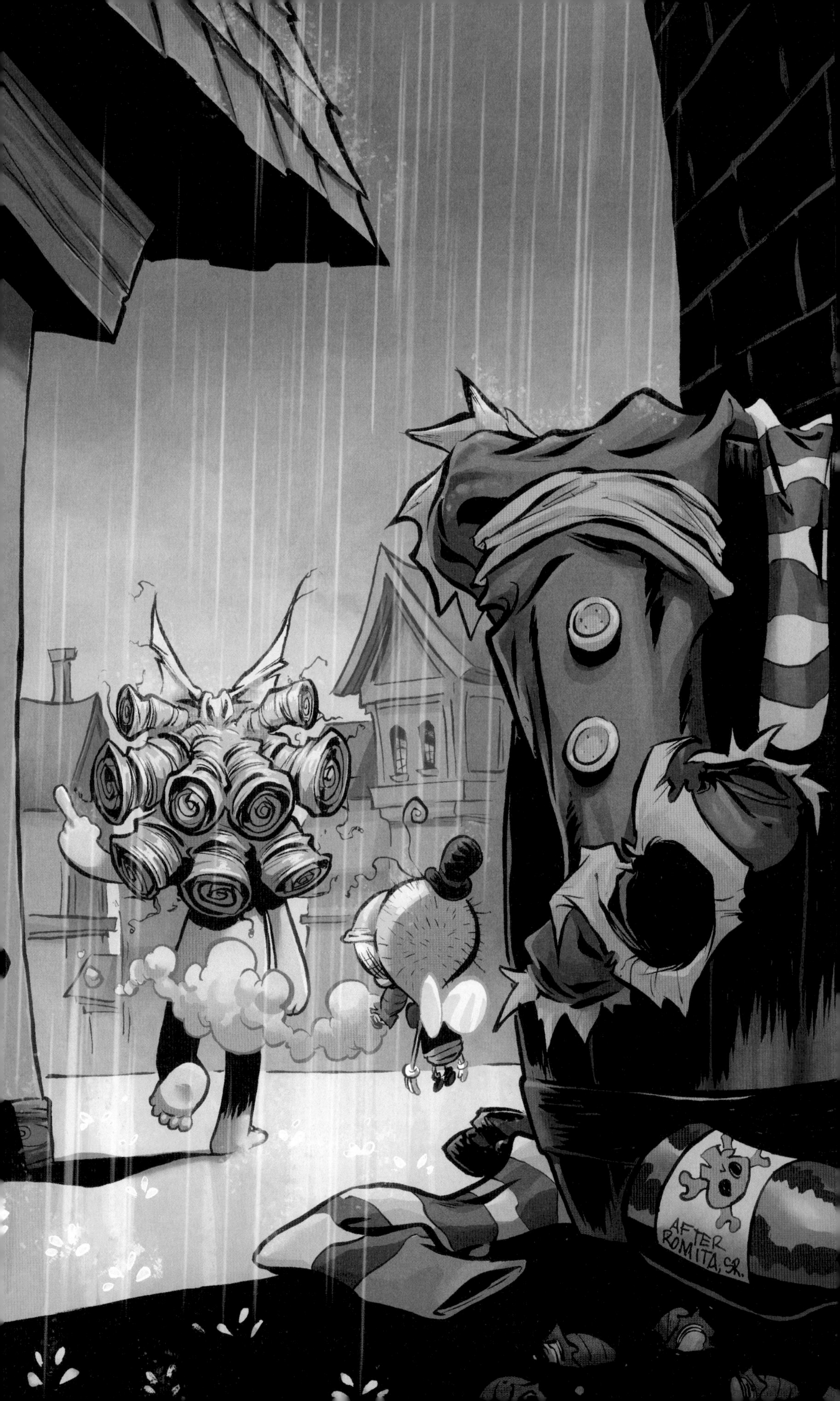
AFTER
ROMITA, SR.

SKOTTIE YOUNG

...is the New York Times bestselling cartoonist behind Marvel's WIZARD OF OZ graphic novel adaptations, ROCKET RACCOON and GIANT-SIZE LITTLE MARVEL, as well as illustrating FORTUNATELY, THE MILK with some writer named NEIL GAIMAN. And in case you have lived in a cave, Skottie has also produced enough Little Marvel variant covers to build a small ranch style home out of them. (Though they are not waterproof, so living in said home is not advised.) He currently holds the record for most Eisner Awards won by anyone born in Fairybury, IL. Skottie lives in Central Illinois with his wife, two sons, and two dogs that drive him crazy (the dogs, not the humans).

JEAN-FRANCOIS BEAULIEU

...is the acclaimed colorist behind Marvel's WIZARD OF OZ graphic novel adaptations, ROCKET RACCOON, GIANT-SIZE LITTLE MARVEL, NEW WARRIORS, NEW X-MEN, and probably other books that Skottie Young didn't draw, but since Skottie Young is writing this we'll keep it to mostly Skottie Young books. Okay, fine, INVINCIBLE. Happy? Jean and Skottie have been working together for over a decade (which sounds way more epic than saying ten years). Jean is considered one of the industry's top colorists and also holds the record for most people who don't know how to pronounce his last name. He lives somewhere in the Canadian wilderness with his fiancé, three dogs, nine cats, and an unknown amount of dope robot model kits.

NATE PIEKOS

...is the founder of BLAMBOT.COM, a company with a much cooler name than any of us could probably come up with. Good job, Nate! He has created some of the industry's most popular fonts and has used them to letter comic books for Image Comics (HUCK), Marvel Comics (X-STATIX, X-MEN FIRST CLASS), DC Comics (NEW SUICIDE SQUAD), Dark Horse Comics (FIGHT CLUB 2, UMBRELLA ACADEMY) . . . and all the other companies that end with the word "comics." Nate has more guitars in his studio than any other letterer on the planet. (That was not fact checked, but I'm going with it.) He lives in Rhode Island with his wife and the previously mentioned guitars.

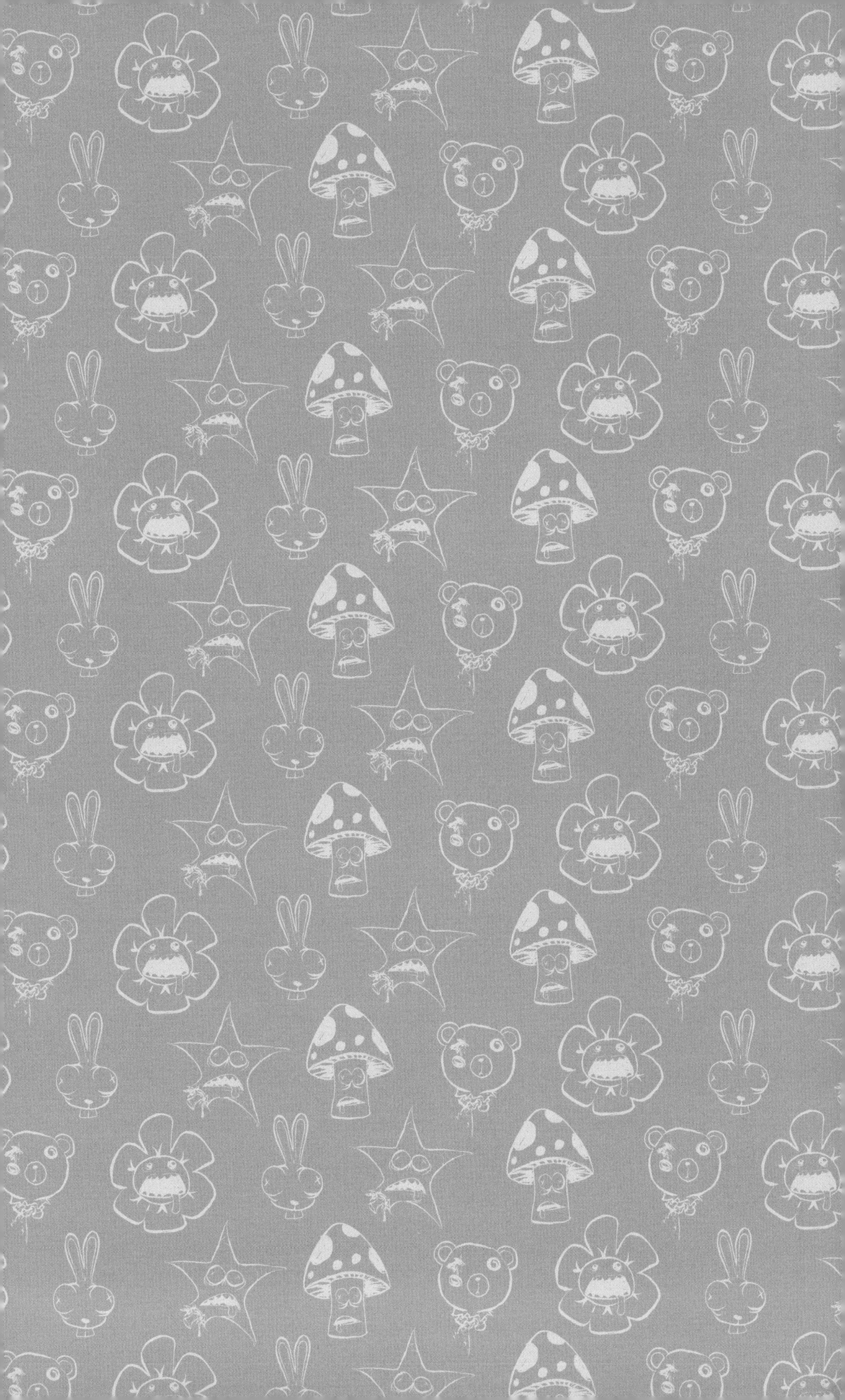

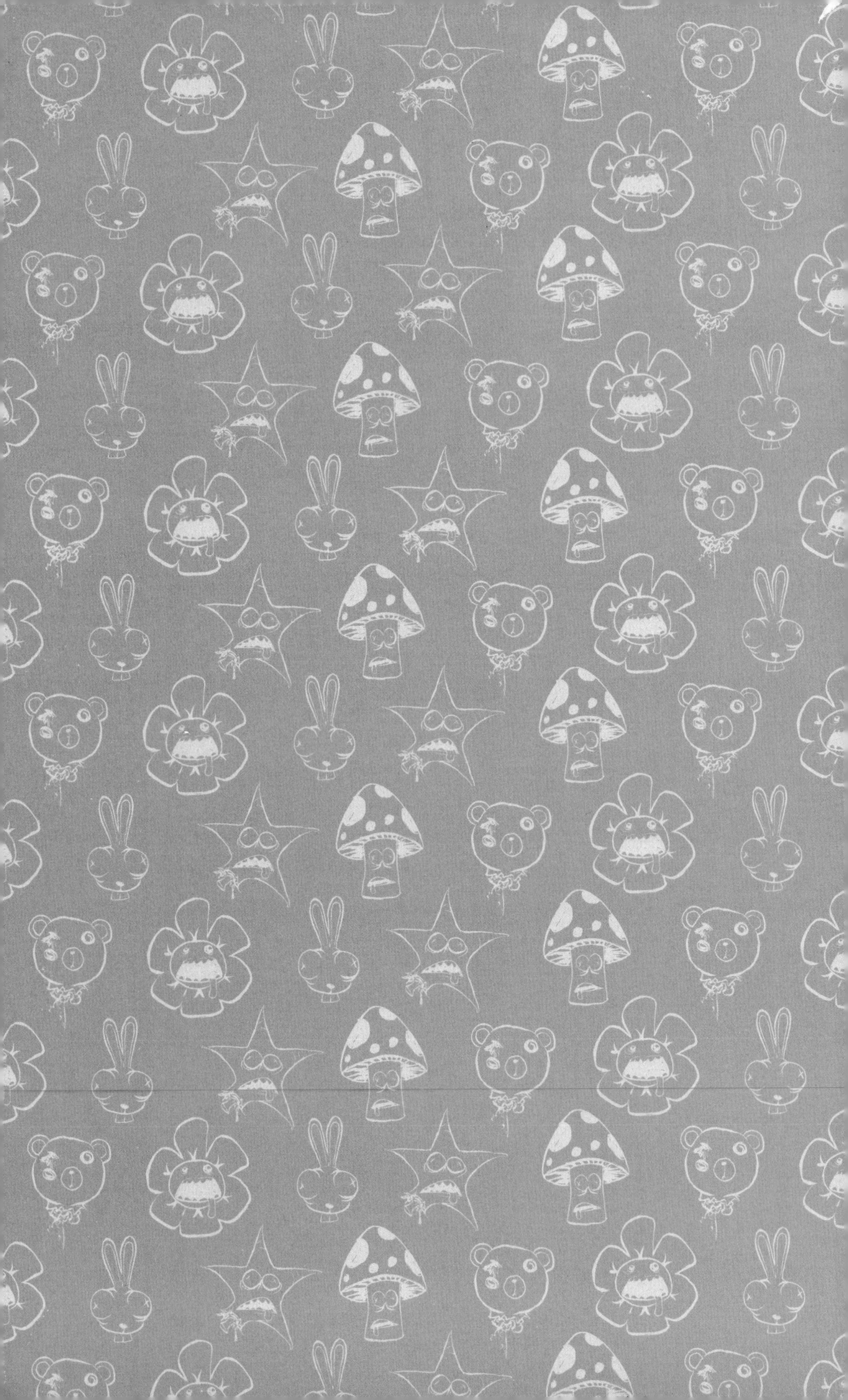